Fiction by James Jackson

Dead Headers
Cold Cut
The Reaper
Blood Rock
Pilgrim
Realm
Perdition

JAMES JACKSON

TREASON

ZAFFRE

First published in Great Britain in 2016 by

ZAFFRE PUBLISHING
80–81 Wimpole St, London W1G 9RE
www.zaffrebooks.co.uk

Text copyright © James Jackson, 2016
Map by Rachel Lawston

A CIP catalogue record for this book is available from the British Library.

Hardback ISBN: 978-1-785-76115-7
Ebook ISBN: 978-1-785-76114-0

1 3 5 7 9 10 8 6 4 2

Typeset by IDSUK (Data Connection) Ltd
Printed and bound by Clays Ltd, St Ives Plc

MIX
Paper from
responsible sources
FSC
www.fsc.org
FSC® C018072

Zaffre Publishing is an imprint of Bonnier Zaffre,
a Bonnier Publishing company
www.bonnierzaffre.co.uk
www.bonnierpublishing.co.uk

For George and Elizabeth Wood

The Key Plotters

Sir Robert 'Robin' Catesby, ringleader

Sir Thomas Percy, coordinator

Tom Wintour, adjutant

Jack Wright, swordsman and enforcer

Guy 'Guido' Fawkes, explosives expert

Robert Keyes, quartermaster

John Grant, acquirer of horses and weapons

Sir Ambrose Rookwood, acquirer of gunpowder and horses

Sir Everard Digby, commander of the mounted kidnap team

Other plotters included Robert Wintour (Tom's older brother and the owner of Huddington Court), Kit Wright (Jack's younger brother), Thomas Bates (Catesby's retainer) and Sir Francis Tresham (Catesby's cousin).

These late eclipses in the sun and moon portend no good to us . . . in cities, mutinies; in countries, discord; in palaces, treason; and the bond cracked 'twixt son and father.

King Lear, William Shakespeare

CHESTER

DERBY

SHREWSBURY

HOLBECHE
(Stephen Littleton)

COLESHILL

COOMBE ABBEY
*(Princess Elizabeth in
the charge of Lord Harington)*

CLOPTON
(Rookwood)

BROMSGROVE

COVENTRY

DUNCHURCH

River Avon

HUDDINGTON
(Robert Wintour)

WARWICK

NORBROOK *(Grant)*

DUNSMORE
HEATH

ASHBY
ST. LEGERS
(Catesby)

WORCESTER

STRATFORD-UPON-AVON

COUGHTON
(Throckmorton/Digby)

OXFORD

LONDON

KEY LOCATIONS
IN THE
GUNPOWDER PLOT

N
W   E
S

0   5   10   15   20

PROLOGUE

New Place, Stratford-upon-Avon, April 1616

Commotion at this hour was unexpected. He would ignore it, the barking of dogs and the whinny and stamp of a horse, and focus on the book before him. Let his servants deal with the matter. He hoped his Anne would not be roused from her slumber, for all their sakes.

He turned another page, adjusted the light cast by an oil lamp and leant to fill again his claret glass. Some fifty years on and a few hundred paces from where he had been born and now he was moneyed and revered and content. What fortune and acclaim his life had brought him, and with what skill he had navigated the treacherous waters of his age. He had served monarchs and yet never lost his head, had played alike to the gallery and groundlings and retained to this day their love. Tonight, William Shakespeare was in a reflective mood.

'Master?'

At the intrusion, the playwright peered towards the doorway. He had given strict instructions that he was not to be disturbed. Yet affection for his staff and the frown of apology on the face of his manservant were sufficient to permit a lapse.

'Why such consternation, George?' Shakespeare smiled at his old retainer. 'You enter the room of a studious man and not the lair of an ogre.'

'I had no wish to trouble you, master.'

'It seems you are the more disturbed.'

'A horseman came, master. A stranger bid me deliver you a package.'

'He would not stay? Gave no name? Offered not a single word of explanation?'

'No, master.'

'Then let us unravel the mystery of the saddlebag.' Shakespeare held out his hand and took the proffered bundle. 'Now get to bed and leave me to the night before our mistress wakes to scold us both.'

Alone once more, he examined the item wrapped in its linen windings. Perhaps it was a manuscript or the letters of an admirer or part of some prank dreamt up by his friend and brother-writer Ben Jonson. He sighed.

Across the years they had caroused and drunk, indulged in trick and escapade of every kind. The ageing should be allowed to reminisce. How he hankered on occasion for the sounds of London, for the urgent energy of its streets and taverns and the excitement of his youth. His past was but a whisper and his present bound by predictability and aching bones.

The small silver crucifix fell onto the open page and his world tilted. With a trembling touch he held the object to the light and turned it in his fingers. In this one tarnished artefact was history, a memory of the old religion and those who in its name would do murder to a king. There was a thick sheaf of papers too, a confession or dossier he freed carefully from its binding. Sleep could wait. As the hearth embers glowed and died and a predawn chill drew in, Shakespeare read. Before him was laid out an intrigue in which many had been ensnared and that had set a deadly trail from the manor houses of Warwickshire to the great Gunpowder Treason Plot of 1605. By the grace of God he was on the side of the victor and through dint of providence once knew the horseman who had ridden here tonight. Faith and passion drove men to heroism or folly. Remember, remember, the fifth of November. He would leave others to judge.

BEGINNING

The Azores, late summer 1591

'Sail ho! Enemy to windward!'

Spanish masts crowded the horizon. They had the weather gauge and advantage, a vast formation of swollen sail inbound for the fray. These were not the laden nau and caravel transports the English had expected, the annual migration of the treasure convoy from the Americas they lay in wait for. Instead a battle fleet encroached from the east. Almost sixty Spanish galleons bore down on a squadron of six English ships. It was the afternoon of 31 August 1591, and the ambushers had been ambushed.

In the crosstrees of the waiting vessels, the lookouts strained to see and hollered their reports, their calls echoing and forcing the pace. Everywhere was action. The English had believed themselves safe, anchoring in a small bay on the northern tip of this small volcanic island of Flores. Here the sick could be taken ashore and parties sent to forage among the waterfalls and meadows; here decks could be swabbed clean with vinegar, ballast replaced, and the hulls caulked with tow and pitch. Everything had changed, for hell was visiting paradise. As whistles blew and crews scrambled to make ready, skiffs splashed a frantic path back to their mother ships and figures swarmed to man the braces. All were preparing for flight.

On the poop deck of the warship *Revenge*, its captain leant on the rail and surveyed the scene. A veteran of close encounters with the enemy, of tight odds and chances seized and of wresting possession from the King of Spain, Sir Richard Grenville, privateer and vice-admiral, was not inclined to panic. At this spot aboard his ship had once stood Drake, the legend who had chased the Armada to its destruction. Three years on and the Spanish had rebuilt and ventured out with vengeance on their minds. Now it was Grenville's turn to find glory.

He straightened to acknowledge a young gallant approaching from the main deck to join him at his station. Ceremony was unnecessary.

There was a bond between them, a trust and familiarity born of combat and strengthened by shared loathing for the adversary and love for the melee. At twenty-four, Christian Hardy was no ordinary seafarer. As a soldier and spy he had lived and taken more lives than most, and killed ruthlessly anyone who threatened his Queen. It had cost him much. Yet there remained the steady confidence of ultramarine eyes, and the swagger and latent ferocity of a natural fighter contained within the armour plates of a faded blue velvet brigandine jacket. With sword and pistols to hand, Hardy felt most alive when in proximity to death.

Grenville gestured seaward. 'It seems we set a trap and are ourselves ensnared.'

'Howard signals we should run to sea.'

'Run?' The captain frowned. 'Our Lord Admiral knows us not.'

'You would fight?'

'I will do as my conscience and nature command.'

'It will be some trial, Richard.'

Grenville smiled. 'Are they not the ones we embrace and our people cheer?'

His companion nodded. The breath of wind on his cheek carried his thoughts back to Drake and the Armada and the fire ships he had led into Calais Roads. Ghosts still wandered here, the images of past friends and flying splinters. Another place and a different commander but Hardy was here again.

Grenville regarded him. 'They complain the *Revenge* is an unlucky ship. What do you say?'

'Ill-fortune may be turned.'

'We have some forty cannon and four hundred tons of leaking oak beneath our feet.' Grenville scanned the tops. 'Perhaps it will not.'

'Then we pray and brawl the harder.'

Grenville laughed and clapped him on the shoulder. 'I am a corsair and you are a gentleman adventurer. Well, we shall have adventure enough this day.'

An enemy admiral named Don Alonso de Bazan would ensure it. He had brought his great fleet from the northern Spanish port of El Perro intent on redressing past ignominy and restoring dignity to his homeland.

He carried seven thousand infantry and was accompanied by giant Apostle galleons with which he would close with and crush the pirates of Albion. Pausing off Terceira, two hundred miles to the east, to gather intelligence and arrange his formation, he was ready for quick victory.

But he had been sighted. Christian Hardy had been gathering information of his own, meeting agents, leading raids across the islands and spying on this Spanish hub. He had watched and tracked the fleet and, guessing at its true purpose, had sped aboard the pinnace *Moonshine* yesterday to deliver his report. A fragment of his soul believed the Spaniards hunted him.

'We aim for the heart of the beast.' Grenville pointed and called out to his officers and men. 'Weigh anchor and make all sail and ready the guns for action. For England!'

The *Revenge* groaned as her tethers loosened and canvas dropped, and cheering eddied from the gun deck to the yards. *For England.* Perhaps they did not yet comprehend their fate, or they did not care.

Hardy glanced back to the slumbering volcanic peak of the Morro Alto, tracing the verdant slopes and black lines of basalt down to the grey sands of the shore. Ponta Delgada they called this protective spur of Flores. It had given only temporary reprieve.

Grenville had followed his gaze. 'No volcano will match the fury we encounter.'

'So let us seize the fire.'

Sails tautened, the helm swung, and the little ship turned into the maw of the approaching host. At least she had distracted the foe; at least the rest of her squadron were clawing to sea. As the sun began its evening plunge and puffs of cannon smoke marked the defiant exodus of Lord Howard, the *Revenge* continued alone. Hardy nodded to Grenville and returned to the main deck. At the step of the centre mast and with his schiavona blade drawn, he would make his stand.

Jostling for the kill, the enemy swept close, the *Revenge* becalmed in their midst as her sails bled wind and her decks bucked to raking broadsides. Smoke rolled in and the world diminished to keening noise and glimpsed morion helmets and falling spars and bodies. Roaring soundless in the din, Grenville directed and stood firm.

Hardy stood at the centre of the fray. He felt the impact of the *San Felipe* as she grappled on the starboard side, her masts blocking the light and her infantry rushing to board. To the flash of muskets and with pike and sword they flowed in and were met with a fury that stalled them. The ache of anticipation was over.

'To me! We have them!' Hardy swung an arquebus and discharged a round, the steel ball designed to bring down rigging and instead removing a face. He was among the enemy now, at ease with their ragged oaths and cries, hewing with his sword and selecting from his brace of matchlock pistols. Fire belched from the pan and muzzle and another Spaniard fell away.

A second galleon, the *San Bernabé*, collided and took hold, her troops racing to seize the prize. Next it was the turn of the *San Cristobal* to ram the English ship, shattering the aftcastle and disgorging a fresh wave of boarders. Hardy moved with murderous fluency through a flickering landscape of bloodspill and wraiths. He was killing as profession and in revenge, for his mother burnt at the stake in a Lisbon square and his wife butchered by an assassin sent to kill the Queen, for his mentors and patrons Sir Francis Drake and the late spymaster Sir Francis Walsingham. In their name he slashed off a head and prised wide a ribcage and thrust through a groin with the point of his sword. The tactics of the alley were not for the squeamish or refined.

Yet they could not stem the onrush. Where one Spaniard vanished to the firefly strike of musketry, others took his place; where resistance ebbed, the enemy pressed in and forced retreat.

Grenville emerged, scrambling low beneath the whine of lead, his face scorched and his doublet torn. 'They bait us as dogs put to a bull.' The words faded in the storm.

'We hold them yet.'

'Though our stern is lost.' Grenville crouched and peered aft. 'I vouch they do not like us, Christian.'

Hardy grinned. 'We hate them more.'

Again the enemy surged and was repelled across the tangled wreckage of men and timber and rigging.

Rudderless and dismasted and with her upper works shot away, the *Revenge* had ceased to be a warship. Yet as daylight leached to dusk, the contest was far from over.

'Now, Christian!' commanded Grenville.

In a clearing framed by debris, Hardy loosed the contents of a fowler cannon into the encroaching ranks of Spaniards. Grey mist turned pink as the cartridge shot plumed wide. The enemy might have seized the colours, but the English counter-attack had begun. Yelling their rage, the crew chased over lost ground, their momentum for a while reversing the flow. Grenville led the pursuit.

More ships clustered around the dying hulk, the *Asuncion* and a flyboat gripping fast to accelerate its demise. It was near midnight when Grenville took a shot to the chest and was ferried to a dressing station beside a toppled gun. Hardy knelt close, his own face lacerated and etched with red.

'What a pretty sight we are, Christian.' Grenville panted shallowly while the surgeon applied a linen compress. 'God is merciful: this is only a scratch.'

'Be still and let the surgeon tend you,' Hardy urged his commander.

'How goes the battle?'

'We endure and shall fight on.'

Satisfaction ghosted through the pain. 'Then we will kill any in our reach.'

'An English victualler probes near to draw their fire, and others seek to aid us.'

'Keep them distant, Christian. I would not have them squander men or effort on our plight.'

With a sigh the surgeon slumped, an entry wound to his temple. Grenville grabbed a rapier and rolled away beneath the cover of the culverin. There were new enemies to greet.

The early hours brightened to the salvoes played into the hull. A relay of Spanish galleons paraded by, brushing point-blank or drifting to leeward, inflicting constant punishment. Below her shroud of smoke, *Revenge* wallowed and replied.

Daylight brought a terrible scene. Ringed by blackened and stricken vessels, the *Revenge* continued to fight. Her firing was desultory, her crew largely dead or injured, her commander now mortally wounded. Propped against a wood block and attended by his diminished band, Grenville lingered between consciousness and death, the old tenacity burnt strong.

'What news?' He stared up at his men.

A lieutenant answered. 'Two of their galleons are sinking and the sea around us is littered with their dead.'

'So there is merit in what we do.'

'They wait on us, sir.'

'Then they must wait longer.' Grenville closed his eyes. 'What are their demands?'

'Their admiral asks that we yield.'

Anger flamed in the captain's face and his voice strengthened. 'We submit to none but God. We throw ourselves on His mercy and not at the feet of a Catholic dog.'

'Our powder is almost gone.'

'You have your teeth and fists. You have your pride. You have the honour of England to defend.' Exhausted, he lapsed to silence. Occasionally a cannon discharged, marking time and magnifying futility, the ball travelling to splash harmlessly in the water.

Grenville roused himself. 'Where is my master gunner?'

'I am here, sir.'

'Gather what powder you can and put a match to it. We have fought too long to go meekly into bondage.'

The men exchanged glances and another officer spoke. 'Have we not been true and steadfast and earned our right to live?'

'And you, Christian? Will you join this mutiny?' Grenville turned his head slowly, his eyes seeking out his friend.

Hardy knelt beside him. 'They have been brave and done more than Queen or country might expect.'

'To surrender the *Revenge* is to commit treason.'

'And to waste these gallant men would be a greater crime.' Hardy took his captain's hand. 'Our ship is spent and no real prize. She will sink and we shall live to tell the valour of this action.'

'Perhaps you speak the truth.'

'I always do.'

'Then pray for me, for it is all I have left.'

In the dismal aftermath of battle and surrender, Spanish longboats shuttled to transport the living and dispose of the dead. The defeated English were worthy of respect. Their *Revenge*, so unequal in size and so ruined, remained afloat only by a miracle. Spaniards gazed in wonder.

Removing his scarred brigandine and abandoning his sword, Hardy sat on the deck among his fellows. Fatigue and desolation weighed on them all. He had survived when others had not; there was little point in questioning the mystery. Instinctively he felt for the silver crucifix at his throat, a talisman from his past once worn by his warrior father. Its contours were as familiar as the grip of his sword.

'What fates we enemies weave.'

The measured words were delivered with a sword tip pressed against Hardy's chest, a hand reaching to snatch away the cross. Hardy stayed motionless, gazing at the face he loathed above all others, recalling the wounds inflicted on the body of his slain wife. He had learnt to understand the darkness in this man's heart. Realm, the Englishman turned traitor, the agent codenamed Reino by his Spanish masters, had returned.

Hardy stared into the pale eyes. 'I believed you dead.'

'I am alive and the Inquisition kind.'

'So again you venture out on a lost cause.'

'But I have a rapier and you are my prisoner.' Realm picked at a thread on Hardy's coat with the blade point. 'Like the *Revenge* itself you are driftwood and flotsam.'

'You failed to kill our Queen.'

'Our religion is patient and all may change.'

'What here is changed? What is altered when it takes a fleet to crush a single English vessel?'

'You alone are consolation.' Steel stroked Hardy's cheek. 'An eternal game is made of many steps.'

'And I will shadow your every one.'

The sword pricked his flesh and Hardy got to his feet. He might be destined for execution or imprisonment, for whatever torture or inhumanity his captors had prepared, but acceptance was part of his calling. There were plantations to work and the rowing benches of oared galleys to fill; there were transports on the Spanish Main to crew and the deep mines of the Americas to dig. Escorted by guards, he was taken to a skiff and transferred to a galleon. Realm was right. An eternal game was formed of many stages.

CHAPTER 1

London, May 1604

'Another stone will suffice.'

In the grim pressing-room of Newgate Prison, a man was being crushed to death. It was a prolonged affair and the audience was small, and yet throughout each groan and permutation there were formalities to observe. Five days had passed already and the stench was as bad as the suffering. *Peine forte et dure*, strong and hard punishment, could be a blunt and heavy means of execution.

'Why bear such pain?' The interrogator leant forward on his stool. 'Why endure so much when reason cries out that you should speak?'

Pinioned beneath the plank, the prisoner whimpered breathlessly at the force bearing down. It seemed the entire English state was squeezing life from his body. He should have known that the dark arts of Protestant subterfuge would ensnare him and drag him here. It was the fate of many Catholics. And he had been willing to accept the risk, to join the English regiment with other believers and fight for Spain in the Low Countries against the heretic uprising there. With fire and sword he had helped cleanse the land. Until the day a trusted brother-volunteer had taken him down to greet a ship of new recruits; until the moment he found himself bound and lying helpless in its hold. That erstwhile friend with his sly patience and charm and searing blue eyes had been in the employ of the chief English spymaster.

Again the voice. 'Some struggle for ten days or more. It ends the same.'

'You want a confession?' The words fluttered out, near inaudible.

'We ask for names before you die. We demand to know the identities of those who would do us harm.'

The prisoner's chest strained, a thousand agonies melding into one. May God forgive him. Confusion infested his mind, stirring false memory.

All the while the voice spoke, reasoned and insistent. 'Speed your journey and give us what we seek.'

'I . . . must . . . have . . . air . . .'

'One name and you shall have relief.'

He heard as if from afar his own thin, high-pitched moan. Perhaps it mattered little now. The plot was already afoot. King James and his satanic coterie would rue their overconfidence.

'Speak louder.' The interrogator tried to interpret the sounds. 'Summon your thoughts.'

A drawn-out, ragged silence and then reply: 'Guido . . . Fawkes . . .'

'Once more.'

'Guido Fawkes.'

The man was dead by the time the messenger rode from the prison and crossed the Fleet Ditch on his way to the Strand. It was a short journey, which saw him pass the taverns and bawdy houses and Inns of Court and continue on through Temple Bar. Not even the screaming inmates of Bridewell or the crowd gathered to view the occupant of a gibbet near Fetter Lane delayed him. His master waited.

On the north side of the Strand, Robert Cecil's large brick mansion was undergoing modification and enlargement. Turrets were being added and a grander entrance installed. It befitted a man ennobled as the first Earl of Salisbury by a grateful King, and marked with stone the shift in power to this diminutive and diligent minister of the Crown. Others had faded and he was ascendant, the spy chief and Secretary of State on whom the monarch relied. No seditious remark would be spoken without his hearing; no conspiracy would develop without his eventual uncovering of the truth. England could sleep soundly and opponents should beware. A constant guardian watched over all.

'A *pressing* matter brings you.'

Cecil delivered the jest without humour or a smile as he took the sealed letter and with a nod dismissed its bearer. He had noted the fear in the man's eyes. People had underestimated him, had thought him nothing more than a short and twisted hunchback worthy only of mockery. Now they flattered and grovelled or begged for mercy. He peered through the leaded panes and glimpsed the apartments of Durham House once occupied by Sir Walter Raleigh, and the tower cupola from which the vainglorious courtier had surveyed his domain before his sudden fall from grace. Another triumph arranged by Cecil.

Guido Fawkes. He read the name again and muttered it aloud. Sometimes the condemned revealed much; sometimes merely senseless babble. Instinct persuaded him there was more to this name. He would set his hounds on the scent. He would send for Christian Hardy.

Gaols tended to unsettle him. At the Tower of London, Christian Hardy surrendered his sword and crossed the drawbridge to the Lion Gate, then continued to the Byward entrance by way of a middle tower and further bridge. Walls within walls and moats encircled by moats. Only kings and traitors took a different route, and only fools came by choice. The Tower was where ambition could end and a head roll for the simple crime of displeasing the monarch. Great men and women had whiled away their years in its stone embrace or been paraded out to Tower Hill to kneel before the block.

He reached the green and its site of execution and headed for the walled garden beside the Bloody Tower. Guards patrolled the perimeter. It was far from the bustle of the streets, further still from his enslavement in the silver mines of Potosì as a prisoner of the Spanish. For three years he had laboured in the viceroyalty of Peru, hacking at the silver ore, burrowing deep beneath the Cerro Rico, the rich mountain, to feed the coffers of the Spanish mint. Though he suffered and many died, he had endured to the day of his escape. There had been a trek with natives and a silver train of two thousand llamas to the port of Arica, passage in disguise aboard ship to El Callao and Panama, the crossing of the isthmus and emergence in the Orinoco delta. Murder and bullion theft had accompanied his ordeal, each step tortuous and fraught with danger. His fluency in Spanish and Italian and the Mediterranean looks inherited from his noble Maltese mother had provided his salvation when on the run. It was the year 1595 when Hardy crawled to the edge of the Atlantic shoreline at the same moment that Sir Walter Raleigh dropped anchor at the river mouth in search of the gold of El Dorado.

Now, over nine years later, Hardy bowed his head to enter Raleigh's open cell door. Raleigh strode to embrace him. 'You came, Christian. Would that you were here to rescue me as I did you on that distant shore.'

'It is not in my power,' Hardy said ruefully.

'A shame.' The ageing courtier pulled a wry expression. 'Thus am I condemned to languish in my tower and to dream of better things.'

'Perhaps better things only inhabit dreams.'

Raleigh gave a melancholy laugh. 'I belong to the past and a dead Queen. It is Cecil and his kind who own the present.'

'To bide awhile here is then your wisest course.' Hardy sensed his friend's brooding restlessness. 'Fortune and tide may shift.'

'Or my head might end placed upon a spike.'

'Risk is part of our calling.'

'I prefer a fair fight.' Raleigh gazed about him, his pride and vitality flaring. 'Though my world is small and I am stripped of everything, I should not complain. I have at hand my wife and children and books, and when they tire of me, my chickens give me welcome.'

He looked back at the younger man. In Hardy he recognised a distillation of himself, another soldier tested and scarred in conflict. 'Let us walk, Christian.'

They climbed the steps to the narrow terrace of the curtain wall, a promenade of fifty paces that marked the bounds of Raleigh's existence. Before them lay the river and its widening vista of wharves and ships to London Bridge beyond. Somehow the bustling scene increased the sense of isolation.

Raleigh waved his hand. 'Do you think they ever speak my name? Do you believe they remember I am here?'

'No one can steal your renown.'

'Yet King James sees fit to take from me my liberty and Cecil my discovery of Virginia.' Raleigh glanced back to his prison home. 'Where once the Bloody Tower was a water gate, those waters are receded. It seems, like the tower, I too am beached.'

'Savour the respite from the storm.'

'The tempest will come soon enough.'

'You write your history of England.'

'In a chamber in which two young princes were once murdered. It reminds us that none are safe from plot and intrigue.'

For several minutes they watched the lighters and wherries meandering between the larger boats and listened to the calls and whistles. In his

JAMES JACKSON | 15

richly braided doublet and silk-trimmed boots, Hardy was far removed from the gaunt man who had emerged on the banks of the Orinoco nine years before. Seed pearls and a hoard of silver could do much to banish the pain of enslavement.

'What of your son, Christian?' Raleigh asked at last.

'We are estranged.' It was safer for Adam that way.

'He is a young man and will find his path.'

'I pray he does not follow mine.'

The older man's hand rested on Hardy's arm. 'You cannot preserve him from all harm, Christian.'

'I can seek to keep him from my own.'

'Fate contrives to trip us in the end.' Raleigh spoke with the authority of his years and of marriage to a Throckmorton. In a climate of suspicion, any connection to the Catholic faith and a leading recusant family could invite a suggestion of treason. He lowered his voice and continued with more urgency. 'Be watchful and alive to danger, Christian. Chained though I am, I see and hear things. Oppression builds and the Catholics will not forever lie quiet.'

'Are you predicting or warning me?'

'I'm rambling. I'm a seafarer and I'm giving counsel to a friend.'

'You forget I labour for the Crown.'

'It will not spare you from the furnace.'

As Christian Hardy left the Tower, another man crossed the City, striding purposefully towards the Royal Exchange. His mind too dwelt on the plight of English Catholics, although his countenance betrayed no sign of his concern. He had learnt to hide both his feelings and his identity, for his flock depended on his succour. Survival came down to luck and nerve, to crouching in priest holes, outrunning pursuit and outsmarting Cecil's priest-catchers, the pursuivants. Father Henry Garnet, chief Jesuit in England and defender of the Catholic faith, fully understood the risks he ran. The heads of his friends adorning London Bridge bore witness. If caught, he would be shown no mercy.

His calling drove him and he hastened on, thanking the Lord for the anonymity and protection afforded by the crowd. He prayed for their souls and for his country, and that their King should be drawn to the light. The tyranny had grown under James. Elizabeth had been an enemy of Rome and yet was not a monster. James was proving different. He railed against what he deemed a superstitious practice and exhorted his bishops to root it out, had encouraged legislation to outlaw the evil and brought thousands before the assizes. Families faced ruin through recusant fines and men and women were cast into prison. It was the harshest of times to be a Catholic and the most dangerous of moments to be a Jesuit.

Close by the churchyard of St Paul's, he had seen a Catholic pamphleteer in the pillory, his hands bound and ears nailed to a board and his face a mask of suffering. What a pitiless place the country had become. There were rumours of future insurrection, of hotheads mounting an armed challenge to the King. Garnet hoped fervently it was a harmless venting of rage, and that it was a stage that would pass. Surely James would discover reason and humanity and a kinder age would dawn. He was certain of it.

'Pins to buy! Pins to buy!'

'What do you want? What do you need?'

'Come this way for lawn and cambric.'

The cries of sellers echoed about him. Any one of these people might be an informant for the state. Spies abounded, trawling the inns, alehouses and theatres and reporting back to Cecil. Father Garnet felt his belly tighten in anticipation of a challenge.

He saw his fellow Jesuit on the far side of the street, a face emerging for an instant in the frenetic flow of people. Their eyes met briefly, and in that moment Garnet detected the hidden warning. A second later he spotted the two young men dressed as apprentices trailing the Jesuit at a distance. His contact was compromised and as good as on the scaffold.

'Halt where you are!'

Garnet's speeding heart ordered him to run, while his cooler head instructed that he stay. With a neutral face and readied excuse, he did as the rest and turned in the direction of the command. But his martyrdom would have to keep: it was his brother Jesuit stumbling to flee, who had diverted leading on the pack in its clumsy stampede. Garnet had no doubt it was an act of self-sacrifice intended to distract them from the greater prize.

'In the name of the King, hold him!'

The shouts of the mob drowned out the cries of the inconvenienced. The promise of violence and summary justice was the finest of spectator sports. Baskets tumbled and stalls gave way as the pressure wave swept by.

May the Blessed Virgin protect and bring stillness in the midst of terror. The hunted priest wept in his exertion, his lungs straining and his limbs aching as he scampered frantically for any alleyway or opening. The tenements rose high around him, and their jetties seemed to close in overhead and channel him to the dark. At least he had lured the enemy away from Father Garnet. He fumbled for his rosary and worked it in his fingers, but dropped it as he sprawled forward.

'You are captured, priest.'

A foot had tripped him and brought him hard to earth. He lay winded, dirt and gravel embedded in his skin and blood starting to flow. These injuries would pale against what he faced. He could do nothing but lie prone and sob in quiet anguish, cleanse himself of hope and commit to future torment. Everyone had their Calvary.

'It seems I have acquired a trophy.' A rapier tip lifted the rosary to slide it on the blade.

The priest angled his head to look up. 'What is a mere trinket to you is precious to me.'

'Therefore you prove yourself a traitor.'

'Not to God.' The priest's voice strengthened with fearful certainty.

'It is to King James you shall answer.'

Isaiah Payne, lead pursuivant, regarded his latest find with satisfaction. Effort and diligence had once more brought results. There were few higher rewards than to ensnare the enemies of the Crown and guard the Protestant body of England from the cancer of Catholicism. Long ago Payne had eschewed the flamboyant attire of a previous age in favour of more sombre and puritanical dress. And like his master Cecil, the priest-catcher found pleasure in his trade.

His voice was scratched and high as he gloated. 'How many of your kind have I cornered in our city?'

'There will be others that escape.'

'Each in turn betrays himself and is discovered.' Payne licked his lips. 'As the swamp is drained, so more criminals are revealed.'

'You revel in your certainty and yet are the one damned.' The priest spoke with contempt. 'One day there shall be judgement.'

Payne leered. 'What should matter more to you is the hour your courage flees and you are drawn and quartered on the block.'

The prisoner was led away through the jeering and shouting throng. Grieving and troubled, a man with a learned face and kindly eyes offered up a silent plea of intercession and hurried from the scene. Father Henry Garnet would not falter in his ministry.

For its part, the English state would not waver in its fight to crush subversion and all that Garnet preached. To that end, among the transports and trading barques moored in the Pool of London, customs men and teams of searchers pursued their endless quest. Everything was suspect: a barrel might contain a false compartment and a length of rope conceal a message. The enemy were skilled in smuggling. Beneath dyed leathers from the Barbary Coast or timber from the Baltics could lie recusant texts. Paper trails that began in the hold of a ship often led to a provincial manor in the dead of night and the arrest of an entire household. There was a cold zeal to the madness.

In the hold of a merchantman, a searcher swung his lantern and followed the arc of its illumination. He was a patient soul, a committed bloodhound and veteran of countless discoveries once congratulated in person by Robert Cecil himself. He tapped a bulkhead with the edge of a chisel and worked his way along. A laborious task, but one he did not resent. He crouched to inspect a cluster of barrels and take his sounding. Salted fish were best left undisturbed. Yet something pricked his interest, a slight variation in the tone of the return, a difference in weight as he tried to tilt the barrels. Complacency had vanished.

'You tread too close.'

The voice hissed behind him as a wire garrotte dropped down to loop fast about his throat. The searcher resisted but was quickly subdued. Deft hands applied pressure, forcing him face down on the ground, relieving him of his dagger.

'Struggle and you will compound your woes.' A knee pressed into his back and leather bindings were threaded around his wrists. 'You were foolhardy to trespass.'

'I do not trespass. It is my duty.' Gasping against the wooden boards, the searcher summoned defiance. 'There are others close, a score of men ready at my call.'

'None will hear your cry.' The ligature tightened.

'There is gold and silver, gems that I keep safe.'

'Still part of your duty?'

'We find things, precious things,' the searcher wheezed from his constricted throat.

'And I find you.' The assailant leant to kiss the top of the man's head. 'You have a name, hoarder?'

'William Birch.'

'So, William Birch. Assist and inform me and I shall let you live.'

Realm smiled to himself as he heard the searcher catch his breath, a subtle sign of relief. Realm had travelled far and for many reasons, for the purposes of revenge and self-enrichment and to aid the benighted Catholics of his homeland. Before his return, he had met those who intended to inflict cataclysm, and he admired the sheer scale of their enterprise. Their ambition was laudable and worthy of support, and Jesuits too constrained and passive in their aims. Where once he had planned to assassinate Queen Elizabeth, he could redirect his artistry to the murder of King James.

The interrogation was systematic and unhurried, Realm keeping a relaxed but purposeful grip on the garrotte. By the end he had gleaned many things and learnt of the corrupt and thieving ways of his victim. Realm felt no pity for him. The man was a dullard whose demise would serve as a waypoint to further acts. He slipped off the noose and rolled the captive onto his back.

'You discover more aboard than you imagined, William Birch.'

'I gave all that you demanded.'

'For which you find me grateful.' Realm gazed down upon the searcher's strained and mottled features. 'In truth, I engage in higher things and you impede my progress.'

Realisation dawned slowly. 'I have a wife and children, sir,' Birch spluttered.

'No doubt they will grieve.'

'We had an agreement!'

'Hush and be courageous.' Realm reached into the pouch at his belt. 'I believe our compact void.'

The stiletto blade was thin and sharp and fashioned from obsidian, the black volcanic glass punching through an eye direct into the brain. Death occurred before shock had even registered. Realm released his grip and studied the result, letting the corpse tremble and settle beneath him. Such a privilege to be present at a departure. He did not withdraw the blade, a weapon last favoured by the Aztecs: he was leaving a message and announcing his presence. Christian Hardy was not alone in having endured years of exile in the Americas.

Carefully, Realm laid a small silver crucifix across the remaining eye of the cadaver. Every Englishman would soon see the truth, arise and embrace the old religion or be cast into the pit, of that he was sure. With his encouragement and the flaming sword of Saint Michael as their guide, the chosen few would begin a process that would lead to the overthrow of government and the downfall of oppression. Any means were justified.

Within minutes, a new William Birch had emerged onto the main deck and crossed to the wharfside, where he mingled with a group of sailors thirsting for the taverns and heading to the City hinterland. Realm had started his mission.

'"Lo, there was a great earthquake and the sun became black as sackcloth."'

Five men were gathered at the table in an upstairs room of an inn off the Strand named the Duck and Drake. There was little remarkable in such a meeting and nothing to draw the eye, for in this fashionable quarter of London the wealthy and connected often convened in private to smoke and drink and play cards. The assembled gentlemen were eager to convey the impression that this was what they were doing, and yet such idle pastimes were far from their aim. Linked by blood or marriage or childhood acquaintance, they were drawn together by common cause and Catholic faith and were intent on doing high treason. It was Sunday, 20 May 1604. Cecil had every reason to fear.

At the head of the table sat Robin Catesby, a tall, vibrant figure. Strong, handsome and charming, he was a natural leader. To his right was Tom Wintour, his cousin and adjutant, clearly in thrall to his command; to his left, Thomas Percy, an older man, grey-haired and slightly stooped, his manner impatient and ill-tempered. Beside Percy sat his brother by marrriage, Jack Wright, a noted swordsman, the group's sentinel and enforcer. And across from him was the soldier Guido Fawkes; quiet and saturnine, he sat observing the rest, brought in to effect their wishes. Catesby, Wintour, Percy, Wright and Fawkes. Companions in doublets and high-crowned hats who had tired of waiting and were now committed irrevocably to the course of violence.

Catesby regarded them. 'Already the fifth seal of the Apocalypse is opened and the cries of the martyrs ring out. It is left to us to open the sixth and unleash a righteous cataclysm.'

'Amen to it.' Percy nodded. 'There is none but ourselves to slay the tyrant.'

Wintour poured claret into his goblet from a leather jack. 'You are right, brother. See how the Spanish offer soothing words and deliver nothing.'

'There is much to divert them.'

'I have heard every excuse from the Constable of Castile himself.' Wintour drank deep. 'Now he prepares to visit London and declare a treaty of peace.'

'Thus do English Catholics stand alone.'

Jack Wright spoke up. 'Scarce do they stand. They are bowed beneath the Protestant yoke, tormented and imprisoned, treated no better than dogs.'

'These dogs may bite.'

Cups slammed down in accord on the plank surface. Catesby leant back and listened to the men speak. He was glad for their fury and passion, for their loyalty to him and their support for decisive action. It would be a monstrous gamble. Yet disease required a cure and their people's desperate plight demanded a radical answer. All at the meeting would need to hold their nerve.

Finally, he sat forward. 'From this moment, there is no retreat. Here, the fuse is lit.'

'It is a wonder we will find the King.' Percy had gained possession of the flagon. 'He runs so scared of pestilence and regicide, he spends his days hunting in the country.'

'I could lead a mounted group and bring him down with sword and pistol,' suggested Wright.

Percy frowned. 'He is well defended and too much would be left to chance.'

'Chance will favour those that seize it.'

Catesby interrupted. 'Both of you are right and in your words are hid the answer.'

'Where then do we strike?' asked Fawkes.

'Parliament House.' Catesby let the silence hang for a moment, his eyes on the soldier. 'Gunpowder is your skill and Westminster our target.'

'You have great faith in me.'

'I have high expectations for us all. With one blow we shall transform the world and rid it of the Beast and his infernal government.'

'What of the aftermath?' asked Percy.

The leader looked at Percy. Mild shock still registered in the chamber, the audacity of Catesby's plan filtering slowly into the others' minds. He knew they would accept his reasoning. Outside, the usual rhythms and murmur of daily life continued unhindered by the words spoken here. One day it would be different; a pall of smoke would spread and his countrymen would notice. Catesby shut his eyes as though imagining the moment. 'Through ash and wreckage we will arise, our brother Catholics join us, our council act swiftly to decide the royal succession.'

'With whom do we replace the tyrant?'

'Princess Elizabeth, daughter of James, survivor of our inferno.' Catesby smiled and reopened his eyes. 'I offer you Queen Elizabeth the Second of England.'

'She is only seven years old,' Wright said doubtfully.

'The easier to be tutored in religion and guided in our ways. The better to be snatched from Coombe Abbey, where she holds court.'

Murder and kidnap were such plausible notions when discussed among friends. They had hoped and prayed that King James might relent and lessen his grasp on the throat of their faith. But his grip became only tighter. There was no alternative to the route they pursued. On his own stubborn head would the small Scots interloper bring down the wrath of his opponents and, Catesby was resolved, the timbered roof of Parliament.

Fawkes was consuming a meat pasty, a soldier attuned to the practicalities of the scheme. 'And what if we should fail and the King live? If retribution is visited upon our fellow Catholics?'

'God wills it we succeed.' Catesby removed from his finger a gold ring and held it up before them. 'Marked here inside are the five wounds of Christ, a symbol of His sacrifice. We act in His name and will see it to the close.'

As it was a Sunday, they took communion from a Jesuit priest brought clandestinely to an adjoining room. Life and death had no value against the power of the sacrament. There were arrangements to make and gunpowder to acquire and men and materiel to gather. Five conspirators received the Host and pledged themselves to holy war and to deliverance.

Unaware of adult machinations or the proximity of her Coombe Abbey home in Warwickshire to the country manor of Robin Catesby, a young princess with fair hair and quick brown eyes sat to dutifully pick out notes on her virginal. She was a diligent and willing pupil. Yet on occasion her thoughts would stray to the things she missed, and in particular her beloved elder brother Henry. The most cosseted and privileged of lives could also be impoverished. Elizabeth paused at the instrument and stared awhile through the window to the moat and beyond to the herds of deer grazing peacefully in the parkland. Unlike her, they had freedom to roam.

CHAPTER 2

Robert Cecil viewed Hardy in silence, appraising him with a neutral eye that managed to convey hostility. Relations between the spy chief and his intelligencer were not cordial. Hardy had been inherited from Cecil's predecessor, the great spymaster Walsingham: the man's independence of spirit jarred with the little hunchback, the historic antics that gilded the legend, the man's effectiveness that might one day prove a threat. Christian Hardy was never fully to be trusted.

Cecil eventually spoke. 'You belonged to Walsingham. I do not forget it.'

'As you once served Elizabeth; we each have former masters.'

Cecil's eyes narrowed. 'Time passes and your insolence remains.'

'Do I not do as I am bid and bleed when I am asked, my lord? Do I not catch and render to you the enemies of England?'

'It is hatred of Spain and not loyalty to me that drives you.' The spymaster had not moved. 'Be glad your usefulness outweighs your tongue.'

'Many comment on my good fortune.'

'A man without a care is incautious. An incautious man may fall and break his head.'

'I will be watchful, my lord.'

'So too shall I.'

They stood in the great parlour of the London mansion, together and yet distant in a scene redolent of a hundred previous taskings. Like Walsingham before him, Cecil could be opaque in his intent. Hardy waited, accustomed to the chill power play and the direction of their business. There were too many ragged ends in the life of Christian Hardy, too much left open to interpretation, to allow him freedom from the hunchback earl.

The spy chief blinked. 'You visit Raleigh in the Tower.'

'He writes his histories and I oblige him with my comments.'

'Take care whom you choose as a friend. It may do you more harm than any foe.'

'My enemies prefer to kill me than converse.'

'To their number you may add one other.' Cecil displayed no emotion. 'Guido Fawkes.'

It was a name Hardy recognised, that of a Yorkshireman, a former company commander once held in high regard, an expert in firearms and explosives. A Catholic, Fawkes had turned rogue, fighting in Flanders for a decade as a volunteer soldier for the Spanish. He was a proficient adversary and had so far escaped the long reach of England and its law.

Hardy felt the questioning gaze of Cecil. 'Where is he, my lord?'

'We believe he is returned to England.'

'To what end?'

'A mystery that is yours to discover.' The spymaster turned and walked to an oak sideboard. 'Yet he is brought by recusants and I have no doubt intends us harm.'

'You are certain he is here, my lord?'

'As certain as the torturer who informed me.' Cecil turned, holding in his outstretched palm a fragment of obsidian. 'I discover other things, too.'

Hardy took the proffered object. 'Volcanic glass.'

'Found in the eye of one of my searchers.'

'A fair way from its source, I vouch.'

'Perhaps this is closer.' The silver crucifix dangled from his fingers, an item once stolen and now returned. Hardy did not reach for it. Cecil fed on any sign of weakness.

The spymaster watched him closely. 'Who is he, Mr Hardy?'

'The traitor known as Realm.'

Cecil's cold eyes registered recognition. 'He wishes us to comprehend his work is yet unfinished.'

'When last in England he sought to kill the Queen.'

'Instead he slew your wife.' There was scant compassion in Cecil's voice. 'It seems that now he comes for the King.'

'Or he acts as a diversion.'

Cecil tossed Hardy the cross and limped slowly about the room. He was mentally sniffing the air, gauging the direction of the scent. Few had a nose for conspiracy like the diminutive Machiavelli. 'Fawkes and Realm are linked or separate; they labour together or apart,' he said as he walked. 'Discover one and you may in turn detect the other.'

'I will bring to justice those who deserve it.'

Cecil paused and turned to look at Hardy. 'You will find that I alone am arbiter.'

'As you desire, my lord.'

'So you will not protest when I join Isaiah Payne and his pursuivants to your endeavour.'

'Their presence is not needed.'

'And yet I ordain it.' Cecil turned to the side.

Hardy saw that the audience was concluded; debate would be to no avail. Isaiah Payne was assigned more as keeper and spy than to assist him in the hunt. Cecil maintained control through division.

The spymaster's eyes were heavy-lidded. 'Enemies to your front and back. Be vigilant, Mr Hardy.'

Hardy considered the remark. As with everything uttered by the Secretary of State, the true meaning was often encrypted.

'There is darkness in your eye, Christian.' They stood close together in the parlour of his half-timbered house, set among the orchard gardens near the Inns of Court.

She spoke without reproach, but her own face betrayed the anguish that he caused. Beatrice had learnt to be resilient. As lover and companion she had grown accustomed to his absence and his homecomings, to the scars he carried and the dangers he met. Hers was a selfless existence bent to aid his selfish one. In return, he adored her, and had promised himself he would one day marry this quiet and beautiful widow. Another deceit to lay upon the rest.

He held and kissed her and made light of her concern. 'You see what is not there.'

'I know that Cecil sends you into hazard.' Her voice was soft in his ear. 'I know you will kill and risk being killed.'

'Have I not survived?'

'In spite of what you do. Fate does not always favour the brave.'

'It smiles on those with wits and swordsmanship.'

'Will you outrun the musket ball, Christian? Or parry the unseen blow to your back?'

'I am an intelligencer and soldier, my Bea.'

'Then you are twice in jeopardy.'

Her instincts were sure and her fears for him justified and yet she had never heard of Realm. On this floor had once seeped the blood of Emma, Hardy's wife, butchered by the English renegade. The stains were gone but the guilt remained, and now the enemy had returned. He shifted, remembering the crimson puddling at his feet.

'Tell me your thoughts, Christian.'

'I believe you are more secure elsewhere. I bid you journey to your home.'

She clung to him. 'My place is here.'

'I cannot guard us both or deal with threats when you are near.'

'Am I to be banished like your son?'

He caught the glimmer of tears in her eyes, but also her recognition that any protest would founder on his determination. He protected himself by shutting out feelings, by concentrating on the task and destroying his opponent. If it helped him towards victory, he knew she would comply.

She sighed. 'Who are they, Christian?'

'No one you shall ever meet.' He prayed it would be so.

'Will you be safe? Return to me alive?'

'You have my pledge.' It wasn't his to give.

She turned her head towards him. 'I release you on condition you hold me in your heart.'

'If I did not care, I would not ask so much of you.' He kissed her once more.

Beatrice trembled. 'I know the ease of words and the nature of death.'

She left him alone to prepare. Behind the buttery and pantry, steps lead to twin cellars. Taking a lantern, Hardy descended to unlock the heavier of the studded doors. He ducked to enter the chamber. It was his armoury and where most of his memories were contained. Before him hung swords and daggers and firearms of every kind, the tools of his vocation and detritus of his past. Some were trophies of war and covert operations and others designed for future assignments. Each was precious to him.

A few of the blades he took down and unsheathed, weighing them in his hand, inspecting the gilding and silver encrustation and the pommels inlaid with gemstones. As a master of Destreza, the Spanish martial skill of fencing, he could put ten armed adversaries on the ground before they had inflicted a scratch. Small wonder the Spaniards dubbed it the true art.

His examination was painstaking. Here, a German rapier with its front guard hooked to catch an enemy blade; there, a Flemish rapier with a perforated basket; an Italian rapier with serpent quillons; a Spanish rapier with an undulating edge. He chose the katzbalger, the cat-gutter, a short, sturdy weapon that would allow him to fight at close quarters in buildings and alleys. On the trail of Realm or Guido Fawkes, an ambush might happen anywhere.

At the head of the stairs, Black Jack acknowledged him with an enquiring stare. He was a man given to few words. Though several of his predecessors had perished in combat and through their close association with his master, it did not daunt the former slave. As servant and friend he had proved the most loyal and effective of shadows. Hardy nodded and Black Jack grinned. The crew were to be summoned.

So the lover was being sent beyond danger. A touching scene, mused Realm. He kept his distance, following the progress of the carriage and baggage cart and guiding his horse through the channelled tumult of the London streets. Only on the outskirts would the flow of humanity and traffic ease. It was rewarding to sit a few paces behind and yet be far ahead. Not only had he unearthed in Clerkenwell the ill-gotten hoard of a deceased searcher to put to use against the English state, but he had arrived at his enemy's home in time to witness the lover's departure. The renegade pulled the cap lower on his forehead. He could not fault the intelligencer in his taste: his mistress was pretty and would bleed as freely as his late wife. There would come a day of reckoning when none would escape. The carriage and wagon headed out for St Giles-in-the-Fields and beyond to the rising ground of Hampstead. The time had come to test the edge and mettle of Christian Hardy.

Nightwatchmen were scarce in these parts. Should people stray or stumble drunk about Holborn without escort, they deserved what befell them. Footpads and cutthroats abounded at this hour and had ready escape in the surrounding labyrinth of alleyways and courtyards. Occasionally a light flared in a window or a tavern door opened to release a gust of sound, yet the prevailing sense was of threat and shadow.

Voices intruded into the quiet, loud in their inebriation, a group of Scots staggering merry on their way. It was their King on the throne and they too had journeyed south, to dance in attendance and inherit the earth. They were the colonists and the English would be forced to suffer them.

'What brings you here?'

The question was not friendly and made the Scotsmen pause. Whoever gave this challenge was unschooled in basic manners. Diplomacy would ease misunderstanding.

'Good eve to you, stranger.' A spokesman kept it affable.

'You will not find it good.' Lanterns were unshuttered and pricked the dark. 'I ask again, what brings you here?'

'We are going home,' the same man offered.

'Would that you did, for your home is not London.'

'Are we not citizens like you?'

'You are dogs and whores. You are prick-lice. You are Scots.'

The atmosphere had changed and the effects of liquor were fast wearing off. Plainly those who accosted them meant ill. Confused, the small band of revellers huddled tighter. Their spokesman tried again. 'We mean you no harm, gentlemen.'

'Yet injury we shall do to you.' The reply came in a mimicked Scots brogue. 'Did you think we would give you welcome? Did you suppose we were lawyers or students?'

'Who then are you, sir?'

'Swaggerers.'

Fear lent the man's voice a higher and trembling pitch. 'We bear arms.'

'As do we.'

'King James protects us.'

'We care not if he knights you for buggery.' Harsh laughter echoed from the gang. 'Your sodomite King is nowhere to be found.'

'In his name we demand safe passage.'

'Because of him you trespass and are damned.'

King James had ascended the English throne only a year before, hailed as the saviour of a nation grown weary beneath the sclerotic hand of the aged Queen Elizabeth. The elderly woman had taken years to die and rotted with her country. The arrival of her successor heralded change and the rejuvenation of the monarchy. Yet there were always detractors, particularly those who went unfavoured, the recusant Catholics chafing at their renewed persecution and Londoners resentful of the influx of the loathsome Scots. The Swaggerers were one response and preyed viciously on the newcomers. Tonight they had fresh pickings.

Their leader shouted, 'Hurt them well and take their purses.'

The attack was brutal and sustained, accompanied by the screams of frightened men and the gleeful oaths of their assailants. The Swaggerers meant to punish and deter and to cleanse the streets of the detested aliens.

A musket shot sounded. 'Put up your weapons and surrender!'

Around the fray more lanterns appeared, hooked on the front of shields. The trap had been sprung. The vagabonds and their targets struggled to disengage. A few lay still; others groaned or spat teeth into the dirt, dazed by the sudden reversal.

Into the light stepped a spry Isaiah Payne. 'What do we catch this night but a sewerful of rats?'

'Thank the Lord you have come.' A Scot rose unsteadily to his feet, his voice quavering. 'They would have killed us all.'

'Be assured they will pay dearly for their crime.'

'It is worse than a mere crime. It is an affront and abomination.'

'You are fortunate my pursuivants on occasion hunt down more than foul priests.'

'Whether these are vermin or Jesuits, they are an insult to the King.' The Scotsman launched a kick into the ribs of a prone Swaggerer. 'See how they cower now.'

A gang member sneered. 'Such courage from a coward who shits his britches.'

Payne beckoned for a light; holding it up, he wandered to the youth who had spoken, studied his fair hair and strong jaw and the blood coursing from his lip. There was a beauty and intelligence in the face that seemed at odds with the venomous hatred in his expression. This lad would make the hearts of women flutter at his public execution.

'You have a name?' Payne asked.

'A friend of England and enemy to the Scots.'

'Your age?'

'Old enough to know my mind.'

'Yet not wise enough to curb your tongue.' The pursuivant stared at the youth. 'King James commands an example be made of your kind.'

'It will not earn him my regard.'

'To attack his countrymen is to strike at the King. To assault the King is to commit treason.'

'The traitor here is you.'

Payne rarely let an insult slide. As his sergeants employed their whips and cudgels, he stood aside, admiring their enthusiasm and how stoically the young man took the pain, uttering not a sound.

Curled up beneath their blows, an eighteen-year-old named Adam Hardy, sometime actor and musician and former student of the law, the son of a murdered mother and an absent father, thought of other things and had no regrets.

A more leisured pursuit was underway in the Mermaid Tavern on Cheapside. In the light flickering dimly through the haze of tobacco and tallow smoke, a fiddler played, games of dice and shove-groat drew rowdy comment, men and women made merry and the house whore plied her trade with aplomb. In a corner, two figures sat in jovial discussion over oysters and strong beer. They were poets and playwrights grown rich on their success, deft at both flattering their patrons and pleasing the populace. The older, balding man had watchful eyes and a listening ear, and a ready geniality that suited his face and drew others to his confidence. His friend was more restless, with the quickness of wit and the energy of a brawler, his features dominated by an aquiline nose. William Shakespeare and Ben Jonson were at play.

'More beer!' Jonson slammed down his emptied tankard. 'My thirst is never quenched.'

'Is it not your thirst that gets you into trouble?'

'I killed a man through anger, not drink. Besides, I was sober enough to escape the noose and plead benefit of clergy.'

'How rare it is to see any benefit in clergy.'

Jonson frowned. 'Find me a bishop and I will show you a thief, a peddler of nonsense in league with the devil.'

'It is the King from whom they take their orders.'

'Each, I hear, has the whiff of sulphur.'

'I will steer a wiser course and keep my thinking silent.'

'Do not forget to cheer me on my way to Tyburn.'

Reciting the scriptures had once saved Jonson from hanging, and yet he was not afraid to provoke or voice opinion or enter into a fight. His Catholic leaning was suspected. Shakespeare's sympathies were better hidden.

'Ben and Will, our greetings!' Robin Catesby and his lieutenant Tom Wintour approached, smiling in pleasure. They were welcomed warmly. These men were old comrades, owning manors close to Shakespeare's home in Stratford-upon-Avon, and Jonson was a long-time acquaintance of the charismatic Catesby. More drink was called for.

Shakespeare reached to grip the newcomers' hands. 'At last a Midlands cure for the maladies of London.'

'Some believe my tonic is too strong.' Catesby smiled at the theatre man. 'You are brave to drink with hated recusants.'

'There is nothing but fondness and regard for you here.'

'While outside lie resentment and ceaseless fines.'

'All things pass, Robin,' said Shakespeare.

'That much is true.' Catesby took his tankard and raised it to his lips. 'I drink to any that bring me cheer and speed a resolution to our plight.'

Jonson swallowed an oyster and belched. 'Moses alone split the sea and offered a promised land.'

'Some would split the world asunder.'

'They are not then a wavering Prince of Denmark.' Jonson glanced amused at the older playwright.

Shakespeare shrugged. 'They may yet end as discarded skulls or diggers of each other's graves.'

He sipped on his beer and lapsed into thought. In his Silver Street lodgings was a manuscript in progress about a tyrant king who ignored wise counsel to reward flatterers and false allies until his fall from grace.

Perhaps downfall was necessary before redemption. God save King James, and God help the people who opposed him.

There was little quiet or contemplation in the cockpit on Shoe Lane, where the straw-covered table glistened with blood. The atmosphere was febrile as fighting birds clashed and the crowd roared. It was a cruel and heady sport. Ranged about the circumference of the platform were the contestants and gamblers, making or losing money and drunk on the moment. Above them in the gallery were the public, pressing to see, baying encouragement and demanding spectacle for a penny. Bottled beer and liquorice spirit could heighten the emotion.

Another two birds were held and released, their spurs enhanced with steel blades and their fury inflamed by brandy wine. In a fluttering rage the combatants locked and clawed and went for the heart as instinct and training instructed. Within seconds a blade had entered a chest and a victor was parading his triumph. The evening was proving a happy one for the favourite.

How quickly a coxcomb was bled of its colour and how decisive a single blow could be. Jack Wright left the clamorous din and climbed the steps to the street. He was a taciturn man and took seriously his repute as a swordsman and his role in safeguarding the plot against King James. Should Catesby demand he counter a threat, he would kill without delay. After all, he had taken a sacred vow to overthrow the state. His solitary pastimes took him to many places and allowed him to sift the chatter and gossip of the street. Security for the operation was safe in his hands.

'Show yourself.' A slight sound or the pricking of his skin had betrayed a presence ahead, and his rapier was already drawn. 'Name yourself or die.'

'Is this a way to greet a friend?' a voice asked from the darkness.

'Step out and reveal your intent.'

Briefly unmasking his lantern, the stranger showed his position and came no closer, preferring to remain beyond the reach of the blade.

Wright stayed on guard. 'You are armed?'

'With sword alone, and I am no match for you.'

'Toy with me and you will end dead as a fighting cock.'

'Such bile, Jack. Such spleen.'

'You know my name?'

'As you know mine.' The intruder's speech was measured, his stance unthreatening. 'It is Realm.'

There was a brief silence. Wright didn't move. 'I was told you would come.' His tone was dark.

'Then Tom Wintour informed you.' Realm was not deterred by the cold reception. 'We spoke much when he was last in Spain.'

'It does not make you a friend.'

'Nor does it suggest I am your enemy.'

'You are sanctioned by Spain?'

'Alas, I am not. Like you, I am cut adrift and rely on my own resources.'

'That brings us no advantage.'

'Though I came close to the murder of the bastard Elizabeth? And that I risked limb and life to seek you out? That I can draw off Robert Cecil and his hounds?'

'How can I tell you are not his agent?'

'For the fact that you are at liberty, Jack.' Realm placed his black lantern on the ground. 'I offer aid and amity and do not pry into your affairs.'

'More is needed to persuade me.'

'Will the word of Wintour or Fawkes not suffice? Would the hanging of my father and mother for marching in the rising of the North against the Queen not convince all where my duty lies?'

Wright knew his visitor was well informed and already vouched for, and had long ago entered the folklore of Catholic resistance. It would be churlish to exclude him and foolish to ignore the skills he brought. The English state enjoyed superiority in every quarter and yet might prove vulnerable to an unexpected blow. Realm could facilitate its execution.

The enforcer lowered his rapier. 'The Jesuits caution against a violent act.'

'But my conscience directs me to it.' Realm threw across a leather bag that landed heavily at Wright's feet. 'You have heard the name of Christian Hardy?'

'He is feared in the fencing schools.'

'He is more dangerous in the street. An intelligencer and swordsman, he is Cecil's man. This is the nature of the foe and what I set out to vanquish.'

'You are very certain of your success.'

'Let it inspire you, and let us go to work.'

A moment later, Realm was gone. He had left a gift, the leather bag through which Wright now rummaged, a trove of gemstones and jewellery. The blackness of the night could not obscure the richness of the contribution. Shouldering his reward, the conspirator walked on. An alliance had been forged.

'My beagle answers to the whistle.'

Should he choose, King James would make the beagle sit up and beg or roll over. Cecil bowed before his master. He did not mind the latent antipathy and barbed remarks, the resentment of a nervous monarch who relied for his survival on the efforts of his spymaster. Both were sly and malformed creatures and each depended on the other. Cecil, the malevolent little hunchback who had steadied England and smoothed the accession of the King; James, the diminutive grotesque with slavering tongue and watering eyes and a predilection for his male favourites. The more fearful the monarch, the greater the influence of Robert Cecil.

A fixer skilled at gauging the mood, he waited for the sovereign to open their discourse. Here in the privy garden of Whitehall Palace, among the statues and fountains and topiary, Cecil used to sit in earnest conversation with Elizabeth. She was gone and her successor arrived and affairs of state were no less onerous. At least he now gave counsel as an earl and had become the most powerful minister and subject in the land.

James spoke, the Scottish brogue thick and coarse. 'Am I not the lieutenant of God on earth, my beagle?'

'By His divine grace you are, Majesty.'

'Why then do men plot against me?'

'Not all are enlightened, sir.'

'Yet England appeared to give me welcome.'

'I venture you are loved and your enemies are but few.'

'Still there is a threat.' James trembled a little at the thought. 'The Catholics are restless and must be purged, my beagle.'

'We shall not rest until they are, sir.'

'Once peace with Spain is assured, then we will destroy the entire nest of vipers.'

'Your council will do as you bid.'

Cecil studied the armoured doublet designed to blunt a dagger thrust. He could not blame the King for his terrors or for suspecting a plot around every corner. Intrigue and violence had accompanied his entire life. His depraved father had been slain, probably by order of his mother, Mary, Queen of Scots, before she later was beheaded for scheming against Elizabeth; at the age of five, he had witnessed the bloodied corpse of his grandfather, the regent, carried from Stirling Castle. The Secretary of State would not trouble him with the details of Guido Fawkes and nascent treason; he preferred to wait until his case was built and revelation would secure the eternal gratitude of his sovereign.

A nerve twitched in the royal visage. 'They would murder me, Cecil.'

'You are well protected, sir.'

'What of my beloved Annie? My children?'

'Your subjects are loyal and your Queen and family are surrounded by the royal guard.'

'And what encircles them?' The King warmed obsessively to his theme. 'What will preserve us from a papist menace as virulent as the devouring angel of the plague?'

'Our informants and pursuivants daily lead us to their lairs.'

'Tell me then of Warwickshire, where my own precious daughter Princess Elizabeth resides, where recusants flourish and subvert my rule.'

'Your writ will carry even there, sir.'

'See that it does, my beagle.'

Weeping eyes could transmit both timidity and threat. The King scratched at his groin. Without Cecil he would be dead or living in fear and exile in Holyrood Palace. There was much to thank him for and every reason to keep him in his place.

'I am leaving soon for the country, Cecil. The saddle and the chase are where I am most safe.'

'As you choose, sir.'

'Ensure my proclamations are enacted and my concerns addressed. Pledge too that recusant fines increase and more baronetcies are sold.'

'Every penny and purse shall be found, sir.'

'And so at the end of my days I will offer to God a Protestant kingdom and a throne bedecked in gold.'

Cecil bent to kiss the proffered hand and left the monarch to his garden. Strange and unappealing the King might be and yet he was no simpleton. He had a nose for smelling danger and the stench was growing stronger.

CHAPTER 3

In June 1604, Sir Thomas Percy had been created a gentleman pensioner to the King. The detachment of fifty trusted and highborn royal bodyguards was commanded by the Earl of Northumberland, who had no qualms in selecting a kinsman who had proved himself as guardian of Alnwick Castle. The appointment gave Percy reason to grace the precincts of Westminster and keep close company with other gentry and nobles. Protocol decreed he should take the Oath of Supremacy and pledge allegiance to the King, and yet the earl on this occasion waived the practice. The plotters now had perfect cover and were a step nearer to their target.

A house had been rented, a small property tucked into the jumble of medieval buildings that formed the Palace of Westminster. It was a sparse apartment, inconspicuous on the outside and cramped within, belonging to John Whynniard, the keeper of the royal wardrobe. Percy would ensure the rent was paid on time and his occupancy caused no trouble. Among the wine merchants and taverns and teeming streetscape, few would notice another tenant. There were the cries of patterers and the sales pitch of whores in Westminster Yard and encounters in the Cotton Garden, the offloading of boats at Parliament Stair and the bustle of people between meetings. Thomas Percy was located at its centre.

He stood with Guido Fawkes at an upper window and regarded the ancient structure of the House of Lords. 'Parliament House has never seemed so sweet to the eye.'

'Or so fragile, brother.' Fawkes had the gaze of a hunter. 'There shall come a day when I level the mountain and turn each brick to dust.'

'For now we wait.'

'A pity, for I glimpsed Cecil himself making for the Painted Chamber. Had I a musket I would have dropped him where he stood.'

'There is greater sport to pursue.'

'Indeed so, brother.' The mercenary squinted at the scene. 'Sport by which we blow the bastard Scots back into their hills.'

Percy nodded. 'The Thames is fewer than a hundred paces from our door. Once the black powder is delivered and Parliament recalled, then you may ply your trade.'

It would not be until at least February the following year that the King visited and the chamber filled again. The absent monarch was the most fleeting and difficult of prey, preferring to rule through proclamation and his Privy Council. Yet it gave the plotters opportunity to prepare, and for Fawkes to become a familiar and unnoteworthy denizen. As a royal body-guard, Percy had ample reason to occupy the site and install the other man there as caretaker and servant.

'Henceforth you are no longer Guido, the soldier we brought from Spain.' Percy retreated from the window. 'You are John Johnson, my loyal manservant, keeping house and performing duties in my absence.'

'I am grown accustomed to change in both my name and my disguise.'

'Then let John Johnson be seen on errands. Let him make acquaint-ance of the porter and the guards.'

'They will love me as one of their own.'

'We must trust they do.' Percy had lit a candle and fixed it in a lamp. 'Come, Johnson.'

They descended the narrow staircase to the floor below and then down brick steps to the cellar. Percy raised the light and studied the vaulted chamber. 'It seems we are tasked with providing the King's funeral shroud.'

'There will be little left to cover.' Fawkes moved aside a heavy chair. 'Ten years of soldiering have brought me to this moment.'

'And every Catholic prayer converges at this point.' Percy tapped the wall.

'How do we proceed?'

'With caution, Mr Johnson. Loosen the stones and clear the cellar and make known that your master and mistress are in need of more storage room. When I return in the winter to London, then we shall dig.'

There would be no great tunnel or excavation, for simply by worming from cellar to cellar they would inch towards the House of Lords. Beside their residence was the home of the porter and his wife, and next to them the Prince's Chamber, in which peers robed in preparation for attend-ance. At a right angle to them all was Parliament itself, its hall empty until the nobles flocked and the King arrived to declare the session open.

Beneath their feet a private servant would be transformed again to Guido Fawkes and make ready with his ordnance.

The mercenary stared at Percy. 'These people are nothing to me. Yet among them will be your friends and kin, and your patron, the Earl of Northumberland.'

'Have we not agreed there will be sacrifice? Do we not each accept grief and loss as the price for our salvation?'

'I have no doubt we are settled on our course.'

'A path dictated by a demon King, and a via dolorosa we gladly travel.'

They surveyed each other with understanding, the choleric Percy and methodical Fawkes, a pair with blood already on their hands. The mercenary had shown little restraint in crushing Protestant resistance throughout the Low Countries, and Sir Thomas had slaughtered reivers and rustlers during his sojourn in Northumberland. One more Scots victim and his acolytes would simply improve the count.

Fawkes blew the dust from an earthenware jug and turned it in his hand. 'Where is my black powder?'

'All in good time, Mr Johnson. We have yet to arrange our quartermaster and supply.'

'Summer I am sure will bring us both.'

'It will also bear the plague and throw the enemy off our trail.'

'Cecil is as dark and deadly as any bubo.'

'Dwell instead on matters here.'

Fawkes released the vessel and it shattered on the ground. 'Mark my words, brother. One day he will be in pieces as the rest.'

Bodies could slip with ease into the Fleet Ditch and no one would pause to look or ask questions. Beyond the north-west bounds of the City was Clerkenwell, the murder lands, the place where millwheels turned and hovel dwellings spotted the scrub landscape and the dispossessed and criminal came to hide. For Christian Hardy it was natural territory in which to gather information.

'Tell me what you hear.'

He had run into his source beside the wreckage of a former tavern. The man, an old acquaintance of Hardy's, was a scavenger of intelligence and taker of valuables. If he was not angling with a rod and hook through the open windows of the rich, he was moving unnoticed among the poor. Both activities could prove rewarding.

The man was defensive and wary. 'What do you want?'

'It is my affection for you and my love for this benighted ground.'

'Do not jest.' The man's eyes darted anxiously from side to side. 'What will you give me?'

'A beating, should you disappoint.'

'There is danger for you here.' Greed and fear were written on the man's features. 'You are far from your territory.'

'While you take leave of your manners.' The intelligencer watched the man grow increasingly uneasy. 'Have I not fed you and kept you from prison and petitioned for your liberty? Have I not guarded your back and saved your worthless pelt?'

'Loyalty costs more.'

Hardy flipped him a coin. 'Speak what you know.'

'You are outbid.'

His informant was already scuttling away, terrified. Hardy drew his katzbalger and turned.

Standing behind him were seven men. They were armed with swords and spiked clubs and exuded the boastful enjoyment of predators on a hunt, confident of their supremacy. There was also the suggestion of a martial past, a soldiering gait and discipline that found new application. Realm had been industrious in his recruiting. It would have been a cheap assignment to arrange, just another killing and a further corpse to throw over the edge. Hardy assessed them, picking out the strong and measuring distances, preparing his moves before they understood their own. These strangers might once have slaughtered Irish peasants but they had never before encountered the precision and geometric artistry of Destreza. He admired their courage and despised their stupidity.

It was Hardy who called out. 'Will you submit?'

'We would rather kill.' The leader identified himself. 'Do not prolong your agony.'

'I will be certain to shorten yours.'

Their eagerness brought them on and Hardy stepped to meet them, the first attacker overreaching and the katzbalger travelling up into his armpit and burying itself deep. With a quick flick, Hardy acquired an estoc blade, thrusting it into the throat behind and carving right to remove a proffered head. Four were left. A man raised his club and exposed his chest and died for his mistake. Rushing forward in a gesture of support, his companion received a dagger to the abdomen, Hardy releasing its twin side blades to spring wide and withdrawing to catch an incoming blow. Again the katzbalger went in. One aggressor remained, slipping on the dead and now hobbled by the backstroke of a blade across his hamstring.

He stared up, bemused by his misfortune. 'You did not lie.'

'I rarely do.' Hardy drove in the blade.

He looked up at the sound of clapping. Isaiah Payne appeared from his vantage on a nearby tussock attended by his pursuivants. Hardy wiped his blade on the canvas jerkin of a corpse and eyed the fidgeting little presence. Their long-held antipathy ran deep. Whether Robert Cecil or Payne, these servants of the state were as malformed as their King.

'Flies are always drawn to the dead, Payne.' He sheathed the katzbalger and stooped to clean his dagger. 'You are late in coming to my aid.'

'Who are we to steal your laurels?'

'When Cecil speaks of our joint endeavour, it seems you would prefer to see me killed.'

'Is loathing for each other not all that binds us?'

'You may add to it mistrust and contempt.' Hardy rehoused his dagger. 'I would rather slay armed men than condemn priests and innocents.'

'There are no innocents. There are merely souls that as yet do not recognise their guilt.'

Hardy contemplated him. 'It is a bleak world you create.'

'A safer one for it. Ideas are always more dangerous than the musket or sword.'

'How many must you consign to the scaffold to feel at peace?'

'Insufficient until you are among them.' Payne approached, strange and almost skittish. 'Look to the blood on your own hands before you judge.'

'Stay back before they redden more.'

'Perhaps I prick a nerve or press a bruise. We each take wages from our master.'

'I guard the people and you oppress.'

The chief pursuivant bowed in mock deference. He would not push Hardy too far, would simply watch and manoeuvre and spy out weakness. Those that followed their own course invariably ended dragged on a hurdle to their execution. He indicated the dead. 'Your brutishness is noted, and the impossibility of acquiring evidence too.'

'Each to his method, Payne.'

'Mine takes me now to Warwickshire, where I intend to hunt the recusant scourge.'

'I thank the Catholics for removing you from my side.'

Payne looked back to his men. 'Be glad instead our current union preserves you from a musket ball.'

Pursuivants were so blunt an instrument. Accustomed to raiding houses and ripping up boards, they were not attuned to the finer nuance of intelligence. In seeing only bodies here, Payne missed clues that directed Hardy in his enquiries. The age and nature of his assailants, the weapons they employed, the hand signals they had used: all pointed to where he should go next.

'A Swaggerer that now has lost his swagger.'

Adam Hardy did not respond to the remark. He had learnt rapidly in Fleet Prison that inmates who spoke out of turn were often found dead by the following sunrise. It was better to comply, to hang in chains and attempt to go unnoticed.

Yet the gaoler was persistent, his breath foul and his scalp alive with lice, a creature born to drag slop or prisoners from one place to another. He prodded Adam in the belly. 'Do you still breathe?'

'More than some others here.'

'Then offer up a prayer of thanks.' A lantern swept close. 'Three of your number are dead and three more set to hang. King James does not like your kind, and intends to punish and make an example of you.'

'His ambition is then realised.'

'Clemency is also in his gift.'

'My fate?'

'Freed and bound on pain of death to keep the peace.'

Adam spoke slowly in his confusion. 'What spares me?'

'That you are junior to the rest.' A key was unlocking the fetters. 'That you are flogged enough and worth a fair price for your release.'

'I have paid no money.'

'Someone must prize your fair skin.' The gaoler's finger grazed his cheek and travelled down his torso.

Too weak to stand unaided, Adam was marched and dragged towards the light. Reality and reason had already fled and he had ceased to question the vagaries of providence. Doors opened, the outside enveloped him, and he landed in the dirt.

Gentler hands took him, guiding him to a carriage, a voice encouraging him to mount its step.

'You must eat.'

They were the first words of kindness he had heard uttered in a while. The stranger indicated a wicker box on the seat and sat in silence as Adam took and ate bread and cheese and tore at a leg of chicken.

'I thank you for your charity.' Adam chewed and swallowed, and rested his head back against the wall of the carriage. 'A Samaritan in a fine doublet. Are you the stranger that paid my bond and won me my release?'

'Regard me as a friend.'

'That I do, and a guardian angel.' Adam reached and grasped his hand. 'Your name?'

'Tom Wintour.'

'I am Adam Hardy.' He watched Wintour closely.

'Ben Jonson, the playwright, has told me of your exploits.'

'Even though he deems me rash and heedless.'

'He also dubs you brave.'

Swaying on the rutted surface, the carriage proceeded from the City and headed for the Strand.

'Why did you seek me out?'

Wintour leant forward. 'Show me your bruises.'

Adam raised the front of his shirt to reveal the mass of welts and lacerations. 'Those jackal servants of the Crown hate me as I hate them.'

'Yet your father sups among them.'

Adam scowled. 'I would kick over their trough and raze their halls. I would hurt him as I would any Protestant or Scot.'

'Is retribution your intent?' Wintour asked, his gaze earnest.

Adam lifted a curtain to peer out. 'What I trust in is their annihilation.'

Hatred grew in many forms, and in Adam Hardy Wintour had found an accomplice with the charms of an angel and a useful rage. Aimless youth had its potential. The young man would not know that a sponsor of their enterprise had killed his mother, that regicide was planned, that should Christian Hardy draw too close, his son would be present as a foot soldier or hostage. All things had their symmetry.

At the Duck and Drake, where Wintour had lodgings, horses had been readied. Within the hour, the two men had mounted up and set off to ride north some eighty miles to the Northamptonshire village of Ashby St Ledgers and the manor belonging to Robin Catesby.

Strangers were not welcome here. The den of thieves off Cock Lane east of Spitalfields nestled uninvitingly between the tenements and brothels, a rendezvous for queer birds and villains. Street gangs and doxies might patrol the territory about, but they were controlled from inside the tavern.

Their master sat at a table playing cards with his lieutenants. He was an Upright Man, head of his underworld tribe, a chief who enforced loyalty and discipline through the relentless application of violence. No challenge would go unanswered or insult ignored, and as the wise chose to pay their tribute so the feckless ended dead. Stakes were high and a deck was cut and the cards shuffled and dealt.

Christian Hardy entered to a widening hush and took up his position on the opposite side of the table. 'What a happy chance that we should meet.'

'Few men would speak so.' The Upright Man had lit his pipe and drew on its clay stem. 'I was not warned of your approach.'

'Then you are ill-served by your kinchin boys and sentries.'

'As you are ill-advised to come.'

Hardy shrugged, observing the hands and faces of those about him.

Smoke wreathed out and the Upright Man gave instructions with his eyes. His men sat up ready. An execution was imminent, though curiosity and the possibility of entertainment might delay the finish.

Hardy had walked such paths before, inhabiting the boundary between his own demise and that of others. He had no right to condemn his son for misspent living and recklessness.

The Upright Man tapped his pipe upon the table. 'What do you wager?'

'That I will depart this house alive and with the things I seek.'

Amusement flared in the man's eyes. 'I am undefeated in primero and prima vista.'

'The game I play is trumps.'

'Your hand is weak.' The Upright Man laid his palm across the cards before him.

'And yours the more exposed.'

'Declare to me or I shall cut out your tongue.'

'Seven of your men were sent against me and I killed each one.'

The Upright Man did not move; he was reappraising the situation and calculating his loss of face. Diminished authority was dangerous for all.

Hardy scouted for weakness and counted time. 'Their clothing was good and their swords and trappings plucked from those naked and diverted.'

'Cock Lane attracts felons of every kind.'

'None with the patter of this haunt or grouped as former soldiers.' Hardy readied himself. 'You directed them.'

Without further warning, Hardy unsheathed a dudgeon dagger from the small of his back and drove it through the resting hand. Pinioned, the Upright Man screamed; his dumbfounded men looked on. His adversary was already behind him as Black Jack, a burly mariner and a gaunt man erupted into the room. Hardy's crew had arrived. They worked efficiently, upending tables, kicking stools wide and dealing violence at random.

Hardy spoke above the groans of the Upright Man. 'My men will slit the throat of any that oppose me.'

In one corner, the sailor Carter cradled a twin-barrelled pistol in the crook of his arm, the weapon primed and loaded with cartridge shot. His face was disfigured by growths. Across from him lounged Swiftsure, cadaverous and hollow-eyed, playing with his knife. Between them stood Black Jack, huge, nonchalant and intimidating.

Their commander spoke in the ear of the Upright Man. 'Bring your dogs to heel.'

'Hark his words.' Almost delirious with pain, the captive called to his men. 'Give them what they need.'

'What I need is a name and a reason you should wish me murdered.'

'Would you not exchange a favour for a bag of gold?'

'The name.'

'He had no name, was nothing but a messenger.' The Upright Man had begun to sob, loudly. 'Yet for his master he demanded as proof of completion the silver cross you wear about your neck.'

Hardy gripped the scalp of his prisoner and wrenched back his head. 'Where was the cross to be delivered?'

'Paris Garden.' Mucus and tears ran down the man's face. 'To the man that tends the bears.'

The Upright Man had shown himself weak and was now compromised and injured. Perhaps he would not last the hour with his men. Hardy and his team withdrew, backing out carefully in case of ambush, Carter covering their retreat.

Vested with the authority of Robert Cecil, Hardy had freedom to roam. Close to London Bridge in Southwark on the south bank of the Thames was the baiting ground of Paris Garden to which people flocked to see animals tormented. Should conspiracy and blood sport be planned, Realm had selected the right location.

'A princess does not run, Your Grace.' The young lady of the royal bed-chamber laughed as she gently chided her small mistress, who had kicked up her heels and run to evade capture. The Lady Anne knelt down and Elizabeth wrapped her arms around her neck.

'Lady Harington has made me sit all morning with her books of Latin and Greek.'

'She is a fine tutor,' Anne admonished.

'She is a stern governess.' The child rested her head against the comforting shoulder and Anne soothed her.

'One day when you are grown and wed and queen of another land, you will thank Lady Harington for the wisdom she imparts.'

'Today I am bored,' the child confessed.

'And you are running.'

'For you, I promise to walk as stately as an empress.'

Anne took the child's arm and accompanied her to the steps lead-ing to the knot garden. At eighteen years old, she, like the princess, was confined, consigned to attend the royal progeny at Coombe Abbey by an ambitious father. Duty had turned to mutual devotion as the little girl with the quick mind and merry disposition won the affection of all about her. In public, Elizabeth carried herself with care; in private, she arranged her dolls and played hide-and-seek with her beloved Anne. The two were inseparable.

'As my mother is Anne, so are you.' Elizabeth squeezed her compan-ion's hand. 'It is no mere chance we are friends.'

'I thank God each day we are.'

'When I am sent overseas, will you be with me?' Elizabeth gave her a quick glance, thoughtful and serious.

'Such things we will address another day.' Anne stepped down with her charge into the sunlit garden. 'Let us enjoy the warmth and tranquillity, and trust we go unseen by the porter Smythe.'

The princess wrinkled her nose. 'He is an ogre, I am sure of it.'

'An ogre that defends you.'

'Why then does he scowl at me so?'

'We shall keep our distance so he does not devour us.'

The Haringtons' home, Coombe Abbey, had been commandeered as nursery and court for the raising of Elizabeth. Hundreds of servants and followers now inhabited the former Norman abbey expanded as a stately dwelling. The costs were crippling and thanks were few. The hosts could hardly be blamed for resenting it, yet they too loved the princess, were glad for her happiness and contrived to appear unruffled.

Elizabeth sat on a stone bench and watched insects busying about the mallow. 'I wish I could sometimes escape my confines here.'

'There are the gardens and the park.'

'What of Dunmore Heath? What of Coventry and Warwick?'

'You have journeyed through them and attended banquets and pageants and been hailed wherever you go.'

'A banqueting house is no real place.' The seven-year-old turned to her companion. 'I would rather see and meet the people and do good as a Christian is commanded.'

'With age you may do as you please.'

'Advisers will find cause to keep me captive.'

Anne took another tack. 'Outside there may be dangers. Close by this house are Catholics and recusants.'

'My grandmother was Catholic and she would not have done me harm.'

'Not every soul is quite so well intentioned.'

'Yet I would like to breathe the air beyond these walls.'

Anne held the girl's small hand between both of her own. 'I will petition Lord Harington to ask that you accompany the huntsmen and their hounds.'

Elizabeth looked at her gratefully. 'No one is a better friend.'

They stood up and wandered on in the July heat. Both girls were elegant and fair-haired; they might have been sisters, aged some ten years apart. A gaggle of courtiers bowed at their approach and a squad of royal guards saluted. Elizabeth acknowledged them with a gracious wave and whispered to Anne of a prank she had just dreamt up.

Anne shook her head. 'Your father the King might hear of such misdeeds.'

'Would he cage me more?'

'We shall turn to quoits and chess and away from any mischief.'

'Those games will not drench courtiers in a surging fountain.'

'It is all to the good.' Anne steered the princess onward. 'Strutting peacocks hate to get their plumage wet.'

The girls laughed and continued strolling between ranks of sculpted hedges to emerge beside a mirror-like pond. Parties and masques were planned and the hosts would further strain their finances to entertain the young daughter of the King. William Shakespeare himself might visit and give readings of his poetry and plays. While plot and plague might swirl about and the monarch find safety on the move, Coombe Abbey at least remained a Stuart stronghold and idyll.

In London, the man with the alias of John Johnson was dining with his neighbours within the bounds of the Palace of Westminster. Guido

Fawkes was the sole member of the conspiracy left in the City. As others sojourned in the country and spread the web of their sedition, he remained as the custodian of a rented house and Sir Thomas Percy's representative. His hosts suspected nothing. In spite of nagging fears of the summer incursions of the Black Death, the mood was jovial and the wine flowed; the talk was of the nobility's antics and of impending peace with Spain. All present were full of hope. Fawkes listened, an imposter at the feast, and was gracious and attentive. He raised his glass and drank deeply to the future health of King James.

CHAPTER 4

'Let joy reign and fires be lit, for peace is declared with Spain.'

Mid-August 1604, and from a plinth set before the great stone cross and fountain of Cheapside called the Standard, a herald proclaimed the Anglo-Spanish Treaty. The Constable of Castile had come to London to mark the end of hostilities and, with banqueting and a procession and formal signing at Somerset House, usher in the dawn of friendship. People listened, cheerful and perplexed. The satanic entity that had once sent against England a mighty armada to impose its papist will was now offering a different future. It would take time to comprehend.

Weaving through the crowd, a member of the Spanish delegation made his unobtrusive way towards Old Change. New-found accord meant no lessening of the espionage game or abandonment of the rules, for agents needed to be nurtured and the body politic watched. The early days of a transformed relationship were often the most fraught.

The man's destination was a timbered five-storey house, hemmed in by others, that gave lodging for visitors to the City. A transient population made it challenging for Robert Cecil's intelligencers and easier for a man like this to cover his traces.

He noted the parallel chalk marks scored discreetly on a lower sill and, after a brief glance around, inserted a key in the door. The meeting would not be disturbed.

'An envoy of peace is among us.' Lounging on a bed, Realm greeted him sardonically. The two men were old acquaintances, had operated together on countless assignments and met in all kinds of places. It was sometimes hard for the Spaniard to rein in the activities of his English charge.

He seated himself in a padded chair. 'You hear the bells and the cheering of the crowd?'

'They rejoice as they are commanded to and it does not suit me.'

'Nothing will be allowed to usurp the peace or undermine the treaty.' The warning came from Madrid itself.

Realm raised himself on an elbow. 'What of the Catholics of England you now abandon? What of their pleas that you should come to their aid?'

'They will learn to love their King and live within his laws.'

'It is betrayal.'

'You will find it is the future.' The Spaniard was emphatic. 'Spain will not interfere in the affairs of England.'

'On your orders I journeyed here to advance the cause of Spain and avenge past wrongs. There are still the treasures looted from the Americas by Christian Hardy. There is still the possibility that he discovered the secrets of El Dorado and plans some later expedition.'

The handler was unmoved. 'No proof exists of his vast wealth.'

'I will find proof and deliver him to you.'

'My concern is with the present, while your wars lie in the past.'

Realm lay back against the pillow. Spain had plainly dispensed with his services and abandoned its previous convictions. No longer did it see merit in plotting overthrow or establishing a Catholic state within the borders of Albion. The rulers sought coexistence of a kind.

The Spaniard was not finished. 'Your work is done here. You are to travel to Gravesend and board our ship for Spain.'

'Am I not trusted to live a quiet life?'

'Your capture would embarrass us and endanger the cause of peace.'

'How quick my labours are forgot.'

'Our gratitude is not in doubt. Nor should be your loyalty.'

Recall to Spain was ignominious and unnecessary, the Englishman reflected. He had only just returned to these shores and already the whipper-in had come to persuade him to his kennel. It would not do. Realm stretched, considering his options and the vicissitudes of life. Agents such as he were ever the ones stranded by a shift in world events.

He squinted at his handler. 'If I should refuse your invitation?'

'You would become an enemy both of England and of Spain.'

'Spain?' Realm considered the idea. 'It is the nation for which I have toiled and faced hazard, for whose religion I have killed in every corner of the earth.'

'Then you deserve your rest.'

'Rest is not my way.' The Englishman moved his hand across the counterpane.

'The alternative is death.'

It always returned to that, to the theme woven into his soul and the fabric of every mission. He had known him for so long and still the Spaniard failed to understand him. Realm rolled to the side and raised the hunting crossbow, discharging its steel-tipped bolt through the draped covers. It embedded in the chest of the Spaniard and hurled him back against the wall. With the satin of his doublet and the crimson splash behind, he resembled an insect splayed out on a board.

For a while, Realm sat with the body. He liked the quiet time. There was no more distraction or chat, no further argument or explanation needed. He would continue the project he had started. Diplomacy was for ambassadors, and all other matters best left to him.

'Here is where everything started.'

In the half-timbered room atop the gatehouse at Ashby St Ledgers, the ringleader and his lieutenant stood in conversation. This was hallowed ground. With its fireplace and leaded panes, the small chamber was where conspiracy was first muttered and the contours of ensuing actions were outlined. On these chairs they had sat, and through this window Robin Catesby had stared at the manor church stolen by the Protestant faith and sworn to wrest it back. King James must die. Treasonous words and sentiments, uttered among friends.

'I recall well our beginnings.' Tom Wintour studied the interior. 'Yet in truth where shall it end?'

'With our salvation or our sacrifice.'

'We have much to do before we reach either.'

Catesby nodded. 'It fills my waking and my sleeping hours. Not one detail must go ignored.'

'Guido at least inhabits his dwelling in Westminster.'

'We will see him supplied with the powder he needs.'

'What about our planned uprising, Robin? Taking London and crushing dissent? Seizing the Princess Elizabeth?'

'In God we trust.'

Yet both men knew that their fates would also rest in the hands of other men. In the aftermath of the explosion and the levelling of Parliament, the enforcer Jack Wright would lead a force to hunt down and assassinate the residual hierarchs who opposed. Meanwhile, five miles north of Ashby St Ledgers, a large posse of horsemen would be waiting to ride to snatch the princess and spread wide the message of revolt. Everything was possible in a time of flux and turmoil.

Wintour gazed with admiration at his leader. 'I have no doubts, Robin.'

'We shall succeed.' Catesby pointed through the windows to his right and left. 'To one side my church snatched by the state, and to the other my home they will contrive to steal.'

Summer had brought more raids and arrests, more recusant fines, more priests hanged and quartered on the block. Still Catholics prayed for a gentler world and Jesuits spoke of peace and reconciliation. In this corner of Northamptonshire, belief in such passivity had long vanished.

Wintour moved to the low adjoining storeroom to fetch out his sword. 'Read the inscription on its blade, Robin.'

Catesby did so and looked up. 'Jesus is indeed our guide.'

'Let us trust He captures the hearts of men and turns them to our cause.'

'May He also deliver the young princess into our care.'

'A daunting prospect, Robin.'

'Less so once her royal guard learns King James himself is killed.' Catesby slapped the sword back into its scabbard.

From below came the sound of an opening door and a quick footfall on the turret stair. Adam Hardy appeared, bearing a saddle. The bruising had faded and his face no longer wore the bitter disaffection of a London brawler but rather the elation that followed a mounted gallop.

'Good day to you, brothers.' Adam set down his burden.

Catesby smiled in welcome. 'Your humours and health are restored since first we met.'

'Outfoxing the pursuivants and spreading word of their approach would improve the temper of any.'

'You have proved yourself a friend.' Catesby placed a hand upon the young man's shoulder. 'We thank you.'

'I am in your debt for giving me refuge.'

'Tell me more about the pursuivants,' Catesby urged.

'I hear they are grown more bold, are joined by men from London sent to stiffen their resolve.'

'They think they will find rich pickings.'

'It is Father Garnet they seek.' Adam snorted his contempt. 'In every quarter they ask their questions and make their threats, pull up the boards in every house.'

'So let us run them ragged.' The light of excitement shone in Catesby's eye. If the spymaster Cecil wished to commit his minions to the shires, they would discover ghosts and empty priest holes. Everything must be done to keep the Jesuits safe and preserve their mission. Every capture was a blow to the Catholic faith and another victory trumpeted by the government, a further step in the annihilation of the old religion. King James believed he set the pace, and yet he had lost the argument. Today the authorities sowed the wind of oppression; tomorrow they would reap the whirlwind.

The eighteen-year-old was eager to assist. 'What can I do?'

'Stay one step ahead and avoid becoming ensnared. You are more use to me free than chained inside a gaol.'

'I have learnt from my experience in London.'

'Then learn also to be patient.' Catesby was fatherly towards the boy. 'You are too precious to be put in jeopardy.'

'Do not spare me the trials others face.'

'In time there shall be task aplenty.'

Adam stooped to retrieve the saddle. 'I will be waiting, Robin.'

'In the morning you must ride to the manor named Norbrook in the village of Snitterfield near Stratford. It is the home of my friend John Grant.'

'He is a quiet man, married to my sister,' Wintour broke in. 'A devout Catholic and true ally of our cause.'

'Am I to carry a message?'

'Take instead two of my swift jennets,' said Catesby. 'A fellow can never have enough horses.'

'Nor the priests he hides show enough gratitude.' Tom winked.

'Travel next to Lapworth and summon Jack Wright here.'

From his command post, Catesby could listen and gauge and lay his plans. Current plotters needed to be kept apprised and future ones cultivated and brought in. To hide a Jesuit was already to break the law.

There was an art to steering those who engaged in gentle resistance to a more aggressive path. The price of two horses was scarcely a heavy burden.

Adam was determined not to disappoint his guardian. He would do as he was bid.

It had been a bloody day in Paris Garden. By wherry across the river or by foot over London Bridge, the public had streamed to the Southwark venue to see animals torn to pieces. They were not disappointed. In the eastern arena, blind bears had been whipped, or set upon by mastiffs, and in the western, bulls baited and killed. The climax of the entertainment was reached when an old nag with a screaming monkey enthroned atop dressed as the pope was brought down by a pack of dogs. Everywhere was viscera and death and the stench of shit and fear.

After the show, the rowdy and chanting masses had departed merrily. In a courtyard between the slaughterhouse and pens, an old man rendered another dog carcass and threw the bones in a growing pile. Over twenty of the beasts had been slain today, disembowelled or crushed by a cornered bear even as they locked their jaws on the larger prey. The keeper admired the tenacity of his charges, their ability to take punishment. With their teeth filed, bears were reduced to clawing their opponents. Here lay the result.

He heard the strange moaning of the bears and barking of the dogs and picked up his lantern to make his rounds. The animals kept him supplied with the good things in life; it was in his interest to tend them and nurture their ferocity, to terrorise if necessary. The persecuted always gave a better performance.

'Eat well, Suleiman.' Standing on the wooden walkway above the enclosure, he threw back the roof of the cage and emptied a leather pail filled with discarded fruit and fish and half-eaten pies. The bear stared up at him, bristling and malevolent.

A second voice joined his own, startling him. 'How Suleiman must resent you.'

He turned quickly in the direction of the voice, stepping back cautiously. 'I keep him fed and watered.'

'Yet things which are trapped so often lash out.' Realm listened to the growls below. 'I swear he voices his complaint.'

'My ears are deaf to it.'

'So in the same way do we treat persons of a different form or creed.'

'Philosophy I leave for others.' The man wiped his nose on a sleeve. 'You choose a late hour to meet.'

'Darkness helps our trade.' Realm had observed Christian Hardy's men loitering in the shadows and understood his security was compromised, but he might yet turn this to his advantage. He had always intended to eliminate the old man, to take over his operation when the time arose. The schedule had been accelerated.

He balanced on the planking. 'Has the silver crucifix been delivered here?'

'Neither word nor trophy has been brought.'

'A misfortune for us both.'

'What matter cannot be resolved by payment?' The keeper was a pragmatic soul. 'What threat may not be defeated by vigilance or force?'

'You do not know my enemy.'

'I hope I never shall.'

His desire was granted with a kick, the keeper flailing backwards and his visitor slamming shut the hatch. Below, the reception was furious and protracted and the victim's screams were loud. Realm walked away, content to have silenced a witness and eager to put distance between himself and his crime.

Hours passed before Hardy arrived with tousled hair and sleep-bruised eyes to survey the grisly scene. The bear was possessive of its prize and the keeper was far beyond questioning.

'Spread wide in your search,' Hardy called to his men. 'Every straw and scrap of bone, each piece of dung, must be examined.'

'What do we seek?'

'Find it and I shall know.'

He stood quietly at the centre of the commotion, imagining the stealthy progress of his adversary and the ease with which he had snuffed out a life. Not a single watcher had detected him, and the result was a mutilated corpse. It might be for a reason – designed to tease or provoke or lure – or none at all, the product of a rational or disturbed mind. Realm's motives were ever opaque.

Hardy paced slowly between the cages. Shutting out the discordant sounds of the agitated animals, he tried to reach beyond the visible. Something had brought Realm here. For an instant, he thought of Isaiah Payne and how the gnomish pursuivant must feel each time he crossed the threshold of a dwelling. In every case there was a hidden truth and in every home a secret to be uncovered. Realm was not sharing his.

He reached a stairway and called to his men. 'Bring your lamps. We'll go below.'

A subterranean complex stretched beneath the arena's animal compounds, the passageways narrow and the chambers cramped. The smell was overpowering. Hardy drew his katzbalger, anticipating ambush, his senses heightened by the murk. So much filth and excrement was gathered here, a flesh wound alone would kill. He prowled on, peering for clues or armed assailants.

Dampness surrounded him. It was not rainwater or the seepage of a marsh, but the rank flow of animal urine dripping from above and pooling on the floor. Sand residue showed where previous deposits had been captured. Hardy crouched to touch the ground, pinching the wet grains between his fingers and bringing them to his nose. Now he understood. In this dark labyrinth was the answer, the by-product of one activity and the precursor to another, the horse piss that contained nitrate salts which when strained through potash created the substance called saltpetre. What Realm sought was gunpowder.

'You bring gifts.'

The lord of Norbrook manor spoke without pleasure, regarding Adam with an earnest stare. John Grant had learnt to be suspicious. As a rich Catholic, despised by the state and a target for its petty spite, he had grown accustomed to the raids and fines and the inconvenience of his faith. A learned man at ease among his books, he was capable of aggression and defiance when pushed to defend his home.

Adam dismounted. 'My name is Adam Hardy, sir. I ride from Ashby St Ledgers.'

'Catesby sends you?'

'He and Tom Wintour both.' The young man gestured to the accompanying horses. 'I bring with me a pair of jennets.'

'As a token of affection or to ease some hidden guilt?'

'The purpose is not for me to guess.'

'Nor for me to judge.' Grant ran his hand along the head and neck of the Spanish mount. 'We are crying out for help and the Spaniards give us horse flesh.'

'Lands are ever conquered by men on steeds.'

'Their people subjugated also.' Grant gave Adam an enquiring look. 'What did you spy on your journey here?'

'Hamlets and fields at peace.'

'It is what I fear. The quiet presages danger.' Grant turned his eyes towards the treeline, his countenance gloomy. Even the addition of fresh horses to his stable had not improved his mood. Adam understood.

The young man broke the silence. 'I first met your wife's brother in London.'

'We hold Tom and his family dear and named our son Wintour in their honour.' Grant swung his attention back to his young visitor. 'He and Catesby must trust you, Adam Hardy.'

Adam met his eye steadfastly. 'I would do nothing to betray them.'

'Then I too will be your friend.' The handshake was firm, though his expression remained serious.

A cry sounded from the rooftop. '*Pursuivants! Pursuivants! Pursuivants!*'

The household had rehearsed for such an event. Already a whistle sat between Grant's lips, and its shrill blast brought servants and labourers rushing. Armed with swords and scythes, pitchforks and clubs, they would do as their master bid them. Previous encounters had left them battle-hardened and prepared. The sharpened edges of their cutting blades would draw blood if required.

Grant glanced at Adam. 'You are not frightened by a chase?'

The young man shook his head with a smile. 'I embrace adventure as it comes.'

'Mount up and gallop for your life.' Grant reached to grasp the bridle. 'A false trail will confound and split the pack.'

Adam swung himself into the saddle. 'Until we meet again.'

'They will not be gentle should they catch you.'

'Then I shall outpace them.' Adam touched his cap and wheeled his horse away, spurring it from the yard.

Across the gently undulating fields the pursuivants bore down, sheep scattering from their path, some of the horsemen peeling away to pursue the fleeing figure and the rest descending on the manor. They pulled up in a clatter of hooves and harness a few paces from their target.

Grant surveyed his visitors without flinching. 'It is customary for my guests to show manners and restraint.'

'I hear it is more usual in these places to harbour priests and traitors.' Isaiah Payne perched crooked and macabre on his stallion. 'Your stubborn ways and opposition alone prove your complicity.'

'While your words display your ignorance.'

There were hoots of derision from the assembled retainers, a jocularity that belied their fierce defiance. They would not be swayed by threat or bend to orders from London. Grant was in armed and loyal company.

The chief pursuivant stared down. 'We arrive to find a fine pair of horses and a spectre fleeing on another. You stand revealed as an enemy of our state.'

'And you exposed as a scavenger of nonsense.' The atmosphere was tense.

'We are officers of the Crown, not some local band of errand boys to be waved off with excuses.'

'Shame then on the Crown.'

'Step aside and let us to our work.'

Grant raised the tip of his sword a fraction from the ground. 'Cross this threshold and you will suffer pain.'

'You will hang when we are done, John Grant.'

'I doubt you shall live to see it.'

Stand off had hardened to impasse, each side regarding the other warily. A horse snorted and another's tail twitched as the battle of wills stretched out the moment. A single false move would lead to death.

Payne backed his horse and with a motion of his hand led his troops away. Any hidden Jesuits would keep. He had gathered information and noted Grant's response, a further glimpse into the treachery of the Catholics. Robert Cecil would hear. Patterns were emerging, and within them somewhere, perhaps even in this house, sat the Antichrist leader of the Jesuits in England.

Adam crouched behind a gravestone. He had ridden hard, dashing between coppice and hedgerow to evade the hunt, feinting and doubling back to sow confusion and divide his pursuers. Luck and superior horsemanship had brought him here. He panted, grateful for the sanctuary of the graveyard and hoping that the danger was past. By now, the pursuivants should be in a headlong rush along the road to Stratford. The village of Snitterfield and its parish church were an unlikely shelter for a fugitive.

'You are too young to seek your grave.'

He recognised the voice and avuncular tone and turned to see his old mentor from the Globe leaning against another headstone. William Shakespeare observed the scene with wry detachment.

'Will? Is it you?' Adam breathed in relief and surprise.

'Unless I am mistaken or a ghost.' Shakespeare was amused by the bafflement on the young man's face. 'I escaped the pestilence of London to be plagued now by youths on leaping horses.'

'But why here? Why this graveyard?'

'I am less an imposter than you. Here in the church my father and uncle were baptised and there my uncle lies buried.' Shakespeare nodded towards a grave.

'Forgive my rude intrusion.'

The playwright checked to right and left. 'Do you play a Capulet or Montague? Or are you a fleeing priest or outlaw?'

'It is no game, Will.'

'I shall not ask and you will not tell.' The older man proffered a hand and helped Adam to his feet. 'You would be wiser to chase some fair maid than be hunted down by men on horseback.'

'Did I not outrun them?'

'Even the swiftest hare may be caught.'

Adam slapped dirt off his clothing and looked towards his horse, cropping grass beneath the east window of the small church. A deceptively tranquil scene. There was still his mission to the manor at Lapworth to summon Jack Wright for a meeting with Catesby. Perhaps his escape from the home of John Grant would not be the only exciting incident today. He relished the prospect.

The playwright stood back and viewed him. 'Your repute for riot and affray is as Ben Jonson warned me.'

'Idleness ill suits my nature.'

'You are a player, so let us play.' Shakespeare smiled. 'Your master and friend Sir Robin Catesby has asked me to engage you.'

'What as?'

'As buck and swain and whatever other guise I give you. We are to visit Coombe Abbey and perform for the court of Princess Elizabeth.'

Of course he had. Adam nodded slowly. Catesby's purpose, he sensed, was larger than he had previously grasped. An avowed Catholic who smuggled priests and lifted a Swaggerer from prison was now focused on a royal household. As a King's Man, sponsored by his monarch, Shakespeare had every right to bring culture to his clients. Catesby had none. In a small churchyard in Warwickshire, Adam Hardy was now certain he was involved in something of great consequence.

Later that night John Grant took a lamp and climbed a back staircase to a remote chamber of the house. His men still patrolled the fields, and inside the manor sleep would be fitful. The pursuivants were likely to return.

Grant felt for the catch and removed a panel, sliding it aside to reveal a door disguised behind rough plaster. The hinges swung open silently and he crawled into the cavity. Expert hands had created the priest hole, conjuring space where there seemed to be none. Grant slithered through the aperture, tracing his fingers along the join until he touched a solid wall. Three knocks and a press of his hand and he reached the innermost sanctum.

Father Henry Garnet emerged from his entombment. In the dismal light of the chamber his skin was yellowed and aged and his thin features seemed more gaunt. Yet his eyes still glowed with certainty. He stood for a while, stretching his spine and kneading circulation back into his limbs, directing his gaze on his host. He noted the change in Grant's face, a tightness to his jaw that showed how angry he was.

Garnet gripped the younger man's shoulder. 'Anger will not save you, my son.'

'Are we forever to skulk in priest holes? To run scared before pursuivants?'

'Evil begets evil.'

'Docility breeds reprisal.'

The chief Jesuit bowed his head. In the darkness there was yet a light, but it was the fiercer glow of battle and resistance for which so many headed.

When oppression reigned it was the centre ground that fell away and fortified redoubts at either extreme which faced each other across the wasteland. Men were sinful and full of hate. Might they find wisdom and comfort in the Word of God, Garnet prayed, for all would suffer otherwise.

CHAPTER 5

Conflagration could not occur without its constituent parts. Near Spitalfields on the north-eastern fringe of the City of London, a vendor negotiated his handcart unnoticed through the throng of a busy market day. While others might summer in the country and look to their affairs elsewhere, Realm had been far from idle. He could admire from a distance the commitment with which Christian Hardy sought his prey, could pity the authorities their fumbling efforts in staving off catastrophe. All were blind and misdirected. On the rolling cart were three kegs of gunpowder, a product of the networks into which he had recently tapped and a gesture of goodwill to the criminals he approached. Uprising required ordnance and trained manpower. His was a small contribution to the greater whole, an element in the blaze that would engulf the King and sweep through the entire country. He trusted the recipient would enjoy his gift.

They fell in around him, men and boys with feral, darting eyes emerging to provide a silent escort. Realm leant on the poles and pushed the handcart on. He knew this endeavour could become a lynching at a single word or stumble. It did not trouble him. Advantage lay with those who calculated and dared, who conveyed their case with enough gunpowder to demolish buildings. Some in England sought to change the future by petitioning the King or pestering Robert Cecil. He adopted a different approach.

In the courtyard stood the Upright Man, ready with a sword. The crime chief's expression was not welcoming. On his own instruction one of his hands had been severed by a blow from an axe, the bloody bandaged stump restoring his authority through a display of raw will. In a world of knaves and villains, it was brute force that held sway. His men stayed back as their leader spoke.

'You have a name?'

'I choose for the present William Birch.' Realm set down the cart. 'My habit is to use the names of those I kill.'

'Mine is to forget, they are so numerous.'

'You will recall the name of the man who impaled your hand.'

There was a murmur of unease from the watching men, and the Upright Man's frown deepened. He needed no reminding. The intelligencer and his crew had maimed and insulted him. There was agony in his arm and hatred in his soul.

Realm gazed at him. 'I gave you payment to murder Christian Hardy, and you failed.'

The Upright Man looked at him in disbelief. 'You have come to collect?'

'To commiserate and make a new offer.' Realm was untroubled by the latent menace in the man's words. 'Our business is unfinished.'

'It shall end with you skinned and your hide run up as a banner.'

'Should vengeance not be turned on Hardy?'

'You are closer.'

Wounded pride could undermine negotiations. Realm sensed the anticipation of the crowd. The Upright Man had grown to be cautious in the wake of his debacle. Yet in his retinue were men who could be trained, the unsentimental and hard-eyed who could incite an uprising and inflict grievous losses upon the forces of the state. They simply required persuading.

Realm threw back the tarpaulin cover to reveal the kegs of powder. 'Kill me and the forces of Robert Cecil will infest these streets in their enquiry. Aid me and I give you the chance to ambush Hardy and spread your influence through London.'

'You promise much.'

'I deliver also.' Realm stooped to rotate a keg and expose the slow match smouldering at its side. 'Each firkin carries gunpowder either as a gift or as a means to blow you to destruction.'

'I will have you seized.'

'Before knowing the length of any fuse? Before knowing what I will propose?'

'Your demands?' the Upright Man snapped.

'Send away your men so we may speak alone.'

A spluttering of the slow match helped to focus attention. The Upright Man could gauge when a stranger preferred to deal and admired the way this one forced the pace. This Birch would make for a clever card player.

The crime chief pointed his sword and his underlings dispersed. In reply, Realm plucked the fuse off the keg and ground it beneath his boot. Alone, the two men could confer without fear of details leaking to their enemy. It was in both their interests to draw a veil on proceedings.

'You are an emperor of felons and I am a lord of misrule.' Realm advanced no closer. 'We are natural friends.'

'No kinship with you is natural.'

'Yet we share a common foe.'

'See how I am mauled.' The Upright Man raised his stump. 'I will not go back for more.'

'Peace with Spain is upon us and soldiers wander idle. You give them food and purpose and in return they swear fealty.'

'Robberies are my domain.'

'Add to it greatness and the power accorded by powder and shot. Garland it with the corpse of Christian Hardy and all others that offend you.'

Temptation flickered in the eye of the Upright Man. A pact with this devil might provide access to fresh influence and territory.

Realm continued. 'Beyond these bounds are men that would do you harm. Better to prepare and take the fight to them than wait for their attack.'

The Upright Man looked briefly sceptical. 'There is no rumour of their hostile intent.'

'Was there warning you would lose your hand? A whisper that Christian Hardy and his band would disturb your lair?'

'Should I lash out, they will disturb me more.'

'Kill them and they shall have no means.'

It was a persuasive argument. In the drastic measures he had taken to shore up his command, the Upright Man had been reminded of the fragility of his estate. The visitor was broadening the scope of his ambition, and his imagination was captured.

He scraped the sword point on the cobbles. 'I have men and you have powder, the materiel for war.'

'Bide awhile and I will offer targets.'

As he walked away, Realm extinguished the second fuse he had held concealed. Had the Upright Man not proven persuadable, the keg would have been minutes from explosion. As it was, a further piece of the strategy had fallen easily into place. Realm was forming his urban army.

On a Hampstead ridgeline north of London, Christian Hardy sat astride his horse and stared down across the heathland and scattered villages to the sweep of the city below. To the east was the blunt outline of the Tower and Gothic edifice of St Paul's, and to the west the cluttered mass of Westminster. Somewhere between them lurked Realm and Guido Fawkes and the beginnings of conspiracy. Along with them was gunpowder.

He patted his horse and rested in the saddle. The trail had gone cold and he could not progress until informants gave more or the enemy broke cover. Known recusants were watched and powder mills visited and the gossip of foreign diplomats noted. There would always be the silt layers of factionalism and dissent to penetrate before genuine threat was found. To that end he had this morning ridden to Highgate to debrief the watchers in their hides monitoring the residence of the Spanish ambassador. A peace treaty did not translate to an easing of vigilance.

Hardy turned his mount to follow the terrain westward, cantering for over a mile past orchards and millponds and descending grassed slopes to the secluded hollow of Templewood. Beatrice would be waiting.

'It seems I am the stranded mariner and you the passing ship,' she called to him.

She came to him as he dismounted, hesitant at first. They kissed long, reacquainting themselves with the touch and taste of the other, freed from their enforced isolation. Hardy held her, drawing strength and giving comfort. She was the light and Robert Cecil the dark, neither of which he was complete without.

He clasped her face in his hands. 'You are fairer than most beached sailors.'

'I vouch I dance a better jig.' Her brown eyes warmed with laughter. 'I have sent my servants on an errand for a while.'

'What would they think of their mistress?'

'That she deserves some happiness.'

He stroked her dark hair and brought her hand to his lips. 'If only it were not so fleeting.'

'I will take whatever is given.' She let her fingers entwine with his. 'And my soldier?'

It was a question he could scarcely answer. The world of knife fights and armed duels, of a mutilated corpse in Paris Garden, were far from the experience of this gentle widow. Hers was a simple life. He would try to protect her, to ensure that one dimension never encroached upon the other. Yet he knew there was no perfect sanctuary, even in a garden mellowed by the August sun.

He pushed his doubts aside. 'Your soldier thirsts, Bea.'

'Inside we shall slake it.'

She led him to the door and into the hall, where they paused to drink wine and divest themselves of clothing on their way to the bedchamber. The days apart fuelled their hunger for each other. In a handsome brick-and-timber dwelling framed by a brook and the woods beyond, Hardy forgot all other things in the arms of the woman he loved. Realm had once taunted him that every life he touched turned to dust. Yet Beatrice proved him wrong, in her fevered passion and with the sweat beading on her face and breasts; here was something alive and good that shut the horrors out. Hardy buried himself deep.

Humidity and the smell of roses billowed through the open window and around their naked bodies. Beatrice clung to him, as if to prevent the inevitability of his departure. She recognised the sudden remoteness in those blue eyes. Duty called and she was left a stranger.

She whispered, 'I give thanks to Robert Cecil that he frees you for these minutes.'

'He is a merciful Secretary of State.' Hardy gazed towards the ceiling. 'He is also a malign dwarf I would rejoice in casting down a well.'

'Your restraint is noble,' she said wryly.

'Perhaps it is misplaced. Yet for all his deformity and faults, he is the devil I know and a shield against worse tyranny.'

'It is you that takes the brunt of any blow.' Her hands wandered on his torso. 'Each scar is a wound you suffer for the Crown.'

'Someone must fight and do the task.'

'I tremble each day it is you.' She laid her head on his shoulder and caressed the scar on his face. 'What history lies behind this mark?'

'Splinters from the battle aboard the *Revenge*.'

'This?' Her fingertip moved to a furrow on his forearm.

He glanced down. 'A musket ball while I campaigned with Drake.'

'And this?'

'More shot.'

Her finger traced the scar tissue on his chest. 'A whip?'

'They beat me well as a prisoner in the mines.'

She had heard enough, could either marvel or despair at the punishment he took. Hardy drew her near, a thirty-seven-year-old veteran more comfortable with danger than in telling its story. At least Beatrice would wait for him and provide some kind of homecoming.

When farewells were done he mounted up and headed out, returning to the heath and the lakes hidden at its centre. Tethering his horse, he stripped again and plunged into the water, immersing himself, drifting free of past cares and troubles to come.

'It grows dark, Anne.'

On the road from Warwick, a carriage had lost its wheel and the occupants stood stranded. A postilion had ridden to summon help while the coachman maintained watch with a musket. Dusk could prove treacherous for travellers. In every town there were priggers and prancers intent on stealing horses, and at every wayside inn resided the watchful and the bold spotting for wealthy quarry. Already a message might have been relayed and highway robbers could be moving through the thickets.

Lady Anne calmed her young maid. She was of a nervous disposition. 'We are well guarded and have sent word. Rescue will come soon.'

'What is soon when we shall be murdered?'

'Hush your fears.' Anne placed an arm about her. 'This is a country shire and not some barbarous land.'

They had left Coombe Abbey earlier in the day, instructed by Princess Elizabeth to distribute alms among the poor and bring succour to the old and sick. It was a mission her young attendants embraced, a chance to escape the confines of court and report back to their mistress of the world outside. Lady Anne was not yet ruing her eagerness.

'Think of the tale of adventure we shall bring back to the princess,' she said encouragingly.

'Should our throats not be slit before we get back.'

'Why this gloom and dread?'

'I saw the faces of some we passed. They did not offer friendship.'

Anne preferred to dwell on the hardship relieved and the good done that day. She would continue to take pleasure in serving her princess, regardless of a coach wheel splintering on a rock.

The coachman called a warning, his tone urgent. 'My ladies, be quick into the carriage.'

'What is it?' Anne's question died on her lips, her eyes drawn to the shapes emerging indistinctly in the gathering dark. Anne stayed motionless, feeling her companion's grip tighten on her arm.

'Seek cover, my ladies. I will protect you.'

Suppressing the impulse to flee, Anne hurried her companion inside and climbed up behind her and bolted the door. Inside the carriage the women held each other tightly, listening anxiously to the muffled sounds of challenge and reply.

There was a single discharge from the musket and a volley in response. Anne huddled with her friend. They had heard the cry, knew their guardian to be injured or dead, and tensed for the next stage of the attack. Anne bent to fumble beneath the bench.

Her companion sobbed in desperation. 'We can do nothing, Anne.'

'We may fight.'

'Fight?' Terror strangled the word.

Anne withdrew a pistol from its case, brandishing it with the clumsiness of inexperience. She was reluctant to submit without defiance; the very sight of the weapon might dissuade them.

A sudden loud crack and her companion screamed. An axe hacked away the shutters. A light shone and the muzzle of a gun appeared through the opening.

The voice was rough. 'A primrose may grow in the darkest place.'

'And a prick appear without warning.' Anne glared at the interloper. 'Our coachman is wounded.'

'Let him bleed.'

'By what right do you assail us?'

The man laughed. 'Privilege of force and superior numbers.'

'They each are trumped by authority of the King.'

'What spirit from the maid!' A hand reached to wrench the pistol from her grasp. 'I see no cavalry or royal person, nor even powder in this pan.'

'We carry little of worth.'

'Value can always be found.' The weapon dipped to press against her breast. 'My men enjoy all kind of plunder.'

'Then they are beasts and not men.'

'You tremble.'

Anne stared at the shadowed stranger. 'Would you not expect it? Will you not have mercy on women whose sole intent is to give alms to the needy?'

'It is we that have need and your *arms* we desire.'

Laughter echoed from the group as its leader bent to unlatch and throw wide the door. Anne and her companion shrank into the furthest corner.

'Come out, my ladies. Resist and you shall suffer.'

'I prefer to die than obey,' Anne cried.

'A false choice, for we will play with you the harder.' A scream rose from the injured coachman. 'Alas, my brothers are impatient.'

'You shall pay.'

'Not so great a cost as you, or your postilion who hangs from a branch some miles back.' The man reached roughly for Anne's arm.

Timing was all. From a distance, Adam Hardy judged his moment, then drew his sword and urged his horse into a gallop. It was time to play his part. He had waited long enough. Surprise and brute force should lend a certain edge.

Blinded by their own lanterns and confused by the onrush of hooves and shouted commands, the gang stumbled back in disarray. Shots were loosed, but the aim was poor and they failed to stem the charge of a foe now in full and slashing pursuit. Panic and shock propelled the rout.

Within moments, quiet descended once more. Unnerved by the silence, her companion having fainted during the commotion, Anne looked up to find a new face at the door. Even shrouded by a cap and cloak, her saviour was revealed to be young and handsome.

'You are a soldier?' she asked, unsure what to make of him.

He grinned. 'A player who acts the part of soldier and captain alike.'

'Are there others?'

'I am alone.' He proffered his hand to help her down. 'We must leave quickly, before the knaves return.'

'Our coachman is wounded.'

'I shall tend to him while you unhitch the horses.'

Restored and warmed by his courage, she followed his instructions without question. He seemed so different to the posturing men at court, so easy and unaffected in his gallantry and with a natural authority that belied his age.

They rode off without any unnecessary delay, a convoy of three roped horses trotting fast for Coombe Abbey. Adam sat on the leading horse with Anne, lightly holding her waist as she sat side-on and moved to the striding rhythm of their mount. Behind them followed the wounded coachman and the maid, Katherine, weeping softly.

He adjusted the reins and spoke in Anne's ear. 'Do you blush in the dark, my lady?'

She swayed against his body. 'You provide a kindness, but our acquaintance is done when I return home.'

'You are sure of it?'

'As certain as Anne is my name.'

'So change it, for I will visit soon with William Shakespeare to perform before the princess and her court.'

Her face warmed and she was glad for the cover of night. For a fleeting breath she imagined this stranger as her lover and then tried to put it from her mind. The thought returned, with shame and pleasure attached. Their meeting could be no coincidence, she decided. Nor the easiness of their embrace.

Seduction, like killing, was another transaction and part of a wider game. In a room off Seething Lane in the City of London, Christian Hardy was meeting a contact. He did not reflect long on the nature of infidelity or the calls that were made on him. There was little he would not do to claim eventual victory. It was ironic that his former spy chief Sir Francis Walsingham had owned a mansion in this street, foiling plots and defending his Queen from the intelligence centre he had created. What happened in this chamber was a legacy of sorts.

She had a hardness to her, an appetite and ambition that had carried her from the gutter to great privilege through the bedrooms of the rich. Now, as wife to a wealthy financier with sympathies for the Catholics, she was well placed to spy and comment on the undercurrents of dissent. Her husband was trusted and respected, relied upon by English recusants to arrange payment of their fines, and had a naivety to be exploited by his wife. One man's folly provided opportunity for another. Hardy was well versed in handling agents.

Her instruction was curt. 'Strip.'

He did as she commanded. It was a barter arrangement and each party knew the rules. Their eyes stayed locked. In turn, she removed her kirtle and bodice until she stood in a silk shift, a perfumed, greedy harlot with a penchant for a dangerous man.

'I do as you ask.' He stared her down. 'What have you for me?'

She stepped towards him and went to strike, the flat of her hand aiming for his face. He parried the blow, grasping her wrist, and she cried out in pain. Her complaint was cut short as their mouths connected, and their struggle went mute for a while.

She breathed. 'You Satan.'

'You whore.' His free hand slipped beneath her shift. 'Tell me what you know.'

'I may tell you are hard and will take before I give.'

She bit his neck and drew blood, her fingers sliding to his pelvis, pulling herself close to straddle and rub damp. Already her hands clawed and she grunted obscenities and threats. He fought her to the bed, flinging her back, tearing her shift and grappling for control. Skilfully she rolled and outmanoeuvred, was overwhelmed again, the ripped cloth binding tight around her arms. A hand escaped and clamped tight about his balls.

'You affront your mistress.' She edged him over and squatted above his groin. 'I demand satisfaction.'

'You have no honour to lose.'

'Then tup me as a harlot.'

He moved as she moved, providing the service she requested. Her enthusiasm was loud. If she wished to be blistered or scourged, he would oblige; should she call on him to debase her, he was ready to deliver. From where he lay, he observed as if from afar her wantonness and rage, her thighs working and her mouth agape and the motion of her breasts. Carnality was no substitute for what she lacked.

He reached and gripped her throat. 'Speak to me of what you know.'

'I will have you first.'

He thrust deep. 'Divulge or you will lose me.'

'Such force.' She rocked and keened and raked her nails on his chest. 'I want no gentleness.'

'Nor shall you have it.'

'Bleed me, dog.' She panted high and groaned.

'What of whispers and secret meetings? What of the purchase of gunpowder?'

'I hear little.'

'You lie.' His hand tightened on her neck.

An ecstatic cry and a shuddering in her belly. 'A young gentleman gathers powder for the English regiment in Flanders fighting for the Spanish.'

'His name?'

'Sir Ambrose Rookwood.'

'Nothing more than a Suffolk landowner.' Hardy held and tipped her hips. 'A breeder of horses.'

'My own mount is bred for rough jumping.' She pressed down and spread the slick across his abdomen.

The encounter continued, bruising and climactic. Each took what they wanted. Though disappointed by the paucity of information, Hardy would not show it. There were many Englishmen who sympathised with Spanish efforts to quash Lutheran rebellion in the Low Countries, and plenty committed to providing weapons and support. One more with money to send gunpowder made no difference. Hardy would wait for further proof and doubtless stray again from the gentler charms of Beatrice.

'A special place, is it not?'

Guido Fawkes could scarcely disagree. With his neighbour and new-found friend the porter as his guide, he toured the great interior of Parliament House, casting a professional eye over the space and discreetly pacing out its length. This was the point of impact, the den of all iniquity, the empty space that would one day be hung with tapestries and echo to trumpets and to which King James and his lords would proceed. What an event it would prove. Secluded in a chamber below the rush-strewn flagstones, a man with a timepiece and slow match would be tending his barrels of black powder. Fawkes looked forward to the moment.

August had decayed to September, the new month encouraging the monarch to establish a commission of privy councillors tasked with exterminating Jesuits and other corrupt influences. Instead they brought on their own obliteration. Fawkes traced the contours of the windows and glanced to the high expanse of oak-beam ceiling. Whatever the level of oppression, it would end here, in the upper house, the Lords, the site distinct from the Commons that sat across the precinct in the old royal chapel. He ground the toe of his boot against the floor. Power flowed through these stones.

He turned to his guide. 'Indeed, you are right. It is a place of rare drama and import.'

'Here the King will sit, and here his nobles.' The man's tone was reverential. 'No finer gathering may be seen.'

'Nor more fitting a spectacle.'

'Perhaps your master Sir Thomas Percy will attend the opening of Parliament.'

'In truth, he prefers the quiet solace of the country,' Fawkes replied with a smile. 'Yet he will be here in spirit.'

'Is he not a royal bodyguard?'

'Our King is beloved and has no cause to hide behind a regiment.'

'Threat lurks and papists conspire.'

'He is safe in an edifice so grand as this.'

'Treason has few bounds,' the porter said weightily, platitude offered as insight. 'We must pray that our vigilance forever preserves the sovereign.'

'Amen to it, friend.'

Fawkes wandered across to the elevation on which the royal dais would rest. He was lost to his musings; in his mind he already walked the debris field and tasted the mired air. But he would not let swagger and complacency undermine his plans. Even a dull-witted porter could develop suspicions or stumble on a plot. He reminded himself that until the fateful moment he lit the fuse, he was nothing more than the servant and caretaker John Johnson.

His companion called to him, 'How does it feel to stand where a divinely chosen King will be?'

'Both humbling and uplifting.'

'You are at the centre of things, the very pivot on which the present and future turns.'

'I am scarce worthy to bear witness.'

'We each have our part.' The man toyed importantly with his keys. 'Monarch or noble, they depend for their survival on those lower born.'

'May the Lord help us to discharge our duty.'

Fawkes had seen enough. He would report to the others on their return to London, would relate his progress. His brother plotters had placed their faith in him and he would not disappoint. He took a final look. It was best to view the impending demolition as just another challenge, a further step in a just and holy war that had started long ago. The soft and pampered elite of England were unready for the blow about to be inflicted. By the time Fawkes stepped from the hall, he had decided on the quantity of black powder he would use.

Nightfall gave cover and opiates had silenced the dogs. On the western edge of Hampstead Heath, a hook gently unlatched a shutter and a figure climbed nimbly through the window. Once inside, Realm stood alert in the darkness, adjusting his senses, absorbing the stillness. His was a reconnaissance and a courtesy call, a chance to study the vulnerabilities of Christian Hardy and his mistress. Beatrice had the prettiest of homes.

He climbed the stairs, listening for movement and the first cry of alarm. At the door to the bedchamber, Realm paused. Her breathing was too light to hear. There was no challenge in slitting her throat, to mutilate and display the corpse as he had the late wife of his old adversary. Like Emma Hardy before her, the lady of this house was nothing but a tool to be used when disruption was called for. Cold blood and a capacity to murder at will distinguished him from others and rendered him invincible. For now, he would let sleeping women lie and an English renegade creep back to his labours.

CHAPTER 6

The plot's enforcer was back in London. At the Bell Savage Inn close by St Paul's, Jack Wright drank beer and pondered what lay ahead. Should Guido Fawkes succeed and the King and his coterie vanish at a stroke, it would be he who swept up the debris and ensured the smooth accession of the young Princess Elizabeth. Yet there were unknowns, and these were what concerned him. Certainly stray nobles might survive the cataclysm, but they could be quickly dispatched in the aftermath as they blundered in shock from their mansions. There was also Prince Henry, the royal prince beloved of the nation, a ten-year-old with his own court at St James's. He could not be allowed to live, would be hunted down if necessary to prevent a rival future to that determined by the plotters. At least the mysterious English renegade codenamed Realm recruited men for such an eventuality.

Wright finished his drink and strolled out of the inn, an establishment in whose galleried courtyard he had often displayed his fencing skills. A wider stage beckoned. Even from here he could smell the stench of Smithfield Market, the malodorous vapours from the stomachs of butchered cattle sitting heavily in the air. Maybe it was a sign, a portent of the carnage he and his companions would bring upon the land. Such was the nature of overthrow.

He crossed the Fleet Ditch and entered the rambling complex of Bridewell. The former palace was home to many things, a prison and madhouse and assorted taverns, but it was the school of swordsmanship he sought. Every gentleman and duellist required training, studying as though their lives depended on it. The Corporation of London Masters of Defence was a repository for fighting talent where prowess with a blade was lauded and encouraged. In this hall, the four governors—of perception, distance, timing and technique—held sway and the distilled wisdom of France, Spain and Italy was taught. Wearing padded jerkins and with blunted rapiers, the students moved to and fro to shouted command. Everything was in the detail.

One man dominated. Wright watched him, observing the contained energy and the subtle motion of the wrist and feet. His artistry was hypnotic. There was experience behind the sword arm, awareness in the eyes, a manner that suggested a wealth of hidden tricks. Christian Hardy would be hard to beat and yet his presence alone pricked the swordsman's interest.

From across the room, Hardy sensed that an opponent was studying him. He had learnt to determine the source of a threat even in the midst of battle. It provided the opportunity for showmanship, for teasing out the level of hostility. He summoned a pair of students and with bewildering speed and little formality proceeded to attack and disarm them. The demonstration drew shocked applause.

Hardy returned the fallen rapiers to their owners. 'This day you lose your blades; tomorrow it shall be your lives.'

'There is no disgrace in ceding to you,' said one of the young men, wide-eyed.

Hardy addressed the wider audience. 'When outmatched or in doubt, employ the ninth parry and Cob's reverse.'

The terms for running away provoked a gust of laughter. But the newcomer at the back of the crowd did not smile. He pushed his way through the onlookers.

Hardy acknowledged him. 'Have you come to learn?'

'To teach.'

Hardy sensed the flicker of antipathy behind the blank facade. The man tried too hard to hide his hostility. In the background, the whip and snap of duelling blades ceased as attention swung towards the centre of the arena.

'I spy a *bravazzo*.' Hardy either praised or insulted by dubbing him a brawler. 'They are often the quickest to yield.'

'Not once has it happened.'

'Your name, sir?'

'Jack Wright.' Wright rested a palm on the pommel of his rapier.

Hardy nodded. 'A swordsman of renown. And a visiting Catholic.'

'It is ground we share.'

'A solitary and unfriendly place.' Hardy raised his chin, alert to danger. 'This is a school, not a forest clearing for affray and *alla macchia*.'

'You run scared?'

'I stand wise.'

'So let us see your vaunted skill.' Wright was skirmishing with words. 'Not for us the safety of blunt tips or the donning of plate jackets.'

'What risks you take.'

'I trust in a wager and my judgement.'

'How is victory to be measured?'

Wright was unbuttoning his doublet. 'First blood.'

Terms were agreed. Hardy watched his adversary. He had seen bravado crumble and bladders leak as he raised his blade and sharp reality bit. It was in the nature of men to pit themselves against the odds. He wondered at the misjudgement.

He twitched his rapier. 'I have your measure.'

'And I yours.'

They were aligned, their stances taken and the space cleared. A senior master would act as referee. Around them the students stood in respectful silence, awed by the promise of virtuosity.

'En garde,' called the referee.

Wright held his rapier at the high vertical above his shoulder, a technique refined by the master di Grassi. Hardy responded with a hanging guard, the blade angled steeply to protect the upper body.

He betrayed himself with his choices, Hardy mused. The textbook fighters always did. Even in a glance, there was a clue; in the positioning of a foot or flicker of an eye there was proof of the next move. On a muscle twitch alone, a great swordsman could reach to block a strike yet to be delivered.

'Murder sits within you, Wright.'

'Killing is not my aim.'

'Is your point to tease? To kiss me on my button?'

'Beware your jesting, Hardy.'

'Forgive my Catholic taste.'

They stood motionless, waiting on a single word that would give them their release. Hardy counted and savoured the seconds.

'Engage.'

Blades chattered, the flow of thrust, parry and riposte carrying the duellists in answering waves across the cramped arena. Hardy conserved his energy, playing Wright and leading him in. His opponent's composure had fragmented, and red spots of fury bloomed on the cheeks of the recusant swordsman.

'You tire, Wright?'

'I do not.' The blades went debole to debole and another lunge was countered.

'Provost fencers would offer me more fire.'

'It is steel I provide, Hardy.'

His pride bruised, Wright attacked hard, jabbing and foining, desperate to close. The intelligencer switched line and deftly flicked away the threat.

'We call it a *botta secreta*,' Hardy said over the other man's rasping breath. 'A concealed move.'

'I am no mere pupil.'

'So what is it you hide?'

'Some talent for silencing my opposites.'

Wright had been lulled by his sense of infallibility, was caught by the patterns and tactics of an undefeated master. Driven to overreach, he fell as a blade slammed behind his knee.

Hardy's voice rang out, amused. 'That too has its name, I believe – a *coup de jarnac*.'

'There is yet no blood and I am not crippled.' Wright sprang to his feet. 'I shall give you coup.'

'As I will give you reason to pay your wager now.'

'You think me some village pugilist?' Wright spat. 'Akin to easy prey in Clerkenwell?'

'Show me what you are.'

Already Wright had done so, confessing unthinkingly to his knowledge of the street fight. He was implicated by association and tied into a wider plot. Hardy met the onrush, absorbing its force and deflecting its aim. Rage rendered the stroke inaccurate and Wright's rapier clattered wide.

'Our theatre is done.' Pricking a finger on his sword tip, Hardy held it up for view. 'Blood appears and salute is given.'

Disarmed and humiliated, Wright shook his head in sullen disbelief. His defeat had been comprehensive, Hardy's triumph achieved seemingly with ease. It was a reminder of the persistent and formidable nature of the foe. Wright was already intent on revenge.

Hardy approached. 'Have more care with those to whom you would present your blade.'

'A giant himself may fall to a hidden move.'

'Or a dwarf submit to ignominy.'

'I am full grown.'

'Then remember well what happened here when next rashness tempts you.'

Wright stared unblinkingly. 'I forget nothing.'

A moment later, still smarting, he stepped into the street and with shoulders hunched headed north up Chancery Lane. He must put aside the humiliation. There was work to do and reconnaissance to perform, a tour of the lodgings of his brother conspirators to ensure they were not watched or compromised. Soon Thomas Percy would return to his rooms near Gray's Inn and Tom Wintour to his accommodation at the Duck and Drake. Robin Catesby would also arrive, returning to his Lambeth home. And all the while, Guido Fawkes remained in Westminster and prepared. Autumn should prove itself an eventful season.

His mind turned to more pressing matters, Wright failed to notice the figure walking some distance behind him and keeping pace through the hurrying throng of clerks and lawyers. He had broken a cardinal rule and brought attention to himself, and had earned himself a tail assigned by Christian Hardy. The intelligencer was not one to ignore a lead.

A third presence fell in behind the follower, Realm shadowing as though he had few cares. It seemed his role was to play nursemaid to conspiracy, to guide the plotters and guard their backs from harm. They did their best. While English Catholics endured and the pallid Spanish creature Philip III hid in the gloom of his Escorial palace, a few brave souls were planning overthrow. Their efforts should be praised and aided as the timidity of Spain should be condemned. In a single year, the country spent eight hundred thousand ducats administering an empire that stretched from the Philippines to Peru. Gold and silver were all and not a single piece would trickle down to support the assassination of an English monarch. Realm continued his leisurely pursuit. It was left to him to help coax his nation back into the light.

'My gracious liege, you won it, wore it, kept it, gave it me: then plain and right must my possession be.'

The audience was rapt. Dressed as Prince Hal and holding aloft a facsimile crown, Adam Hardy delivered his lines. For over an hour he had entertained as Hamlet and Romeo, played the fool and sprite and, with Shakespeare, enacted scenes that drew gasps or cheers or laughter. Royal courts were places in which themes of kingship and treachery were guaranteed to resonate; Coombe Abbey was no exception.

Shakespeare stepped out of character and bowed to those assembled. 'Your Grace, my lords and ladies. You have heard and we have told and we assail enough your senses. May we give our thanks and say God bless as we bid you well this night.'

Applause echoed in the hall, and Shakespeare turned smiling to his protégé. 'You bring them both tears and joy, Adam. It is a potent gift.'

'Not as great as is the writing.'

'Look at them.' The playwright gestured with his eyes. 'All is pride and vanity and all humanity is here.'

'They are generous with their kindness.'

'Some are stirred and some unmoved and full of jealousy and spite. Others may view you with charity and a few yet with alarm.'

'Alarm?' Adam looked at him in surprise.

'You are young, handsome and brave, and it provokes.'

'Perhaps it is the nature of a royal house.'

'Learn quick, boy.' Shakespeare patted him on the shoulder. 'Enjoy praise and favour and take them all with a pinch. A golden boy is next day a chimney sweep or a victim on the block.'

'I ride fate wherever it takes me.'

Courtiers clustered to meet the famed playwright and his companion, pressing in to give opinions, offer compliments. Adam studied the faces turned to him in approval or vigilance. To most, he was yet the hero who earlier had put brigands to flight and saved two of the princess's attendants. It provided currency for a while.

A pathway opened as Princess Elizabeth and her ladies advanced to greet him. He was the talk of her court and worthy of inspection. He bowed, an eighteen-year-old no better than a humble servant before a child of eight. The princess's response was dignified and then interrupted by a fit of sudden mirth.

'You are as handsome and strong as I have been told, Mr Hardy.'

'I claim no merit for what a parent bestows, Your Grace.'

'Then you may accept our thanks for your daring.' Elizabeth's eyes were lit up with humour. 'You delivered Lady Anne safe back to our care. My ladies are precious to me.'

'It is my privilege and honour.'

'You bring adventure where there was none before, Mr Hardy.'

'Quietness is my preference.'

Elizabeth peered doubtfully into his face. 'Shall we be friends?'

'Such decision is not for me, my lady. I am nothing but a vagabond travelling player.'

'Is wandering your pleasure?' the princess asked, intrigued.

'I find it is my life.'

Murmuring and whispers arose from the surrounding crowd, the sotto voce exchanges of courtiers disconcerted by the presence of a lowborn buck. Yet the princess was ruled by her tender spirit and should on occasion be allowed her head. The youth in his princely costume was a harmless diversion and plainly posed no threat.

Elizabeth sighed, her eyes wistful. 'For an instant I saw on stage the commanding prince I would wish my brother Henry to grow to be.'

'All that I offer is illusion, my lady.'

'We each have our part and you act yours well.' Graciousness again replaced impish charm as the child princess moved to leave. 'You are most welcome to Coombe Abbey.'

In Elizabeth's wake stood Lady Anne, briefly reunited with her champion. Adam detected the shyness and defensive formality, the transparent delight she tried to hide. She was as fair and as fascinated with him as on their last meeting.

'My Lady Anne.' He bowed. 'It pleases me to find you safe and content behind these walls.'

'Contentment is a fickle thing, sir.'

'Am I to bear the blame?'

Her eyes dipped. 'I would not lay complaint against a man who saved my life.'

'He is no stranger and has a name.'

'Which one of his characters should I believe?'

'Suitor and lover, I commend.'

Her cheeks flushed pink. 'I must bid you farewell and go to my mistress.'

'She is fortunate for your company and blessed for your concern.' Adam kept a steady gaze. 'As I am fortunate and blessed she wills it I return.'

They parted, their encounter unobserved amid the general din. Musicians played and dancing started, and jugglers and tumblers performed. Should the princess be amused it would make the King glad, and honour and reward for the hosts might follow. There was a fine line between gain and financial ruin. Adam surveyed the spectacle.

'You appraise them as a husbandman or hunter does a herd.' Shakespeare's voice sounded merry in his ear. 'Is your intent to slaughter or to breed?'

'Observation is enough, Will.'

'So study and digest and remember that we serve.'

'They like what we provide.'

'Gratitude may turn. Tonight they toast us with fine claret and tomorrow might toast us on a spit.'

'Such is the experience of a playwright.'

'Even a groundling is more loyal than a courtier.' Shakespeare took the young man by the arm. 'Now come play the lute and further charm our masters.'

Adam did as he was ordered and sang and played his minstrel tunes. When people responded with their hearts they rarely stopped to see or think. Shakespeare was correct: they really did resemble cattle. It suited Hardy's purpose. He was precisely where he wished to be; from here he would report back to Robin Catesby and show himself of use. And he had aroused interest and passion in Lady Anne's eyes.

Ancient skills, like the old religion, were still practised in the land. On the lawn at Ashby St Ledgers, a target butt had been erected, and from a hundred paces Adam loosed arrows at it with a longbow. The ritual and focus, draw and release, helped to clear his mind. In these closing days of September, when the weather turned and plague receded and the thoughts of gentlemen strayed to London, there remained the business of keeping priests and seminarists out of the clutches of the law. The rich might disport themselves at Coombe Abbey, but in the shires around, the life or death of Catholic preachers was daily being decided. Adam raised the weapon and lined up the mark.

A different arrow shot over his head and struck the centre, an exultant shout from the terrace above confirming the presence of Catesby.

The younger man called to him, 'What ploy is this, Robin?'

'A simple trick to prove the unexpected triumphs.' Catesby descended with his bow and quiver. 'Yet it is gunpowder and not archery that wins the battles of today.'

Adam turned back to the target and let fly his arrow. 'I prefer a nobler art.'

'Promise shows in everything you touch.' Catesby leant on his bow. 'Priests are alive because you intervened, gave warning or escorted them to sanctuary.'

'How else is a boy to spend his summer months?'

'Few would embrace such hazards.'

'Blame an appetite I gained in London.'

Catesby shaded his eyes and looked towards the target. 'From common street brawler to strutting and supping in the hallowed halls of a Stuart princess. By any measure, your rise is astounding.'

'You played a part in it all.'

Master and apprentice acknowledged each other with a smile. Whether a release from gaol or an apparently random attack on a stranded carriage, the deft hand of Catesby had nudged events along.

Catesby's eyes narrowed. 'I depart south in three days.'

'To abandon me here?'

'In London, bad company or a justice would lure you to their grasp.' Catesby selected an arrow and tested its tip on his thumb. 'You are too important to squander in that fashion.'

'Condemning me to languish is itself a waste.'

'Be patient, Adam. The call will come.' Catesby fitted the arrow and raised the bow.

'Meantime?'

'Ride out each day to exercise the horses and thwart the efforts of the pursuivants.' The arrow sped home. 'Visit Coombe Abbey and woo the Lady Anne.'

'Once more you hide your deeper purpose.'

'As again you ask too much.' The ringleader would not yet expose Adam to the pressures that full knowledge might bring. Exploiting others demanded finesse. Catesby was fond of the young man and considered him an asset to be preserved. Those in search of a home and cause were the easier to lead. He spoke again, more gently. 'You trust me, Adam?'

'On my life, I do.'

'And with my life I shall defend you. Should I confide in you, it could invite on you the horrors of the state.'

'I would not buckle before them.'

'Many a recusant has thought the same until the steel gauntlets crushed his hands or he was laid out on the rack.'

'We shall succeed, Robin,' Adam said earnestly.

'I have never doubted it,' Catesby said with calm authority. 'Now back to our contest.'

In rapid salvo the ash shafts flew, their feathered flights patterning the target. The men stood side by side to unleash the final volley.

Catesby was generous in his praise. 'Not once do I outshoot you.'

'There is yet much I have to learn.' Adam furled his bow, content. 'I know no kinder tutor or replacement for a father.'

'Nor I a truer pupil or a son.'

A servant appeared through the open doorway and hurried towards them. He spoke breathlessly. 'A party of horsemen some twenty strong is sighted at the Dunchurch crossroads.'

'Pursuivants or militia?'

'Their identity and intent are unknown, sir.' The man's eyes were wide with alarm. 'But I wager they raid a Catholic house.'

'Unless we manage to thwart them,' Catesby said calmly.

Adam was already running for the stables to mount up, but Catesby knew there was little cause for panic. The forces of Protestant tyranny were irritant gadflies to be avoided or kept distant. In time their nests would be smoked and their leaders killed and the country left in peace.

At the tables around him, young men laughed raucously. Christian Hardy nursed his pot of ale and swallowed back the memories and his worries for his son. He had been a poor father, absent, immersed in intelligence and war, afraid to involve himself in the life of a little boy whose mother he once loved and who had been destroyed by that love. As Adam grew up, the pair moved apart. The sense of loss was keenest when Hardy saw the youth and fellowship of others.

It was the third night of waiting at the inn beside Tyburn, breathing air thick with the fumes of tallow, sea coal and tobacco. There were a hundred varied factors that could make an operative disappear. Perhaps rain had slowed him. The bleak weather outside churned the gravel and mud and added to the melancholy. This was the site of public executions and the stalking ground for ghosts, the place where paths and destinies converged and crowds and tumbrils gathered. Hardy himself had sent enough people on that route.

A spray of water and evaporating dampness announced a new arrival. Wearied and mud-spattered, his man slumped into a chair without speaking. The great north road was a punishing trek. Hardy ordered beer. They sat in silence, the other man gratefully taking in the warmth. Finally he reached into a leather pouch and withdrew a waxed canvas envelope.

Hardy slit open the canvas and took out the folded sheet of paper within. He unfolded the page and held it to the candlelight. It was a list, names copied from a register of those who had once attended St Peter's School in York. A cradle of militant Catholicism. Hardy's eyes settled on a familiar name. Jack Wright had betrayed his intentions through his arrogance and pride. Now his background was identified. Another name was here, *Guy Fawkes* scratched in ink like the rest, a boy who would later fight for Spain and against the interests of England. Cecil's intelligence had proven worthy. Fawkes and Wright shared common heritage and cause.

Donning his cloak, Hardy thanked the man and left. Outside, he slung himself up onto his horse and rode away through the dark, wet streets.

In the threads of thought spooling in his mind were captured other persons linked by blood and faith to the two already unmasked. Security dictated they would keep their enterprise tight, would not build alliances far from the core. He was glad: it would limit the casualties.

A severed head confronted him, hung from a tree close to his house. Warning, taunt or gesture of intent? As always, it was difficult to gauge motive with Realm. Hardy stayed in the saddle and studied the object lit by a lantern hung on an adjacent branch. Again the renegade had miscalculated. In slaying the agent who had tailed Jack Wright, he had showed his hand too early. Gunpowder would be the vehicle for their murderous ambition. Hardy gently eased the item from its resting place and snuffed out the lamp. Let the bodies fall where they may.

Saltpetre boys were busy on the Strand, their convoy of wagons travelling to collect horse urine from the stables of the rich. Theirs was a menial trade made harder by the peace with Spain and a resulting collapse in demand for gunpowder. Yet they persevered, would carry off without complaint the stinking waste of the hierarchs. The likes of Robert Cecil would pay them no attention.

After collecting a load, their route took them in slow progress north and east to pastures near Epping Forest and a collection of disused barns set discreetly on an estate. Once they would have passed their casks to buyers and middlemen sent by the powder mills of Essex and Kent. But circumstances had changed since their overseer had vanished from his post at the Paris Garden baiting pit. His loss to Southwark was their gain, for their new master paid well and few questions would be asked.

The boys waited patiently at the barns. Soon horses and another cart appeared, escorted by a finely dressed young blade at ease on a black charger. Sir Ambrose Rookwood had come to take delivery. He was in his mid-twenties, wealthy and committed, a vigorous Catholic entrusted by Robin Catesby with acquiring supplies of gunpowder. Believing it was bound for the English volunteers fighting for Spain in Flanders, he was happy to assist. Recruitment and revelation would be a gradual thing.

He threw a purse across. 'In a fortnight I shall return and demand a further load.'

'Whatever you desire.' The spokesman tipped the bag and counted the silver pieces in his palm. 'You will find us ready.'

The goods were transferred swiftly, the parties aware of the need for discretion. Rookwood tugged the canvas cover into place. He enjoyed the element of intrigue, the chance to strike a blow and to explore the world beyond the confines of horse breeding. He was not to know that his name had already been passed to Christian Hardy by the viciously amorous wife of a City financier.

A whip flicked and the small cavalcade departed on a different heading. The burden it carried would in time be turned into gunpowder destined not for the Low Countries but for a modest dwelling close to the Thames in Lambeth. A ruling class had planted the seeds of its own obliteration and provided the means by way of the scrapings from its stable floors.

CHAPTER 7

Christian Hardy disliked Westminster. He preferred the honesty of a straight fight to the machinations of statesmen, enjoyed the company of whores and thieves over that of preening and ambitious nobles. The King decreed and his ministers scrapped like dogs about his feet for morsels of influence. It made no difference, for power flowed inevitably into the grasp of Robert Cecil.

Hardy wandered the environs, observing the frenetic flow of people and business and the wayward gait of those departing the taverns. Everyone had their pace and purpose and they all had sound reason to be drunk. He moved aside for a stranger manoeuvring a barrel, the man bending to guide the hogshead across the cobbles. A servant rather than a vintner, Hardy decided. And not always a servant. Even with his back turned and the brim of his beaver-felt hat pulled low, the man's manner and bearing suggested a soldiering past. Quick hands and confident movements, a certain disregard for civilians in his path, all pointed to his history. It took a trained and combat-seasoned eye to recognise the signs.

There was a rumble of wheels and a warning cry and people dived out of the way of an approaching delivery cart. The servant's reaction was swifter than most, his arm sweeping to safety a maid with her pail and his foot sacrificing the cask to a steep flight of steps. The hogshead fell heavily, and shattered at the bottom of the stairs. People stared, some laughing or shaking their heads, absorbed in the sight of claret wine gone to waste. They marvelled at the expense and anticipated an outburst against the driver. Yet the servant hesitated, his hand on a sheathed dagger before retreating from view down an alley. Hardy glanced after him and back to the remains of the barrel, his interest pricked by someone with the discipline to choose the time and ground for confrontation. Maybe he too had a pressing appointment.

'I see you keep your head, Mr Hardy.'

Cecil sat behind a desk, inscrutable and dressed in black. Attending his government offices provided some relief from the suppliants and petitioners clamouring at the door of his London mansion and allowed him to place himself at the centre of the web. As Secretary of State and representative of the King, there was no detail of political life he did not wish to hear. Intelligencers existed to make report.

He viewed Hardy. 'Realm toys with you.'

'His conceit is his weakness.'

'Is it not justified?' Cecil could accuse without a change in tone. 'A whole summer is gone and all you have done is litter the ground with corpses and find a severed head in a tree.'

'My methods have never failed you.'

'They continue to disturb.'

Hardy stayed sanguine. 'Do I not find a connection between Guido Fawkes and Jack Wright?'

'One a mercenary and the other a swordsman.' Cecil was dismissive. 'I'm searching for the generals and you have given me mere foot soldiers.'

His intelligencer continued. 'Whatever blow our enemies intend, I have reason to suppose it is gunpowder they will use.'

'There is no point in speculation.'

Hardy had expected the response. 'Conspiracy has been foiled with less. Realm has discovered a ready supply, and young recusants such as Sir Ambrose Rookwood are scouring the market.'

'You have built a tale from fragments and guessing.'

'Is this not our world, my lord?'

The spy chief ignored the mild insubordination. 'Gunpowder alone does not indicate overthrow.'

'It may still provide the spark.'

'For a few muskets and occasional cannon?' Cecil would not concede the point. 'For a disorganised rabble of malcontents?'

'What of hellburners? What of mines and infernal devices?'

'They cannot bring down a kingdom.'

Yet Hardy thought the Secretary of State was turning matters over in his mind. Hellburners were explosive ships sent by the Dutch against Spanish invaders with devastating consequences. Mines and bombs could be created from barrels packed with powder and naphtha and sheathed with nails and shot. When the mighty were brought low it was often by the unexpected.

'We are surprised in the present for we are besotted with experience of battles in our past,' Hardy said.

'Your remedy?'

'Awareness, my lord.'

'So how would you proceed should you seek to kill the King?'

'With preparation and guile and every manner of diversion. All leading to a single awesome cataclysm.'

'Why not the stiletto blade to the back?'

'A dagger demands close approach and leaves too much to chance.'

'Is there not the pistol or arquebus?'

'It would not paralyse the body politic or bring the populace to heel. Nor would it ensure a seizing of control.' Hardy was persistent. 'Only with apocalypse will the zealots create their new Jerusalem.'

Cecil returned to sifting through his papers. His intelligencer was accustomed to this tactic. It was designed to unsettle and to reinforce authority, to remind any who might mock that the little beagle had bite. Hardy listened to the scratch of the quill and the turn of the pages. Whether devil's advocate or the devil himself, the ennobled spymaster had a vested interest in keeping the King alive. Twenty minutes passed.

Finally, Cecil looked up. 'Some would call your musings reckless and misplaced.'

'Others will recall I once saved the life of Queen Elizabeth.'

'It is the health and future of the King we debate.' Cecil laid down his pen. 'Who shall be consumed in this supposed apocalypse?'

'Those that placed James on the throne and strive to keep him there.'

'Then I am a marked man,' Cecil commented drily.

'High office and espionage invite such risk, my lord.'

'So we must beckon the threat.' The spy chief had made his calculations. 'When the plot is ripe, we shall begin our harvest.'

It would doubtless be a bloody affair involving the round-up of conspirators and their supporters. Cecil was a methodical and callous man. He would spread the net and hold it tight while his rivals fell in. Dukes or earls or baronets, all in time might be implicated. Every story had a victor, and the Secretary of State was determined he would settle scores and write its ending.

'I want no trouble, sir.'

Confused by the sudden presence of the stranger beside him on the box, the carter attempted to negotiate. It seemed the unwelcome visitor was not about to move. He had climbed up without warning to take his seat, and appeared content to act as escort for the length of the journey. Madness had its many forms.

'You want no trouble and yet you are causing it.' Guido Fawkes threatened in a low voice and stared ahead. 'Maintain your pace if you value your life.'

'I have the whip.'

'And I a blade.'

'There is little of worth here.' The carter guided his horse on. 'I fetch and carry and that is all.'

'In between you broke a full cask of Bordeaux wine.'

The pause signalled recognition. 'The fault may lie with us both, sir.'

'It rests with you.' Fawkes was in an uncompromising mood.

'There is no need for this.'

'It is what I think that counts.' The mercenary placed his arm about the man's shoulder. 'Would you have me in bad humour? Insult a soldier who has done all acts of violence?'

'All I want is to see you gone.'

'So purchase your liberty and win my trust and we shall depart as fellows well met.'

His offer was persuasive. There could be no doubt the stranger would deliver on his word; he was a dark and vicious type unlikely to be mollified by any manner of excuse. Accidents happened and a smashed barrel was as common a sight as a shattered skull or corpse. The wisest course was to pay.

'How much do you want?'

'Both the purse at your side and its brother hidden in your jerkin.' Fawkes's grip tightened. 'Fair exchange for my embarrassment and loss.'

'I am not a wealthy man, sir.'

'Your delay will render you poorer.'

Fawkes grabbed the purses before jumping off the moving cart. He had learnt that action provided an answer to most wrongs. It paid to make a stand, to drive a point home with a knife or lit fuse. Yet he would be careful, for the enemy watched. In the precincts of the Palace of Westminster he had spied a man with bright blue eyes and knew him to be Christian Hardy, the intelligencer of whom his old school friend Jack Wright had warned.

They had slipped unnoticed and by different routes to gather at the Duck and Drake, comrades reunited in London after a summer absence. Their commitment was still strong and confidence high; each could see that a crusade begun as a conversation in a Northamptonshire gatehouse was developing apace. It was October 1604, and Robin Catesby was in an ebullient mood.

'God willing, all is well, my brothers.' He gazed at his fellow conspirators, Tom Wintour, Thomas Percy and Jack Wright. 'And Christ willing, James will die and the world forever change.'

Wintour raised his cup and drank. 'These months have brought it closer, Robin.'

'In every part and in every way.'

There were murmurs of agreement and self-congratulation.

'We have found our supply of powder, and Guido resides at the very heart of the Beast,' Catesby continued. 'Our future queen is brought within our grasp. Yet we cannot force the pace,' It is rumoured the King plans to delay the recall of Parliament from February next to the last months of the year.'

Percy sliced and chewed on a slab of gingerbread. 'He is no lover of Parliament, as we are no admirer of his.'

'Then perhaps he would welcome our plan of demolition,' suggested Wright.

'He will be in no state to thank us.' Wintour waited for the mirth to settle. 'It gives us time, brothers. Time here to ready ourselves and to build our force in the Midlands.'

'Time also to be captured.' Percy stared at his brother-in-law. 'Was there not an incident with an intelligencer, Jack?'

'None that would lead him to our business,' Wright said sharply.

'How sure you are.'

'As certain as a man who guards your backs and would challenge every danger unto death.' Anger flashed in Wright's face.

Percy continued to eye his brother-in-law. 'Your task is not to tempt it to us.'

'I will do as the moment commands.'

'Or as rashness dictates.' Heat had also entered Percy's voice. 'In future we should sheath our swords and keep our heads low and let wisdom rule our actions.'

'And keep opinion to ourselves,' Wright shot back.

'What hope have we should we quarrel now?' Catesby interrupted. 'What chance if the family and faithful are at daggers drawn?'

Percy grudgingly conceded. 'I make my point.'

'As I make mine.' Their leader spoke firmly. 'Our grievance is with the King and our loyalty to each other.'

'There remains the threat of Christian Hardy,' said Wright.

'He will be dealt with in good order.' Catesby smiled.

His accomplices believed him as they always did, silenced by his authority. Whenever doubt appeared, Catesby would quell it; whatever friction arose, he would remind all of the higher purpose. Catholics were in need and the plotters had taken their vow. God called them.

Catesby steered the debate. 'Think not of Christian Hardy but of his son. Driven by resentment and hot blood, he is a gift to us and a thorn in the side of the state.'

'Will he deliver us the princess?' asked Percy.

'Adam would lay down his life to do as I bid him.'

'Then he is our friend and equal.'

'A friend who cannot carry the day alone,' Wintour warned. 'To spread revolt and snatch Elizabeth, we require houses and money and horses.'

'All are matters we address,' said Catesby. One day soon, a clutch of manors near Warwick and Stratford would be commandeered as armouries and mounting posts, and further recruits would join the venture. This and more Catesby promised.

He spread his hands flat upon the table. 'I was eight years old when I first witnessed my beloved father imprisoned for his faith. He was a pious man accepting of his torment. For his memory and the future of our religion, we shall not be so meek.'

'Blood will rain, be sure of it.' Wright rapped his cup upon the table. 'With the agent Realm ready at our shoulder, we are well equipped to break the foe.'

Wintour nodded. 'While Spain sleeps, he alone shares our danger to lend succour and support.'

'As he alone once journeyed as assassin to kill the bastard Queen,' Percy said.

'Indeed, we are blessed by his example.' Catesby rose and stepped to the window, peering through it to the street below. 'Yet it is stealth that is our shield and the cloak of our approach, the reason we can sit but a few hundred yards from the home of Robert Cecil.'

Percy threw back a tumbler of wine. 'Our petition to him is not one he will like.'

'First we must arrange to deliver it.'

The ringleader continued to gaze down from his vantage, a man sure of himself and the course he had set. Out there was the Secretary of State going about his trade, spreading poison and malice and directing the forces of oppression. His was to be a glittering and short-lived career. Catesby found himself tracking the movement of an aged beggar unsteady on his feet, then switched to follow a pair of maids on an errand. The thought of Cecil always brought on additional wariness. Perhaps the pygmy already detected signs of their endeavour and was in conference with his staff, planning arrests. Mercifully, even a spy chief was not privy to everything.

'Another drink for our brother.'

At the Roebuck Tavern in Stratford-upon-Avon, pursuivants had met to boast and swap tales. They were among friends, secure in the company of like-minded fellows who applauded their efforts on behalf of the state. The Catholics must be watched and the Jesuit priests they harboured rooted out. Yet the hunting season had been poor and the catch small, their quarry forewarned and nowhere to be seen. It was wearying and thirsty work.

Adam took his brimming cup and raised it in gratitude to his companions. They made for excellent drinking partners. He had sung and played for them and been befriended, ingratiating himself with his wit and charm. Able to imbibe with the most hardened drinker, the handsome young man was a good listener to their talk.

'How do you find our local ways?' A hand gripped his forearm and the words slurred. 'Are they too coarse and rough? Too crude a diet for a refined southern boy?'

'It is to my liking.'

'As you are to us. Yet papists do not suit, for they give me bile and wind.'

'I know no proper remedy save to see them hanged.'

'The lad speaks true,' spoke up another voice. 'What cure is there but the just medicine we deliver?'

'We are physicians of a kind,' the first man agreed.

'Loyal and trusted men fighting a foul sickness.'

A third pursuivant joined in. 'And what a disease it is, my brothers. A pestilence spreading virulent and fast, a canker that grows beneath the surface and erupts in every part.'

'It will be met.'

'When we are blinded? Outwitted? Defeated by guile?' An arm waved in drunken emphasis.

'On occasion we win.'

'Most times we do not.' The fist slammed on the table. 'Women and servants are all that we find, and they are as mute as the dead.'

Another man called out placatingly, 'Rest tonight and drink, for tomorrow we raid again.'

'You think there will be a plump lay brother at Thrumpton? A cowering priest waiting at Kingston on Soar?'

Discussion and ale flowed and Adam listened closely. The tavern was proving a useful source of information. This town stood at the centre of recusant activity; from here, the pursuivants could ride north to Warwick or west towards Worcester or spread down to the honey-stone villages of Oxfordshire.

'What of London, young cousin?' The enquiry was directed to Adam. 'I hear it is a place full of wonder.'

'If by wonder you should mean the shit emptied each day from three hundred thousand stomachs.'

The man smiled. 'You do not yearn for the adventure of the city and noise of the street?'

'There is sufficient here to divert me.'

'Ignore these fools. We are simple men who boast and jest and would as soon kick a Catholic head as any football.'

Adam laughed. 'I am better with a song.'

'So give us what you promise.' A request rang out, accompanied by a clattering of tankards.

Whether in Coombe Abbey or an alehouse, performing gave Adam licence to roam and his easy nature an open invitation to return. But before he could begin his song, the tavern door opened and a new group arrived, sober outsiders who regarded the local men with contempt. Isaiah Payne stood at the head of his band of pursuivants and made no attempt to hide his disdain as he looked around the tables. Were it not for these locals and their fumbling ineptitude, he would be comfortably residing in London.

He stared at Adam. 'Let us hear your voice.'

'My throat is dry and the occasion is lost.'

'It seems wherever I journey a silence greets me.' Payne continued to stare at Adam. 'Are we acquainted?'

Adam bowed his head. 'I would recall. You could be mistaken for no one else.'

Adam watched his remark bite, the man's sensitivities betrayed by a facial tic. Unlike Payne, he remembered their last meeting clearly: a chaotic night in London, a brawl interrupted, he a Swaggerer and Payne the architect of his arrest. He could see from the chief pursuivant's frown that he still reached for the memory. The longer Adam stayed, the more likely that Payne would grasp it.

Making his excuses, the young man strode confidently on his way. Only for an instant did the glow of his lantern on the high street chart the course he took. It confused the two men who emerged from the tavern to trail him, assigned by Isaiah Payne to question and beat the youth.

In the dark and quiet hours when the nightsoil men brought their cart and cloth-shoed horses to clear the local cesspits, a figure mired and rank with human waste climbed from beneath the outside privy of the house named New Place. Once more, Adam had found refuge at the feet of the playwright and immersed himself in his works.

Generals not foot soldiers, Cecil had said. At his home near Fetter Lane, Christian Hardy stood before a corkboard and pinned to it slips of paper on which were written names. He was drawing connections. In the centre was the legend *Powder* and about it he had placed the glimpsed and likely players in conspiracy. Alongside former schoolmates Guido Fawkes and Jack Wright he added the younger Wright brother, Kit. Prediction and guesswork had their place. Directly above them on the board he placed another name and linked it to the brothers with a piece of thread. Sir Thomas Percy was married to their sister Martha Wright, and had perfect cover and a powerful ally in his patron and kinsman the Earl of Northumberland. Maybe Percy was one of the generals or perhaps nothing at all. Then there was Sir Ambrose Rookwood, scion of Suffolk Catholics and brother of seditious priests, purportedly collecting gunpowder for use in campaigns in the Low Countries. Each name was an element in the uncompleted picture and worthy of investigation. A stack of papers remained.

Hardy paused to study the display. He had never favoured trawling the shoals of the innocent to uncover the true enemy; indeed, he had once been at pains to destroy Spanish records detailing potential allies in England should the Armada invasion have succeeded. Too much blood could be shed through a frenzy of suspicion.

A name was missing. He placed it at the top, unconnected to the rest. Realm was no stranger to attempted regicide, and had proved himself adept at evading capture and at mustering forces. Still, his role in this conspiracy was unknown. Hardy increased the flame of the oil lamp and bent above the parlour table to peruse the files. There would be identities here of those who as yet went unrecruited and patterns which might emerge. An intelligencer existed to pre-empt.

Needing air, he climbed the stairs and by way of an attic chamber stepped out onto the platform set atop his roof. Up here he could clear his head and keep watch on the approaches, as he had once stood with Drake in the fighting tops of the *Revenge*. It was second nature to observe for the jarring or the ordinary. He breathed deep, scenting the air, his eye tracing the progress of a lamplighter through the trees.

There it was, a glow faint and almost imperceptible that showed somebody was close. They wanted him to know. Hardy was already descending from the roof, leaping down the flights and reaching to buckle on his katzbalger, calling to Black Jack to cover the encounter with a musket on the roof. Realm was paying him the compliment of a visit.

His hunch was confirmed by the tautness in his spine and the flash of a lantern as he opened the door and walked slowly outside.

'Step any closer and you will die.'

'A musket is aimed at your position.'

'Several pistols are trained on yours.' Realm, too, spoke calmly. 'Our encounters show you are better mannered when ringed by superior force.'

'I would have taken victory each time.' They had faced each other in the dark before, had fought in a Lisbon alleyway and in a royal tent at Gravesend where Queen Elizabeth journeyed to review her troops. Their history spanned the hostilities of their age.

'Yet I live to hang a head from a nearby branch.'

'Your methods are as black as ever they were, Reino.'

'And my commitment to my cause as strong.'

'What type of a cause is murder? What cause is villainy and destruction and the butchery of women?'

'You still mourn your wife,' Realm said with mild interest, a passing observation.

Hardy balanced on the balls of his feet, ready. 'Spain is at peace with England.'

'Alas, I am not. Men such as you and I are least content when surrounded by accord.'

'You and I? We scarce breathe the same air.'

'But we each embrace peril and are driven by the will of our masters to barbarous deeds.'

'You enjoy your sport too much.'

'It is merely part of our eternal game.' Realm was hoping to goad and probing for weakness. 'A game to which you cling as surely as you guard the silver cross about your throat.'

'Why do you come, Reino?'

'To salute you before you die.'

'For one who fails in past endeavour, you speak with great certainty.'

Realm spoke lightly. 'How is your son, the boy I let live and left without a mother?'

'He is a finer soul than you.'

'Though he stands in opposition to you?'

Hardy tried to decipher Realm's meaning. His adversary might be twisting the knife or laying a trap or mounting a reconnaissance. It was wise not to engage, to steer the conversation away from the subject of his son. The less Adam had to do with him the better.

He peered at the shadowy presence of the renegade. 'A Spanish agent was found dead and transfixed by an ash quarrel in lodgings in the City. You are poor at keeping allies.'

'I have found new friends.'

'Those you sent against me in Clerkenwell? That feeder of bears in Paris Garden you pitched to his death? How wasteful you are in your dealings with others.'

'Each to his own lifespan, Hardy.'

'You would not gather men to your side without a deeper purpose.'

'Yet neither you nor Cecil may guess it.'

'King James dwells beyond your reach, Reino.'

'Then sigh relief and sleep free of all your cares.' And Realm was gone.

Hardy withdrew to the sanctuary of his home and paced around the room, replaying the conversation in his head. Whatever Realm's true motive in coming here tonight, Hardy could not ignore the warning in his words. From the stable block behind the house, he collected lengths of thick bamboo and supplies of linseed, turpentine and pitch. He and Black Jack would be working late to prepare for whatever Realm brought against them.

The tall red-haired man paced with nervous energy in the confines of the house. He was a recent arrival to Lambeth, taking up residence in the London home of Robin Catesby with the convenient cover of a servant. There was no reason why anyone should doubt his story or question his credentials. Yet he was in possession of a secret, had been briefed on the epic conspiracy and become its sixth volunteer. It was both a privilege and an onerous undertaking.

Robert Keyes again checked the time and peered through the window. Discovery would mean his death. As Guido Fawkes prepared across the river, on the south side there were matters of supply and transport to address. Everything turned on this property. He had promised Catesby he would overlook nothing, would play his part and guide the scheme to its conclusion. Others might talk or dream, but he, like the former soldier in Westminster, was of a more practical bent. Results were vital.

The stamp of hooves and loud hammering on the door announced the arrival of his cousin-in-law Sir Ambrose Rookwood, the young gentle-man unusually shorn of his finery and dressed in the mean clothes of a labourer. Behind him was a humble cart with a collection of securely tied barrels, filled with gunpowder.

The men embraced in greeting on the step, and Keyes checked the street. 'I was worried.'

'Caution is the ruler of speed.' Rookwood tugged at his apparel with an expression of exaggerated distaste.'

'There is a reason for disguise.'

'To humiliate me?' Rookwood prodded Keyes in the chest with a good-humoured finger.

'Let us bring in your wares.' Keyes again looked out furtively.

They stowed the powder behind the house, the hogshead and firkin barrels arranged and hidden in a woodshed. Were they to explode, the street would disappear.

'Until next we meet.' Rookwood leapt back onto the cart and took the reins.

'God speed you well.'

Keyes watched the departing cart and turned back to his duties. From now on, he was more than just a devout Catholic or Jesuit with a grudge. He closed the door. The gunpowder treason had recruited its quartermaster.

CHAPTER 8

In a forest clearing north of London, training was underway. Beside Realm stood the Upright Man and before him the men recruited from taverns and street gangs to form the body of his army. Figures ran and practised with sword and pike, pursued by the bellows of instructors. Money and drink guaranteed allegiance, and relentless drilling ensured proficiency.

The renegade watched as a sergeant wrenched a crossbow from the arms of a recruit and kicked him to the ground. They had to learn. In Lisbon, Realm had once trained former janissaries, the Ottoman sultan's shock troops, as marksmen to assassinate Queen Elizabeth, honing their skills against live targets drawn from among captured English crews. It was possible the hapless wastrels gathered here might survive long enough to surprise both him and the authorities. None of them had an inkling of their role.

His companion was impatient. 'What are we without musket and shot? When will we end this play?'

'These men will be blooded, you have my word.'

'The word of a rogue I do not know? A rogue that today is William Birch and tomorrow another ghost?'

Realm ignored the threat, striding forward to seize a quarterstaff and wield it in a challenge to a student. Tips met and the wooden shafts collided as the pair battled briefly, a blow to the leg quickly felling the student. Realm drove the staff hard into the man's ribs and discarded the weapon to return to his conversation.

'Training proceeds until I am content.'

The Upright Man stared ahead, his expression dark and mutinous. 'Are we to be slaves waiting on your word?'

'Walk from me and you gain nothing. Stand and you may own the world.'

'Or I chance my remaining hand.'

Realm shrugged. 'Contest has no worth without risk.'

'A risk that bears the face of Christian Hardy.' The Upright Man glanced at Realm. 'Tell me more about him.'

'He is the best in Robert Cecil's stable and also his bane, and avoids the wrath and censure of his master only by his daring and resolve.'

'You admire him?'

'I despise him and detest his ability to endure.' Realm paused. 'Each time I believe him buried, he returns to haunt me.'

The Upright Man gazed across the clearing. 'He has a weakness.'

Realm nodded. 'An instinct to protect others.'

'I thank God we are not so cursed.'

A whistle alerted them to the approach of a horseman. The newcomer guided his mount past the thicket of trees and reined to a halt. Jack Wright had responded to Realm's invitation. The three men regarded each other, a wanted renegade, a crime chief, a swordsman and enforcer. Outcasts driven by different aims and brought together by a common foe.

The Upright Man responded to the new arrival with innate hostility. 'When I last encountered a gentleman, he shat his britches and begged me to kill him quick.'

'When last I met a cur I split its belly wide.' Wright would not be threatened by a gutter dweller.

Realm intervened. 'I offer you both a better target,' he said quietly. 'Remove the intelligencers and you blind the state and damage Robert Cecil.'

Wright was wary. 'Stamp on a serpent and it will strike.'

'Cut off its head and it cannot. We hunt the hunters.'

The Upright Man nodded. 'Should I have the chance to tear out the heart of Christian Hardy, you would find none so eager.'

'Let us first punish him,' said Realm.

'You think he will be meek?' Wright snorted. 'You think he will put up his sword without a fight?'

Realm studied Wright calmly. 'What I know is that a wounded body is less able and backs from outside danger. I also know we each have reason to kill Hardy.'

'Perhaps he does not yet detect us.'

'You suppose too much. We pay and train men who must eventually be tested.'

Convincing them was easy. Catholic or criminal, Jack Wright or Upright Man, every party had a stake and a hatred that needed his direction. Realm waited as the swordsman dismounted, and then led him on a tour of the site.

On reflection, Christian Hardy had one further flaw. He retained a touching loyalty to the King.

Information was expensive. In an alleyway near Gray's Inn an intelligencer met his contact, a thrupenny boy with attitude and few scruples who preyed on or serviced the city folk. He heard things, listened with casual attention to the boasts of a libidinous soldier who unbuttoned his britches and whispered desire. The man had grunted and paid and taken his leave, forgetting he ever spoke of martial practice in the woods. With luck the boy could double his earnings here.

'You have a report?' The intelligencer was curt.

'I bring you precious fact.'

'Better than precious little. Gold begets gold, as lies earn you a beating.'

'No lies, uncle. Simply the truth from my labours.'

'Truth may vary in the telling.'

The boy sounded aggrieved. 'How harsh you are when I have shown you tenderness.'

'Save your ways for another night.' The man's irritation was growing. 'Our time is brief.'

'I will let you touch me for a penny.'

'Give me names and places or be gone.'

The boy sighed. 'I have heard of preparation for attack, the gathering of men and arms in readiness for some dark act.'

'What is its nature?'

'My thoughts are somewhere else when I am coupling.'

'I urge you to gather them.' The intelligencer reached to grip the boy's throat. 'Prison is not easy to your kind.'

Both were accustomed to the rituals of bargaining. In alleys and shadowed corners across London, informants and their handlers were sharing secrets. Drink and debt and sexual indiscretion were reliable instruments for blackmail and control. It was how Robert Cecil operated and how the state survived. Allegiance of the populace could never be assumed.

The intelligencer let go of the boy's throat and counted out the money. 'Find your voice.'

'An Upright Man has been recruited and assigned to spread discord and unrest.'

'Who stands behind this Upright Man?'

'My rough soldier murmured something about Catholics.'

There was a pause. The boy waited as his paymaster moaned and seemed to struggle physically with the mystery. He was in no hurry. Intelligencers were a rare and distinctive breed.

But the man's body slumped to the ground and an unfamiliar voice sounded in the dark. 'Sadly, he departs us.'

'He is dead?' The boy stared blindly and stammered.

'Play with a furnace and somebody burns. You were unwise to tell tales for gain.'

'I do no wrong. Have pity on a homeless boy.'

'Pity is kept for those with value.'

This last statement put the boy to flight, yet he did not run far. He yelled and fought and clawed for a freedom beyond his reach. Then he wept silent tears of defeat. Of everything heaped on his short existence, he recognised that this would be the worst.

At daybreak the scene was discovered and a posse of horsemen arrived to bear the bodies away. The intelligencer had suffered multiple wounds and a slashed throat, and a street boy was crucified to a door, his tongue cut out. Although Cecil did not yet understand it, yet the opening move was made.

Wrapped up warmly against the easterly wind and occasional flurry of snow, the two women had braved the November weather to take the air and exercise their horses. A manservant, obliged to ride as escort, rode a distance behind, muttering disgruntled beneath his vapour breath. With her charming smile, the young and beautiful Lady Elizabeth Tyrwhitt, wife of Sir Ambrose Rookwood and first cousin to Robert Keyes, generally got her way.

'Your servant feels the chill, Elizabeth.' Her companion glanced over her shoulder. 'I can almost hear his oaths and chattering teeth.'

'Are not we women hardier creatures?'

'On occasion cruel.'

Elizabeth gave a gentle laugh. 'Do not be fooled by his grimace. He complains as much when it is warm.'

'It is akin to dragging behind us a sleigh full of rocks.'

'Yet I would despair without him.' The young mistress pulled the fur hood closer to her face. 'When Ambrose is away, I am happy for his company.'

'Now you are alone once more.'

A weary acknowledgement. 'Blame it on pursuivants.'

Those bloodhounds of the state had raided Coldham Hall, the family seat in Suffolk, threatening the household and spurring Sir Ambrose to respond. He had travelled ahead and she would soon join him, and then return with their children to stand firm against the tyrants. At every turn the government sought to catch them, fine them, find reasons to oppress. She was inured to their hateful scheming, born of an ancient line of Lincolnshire recusants who rejoiced in their defiance. King James should have made enemies of more timid souls.

She steadied her mount with expert hands on the icy approach to the River Lea. It had been a two-mile ride from the small manor near Homerton, the forward vantage close to London from which her husband could conduct his business and stable his horses for onward sale. Wealth and scattered property allowed the Rookwoods to hide and convey priests and do their duty by the old religion. Cecil and his intelligencers were woefully slow on the scent.

Wiping a snowflake from her eye, she paused to view the misted scene. 'How tranquil the marshes appear, and how treacherous they are underfoot.'

'Is it not the same for England?'

'King James would make traitors of us all.' There was resignation in her voice. 'We can but pray for change.'

'Some would use force.'

'Then they are fools, for only a fool would bring on our heads the full wrath of the sovereign.'

Her companion regarded her. 'Yet you worry for Sir Ambrose.'

'My husband is loving and devoted and also quick to anger. He is heedless of danger when his blood is up.'

'Many young men are of such quality.'

'As most too are the cause of young widows.'

Their conversation was interrupted by the sight of a strange figure crawling half-naked from the frozen bog. He was blue with cold, his hair and beard matted and frosted and his body convulsed with spasms of pain. Even at a distance they could hear his cries.

'We must go to him,' said Lady Elizabeth.

Her companion held back. 'What if he should be an Abram man? A rogue and robber feigning madness?'

'We must show compassion.' She unhooked her cloak and swung it from her shoulders. 'Come, let us help him.'

'For my sake, let your servant go near.'

Elizabeth reluctantly agreed, and the two friends stayed back as their escort dismounted to proffer the warm cloak. There was bread too and a flask of wine and, from a distance, the blessings of young ladies bestowed with a smile. The unfortunate man appeared grateful, snatching at the offerings and mumbling his thanks, his blue eyes pleading.

Pulling the cape tightly around him, Christian Hardy gnawed on the loaf and observed the onward passage of his benefactors. His ruse was simple and had won him fleeting contact and instant possession of the prize. Out in East Anglia, Sir Ambrose Rookwood's home was circled and watched and in need of its master. East of London, a secondary residence would any day be empty and deserving of investigation. In his hand the intelligencer clutched a key lifted from the servant's belt.

Adam Hardy, too, was in a state of some undress. They called it Lady, Come into the Garden, a game of dare and teasing flirtation where a young blade was disrobed in stages for the entertainment of the ladies of the court. At Coombe Abbey they had found a willing and athletic victim and an outlet for their boredom. Weeks earlier he had recited Shakespeare and played the lute, and now he was stripped to his undershirt, dancing. For his handsome face and strong young body, they applauded.

'You dance well, sir,' a woman called. 'Turn for us once more.'

'I leap enough, my lady,' he demurred.

'Our poor cub tires,' said another woman. 'We too are exhausted.'

Their cries had swollen to a chorus, the group reluctant to abandon their pursuit. Few other pastimes could match the reward or be so pleasing to the eye. Adam was trapped by his own success.

'How you betray our devotion, sir.' An elderly dowager swigged from a bottle. 'You taunt us with your artful ways.'

'No mockery is intended.'

'So show yourself as a newborn babe.'

Delight followed as Adam yielded. He paraded before them, venturing on the bounds of taste and decorum. He needed the women as friends, was commissioned by Catesby to penetrate deep. Disarming the feckless and jaded was part of the entertainment.

A door opened and Lady Anne stepped through, surprise and consternation rising vividly in her face. Adam stopped mid-leap and their eyes met. 'In the second before she turned blindly towards the door, muttering an excuse as she fled, he saw her disappointment. A trust had been broken.'

Hastily pulling on his clothing, Adam stumbled to give chase, negotiating the same rooms and passageways through which he had recently led his admirers. He didn't hear the protests of the women left behind. Only Anne mattered. Yet she had stolen from the building, removing herself in rage or disdain. Adam called and hurried after her.

It was cold in the arbour, the high yew hedges giving privacy but little shelter. She was standing deep in its hidden recess. In the clamour of court life, few places provided such seclusion. Adam hesitated, feeling like a trespasser.

'Do I intrude, my lady?' he called softly.

She didn't turn but he saw the stiffness in her shoulders. 'No law prevents you entering the garden or playing any game.'

'You will catch a chill.'

'It is you who discards his clothing,' she said aloofly. 'How versed you are in both recitation and bawdy manner.'

'A man must eat.'

'Some would still guard their dignity.'

'Forgive my vulgar ways, my lady. A boy raised in hay and dung so often plays the ass or ox.'

'Some here may covet you in harness.'

'You, my lady?'

She did not answer, yet he detected a faint smile in her coolness.

He moved closer. 'I beg you wear my cloak, my lady.'

'As presumption and token?'

'For warmth.' He slipped the cloak around her shoulders. 'I rode once to your rescue and would be wounded should you now condemn me.'

The reminder of his past service had the intended effect, Anne relinquishing any pretence of distance. 'Then I must be beholden.'

They kissed and embraced breathlessly, both pushing from their minds the implications of what they did. Adam caressed her tenderly but did not overstep, inviting her response. Once released from constraint, she was unlikely to pull back.

'I cannot. I cannot,' she repeated, attempting to convince them both, even as she clung to him.

'You can.' He could be persuasive.

Minutes elapsed. Anne resurfaced.

'Adam, I must go.'

'Must?' He kissed her again.

'Visitors are expected, the London chief of pursuivants is paying respect to the princess before he departs. I must be there.'

'You imagine he will find the enemy here?' He brushed her neck with his lips and reflected on the deformed spectre of Isaiah Payne that seemed to haunt his every move.

'My duty is in the house, Adam.'

'Your love stands here.'

'He will have to rest and curb his ardour.' She let him draw her close again. 'What we do is wrong.'

'Nothing which pleases the heart is wrong,' Adam said with certainty.

After a lingering farewell, during which she fought laughingly to extract her hand, he remained behind. Returning to the house together would attract attention, but more importantly he wished to avoid the Jesuit hunters. Should Payne finally remember him, all would be lost. The danger of his position was sufficient without his fuelling the risk.

'A garden nymph.'

Adam found his way barred. The man was a giant, bearded and malevolent and spoiling for a fight. As porter of Coombe Abbey, Smythe jealously guarded his role and patrolled with a vigour that bordered on obsession.

Smythe pushed him back. 'You offend me.'

'Yet my wit and charm are renowned.'

Another push. 'I will not take insults from a boy.'

'A guest under the protection of Princess Elizabeth.'

'Protection is void when you step into my domain.' He pushed Adam again, harder. 'You sneak about and I watch.'

'Find better entertainment.'

'Instead I find you skulking after the Lady Anne.'

'You are jealous?' The question drew a punch and Adam doubled over.

A huge hand clamped on his scalp. 'None would ever wish to be you.'

Strength could breed complacency. Adam exploited it, moving fast and sliding behind to force Smythe off balance. A well-aimed knee and reverse hold transformed the situation. The beast toppled and the young man added his weight as they crashed onto paving. Seated astride the big man, Adam slammed Smythe's head against the earth until blood flowed and the struggle and groans abated. In truth, he preferred the company of Lady Anne.

He leant in and whispered, 'Keep silent on this matter, Smythe. You would not like to suffer worse.'

Infiltration was in train elsewhere. Overlooking a small brick manor near Homerton, Christian Hardy had abandoned his disguise and lay hidden to watch for movement. Sir Ambrose Rookwood and his family had departed and the house had returned to a somnolent state, guarded by a servant and his wife. They posed no threat. In London, intelligencers were dying, cut down by forces unseen. Out here they still operated and would not cease in their search for evidence. Hardy possessed the key.

The family's absence had brought scavengers. The figure was nervous and quick on his feet and Hardy observed his scampering, alert progress. All was quiet. Feral and instinctive, the visitor flitted across the yard and vanished into the stables. Hardy considered. The man might have seen or heard things, could provide a record of events. Yet he could also draw attention and prove more trouble than his stalking merited.

'I have you.' Hardy had expected the attack, and was ready as his assailant dropped from the beams. He easily threw the man to the ground. The creature hissed and spat and clambered away fast, and Hardy hauled him back. The wild man had plainly survived on his habit of escape.

'Be quiet now.' Hardy stared into the glistening eyes and held his blade close to the man's neck. 'Move and I shall stick you.'

A whimpering laugh. 'He does not like it, does not like it.'

'I too have played mad.'

'They scourge me, scourge me.'

'I know you to be a mariner. It is in your eye and gait and your scramble for the tops, in your face scorched by the sun and your palms scored by rope marks.'

'Wise man, good man.' The creature's torso was shaking.

'Tell me.'

'It burns, burns.'

'On which vessel did you serve?'

'A white bear, a bear. The very whitest bear.'

Hardy nodded, recalling the *White Bear* of the English fleet that had once sailed from Plymouth to give battle to the Armada. The glory days had passed forever and for all the men who had served. The veterans often ended like this, in hardship and vagrancy. Peace had as many victims as war.

He eased the pressure of his knife. 'I am your friend.'

'They beat me here, beat me.'

'Do they feed or clothe you?'

A shake of the head. 'Threaten and beat. Threaten me.'

'Yet they have food? Provisions in barrels?'

'Barrels upon barrels and barrels upon barrels. Stowed in my home.'

'Here?'

'All gone, all gone. Fish that is too fishy and meat that has no pork. Yes, yes.' A toothless smile of rapture creased the face. 'I know a keg of powder when I see one. Know it. Know it.'

From his rafter's eyrie the itinerant had studied the comings and goings, been drawn to the hidden stores and covert proceedings. More proof might rest in the house.

'In which direction did the powder journey?' Hardy asked.

'A cart goes to London and the master is its driver.'

'Sir Ambrose Rookwood? You are certain?'

'No, no.' The man's grin had faded and he began to cry.

'There is money if you help me.' Hardy had sheathed the knife and now dangled a pigskin pouch. 'Divert the servants and create a din and you shall live like a monarch.' The intelligencer would probe deeper into the life and habits of the Rookwoods. A name was about to gain more prominence on the corkboard at home.

'Thou shalt not kill.'

The statement was blunt and heartfelt, for there was too much at stake for compromise. Father Henry Garnet regarded his old friend anxiously and waited for a reply. He would never have taken such a terrible risk in granting audience to Robin Catesby without an urgent reason. Of course he admired the man and loved him as a brother; Catesby's family had often given Garnet sanctuary against the grim marauders of the Protestant state. Yet he suspected Catesby planned some extreme act and wished for his blessing or absolution. Neither would be forthcoming in this low-ceilinged room on Thames Street close to the Tower of London.

Catesby leant forward in his chair. 'The King must go.'

'It is for God alone to decide, Robin.'

'We deny Him and abandon our religion by allowing the Beast to reign.'

'"The powers that be are ordained of God."' Romans 13 was a useful tool. '"Whosoever therefore resisteth the power, resisteth the ordinance of God."'

'He would not intend evil to prevail.'

'James is crowned ruler of England.'

'My loyalty is to the King of Kings.'

'Our duty is to endure.'

'I believe it is to fight,' Catesby said. 'You bear witness to our plight and see the murder of the innocents.'

'You seek to right injustice with a further wrong.' Garnet shook his head. 'Christ told his disciples to lay down their swords.'

'He accused Peter of turning away.' Catesby was adamant. 'The cock again crows and I will be no Peter.'

'Beware of Judgement, Robin.'

They faced each other, the learned Jesuit and the obdurate member of his flock at odds over the direction and future of their cause. Garnet had long expected this moment. In every recusant house he visited and in every Catholic face, he detected fear and anger. It sometimes felt as though they blamed him for the heaviness of their burden. But what Catesby offered was false hope and mindless fury that would bring down worse upon them. He needed to be stopped.

Garnet studied his friend, aware of why others followed him. 'There are better ways to wage battle, Robin.'

'With passive and soothing words? With gestures of piety and plaintive prayer?' Catesby spoke scornfully. 'They have been tried.'

'Christ showed a different path,' said Garnet.

'In His name I would martyr myself.'

'And for yourself you would create thousands more.' The Jesuit's gaze had hardened. 'Too many will be devoured by your folly, our fortunes blighted by the wrath you will bring.'

'Providence favours the bold, Father.'

'It punishes the rash. You worship a false idol and pursue a corrupted dream.'

'Do not doubt my resolve.'

The chief Jesuit felt hope slipping away, despair settling on him. For years he had pursued his mission, dodging every hazard to bring succour and wisdom and spread a message of understanding. It was to no avail. Men of action had seized control, commanding figures such as Robin

Catesby silencing the still small voice and leading the charge towards destruction. The argument was decided.

Garnet stared sadly at the younger man. 'You are become a stranger, Robin.'

'I am no stranger to the truth.'

'So what brings you here? Ancient ties and curiosity? A belief that I would praise your enterprise?'

Catesby did not answer. He stood up, perhaps recognising his mistake in seeking out the priest. Nearby was the Tower, the site of imprisonment and torture to which enemies of the Crown were brought. Should he or Garnet end their days there, so be it. He at least would not waste the time remaining.

'Know this, Robin.' Garnet was bidding him farewell. 'I have written to His Holiness in Rome urging him to excommunicate any engaged in plotting regicide and overthrow.'

Catesby paused. 'Paradise will be denied only to the cowardly and weak.' He turned and walked out of the room.

CHAPTER 9

He had added the word *London* to the display, placing it beside *Gunpowder* at the centre of the board. Hardy stood back to review his work, looking at the names of places and people and the coloured threads of interconnection. The picture was building. From his clandestine visit to the small manor east of London he had learnt that the explosives were being transported not to the ports for overseas shipment but to the capital itself. It changed things. Sir Ambrose Rookwood was intimately involved, had seen fit to don a disguise and personally arrange the delivery. While the jabbering itinerant distracted the custodians, Hardy had explored the painted and panelled interior and chanced upon a cedar chest in which, amongst the finery, lay the humble and incongruous apparel of a drover. Something jarred.

Hardy traced his finger to Sir Thomas Percy, brother-in-law to the swordsman Jack Wright; the connection was too great a coincidence to ignore. On the table behind him was a leather-bound volume in which Percy was listed as a gentleman pensioner, a member of the elite and high-born cadre of royal bodyguards entrusted with protecting the life of King James. A convenient cover. Each of the bodyguards had sworn the Oath of Supremacy, recognising the divine right of their sovereign to rule, and all were commanded by Percy's kinsman the Earl of Northumberland. Should Percy be implicated in treason, it would mean the fall from grace of Northumberland and another notable consigned to the Tower. Cecil would relish that.

Another thread and a different name. Pure conjecture had inspired Hardy to add Robin Catesby to the board. As the class ledger of St Peter's School in York had shown, the most tenuous connection could be relevant. An acquaintance of Percy's, Catesby was a known recusant, a man of firm belief and action once gaoled for his part in the Essex rebellion against the ageing Queen Elizabeth. His family seat of Lapworth was now occupied by Jack Wright. He was one to watch.

Then, as always, there was Realm. In the months leading up to his attempted assassination of Elizabeth, many intelligencers had been snuffed out. It was happening again: agents and their handlers had been stabbed, garrotted or shot, or fatally bludgeoned during tavern brawls that dissipated as quickly as they arose. Realm either directed or rode on the slaughter and would avoid revealing his hand until the very close. And his death squads were bound eventually to come for Hardy.

He crossed the room and poured himself a glass of wine. It was in these early hours that he most felt Beatrice's absence. The bedchamber had few attractions without her soft breathing beside him. The background snores of Carter asleep in the hallway provided an unworthy substitute. He listened. If there were to be an attack, it would come before dawn.

A footfall on the stairs signalled the descent of Swiftsure from the roof. The gaunt knifeman had been keeping watch with Black Jack for the long shift. He was too hardened to be easily spooked, and would not raise the alarm without good reason. Whatever was out there had arrived in strength.

Hardy covered the corkboard and dimmed the lamps. 'How many?'

'It is too dark to say, Christian. Yet they are there.'

'Front or back?'

'I spy them all about.'

'So let us be the generous hosts.' Hardy reached for his sheathed katzbalger and buckled it on. 'Rouse Carter and stay low and out of sight.'

Everything was prepared. Their enemies had already lost the element of surprise. In mounting their raid, they would seek to overwhelm with sudden violence and depart before an armed response could be formed. Setting fire to the building would only betray their presence and serve as a beacon for the counter-attack.

Carter was awake, his bulk filling the doorway as Hardy hooked a lantern on a beam in the ground-floor parlour and manoeuvred a wooden mannequin into place. The dummy, scored from a thousand encounters, belonged to a set he employed in refining his rapier skills against multiple targets. Now it would face a different foe.

Hardy glanced at his lieutenant. 'You are ready?'

'Always, Christian.'

'Reserve your guns until they enter, and make each room cost them dear.'

'It will cost you more to cleanse their spill.'

'I would not begrudge it.' Hardy scanned the chamber and nodded. 'Mark time and start your theatre once I climb the stair.'

Accompanied by Swiftsure, Hardy headed for the roof. Behind them, their large and brutish friend would be caressing his twin-barrelled pistol and relaxing in the expectation of an imminent bloodletting. The house was in capable hands.

On the rooftop, the three men spoke in whispers. To the untrained eye and ear there was little beyond the scurrying of a rat or the strangulated barking of a fox to suggest nocturnal life or movement around the house. Yet Black Jack had sensed things; he squatted cowled against the chill, holding a musket and staring into the dark.

Hardy tapped his shoulder. 'To your station.'

For the moment they had the high ground. Laid between the house and its outbuildings was an aerial walkway, a network of planking that sprouted at night to allow for a rapid response to attack. For men schooled in piracy and conditioned to life at sea, it was second nature to run nimbly across the perilous structure; the same techniques had provided Hardy's escape above the streets of Lisbon. Battles were so numerous, the patterns rarely changed. Now they crossed to the stables on their overhead route and crouched in the lee of the parapet.

Hardy cupped his hand and put it to Swiftsure's ear. 'You have your knives? Your flint? Your arsenal of mischief?'

Swiftsure nodded. 'All I need is here.'

'Wait on my word and we shall put it to use.'

Below them, invasion had begun. In the parlour, Carter had completed his preliminaries, opening the drapes a fraction to permit the subdued glow of a burning candle to shine out and silhouette the shape of an insomniac seated at the window. Tobacco smoke wreathing the head lent authenticity to the tableau. It was sufficient to convince. Three crossbow quarrels struck simultaneously, shattering the glass and splitting the carved torso and announcing the attack. Behind them came the blow of axes to remove the window frame. The inrush of cold air brought the invaders.

'Make haste.' The leader hissed instructions. 'Spare none.'

A lantern swayed in the gap as another man clambered through. 'Take what you like, brothers.'

'All is laid out for us.'

'A short trip to Tyburn if you do not hurry,' snapped the leader.

Twin muzzles flamed with a loud report. The screams of the leading man were pitched high, the mission briefly stalled in a confusion of blood and smoke. The sleeping prey had woken and appeared determined to resist. Still, reinforcements crowded in, driven by the promise of reward and convinced of the outcome.

They were no match for the unhurried ways of Carter. A wildfowling gun discharged, the spread of shot removing a face and punching a hole in the chest of a further victim. Casualties groaned and floundered on the ground. Carter stepped forward and reversed the weapon to club them into silence. Then he withdrew to the corridor to reload and wait.

'On my count.' Above the stable, Hardy murmured the timing. 'Now – sweep wide and catch them all.'

Gathered to storm the rear, the motley band of attackers were un-tutored in the finer arts of siege and war. Some might have butchered Irishmen in previous campaigns or dabbled in supporting continental rebellions against the Spanish. But none had anticipated what hit them now. Fire swept down upon them, lancing bright from the mouths of flame-throwing trumps, the roaring incendiaries mounted on pikes and projecting burning fuel some twenty feet. Few of the men below escaped their reach. A blazing figure attempted to flee before collapsing. Another got further until a grapnel struck him in the back and slowly reeled him in. With a grin, Black Jack hoisted the kicking man high before cutting his throat and letting him drop. It was good to be involved.

Hardy shouted to him, 'Movement beyond the stable wall.'

Jack's response was swift, a couple of wildfire pots arcing to the far side of the yard and bursting in an oily incandescence that consumed trees and humans alike. Hardy and Swiftsure had swarmed down ropes and were pressing home with blades.

Inside the house, Carter stalked a lone survivor to the kitchen and found the man kneeling and praying and begging for mercy. His pistol levelled. The place was no church.

'Again carnage and devastation, Hardy.'

Isaiah Payne's voice was disapproving. As another corpse was dragged from the building, the chief pursuivant stood in the midst of the blackened early morning scene, a perfumed handkerchief pressed to his nose. He was an uninvited spectator, directed by Cecil and his own curiosity to walk the ground and pry.

Hardy dismissed the jibe. 'Is your service not better rendered chasing priests across the Midlands?'

'His lordship the Secretary of State bids me come.' Payne gave an exaggerated wave of his hand. 'Everywhere is awake and full of fear and consternation. The militia has been called and the constables send patrols and citizens in their nightclothes gather on street corners.'

Eleven bodies were laid out for disposal, cadavers disfigured by fire and gunshot. Garments still smouldered and the stench of pitch and charred flesh hung dense in the air.

Payne nudged a corpse with his toe. 'Once more you choose the path of battle over detection and enquiry.'

'These men seemed deaf to my blandishment and reason.'

'As you appear ignorant of the kind of war we fight.'

'So speaks a huntsman ever late to the fray.' Hardy strode to fetch a bundle of discarded weapons and returned to drop them at Payne's feet. 'Ignorance lies with those who face nothing more dangerous than a fleeing Jesuit.'

'Strange, is it not, that wherever you reside, the result is alike to the deck of your *Revenge*?'

Perhaps the pursuivant was right, for the scene had been replicated a hundred times. Human remains and the scorched trunks of trees as stark as ship masts shorn of rigging. These were the situations he created and against which he measured himself. Sir Richard Grenville was thirteen years dead, the casualty of a long-forgotten incident. Yet ghosts still walked and the conflicts of the past lingered in the present.

Hardy watched Swiftsure coil a length of rope and turned back to Payne. 'Put your men to work or I shall.'

'They answer to my word alone.'

'They will pay heed soon to my boot.' Hardy gave a sharp whistle and pointed, and a gaggle of pursuivants ran to lift the bodies and fling them on a cart. 'In killing them we preserve the peace, guard intelligence and remove an enemy force.'

'Your foes multiply, Hardy.'

'The result each time will be the same.'

Whether Cecil would condemn or praise, Hardy did not care. He did what was demanded and intended to continue until the crisis was averted or a musket ball embedded in his skull. People wished him dead, and it told him he was closing on conspiracy. The road to revelation was always paved with bones.

Adam Hardy was engaged in more civilised pursuits. As Princess Elizabeth played on her virginal, he accompanied with his lute and encouraged her with gentle words and lines of song. While the porter Smythe prowled the grounds with blackened eyes, a broken nose and a mouth liberated of several teeth, in the comfort of the music room the young man from London won favour and smiles and consolidated his influence. Accomplished and a natural wit, he had ease and charm and style, and could be relied upon as a friend and mentor to the young girl. Lady Anne vouched for him and the court appeared to defer to the enthusiasm of their most precious charge.

The princess stumbled on a note and tried again. 'I shall blame the instrument rather than myself.'

'And why not, Your Grace?'

She seemed a little crestfallen. 'Hours of practice scarce improve my playing.'

'Your ear is good, Your Grace.'

'As yours must be poor that you praise me.'

They laughed and she left her seat to join him in conversation. There was both lightness and earnestness in her manner, a confidence that never strayed to arrogance. She desired to learn and he was happy to teach. For the princess, the musician and player was the answer to her prayer for greater excitement. He was not bound by the dreary conventions of court.

She peered at him. 'Do you love my Anne?'

'I could not presume, Your Grace.'

'Why so?' she asked, surprised.

'I am not blind to my station.'

'But I am your friend. And I am a princess.'

'It is no counter to my lack of noble blood.'

'Some of the most noble are the dullest.' The princess spoke emphatically. 'I live among them and know it well.'

'Then as your jester and fool I will endeavour to divert.'

'I would rather have you as my brother, Adam.'

'You flatter me, Your Grace.'

The mention of family led her to silent musing, a shadow of loneliness crossing her countenance. She was at once the dutiful representative of the King consigned to dwell in a corner of his realm and a child kept remote from her parents and siblings. Everyone was so far away.

She regained her composure. 'I should have a penny for every strange sight presented to me.'

'Your coffers would be filled, Your Grace.'

'So they would. A loathsome man named Isaiah Payne came here.'

Adam gave a theatrical shudder. 'Are they not created to strike terror in all?'

She giggled. 'I almost hid for my protection behind the giant Smythe.'

'Monsters appear in many forms.'

'Our porter's face is broken and he lurches about more miserable than usual.'

'Let us trust he soon returns to his carefree and happy self.'

The princess laughed again. Creating trust and dependency was an art. Adam plucked at the strings of his lute, letting the mellow sounds lull and soothe. Music was the surest way to the heart.

The door opened and she sprang to her feet in pleasure. 'Anne.'

'I mean not to intrude.' The young lady of the bedchamber performed a curtsy before embracing her mistress, her eyes seeking Adam's above the girl's head. 'Sweet melodies drew me to enquire.'

'I have learnt that I am more a princess than musician.'

'There are years aplenty to master both roles.'

'But I must stay imprisoned.'

Adam interrupted, young and bold enough to cut through royal protocol. 'We shall ride out, Your Grace.' He put aside the lute. 'We will roam the heathland as free as any spirit.'

'That is forbidden.'

'With royal guards and gentlemen attending? A retinue that could put to flight an army?'

'Lord Harington is against it,' said Elizabeth.

'Yet I am in favour.' Adam returned her grin. 'As you are a princess and I a man of my word, we shall slip from the abbey and sortie out to pastures new.'

Where there was a will, there was the ability to force the pace and manipulate events. It was December 1604 and the land was encrusted with the ice chill of winter. A new year and season would bring change and reactivate things that for the while appeared dormant.

'My beagle does not forget me.'

The sneer was in the eyes. James studied his Secretary of State, reimposing his authority over the minion on whom he relied. Cecil bowed, a statesman and spymaster arrived at Hampton Court to brief his ceaselessly travelling master on the state of his nation.

James's tongue bulged clumsily in his mouth. 'How fares my hunt for Catholics, beagle?'

'Fines increase and imprisonments rise, Majesty.' Cecil was glad to deliver positive news. 'We expect several thousand pounds more in the year to come.'

'A contented king is a benevolent one.' The watery gaze displayed no irony.

'Indeed, sir.'

'I have in my progress seen my subjects weep in their loyalty and affection, heard their cheers of affirmation.' James either grimaced or smiled. 'I cannot betray them or cease my fight against the wickedness of popery.'

'You cannot, sir.'

'"Long live the King," they cry.'

'It is most heartfelt, sir.'

'Am I to live long? Will I escape the dagger-thrust of treachery and the schemes that hatch against me?'

'Not one adversary possesses the strength to strike a mortal blow.'

'Be certain you do not regret such words.'

James began his perambulation, a small Scot garbed in silks and sable attended by a yet smaller and hobbling Englishman. An odd yet effective pairing. Cecil determined to calm the royal nerves and put his sovereign's mind at ease.

They reached the private chapel and stood on its balcony to gaze on the interior. Everything began and ended with religion, Cecil reflected. Here was the former haunt of King Henry VIII, Defender of the Faith and architect of total schism with Rome. Still the consequences of those days played out and the forces they unleashed duelled for the hearts and minds of England. He was in no doubt as to who would triumph. Cecil was always on the winning side.

The King was similarly contemplative. 'Is not my first duty to survive?'

'I shall ensure it, sir.'

'A ruler that dies cannot rule. A ruler who does not rule cannot be remembered.'

'Our eyes watch and our ears listen and everywhere the threat is cornered and contained.'

'You are found wanting with the truth.' James swung on him, savouring the chance to prove his adviser wrong. 'I know that in every quarter our intelligencers are killed, those eyes of ours put out and those ears struck from our heads.'

Cecil paused. 'It shows where we must search, sir.'

'Rather it proves that we are weak, that something is planned for which we have no remedy.'

'There is ever a cure, sir.'

'You have not found it yet.' The monarch whimpered a sarcastic laugh. 'In towns and villages the foe readies and arms, and we glean nothing of the facts.'

'The fact remains each plot is foiled. The fact is proven we win all encounters.'

Whether observation or implied criticism, Cecil's words took a moment to digest. The King was content to let the matter pass and proceeded on towards the Watching Chamber. Beyond it was the great hall and the fawning clusters of courtiers and favourites waiting on a generous remark or roving eye. Young men were prostituted by their fathers for advancement. Such was the divine right of a sovereign and the gilded cesspit of the age.

'I lean on you, my beagle.'

'My purpose is to serve.'

'Some say it is to gain enrichment.'

'Vicious tongues forever jibe and cut at the heels of success, sir.'

'I shall give them other things to talk of – I will improve their mood and bring down to join us my younger son from Scotland.'

'The rejoicing will be loud, sir.'

The lie was a mere formality. No one expected the tiny and sickly Charles to live or would rush to join his nursery court. Like James himself, he was just another unappealing Stuart specimen to be found north of the border. The English would groan. Yet at least he provided an additional target to confound the calculations of assassins. Cecil was keen to accentuate the positive.

He gave a diplomatic cough. 'What of Parliament, Majesty?'

Petulance flashed across the King's face. 'I am not minded to recall it. Proclamation is better than exposure to the plague or dealings with recalcitrants and fools.'

'London will glitter the more for your return, sir.'

'At the moment, it stinks.'

'Think of the power and pageant you would bring, sir. Think of the loyal acclamation your presence would unleash.'

A pause. 'October next, it is.'

An invisible king would eventually go ignored. Queen Elizabeth had understood the necessity of occasionally mounting a parade through her city. Her successor had much to learn. Popularity required the style this gutter Scot was lacking.

The Secretary of State was deferential. 'Your wisdom is unsurpassed, sir.'

'While your devotion is to be commended.' It was more snub than thanks.

The doors were flung wide and a trumpet sounded as James beckoned his retinue close and entered the opulent vastness of the hall. Cecil stayed behind, the manipulator and shadow presence on whom this theatre depended. He had promised the King the praise and affection of his subjects and hoped there would be nothing else lurking in the crowd.

Two of the disloyal kind to whom the King referred were toiling in the basement of the rented dwelling in Westminster. Mining had started and the first bricks had been removed. Thomas Percy and Guido Fawkes stood in whispered conference encompassed by the gloom. There was little dashing or romantic in what they did. It was also beset with risk. Yet painstaking excavation was critical to their plan.

'We have our breach, Guido.' Percy wiped the grit from his eye.

'So long as it is Parliament House we bring down and not that of our neighbour upon our heads.' The explosives man leant to test the wooden frame he had inserted into the gap. 'We will either launch the greatest attack in history or dig the entrance to our grave.'

'Nothing significant is ever achieved without risk.'

Fawkes continued to stare at the remaining layer of dividing bricks. 'Imagination plays on the mind, conjures visions of soldiers waiting on the other side.'

'Little awaits save another cellar and at worst a porter and his wife.'

'If they should investigate or resist?'

'You have your blade and I a sack and we shall dispose of them as spoil.'

It would complicate the business greatly. But when set against a massacre, a couple of deaths seemed inconsequential. Holy war played by different rules, and Fawkes had seen sufficient corpses in Flanders to be hardened to the unpleasantness. The persecution and extermination of Catholic priests in England far outweighed in horror any act he perpetrated.

He felt for the haft of his knife. 'Those who block us are destined to perish.'

'Intelligencers already have.'

'Not Christian Hardy.'

'Fresh traps will be set, Guido.'

'I do not seek to be the lure.'

Percy clapped him on the shoulder. 'Once we stood at the window and observed. Now we stand at the gate to deliver our promise.'

'A moment for which we have waited.'

'Angels are at our shoulder and the hopes of all believers at our back.'

'Then we cannot disappoint.'

Crouching low, Fawkes crawled into the opening and began to apply the tip of a small pick to prise away the mortar. The loosened stone and filling displaced by his ongoing labour were strewn about, and collecting sheets were draped around the space in a hanging shroud. The sound was kept to the level of a scratching rat. Still, it was fortunate the mercenary had befriended the porter and his wife and learnt their daily routine.

A third figure appeared at the head of the cellar stairs, bearing a candle, and descended to join his companions. The seventh plotter had been recruited. Thomas Bates, a manservant to Robin Catesby, was a devout Catholic and a valued and trusted asset. A newcomer he might have been, yet he was practical and courageous and served as courier and liaison between the gunpowder treason in London and the kidnap attempt further north. He was among friends.

He stepped across to give his report. 'All is quiet above.'

'Long may it remain so, for we burrow hard below.'

'I bring my tools and will scrape here at the face.' Bates got to his knees. 'As in Coombe Abbey, they do not see the inroads we make.'

'Adam Hardy?'

Bates nodded. 'None are so adept at subverting the foe and casting a spell. By the day the princess grows fonder of him, treating him as a brother. By the hour his position grows unassailable.'

'As each day we draw closer to explosion.' Percy turned to leave the cellar. 'Dig well and I shall mount watch from the upper chambers.'

'Brick by brick we shall reach our goal.' Bates crawled in alongside Fawkes.

Percy left them to their work and climbed the steps towards the light. The cellar was too much like a tomb for comfort; it was the reality written in dust and dirt of what they had pledged in the gatehouse at Ashby St Ledgers. He reflected on the sheer audacity and magnitude of their scheme. A quartermaster stored black powder in Lambeth and Fawkes lived here, while an agent in the Midlands smoothed the way for the seizing of a girl. All because the ringleader Robin Catesby ordained it. On the surface, life was normal, and a new year would soon arrive without a hint or murmur of impending cataclysm. It was just as they desired.

He glimpsed through the window the distant procession of body-guards and secretaries that marked the businesslike progress of Robert Cecil. The Secretary of State must be taking his exercise or boarding his private barge for an appointment. Upriver or down, whether squeezing City financiers or fawning to the King, he would return the richer and with his power enhanced. Percy closed the curtains on such theatre. It would be a joy at some later date to truly ruin the day for the Catholic-hating pygmy.

Back in Seething Lane, at the discreet safe house to which he often brought his mistresses and informants, Christian Hardy removed his cloak and settled down to wait. Since the armed assault on his home, he had stayed only fleetingly in one place; in that respect, he reflected, he resembled the nervous little King he served. Intelligencers who remained alive were at a premium. Yet the scale of the attack on his home confirmed that his enemies saw him as a threat, which was to the good, and his continued existence would further provoke and dismay. They would be licking their wounds and counting their dead while he manoeuvred to outflank them.

The gunpowder took priority, and its covert journey led to London. Now he was offered intelligence that could not go ignored, by a source who had shown herself reliable and was willing to trade. Everyone had vulnerabilities and diverse motives and Hardy was the master of exploiting both. Either through desire or greed or love or fear, humans were instruments demanding to be played. Some were trickier to handle than others.

She appeared, the product of privilege and prostitution with a ready snarl on her lips and self-loathing in her eye. The banker's wife was a troubled soul who had not mellowed with time.

'My soldier boy is as handsome as he is hard.'

'And my lady is as beautiful as she is dangerous.'

'How well you know me.'

'I bear the marks of our encounters.' Hardy indicated a chair. 'Be seated.'

'Our trade is better done in bed.'

He continued to stare at her. 'Do as I command or leave this chamber.'

She scowled and slumped moodily in the chair.

They faced each other, the struggle of wills already begun. It generally ended with bruising or blood. He would not reward her unless she complied, would not take her punishment or cede ground until she begged and wept.

She eyed him and rubbed two fingers between her thighs. 'I have what you want.'

'You are not the judge.'

'Yet I am your lover.' Her hand moved. 'What a prize you are, a trophy any woman might covet.'

'My skin is not for sale.'

'For you are beyond reproach as I am beneath contempt.' Her tone was mocking and her legs spread wider. 'You will find me true and my word good.'

'Though your soul is cheap.'

'Would you have it any other way? Would you have me quiet and sweet and fragile as a rose?'

'I would like you to tell me why you are here.'

A whore was rarely tamed by wealth and jewels and an embroidered bodice. The dark always chased them down. She wanted to be noticed and acquire respect, to feed and silence her demons by debasing herself. Informing on others gave her control.

'Gunpowder.'

'That tells me nothing.'

'Your look suggests it does.' She smirked. 'You love me now, soldier boy.'

'Proceed and I may despise you less.'

'Did I not give you the name of Sir Ambrose Rookwood? Did I not state that he and other Catholic gentlemen gathered the black powder for onward shipment to Flanders?'

'You did.'

'Then note this.' She was almost aroused by her own revelation. 'Barrels are stowed where they would least be suspected, arrayed for grave and future incident beneath the very nose of the state.'

'How do you know?'

'With guile and cunning and a husband whose spine I could break on my knee.'

'He is a man of finance and no traitor or smuggler.'

'A man who lends money has insight into much and power over most.'

'Still he would have scant knowledge of such matters.'

'Scant knowledge is enough.'

She lifted her skirt and linen shift, playing with herself. Recreational lewdness was part of her game. Hardy sat with his gaze on her face, ignoring her efforts. Eventually she would tire and return to her story.

'Grave and future incident?' he repeated. 'Arrayed beneath the very noses of the state?'

'My soldier boy asks questions.'

'And my harlot will provide the answer.' He lashed out with his foot to kick away her chair and send her sprawling to the floor. 'There is no thanks for delay or deceit.'

Shocked, she attempted to rise. 'I do not lie.'

'So give voice to the information in your head.'

'It will cost.'

'Defiance will lose you more.' He stood and bent forward to haul her upright. 'My patience is flown and you will soon follow.'

'You dog.' She spat and tried to claw him.

'Name the place, you vixen.'

She gave up her secret sullenly. 'The Globe.'

Another recipient of her favours later greeted the banker's wife in rooms close to the Royal Exchange. Betrayal and subterfuge were addictive and she had grown adept at serving those who fascinated or paid her. This man intrigued her. He was ordinary enough in appearance to melt into the backdrop in any street or tavern. Yet he had a controlled intensity, a latent violence that expressed itself through an emptiness in his eye, an absence of emotion. Few things were more appealing to her. It didn't matter that he had no name or that he should hurt her, for the fight was all and tenderness was far from what she sought. She was the prettiest of bait, decided Realm.

CHAPTER 10

The revelry was loud at the Mermaid, the Cheapside tavern soaked in the stench of ale and smoke and pulsing to the noise of conversation. It was a busy night. Writers and thinkers converged here to argue and play cards, to mingle with their peers and trade banter and joshing insult. At their centre, acting as host and accompanied by his friend Ben Jonson, sat the beaming figure of William Shakespeare.

An acquaintance moved unsteadily towards them, a flagon of beer in his hand. 'Good evening to you, boys. I bring you the gift of cheer.'

'Each drop that you spill is a drain on it.' Shakespeare pushed back a chair and bade the man sit. 'I would rather a wench bring me my drink.'

'Fellowship is not bound by things so shallow as beauty.'

'Praise God for it, or we would be foes. Then there is Ben.'

Jonson laughed. 'I may have a wart on my nose, but I defy any common arse-pimple to better me with pen or sword.'

'His blood heats and we shall suffer for it.' Shakespeare raised his horn cup. 'I give thanks he is my bodyguard and not my enemy.'

Jonson proposed a toast. 'To friendship.'

'As good a reason as any to be drunk.'

They joined in song, Shakespeare leading in a loud refrain. He was happy to be returned from country exile, to be back once more among his fraternity. A town such as Stratford-upon-Avon could never match the febrile atmosphere of London. Yet even in the country there was still the underbelly and the darkness, the mutterings of dissent and the shadow of persecution. He had seen the pursuivants riding by and heard the whispers in the local inns. People tried to forget or ignore the lurking threat.

He hailed another friend. 'Be no stranger – come and drink with us.'

'I see the country straw clings yet to your hat, Will.'

'Better than the city dung lodged fast between your ears.'

'The shires do not dull your wit.'

'Nor these streets improve yours.' The playwright rose to embrace his comrade. 'I am glad we again gather and the plague takes none from our communion.'

'We happy few, Will.' Jonson leant back and surveyed the throng with a benign air.

'Cling to happiness where you may, Ben. It might be fleeting or illusion.'

'I mind neither, so long as there is wine and vice.'

'Like a mistress, they will leave you hurt.'

'Should we bow to her or enslavement by our master?'

Shakespeare avoided replying. He had spied Robin Catesby in the crowd, and observed the ease with which he drew others to him. The man was a rarity: he had presence and authority and a gift for bending lesser mortals to his will. Such powers could be misdirected.

Jonson swallowed his drink and followed his friend's gaze. 'Robin as ever delights the crowd, Will. He is loved by many.'

'And as soon will be deserted. A multitude is fickle. Remember where his sympathies lie, Ben.'

'They are not so remote from our own.'

Shakespeare had grown serious. 'Be cautious and play wise, for popish leanings will ill serve you.'

More beer was summoned and cards were cut and dealt. It was an evening to discard doubt and enjoy the company about. Matters of religion and politics would not be permitted to intrude.

Only when the lights were finally doused and the tavern lapsed to silence did Shakespeare walk back to his lodgings. Friends accompanied him some of the way and a nightwatchman with whom he often spoke escorted him to his door. The favour earned the man two pennies. Wearily the playwright climbed the stairs, sober enough to bolt the door behind him and hushing himself at the squeak of a board underfoot. Fortunately, his landlord was an understanding fellow.

There was a glow coming from his room. No real threat existed within a locked dwelling, he reasoned; if he were to be a victim, it would be of his own imagination.

'William Shakespeare?' A stranger was perusing a manuscript and placed it down as he entered.

Shakespeare looked at him warily. 'My presence is less surprising than your own.'

'I am sorry for the intrusion and will explain.' The man gestured to a chair. 'Let us speak.'

'It is late and I prefer to snore.'

'Then we have much in common.'

Shakespeare doubted it. However, he did as he was asked, never removing his gaze from his unexpected visitor. Disconcertingly blue eyes stared back. The man was scarred and handsome, with a casual hardness and economy of movement that proved he was tested in battle. There was no menace in his air, yet his presence alone created an atmosphere that encouraged cooperation.

The playwright was alert, the effects of alcohol burning off. 'You are no chance intruder.'

'Chance is for those in other kinds of trade.'

'What is yours?'

'Less public than your own.' Christian Hardy had no wish to frighten his host. 'I am a servant of the state.'

Hardy drew from a pouch a folded letter and passed it to the playwright. Shakespeare had no need to read it in full; he knew the lines carried no ordinary message of introduction. The signature of Robert Cecil was enough.

He looked up. 'It seems I am visited by an intelligencer.'

'You are vexed?'

'Bafflement is the human condition,' Shakespeare said diplomatically.

'I shall explain.' Hardy took back the letter. 'You are under no suspicion or threat.'

'I am accustomed to an audience of a more . . . generous disposition.' Shakespeare's eye flicked to the sword.

'You do not know mine.'

Shakespeare leant his chin on his hand. 'Now is as good a time as any for revelation, intelligencer.'

'I come to ask for assistance.'

'Of me?' The playwright did not move. 'Why not seek me out by day? My generosity would improve.'

'Daylight holds peril for us both.'

'You are the intelligencer; I am a mere writer.'

'That would not spare your life.' Hardy had now guaranteed Shakespeare's attention. 'Enemies circle like carrion crows.'

'Who are they?'

'Desperate men who yearn for violent overthrow.'

Shakespeare pointed to his manuscript. 'When have I been involved in such things except in the realm of make-believe?'

'You own a theatre.'

'I have a smaller share in it than the Burbage brothers and others I might mention.'

'It is a place you call the Globe.'

'They say I am a worldly man.' The playwright regarded Hardy with understated interest. 'No drama at the playhouse is so strange as this encounter.'

'All may change.'

'Cecil bids you speak in riddles?'

'He pays me to guard the nation.' Hardy was not there to negotiate. 'I need access to the Globe.'

'Why?'

'Gunpowder may lie hidden deep inside its bowels.'

The statement drew no exclamation, and the playwright's chin stayed perched on his fist. All the world was a stage and beneath a Southwark theatre plainly lay another. Shakespeare was hardly a stranger to the wilder shifts of fate, and he considered this new information without histrionics or alarm. 'Tell me it is not my sodden mind that plays these tricks.'

'It is an intelligencer that informs you.'

'One who might be mad.'

'Insanity on occasion would give relief.' Hardy smiled wryly before offering clarification. He would be sparing with the detail. 'We believe traitors have persuaded a storeman to lay down powder like casks of wine, to ready them for a later uprising.'

'You believe? Where is the evidence?'

'Instinct that should be acted on.'

'Or blind folly that misleads.' Although his face remained calm, Shakespeare's knuckles had whitened. 'I am a King's Man, a theatre owner, a loyal scribbler and player feted of late in the household of Princess Elizabeth.'

'The Globe draws crowds, and crowds include the angry and seditious.'

'They are called to watch, not called to arms.'

'Let us then investigate.' Hardy rose, aware that he had ruined the evening and sleep of a man he much admired. The playwright was indeed worldly, but he had yet to encounter traitorous zealots like Guido Fawkes or killers such as Realm.

A thought occurred to him. 'You know Sir Robin Catesby?'

'I have drunk with him and once or twice played cards.'

'Watch him and be careful.'

'My concern is for my playhouse and some imagined mob.'

'Matters will be resolved.'

'Not always for the best, intelligencer.' Interest was giving way to fatigue. 'Not always without damage and bloodshed and death.'

Hardy revealed the silver cross at his throat and dangled it before Shakespeare. 'Should harm befall what is precious to you, I shall surrender what is most precious to me.'

Whether fair or obtained under duress, a bargain had been struck.

Wherry oars dipped and pulled, steering the craft for the Lambeth bank. Only one passenger occupied the stern, shrouded by his hat and cloak and hunkered low against the wind. Fawkes was making a journey. Acting as shepherd, another boat ploughed a distant and parallel course across the river as Jack Wright, guardian of the enterprise, kept watch to ensure a smooth and uninterrupted visit. Events were too important to leave to chance or allow a mistake to let in Christian Hardy.

The explosives man alighted at the jetty and walked the short way to Catesby's home.

'Our brother visits from the other side.' Catesby stepped to embrace him. He took the mercenary by the arm to usher him to the parlour. Waiting to greet him warmly were the adjutant Tom Wintour and quartermaster Robert Keyes.

'I trust Jack kept watch on your progress?' Catesby poured a glass of wine and handed it to Fawkes. 'We cannot let fate or lazy error trip us in our game.'

'None will trip me, Robin.'

'Yet the closer we are to killing the King, the more exposed we shall be to the wrath of his servants.'

'Some we have already dealt with.'

'Others we have not.'

'They will soon be consumed in the flames.' Fawkes took a gulp of claret. 'As we lay our foundations, so we undermine theirs.'

'You push forward with the tunnel?'

'Enough to be satisfied and too little to claim success.'

'To the home of the porter?'

'And beyond it to the robing chamber. But caution slows us to the speed of a worm.'

'How sure can you be that you go undetected?'

'As certain as a man who inches on his belly and scratches at a wall for his living.' Fawkes proffered his cup for replenishment. 'None of my lookouts witnesses any disturbance or a change in mood or pace.'

'It does not mean we go unwatched.' Catesby withdrew momentarily to his thoughts. It was possible the snooping apparatus of the state had been impaired or distracted. It might lend them time or provide an edge, yet the forces of the hunchback Cecil were resilient. Fawkes looked around the room. 'Where is Bates?'

'He bears messages for me and ranges wide.'

'A pity, brother. He is strong with a hammer and chisel.'

'Learn to labour without him.'

'I do not complain.'

'Nor would I expect it.' Catesby gestured to Keyes. 'Our store of powder grows and Robert tends it as a physician does his patient or a soothsayer his runes.'

Leading them through the house, Catesby brought them to the wood-shed, revealing the hidden cache with pride. A plot hatched in another place here took solid form. A prayerful hush fell on the gathering.

Fawkes murmured in satisfaction, 'Few sights are so full of beauty.'

'All that we are is here and all that we shall be.' Catesby rested his hand on a cask. 'We depend on you, Guido.'

'Your faith will be rewarded.' The man bowed his head.

'It is faith that wills us on and God who shall grant us grace. For we are the sons of the Covenant who are freed.'

The mercenary gave the barrels an assessing look. 'If annihilation is our business, we will need more than this.'

'You shall have whatever is required,' said Keyes.

'We are then in accord.' Catesby gripped Fawkes's shoulder and that of Keyes, a commander exuding confidence and eager for the fight. Only a fool would think they were unequal to the task. It was always the same, a state that trusted in its invincibility and a royal circle blinded by arrogance to the nature of the threat. Long might their search prove fruitless.

Keyes passed Fawkes a powder horn, and the explosives man unsealed it to sniff the contents and pinch a sample between his thumb and forefinger. Some men knew tobacco and others the intricacies of black powder.

'Fetch a match and we will test the fury of the flame.' Fawkes stepped out of the shed and moved to the far corner of the yard. 'No alchemist could produce the magic we perform.'

'Nor create such a trick of disappearance.'

Muttered laughs greeted Catesby's quip. The other three men stood back as Fawkes tipped the powder to lay a trail and put the slow match to its end. It flared bright and burnt well. There were smiles of relief among the men, their fears allayed. How seamlessly their enterprise proceeded.

Back in the parlour, they talked with renewed animation of their mission. Further down the street, Jack Wright patrolled, and across the Thames at the Palace of Westminster the business of the day continued.

'So this is what it means to be a lady of the bedchamber?'

Adam lay with her and held her naked in his arms. He was exultant, a young man who had worked at the seduction even as he knew it would succeed. Now Anne was his. She had been tentative at first, nervous and pretending to resist, a lover entranced and submitting to her own desires and his.

He kissed her again and looked into her face. 'You are happy, Anne?'

'I could be nothing else.' She stretched out on his torso and let his fingers trace her lower back. 'Yet I am a sinner and it fills me with dread.'

'Though our exertions banish most doubts?'

'Some may linger.'

'Will you return to me or is virtue your true calling?'

'It seems I am ensnared.'

She could not possibly imagine how deep. The day had been spent following the chase and attending to the princess, sometimes idling and sometimes riding at the gallop as the hunting party and its pack traversed Dunmore Heath in pursuit of deer. Adam knew the ground and, encouraged by Robin Catesby, had often set out from Ashby St Ledgers to explore and map the area. His endeavours had not been wasted.

The heat was dying in the grate and the afternoon light was receding. It was almost time to leave the inn and merge with the stragglers heading home to Coombe Abbey. Slipping away from the hunt had presented no challenge, and continuing the deception should be as simple, the participants immersed in the pleasures of their sport. Adam had found a different delight.

He stroked her face. 'We are taught honesty and Christian truth, yet the serpent finds us.'

'My father is an unforgiving man. He would have you flogged, would see you hanged.'

'You are worth such a risk.'

'He is powerful, Adam.'

'Am I not?' He rocked her in his arms.

'Do not make light of things.'

'Why so?' He let his hips move slowly. 'If I am to die, I shall have the memory of this day.'

'I would rather that you live.'

'Tell me where your fearsome father might consign you.'

'To avoid the shame, he would send me to a convent.'

'I will break in.'

'Save that you are dead or languishing in a dungeon.'

'Where there is a will, there is I.'

He rolled her over and silenced her laughing remonstration with a kiss. On the chair and floor lay their discarded clothing, proof of their untidy descent to making love. Emblems of rank and privilege were easily shed when desire took hold. He had the confidence to steady her nerve, could coax and encourage and create the illusion she was no victim but the mistress of her decision. There was artistry in subterfuge. Anne groaned and her fingers dug deep into his shoulder.

Afterwards, as they hurriedly dressed, they were almost shy, the furtiveness of their deed lending an awkwardness that had earlier been masked by passion. Yet even if reflection brought regrets, they both understood that this would not be the last time, and whatever the risk they would snatch another moment together.

They emerged from the rear of the inn, intent on returning unseen to the hunt. But their path to their horses was blocked. A group of four or five, ruffians who could as easily cut the throat of another man as poach and gut wild game. Their lookouts had been watching the progress of the hunt and their scouts had followed the pair who ducked away. Word travelled quickly in these parts. Now a couple of Protestants were delivered up and would be made to pay.

'What have we found, my lads?' jeered a thickset man, a cudgel clenched in his fist. 'Two sucklings who will squeal well.'

Adam pushed Anne behind him. 'We do you no wrong.'

'You walk on land that is not yours.'

Adam gestured towards the horses. 'So we will take our leave and ride.'

'I think you do not understand.' The big man tapped the cudgel against his callused palm.

'Harm us and the blow will fall greater on you. Touch a lady of the court and you and your families will hang.'

'Our suckling threatens, would do us mischief.'

'I speak as it is.'

Adam himself had menaced Protestants; as a roving Swaggerer in London, he had set upon visiting Scots. He would consider the irony later. He could not break cover and admit his loyalties or confess he was one of them. The joy and intimacy in the chamber above were memories as cold as dead embers.

He attempted to bargain with the men. 'Your argument is with me. Let the lady go.'

'Both of you are Lutheran dogs and both will suffer the same.'

They circled closer and Adam counted their number, noted the makeshift weapons roughly concealed beneath clothes. Having survived encounters with the oafish porter Smythe and with Isaiah Payne and his pursuivants, he briefly wondered at his misfortune in adding to his enemies. 'The innkeeper will not thank you.'

'He already does.'

'Are none of you bound by the law? Is this a place of brigands?'

'You will soon discover it.'

'Then I am driven to fight.' Adam drew his knife. 'I ask you to save yourselves.'

'It scarce persuades me, suckling.' There was coarse amusement in the man's voice.

'I am not some soft and pampered courtier.'

'Yet you are as fair as any maid.'

Adam adjusted the grip on his blade. 'You are warned.'

The locals had reached for their arms and were poised to attack. For an instant, Adam wondered what his father would have done in his place. He stared at the leader. 'You do not wear a mask.'

'When we are done, you will scarce recall my face.'

'I shall commit to memory your screams instead.'

'Brave words from the suckling.'

Adam struck hard and fast, the stirrup iron Anne had pressed into his hand arcing down between the eyes of his adversary and felling him with a single blow. The group had expected easy victory, had not anticipated such fighting spirit. As Adam moved swiftly into the attack, several dropped their weapons. The bravado of bullies was a fragile thing. Without their chief, the men were lost, each reluctant to be next as sacrifice. They backed away, shouting in alarm as their retreat picked up pace.

'Holy Mother, he is the devil.'

'A devil and his bride.'

'I shall prick him yet.' A pitchfork jabbed towards the youth and was quickly beaten aside.

'Run, my brothers. Escape with your lives.'

'He's on us!'

The young pair quickly mounted up and charged through the confusion in a fury of hooves. Kicking aside a token attempt to stop him, Adam led the way. They galloped a mile before they slowed, breathless and elated, amazed by the changes the day had wrought.

'You are bleeding, Adam.'

'They bleed more.'

'What men could do this? What beasts could summon such vileness and hate?'

He looked away. 'I do not know. We must return you to the safety of the hunt before I go to lick my wounds.'

She regarded him with concerned and loving eyes. 'Twice now you have saved me from danger.'

'And twice I wish you had not been placed there.'

'We should pledge ourselves henceforth to a quiet life.'

It was not a promise he could keep.

Beatrice was more sedate in her horsemanship. Christian Hardy's lover crossed the heath towards Highgate with a party of friends, happy to be out on a crisp and clear winter day with the prospect of a visit to the pleasure grounds. A game of quoits was planned and a trot along the bridleways and perhaps an opportunity to watch archers at the butts. If her beloved Christian was away, she would create entertainment for herself and lessen the burden of his absence.

A female friend rode alongside. 'What charms we shall discover, Bea.'

'I haven't ventured so far since the summer.' Beatrice thrust her hands deeper into the fur cover. 'Though it is still cold. . . .'

The other woman gazed about. 'We are quite the spectacle.'

Beatrice smiled at her. 'I am glad I bowed to your entreaties.'

It was a peaceful scene, gentlemen and ladies winding unhurried through the landscape. London was no distance and yet could have been a hundred miles away. Up here, life was free of the bustle and tensions of the city and remote from the workings of the state. Beatrice was almost grateful for the exile imposed on her by Christian.

A young gentleman on a handsome gelding formed up on her right. 'I trust we men do not shun you, ladies.'

'You have much to discuss and sporting prowess to deliver,' Beatrice teased gently.

He smiled in acknowledgement. 'Where there are men there is boastful contest.'

'I vouch we would have it no other way.'

'Will you cheer for me?'

'What luck I bring is uncertain.' Beatrice smiled modestly. 'Yet should it spur you to great feats, you have my notice and my blessing.'

'It is an honour, mistress.'

That the man had gaming debts and a reputation as a scoundrel and philanderer could not be discounted from his attentiveness. Yet Beatrice was a generous spirit and willing to be kind. Without her lover's presence, she was destined to become the target of unwanted attention. Might God grant her the wit and grace to tolerate lesser mortals than her Christian, she thought.

'Hail to our travellers,' another man called as the riders approached. He was a recent acquaintance of the group, a cheerful merchant with money to spend and an easy manner that could disarm even the haughty or indifferent. They were pleased to see him and invited him to ride with them. There would be sweetmeats and bottles of fine wine in his saddle-bag and a host of tales of travel and adventure. All were in agreement that he would add to the enjoyment of their excursion.

Realm indeed had stories to tell. He had assiduously cultivated the group's goodwill, and under the adopted name of William Birch moved easily among them. Fools and innocents, they laughed and cavorted, oblivious to what would come.

'Mistress.' He doffed his hat to Beatrice. 'I intrude?'

'You are welcome to our caravan, sir.' She steered her horse on and let the merchant replace her unwanted suitor. 'The more of us, the merrier the diversion.'

'I cannot say I will excel in competition or feats of arms.'

She looked at him in approval. 'Your honesty alone has merit.'

He concentrated on the route ahead. 'Not for me bluff and swagger. It is better to be as one appears.'

She supposed from his age that he too was widowed. There was a warmth and decency to him, an unaffected air that could make the time pass and conversation flow. He was plainly not a man for secrets.

What discernment Christian Hardy possessed, Realm reflected. She was a kind and gentle woman, quick to laugh and too trusting. There would be tears. He had listened to her sleeping in the quietness of her home, had plans in which she would one day feature. It was important to reconnoitre close and gauge each aspect of the enemy's situation. Attention to detail had brought him this far and provided all manner of opportunity.

She shaded her eyes to study the vista reaching south to the capital. 'A magnificent sight, is it not?'

'Few compare.'

'Yet to dwell at its edge is ever to be an observer.'

'I leave others to their excitement,' said Realm. 'For me, it is time for gentler pastimes and pursuits.'

'From a man in fine vigour and health?'

'Forgive my dull and timid nature.'

They exchanged smiles at his self-deprecation, each glad for the other's company. The renegade pondered how she might die. Back in the city, Hardy would be considering his own next moves, forgetting how exposed was his flank.

Outside the Globe, Hardy crouched with Black Jack at his side, ignoring the cold and drunks and feral dogs and studying the shadowed mass of the theatre. Within were more galleries than a warship had decks, a multitude of places from which an enemy could launch an attack. It would have been a reckless oversight to dismiss intelligence regarding gunpowder, but it was just as misguided to rush in. Small wonder the spymaster Cecil had shown a certain relish when giving his assent.

Black Jack nudged him, gesturing to the stumbling approach of an inebriate. Their presence had aroused the man's interest, his territorial belligerence growing and his unsteady gait propelling him until he fell. With loud oaths he blamed the cobbles and sought to right himself.

'Keep away from us, stranger,' Hardy hissed.

'I will not,' the man slurred.

'Hardy moved quickly, was upon him before a protest left his mouth. 'Listen well, knave,' he whispered harshly in the drunk's ear. 'You wish to earn a shilling or to perish where you lie?'

'The shilling is preferred.'

'Then do as I bid, for this night you acquire greatness.'

The man set forward his terms plainly. 'My desire is to drink.'

'Help me and you will have numberless flagons of ale and wine. Resist and I shall have you driven from these parts.' Hardy's grip stayed firm.

'Summon your comrades and earn your pay, for within the hour your fortunes turn.'

As a screening force they were unimpressive, a quarrelsome gaggle of beggars convinced by coins and desperation to chance themselves on a mission. Yet they had lanterns and the courage afforded by liquor and their task as set out was simple: enter the Globe, seek out miscreants who might be lurking and recover any stolen property. Wealthy patrons, Hardy had explained, were concerned that the site was in danger of becoming a den for rogues and thieves.

The volunteers filed eagerly through the outer gate, the flicker of lights scattered and uneven, stumbling footsteps announcing the incursion. It would wake the dead, let alone the primed and waiting. They pushed on, crossing the outer yard and streaming through another gate, excited to partake in the venture. Attention would be on them.

Discarded nutshells and the littered debris of shellfish crackled underfoot as they progressed to the amphitheatre. Before them in the gloom was the apron stage and about them the triple bank of galleries. A ghostly place that by day throbbed to the gathered voices of three thousand souls and at night was as closed and deserted as a mausoleum. Sound would not travel far beyond the thatched roof and twenty-sided enclosure. In the cellars beneath the stage or in the tiring house behind, rich pickings might be had. Greed was a powerful motivator.

'Be watchful, brothers.' An itinerant held up his lamp. 'Ghouls and fiends abound.'

'We shall chase them off,' said another.

'You are right, friend.' One of the volunteers strode for the pit before the stage. 'A few shadows and echoes of speeches hold no fear for us.' He hauled himself onto the platform and strutted along its length, a vagrant performer who had missed his vocation. Within this building of some one hundred feet across, magic had often been created and audiences moved to shout or weep. No harm was done by a little improvisation. He gave an exaggerated flourish, and his friends laughed and cheered.

Suddenly the surrounding tiers erupted in smoke and flame as muskets opened up and the killing began. The enemy was revealed. How often history repeated and how obvious that Realm would train his recruits on live and running targets. The contest was unequal and most of the beggars were quickly torn to pieces in the raking crossfire. But their sacrifice was not in vain, for the counter-ambush had started, musket balls aiming for the firing points and ricocheting among the timbers. Christian Hardy and his force were surging through the entrances in a melee enveloped by smoke and splinters.

On stage the lead part had lost first his voice and then his head as the Upright Man leant forward with a firearm from the balcony behind and proceeded to blow out his brains. The crime chief held a commanding position. It was not going his way or as the mysterious English renegade had promised.

'Take the sons of whores, my boys.' He bellowed his encouragement. 'Let not one of them crawl alive from this theatre.'

His words were drowned out by the shouts of men and report of guns. Somewhere in the confusion, leaping from bench to bench with his katzbalger drawn, Hardy fought towards the upper levels. Evading his hacking blows, an adversary dodged to right and left behind a pillar and jabbed at him with a shortened spear. The intelligencer jumped, swung high on the post and kicked the man unconscious. Amid the toppled seating, his dagger soon claimed another kill.

'You take my hand and now you take my people,' the Upright Man roared from his eyrie. Shrouded by darkness the intelligencer might be, but he knew he was there.

Hardy called back, 'You shall be next should you not submit.'

'Submit?' The Upright Man laughed. 'Submit to the law? To prison and the hangman?'

Their conversation was briefly interrupted as a man charged from a doorway at the rear of the stage and was felled by a single shot.

'Enough blood is shed,' Hardy continued. 'You are surrounded.'

'What does it matter?'

'You will all be killed.'

'My men without me are as good as dead.'

A trapdoor opened in the ceiling space above the stage, a rope dropped from the heavens and a single figure swarmed down. Within a moment, the Upright Man was dead and Swiftsure had added to his tally. Others were clambering out from below, reinforcements for the operation stiff from their hiding places and spilling wide to crush resistance.

As smouldering rushes were doused and the dead thrown carelessly from the heights, Hardy was thankful the damage was contained. At least for the moment the threat was neutered and a slew of potential assassins removed. He wondered if the incident would mean the forfeit of his silver cross.

Intrigued by activity on the water, the prisoner smoked his pipe on the rampart walkway and watched as boatmen struggled to retrieve a headless corpse. Among the frenetic trade and traffic, it was a detail almost unnoticed by most. Plainly the corpse was that of a wealthy female, Sir Walter Raleigh observed. Whatever the rank and wherever one dwelt, a person could end as flotsam. He turned away, glad for the company of his books.

The wife of a leading banker had simply ceased to be.

On Christmas Eve, the King announced a further delay to the recall of Parliament to October the following year. At court the revels continued, culminating on Twelfth Night with Queen Anne and her ladies darkening their skins with paint to perform *The Masque of Blackness* by Ben Jonson. The new year was full of promise and the gunpowder plotters still dug.

CHAPTER 11

A longboat was making the Thames crossing, edging through the predawn mist from the south bank to the foot of the stairs at Westminster. The two men on board had chosen this hour for good reason. They carried with them a consignment of gunpowder, twenty barrels brought from the Lambeth home of Robin Catesby and destined to be stowed beneath the House of Lords. It was April 1605 and the next stage of the plan was underway.

Waiting at the steps, his lantern held aloft, Guido Fawkes guided his comrades in. There was no need for talk as they transferred the load quickly to a large handcart. Jack Wright remained ashore as the quartermaster Keyes cast off and returned into the gloom. Should there be an ambush it would happen here and now. The swordsman peered into the shadows blanketing the silent halls and empty buildings. It was as though he had landed on some foreign shore, was come to do battle with a distant foe. Like the natives of the Americas who tried to stem the incursion by the Spanish, the incumbent regime stood no chance against invasion. When he was satisfied no one was watching, he took up position on one of the poles. Fawkes grasped the other and they pushed the cart towards the passage with some difficulty.

'Our ordnance is here at last.' There was a note of wonder in Thomas Percy's voice.

They stood in a corner of the ground-floor undercroft set beneath the raised hall of the House of Lords, a storage area almost forgotten and generally ignored by the denizens of Westminster. Percy was glad of its existence. It meant that they had been able to abandon the dangers of mining and instead rent space from a coal merchant directly below the target. As a gentleman and official bodyguard to King James, he had reason and right to be there; as a married man with lodgings a few paces distant, he had excuse to seek a convenient overflow for his possessions. Twenty hidden barrels of explosive were now added to his inventory.

He turned to Wright. 'When will Keyes bring the rest?'

'There is no need for haste.'

'Yet we must be prepared to create a blast to devour all. The King brings to London his youngest maggot Charles and it seems we have no longer have a street army.'

The swordsman was as taciturn as the mercenary beside him. 'We have sufficient force to hunt them.'

'To erase Charles and his elder brother Henry? To prevent their flight or the survival of any loyal member of the court?'

'A beheaded regime cannot resist. When the King is blown to bits, confusion will be our friend.'

'Numberless enemies for the present remain.' Percy rearranged a bundle of firewood to better screen the stockpile. 'But I cannot deny we are closest yet to our aim.'

In the preceding month, Pope Clement VIII had died, a pontiff who went to his maker still convinced that the King of England would repent his ways and convert eventually to Rome. It seemed a forlorn hope and one that scarcely concerned the plotters. Already new members had joined the group. The course was set and the gunpowder secured.

Percy stepped back with a lantern to review their handiwork. 'Neither the new pope nor Spain will help us. We alone shall bear this burden.'

'James will wish he had never ventured from Scotland.' Fawkes contemplated his new responsibilities. 'Would that we had not spent these past months digging.'

'At least our goal is reached, Guido.'

Wright peered into the further reaches of the undercroft. 'What now?'

'We wait and listen. We ensure we are not captured,' Percy replied., 'Christian Hardy still breathes.'

'He is but one and we are several. And we keep beyond his reach.'

'I am ready should he draw close.'

'Have you not suffered enough at his hands?' Percy could not resist the barb at his brother-in-law. 'None of us should doubt his persistence or the guile of his master Cecil.'

Fawkes intervened. 'For myself, I will not sit and be their target. I will go to Flanders to gather horses and recruit friends from my old regiment.'

'Take care in whom you meet, and what you say,' warned Percy.

Abroad or at home, every tavern had its spies and every comment could be noted and relayed by an informant. The Secretary of State had invested heavily in his networks and penetrated to the highest levels of the Catholics. An unguarded remark in some foreign city could lead directly to the gallows at Tyburn.

Percy turned to leave. 'All is secure and our labour for the while is done. I shall report to Robin that my residence lies quiet and its storage undisturbed.'

'The Lord keep it so.' Wright made the sign of the cross. 'The Lord speed us in our endeavour and to do His work.'

They left before the day rode in and the precincts of Westminster filled. The lower their profile, the less likely a chance encounter might spoil their wider plan.

'The Queen again is heavy with child.'

Robin Catesby stared out of the window at the apple blossom and made his remark to no one in particular. The returned Robert Keyes busied himself in the yard as Catesby waited inside with Tom Wintour for word from Thomas Percy and discussed the progress of the plot. How remarkable it was that they had so far evaded the clumsy blows of the state. So the courtiers played and Queen Anne fell pregnant and the Stuarts believed they were untouchable. All would be consumed in the fire.

'Born or unborn, no royal issue but Elizabeth will live,' Wintour said calmly. 'It is likely Queen Anne will be with her husband when our powder ignites below.'

'Better death by explosion than cruel and cold steel, Tom.'

Between the plotters, murder had become the most prosaic of subjects and its method an everyday matter of debate. Hatred and faith would prevent any deeper consideration. Conspiracy was all-consuming.

Catesby retired from the window and bent to move a chess piece on the board set out on the table in the embrasure. 'As each day we grow stronger, so they become more confused and blind.'

'My elder brother Robert is glad to be among us.'

'His house alone adds immeasurably to our cause.' Catesby stayed focused on the game. 'Huddington Court will play its part in our tale.'

When the time was right they would gather forces there to spread revolt and word of what they planned. 'John Grant too adds his manor of Norbrook,' he went on, foiling a move by Wintour and swiftly toppling a knight. 'Slowly we edge closer to Coombe Abbey and our grip tightens on the weasel throat of the King and the future of his daughter.'

'Let us hope Guido wins us succour in Flanders.'

'We will fight with whatever we have, Tom. And we shall win.'

Confidence radiated from the leader. Ever suspicious and yet oblivious to the threat, the monarch cavorted and indulged himself as the surrounding pieces slid into position. A pity there was no depiction on the chessboard of a keg of powder or a Catholic plotter or a horseman riding to snatch a princess. Catesby pondered and reached to break through the defence. The King was down.

In the fields of Suffolk, James was very much alive. Attended by his retinue, he had found a fresh diversion, deciding on a whim to create an estate and erect a palace close to the village of Newmarket. At a stroke he could conjure magnificence and command architects and gardeners to do his extravagant bidding. If it added to the sum of his pleasure or gave him further excuse to keep from London, so much the better. There would be coursing and racing and sybaritic pursuit, the space and opportunity to hide or parade, in a gilded environment devoted to male dalliance. A representative of God on earth could do such things.

'What a mean and dismal hamlet.' The King sat in the saddle and waved a silken handkerchief. 'By the grace of God we shall transform it.'

A courtier responded. 'It will be a blessing for all about. Your Majesty has no rival in matters of taste and beauty.'

'Yet I must fund such vision by fining Catholics the more.'

'They will not complain, Majesty,' another courtier assured him.

'Do the natives applaud?'

'Should they resist, they shall be removed or hanged.'

'Some cannot see I improve and raise up their lives.' James called to a gaggle of surveyors and draughtsmen, 'Here I desire a pond and a fountain rising from it.'

He continued his tour, his enthusiasm boundless as his nobles trailed weary and resigned. Astride a horse he was their equal in stature and able to forget his limitations. They did not laugh when they saw him take a jump, could not complain when he beat them in the chase and controlled the drawstrings to their purses. How loyal and respectful they were.

Reining to a halt, he peered towards a distant church. 'Though we pursue an earthly course, it is right we maintain our eyes on the heavens.'

'None doubt you are guided by the Divine, sir.'

'Our Lord decreed I came from Scotland and now He brings me to this place.'

'You will create wonders, sir.'

'That is my intent.' The monarch had spied something new and directed his horse towards it. 'I vouch my sport for the day is arrived.'

A cluster of functionaries had appeared near a copse, officials sent from London with petitions and dispatches. Government continued even as the King and his favourites caroused. The earnest and dust-clad visitation was at odds with the flamboyance of the travelling court. James had been expecting them.

'You are as ragged crows standing in our midst.'

'We seek to serve and not offend, Majesty.' A secretary bowed obsequiously from his mount. 'Yet we have ridden nearly seventy miles and are somewhat travel worn.'

'That you do your duty is beyond complaint.'

'As your humble servants, we give Your Majesty our thanks.'

'And as your King I offer you wise counsel.' James hawked a ball of phlegm into the dirt, a ruler at ease with both refinement and coarse humour. 'Bear yourselves with dignity and you will earn reward.'

They laughed on cue, eager to please and to follow his lead. The little Scotsman enjoyed his jests and petty triumphs. It kept everyone alert and in their place. Yet he noted that one newcomer did not play, a handsome, self-assured man separate from the rest and unresponsive to his antics.

The King's moist eyes viewed the stranger. 'Christian Hardy?'

'Yes, sir.' The intelligencer gave a perfunctory nod.

'You do not flatter your King.'

'I prefer to guard him.'

'Thus does Cecil send us an untamed and savage mastiff.' The royal eyelashes dipped. 'Are you fed on raw bones and meal?'

'I dine as any other.'

'Though you defy crude comparison. For you are the keeper, the avenging angel, the lauded saviour of Queen Elizabeth.'

'My desire is to go ignored.'

'A man who shies from praise and shuns the light.' James gazed about at his coterie. 'It is unnatural.'

Hardy contradicted him without hesitation. 'As intelligencer, it is convention.'

'Perhaps you are no mastiff, but Cerberus at the gates of hell.'

'Some say I am the boatman that ferries souls across.'

Silence followed, the King's mouth agape and his tongue lodged in his cheek as he studied his uncowed subject. Hardy was a rarity, a collectable to be viewed either with gratitude or unease. He should be put through his paces.

James stroked the horsewhip in his hand. 'How obedient are you to your King?'

'Enough to lay down my life.'

'Today I ask only that you race me to the poplar yonder and back.'

That God had ordained the runt of a litter should become King of England was either a celestial joke or an aberration, Hardy supposed. There could be no retreat from the contest or doubting the result intended. James wished to prove himself and show his mastery, to teach a lesson to all. The King spurred away without warning, Hardy in sudden pursuit.

'You have caught me.' As they rounded the tree, the King saw fit to change the rules. 'Let us try the distant oak.'

Again Hardy gained ground and overtook before pausing for the monarch. He would not upset his master for the sake of it. It earned him a panting nod of gratitude.

'Your beast is less winded than I imagined, Hardy.'

'He responds well to the touch.'

'Perhaps then I should invest him as a favourite.' James was regaining his breath and composure. 'Prerogative decrees you shall cede to me the lead.'

Hardy inclined his head. 'I will not forget.'

'Few else would dare abuse my station and authority.'

'A race is but a race, sir.'

'It is never so pure or simple.' The King leant to peer close. 'You are at once experienced and an innocent.'

'Some are born to soldiery and others to be diplomats.'

'Why has Cecil sent you?'

'To see that you are safe. To ensure no malcontent or traitor lurks smiling in your company.'

James pointed. 'Tell me what you espy.'

'A glittering array of nobles and loyal faces.'

'Each drawing on me for their comfort and rank. Every one of them depending on my longevity and mortal breath.'

'It gladdens me to hear.'

'Should I fall, they will fail. Should I rest in one place too long, the Catholic assassins may scent my blood.'

'We shall keep you from their reach, sir.'

'Is that so?' The tone was almost accusatory.

'All the plots we have discovered so far have been foiled.'

'There will be more.' The King fidgeted with his reins, eager for distraction. 'More to crowd my dreams and upset my peace.'

'I have come to reassure you.'

'How strange, then, that your visit serves to trouble and unnerve. Look to London, for my enemies will strike there.'

'Whatever you command, sir.'

'Find them, Hardy.' James whipped his horse into a gallop. 'Find them.'

Christian was not the only one with secrets. At her Hampstead home, Beatrice studied herself in her looking glass and smiled. Vanity was a sin and unfaithfulness far worse, and yet she should be permitted on occasion the chance to rejoice in her womanhood. The absence of her lover and the loss of human warmth had reinforced her loneliness and reminded her of those painful months of solitude after her husband's death. Her beloved intelligencer might not survive, and was in any case diverted by more important matters. He would wish her to be happy.

She heard the rumble of wheels and hurried down the stairs, mildly disconcerted by her own sense of expectation.

'A carriage for my lady.'

She laughed in delighted surprise. The wagon, driven by the friendly, good-natured merchant she knew as William Birch, was filled with spring flowers. The sight seemed to encapsulate the contrast between the two men. Where Christian could be closed and silent, Birch was open and wreathed in smiles; where Christian spied and killed and answered to the darkness of Robert Cecil, this man had a lightness and honesty that shone. It was as though he understood her, valued her as did few other casual suitors. No harm was done or wrong committed by idling awhile in the sun.

Birch offered his hand and helped her up beside him. 'I could not wish for fairer company.'

'Nor I a kinder or more solicitous friend seated at my side.'

'We have breads and meat, sweet pastries and wine, everything for our pleasure and repast.'

'I am undeserving of such favours, Will.'

'Who are you to judge?' He flicked the reins and walked his horse on. 'For this afternoon we will be as king and queen.'

'Each widowed and both charmed in their nearness to the other.'

'We shall drink a toast to companionship when we reach our glade.'

'Where do we go?'

'To places unimagined.'

Sitting contentedly, she did not ask for further explanation. The ease of his manner calmed her and made her feel protected.

Realm guided the horse and let Beatrice lean against him. Christian Hardy must be congratulating himself on the progress of his enquiries and on outfighting the armed rabble sent against him. Let him enjoy his moment. The sacrifice of the Upright Man and his followers had not been entirely in vain, for it had provided a feint and kept the state guessing. While Hardy chased shadows elsewhere, his Beatrice engaged in projects of her own. Realm hoped it might bring them closer together.

Cecil sat unstirring at his desk and listened to the noise of carts on the Strand and the murmur of petitioners queuing at his gates. All things had their rhythm and every action its pattern. It was a question of sifting out the background clutter to isolate the individual sound so meaning could be determined. The spymaster was accustomed to listening for the extraordinary or important.

Before him lay bundles of digests and dispatches, secret communications penned by ambassadors and agents and detailing the gossip and indiscretions of the power elite of Europe. The smallest morsel of intelligence could provide an opportunity for blackmail; an overheard remark could signify a change of policy or the reneging on a peace deal. Puzzles existed to be deciphered. In a world beset with enemies and bounded by fragile truce, vigilance and forewarning were required.

Yet it was a stained canvas shoe to which he directed his attention, turning it in his hand as though it were an object of exquisite beauty. Its value was not immediately apparent. But the footwear had been worn by a seaman aboard a trading ship sailing from Flanders, and that gave the item provenance and interest.

Cecil reached for a knife and slit the stitching, peeled back the sole and deftly removed the wrapped papers hidden within. One of his most reliable sources was making his report, writing urgently and unencoded to avoid the need for any cipher and codebook. The Secretary of State teased open the pages and read. He stared for several minutes, reading again, committing everything to memory before putting the paper to the flame of his candle and watching it flare and die to ash in its descent to the stone hearth. Then he rang a bell and summoned a secretary to convey a message to a distant corner of the house. His forces would be redeployed.

Isaiah Payne stood eventually before him, the chief pursuivant both honoured and frightened at the privilege of an interview. Payne was glad that he and his powerful master fought for the same cause, and was ever anxious to be of service.

Cecil rested in his chair. 'Summer approaches and you will soon return to the hunt.'

'Whatever is your bidding, my lord.'

'As the ground hardens, so Jesuits travel and sedition spreads.'

'We will be waiting for them, my lord.'

'They often prove your match.' Cecil noted the pursuivant's slight tremor. 'We cannot let them grow in strength or in the scale of their audacity.'

'One of their kind bleeding and in chains will loudly declare the authority of the King.'

'Alas, it does not stop them.'

The minister pressed together his fingertips and continued to study his underling. Payne had been a useful instrument of control, harrying the Catholics and pursuing their priests. There was much to thank him for, were Cecil inclined to gratitude.

He did not blink. 'There is talk again of insurrection, chatter of papists eager to take up arms and agitating to depose the King.'

'They shall not prevail.'

'Your confidence accords with mine. Yet we must attack in every quarter and force them to expend their energies in a fruitless quest to survive.'

'Have faith in my pursuivants, my lord.'

'It is for no other reason that I call you. Increase your efforts in the Midland shires, maintain the tempo of your raids. Search under every stone and in each hollow for these poisonous Jesuit snakes.'

'I shall not fail you.'

'Look too for signs beneath your nose, for proof of mischief and preparation for deeper conspiracy.'

'You have particular matters of concern, my lord?'

'Horses.' The Secretary of State laid his palms flat upon the desk. 'Where there is stabling, there are men willing to ride. Where there is stabling filled to abundance with coursers and war chargers, there is a darker plot afoot.'

'Equine flesh is as easy to follow as the stench of Catholic priests, my lord,' Payne offered.,

'Commit to seeking both.'

Orders received, Payne left to execute the plan. Cecil resumed his silent musing on the contents of the letter, which described a Catholic plotter sent from England to acquire horses in the Low Countries. Guido Fawkes was on the move and returning briefly to his old campaigning ground. Another name was mentioned, that of a man on whose authority the elusive mercenary travelled. At last the identity of the mastermind was revealed, and Cecil would share it with no one. It was his insurance, his tool for manipulating events and consolidating power. Robin Catesby was more than just the prize. He was the very key to the future.

Four miles north of Stratford-upon-Avon, Adam Hardy again brought horses to the village of Snitterfield. Only a summer ago, fleeing from the pursuivants, he had crouched low in the churchyard as his pursuers rode by. In this new year the pace had quickened once more. The owner of the manor of Norbrook expected his arrival.

'When we last met, you made a hasty exit.'

John Grant remained a bookish and unsmiling figure whose thoughts were hard to read. Tom Wintour's brother-in-law was not given to levity. Yet, newly recruited by Catesby to the plot, he was a valued member, and his proximity to Coombe Abbey and the young Princess Elizabeth rendered him indispensable. He appreciated the significance of the horses.

'Last time you brought me two.' He stared from the young man to his steeds. 'It since multiplies to four.'

'All fine coursers sent north from the stables of Sir Ambrose Rookwood.'

'He has a good eye.'

Adam leant from his saddle to pat the nearest. 'Sixteen hands and strongly haunched.'

'They seem well-tempered and in health.'

'I have ridden each and can vouch for it.'

'You will bring more?'

'As supply and security allow.' Adam gazed out to the treeline. 'Rumour has it the enemy bloodhounds again infest this area.'

'Fear not. Their hunt will come and go and still we shall outwit them.'

Adam remained cautious. 'I have cause to be wary of their ways.'

'We will brazen it out and maintain our watch.' Grant blew a note on his whistle to summon a steward with a flagon of wine. 'You must be thirsty from your travel.'

Adam nodded gratefully. 'A cup and then I ride.'

At the gates to the Norbrook estate, Thomas Bates would be waiting patiently. Catesby's trusted manservant was the communications link to his master in London. Coordination was imperative. The new year had intensified the pressure, fuelled the pace and sent the loyal courier travelling wide. Adam did not enquire where or why.

Grant was watching him. 'How fares your life of dance and dalliance at Coombe Abbey?'

'As well as I could wish and more blessed than that of a stable hand.'

'Don't forget your friends, nor who are your enemies.'

Adam made a wry face. 'I need no reminding when the likes of Isaiah Payne chase at my heels.'

'He is all that is rotten in this state.' Grant spoke with an air of sombre acceptance. 'Yet he is not alone in his vile endeavours.'

'You would surrender to it?'

'May God smite me should I not defy them with every fibre of my soul.'

'Brave words, sir.'

'Simply the truth.'

His delivery made, Adam departed. To loiter was to invite risk and neither he nor his host sought to draw attention. The summer would involve many such meetings.

At the edge of the grounds, Adam encountered the waiting Bates. 'It is a scene more tranquil than my past excursion.'

'I have seen nothing to alarm.'

'Perhaps it is meant to lull.' The young man turned his horse onto the track. 'Cecil has his devils in every corner of the land.'

'You made fools of them before.'

'Even dullards such as they may strike lucky. Yet we will enjoy our sport before they have us hanged.'

Bates did not reply. His silence spoke of matters hidden and things decided in another place. Like the upstairs chamber of the gatehouse at Ashby St Ledgers, it was a world of alcoves and hinted secrets. Robin Catesby directed events and he kept his own counsel.

They trotted on, heading for Stratford-upon-Avon. Their route would take them past Clopton House, a manor available for rent and of interest to Catesby. With large stables and a deep cellar, it was another potential redoubt and a further link in the chain of conspiracy.

CHAPTER 12

He drank because he was weak and had a thirst, because life had dealt him a hand he deemed unfair, and because he was entitled to behave as he pleased. Sir Francis Tresham swallowed more wine and slammed his empty cup upon the table. The Jack of Blood was as foul and rat-infested as any tavern in St Giles, but none visited this part of London for the sweet smells and aesthetics. On a makeshift sand-strewn stage, a pair of bare-knuckle fighters traded blows with an alacrity that drew cheers and smeared blood across their torsos. Maiming was not pretty and yet could earn reward.

'More wine to my table.'

Tresham watched the fight and its supporters with a degree of aloofness and contempt. He was careful whom he chose to back. The debts he would inherit taught him to trust few, to avoid committing until the likely outcome was clear. His recusant father was principled and thus a fool and had brought fines and confiscation upon his family. It was wiser to box clever and dodge the low punches of the state.

'You have money on them, Francis?'

'I wait for a bout I may more easily call.' Tresham replenished his goblet. 'It is the snarling underdog that generally triumphs.'

His companion slid onto a bench opposite. 'Why so?'

'The favourite becomes soft and preening, basks in the adulation and applause. Meantime, the less favoured studies his rival and awaits his chance. One has everything to lose and the other nothing.'

'If your underdog is wounded early in the fray?'

'There will be others to replace him, and I still have my table and my wine.'

The crowd yelled its delight as a pugilist staggered beneath a flurry of blows and lost teeth and blood before he fell. Perhaps he could be revived with a pail of water and reclaim some dignity with a stumbling comeback. He was in no state for a quick recovery.

As money changed hands and drinkers idled between contests, Tresham settled in for the evening. He was most at ease when surrounded by those who looked up to him. Not for him the intellects of the Mermaid on Cheapside. For men like his cousin Robin Catesby, it was a simple trick to lead and inspire and draw others to his side. Tresham found it harder.

He stifled a pang of envy at the thought of his cousin and rose to answer a call of nature. 'Keep my seat guarded and my glass untouched. I have an appointment with a wall.'

Outside in the alleyway, he emptied his bladder with a groan of relief and listened to the noises spilling from the haunts nearby. Even low life could dance and play. He fastened his britches, a gentleman standing in the midst of squalor and putrefaction.

The attack was sudden. The men's moves were orchestrated, hands swiftly pinioning and wrestling him to the ground. He tried to resist, to shout, to twist and face his assailants. The strike to his kidney and the hood forced over his head put an end to his efforts. Dazed, he felt himself lifted, sensed the ordered flow of the operation as he was ferried and thrown onto the floor of a carriage. Distantly he registered that a kidnap was in train and that he was the victim. It defied everything he comprehended of his life. Snatched from the comfort of the known, he was transplanted to a place of total mystery. Wheels rolled and the carriage rocked and he lay curled inert and weeping. Confusion did not mean he failed to fear.

Random sounds broke through his stupor, the clanging of a bell and the call of a watchman receding into the night. The unseen enemy was taking him to the City. A foot pressed him down as he sought to rise and gain a bearing. But he had heard an echo and it suggested a proximity to buildings and a narrowing of the streets.

Finally, the journey ended. He heard the challenge of guards and the rattle of chains and the clop of hooves on bridges. Hands dragged him again, now bearing him up flights of steps and through a doorway. Even stones could reflect despair and desolation. As he was pushed down onto a chair and expertly secured, Tresham began to pray.

'You tremble.'

He blinked at the speaker in the sudden light as the hood was roughly pulled off. His thoughts were overloaded by terror and the image of the deformed little man standing before him. Robert Cecil, the first Earl of Salisbury, could be the most menacing of hosts.

Cecil again broke the silence. 'What do you see?'

Tresham found his voice. 'A vision of hell.'

'Many have said as much.' The Secretary of State motioned to the instruments and hanging bars about him. 'The manacles, the gauntlets, the thumbscrews, the wheel, the scavenger's daughter.'

'They are fit for traitors and I am not among them.'

'So often we must dig to discern the truth.'

Tresham shook in his bindings and retched.

They always settled eventually, mused the Secretary of State. At first visit, the basement of the White Tower that dominated this prison fortress beside the Thames was a disconcerting place. He let his hand rest on the crank lever of a large oak-framed device beside him. 'What is the name of this instrument, Tresham?'

'The rack, my lord.'

'A thing of beauty and horror combined. A tool for mining gold and plucking gemstones from the mire. A necessity in a dangerous age.'

'I am no danger, my lord.'

'It is then your word against mine.' The Secretary of State did not smile. 'My inclination is to believe my own.'

Tresham let out a sob. 'None could challenge my loyalty or devotion to the King.'

'And yet you are a papist whose record tells otherwise.'

'Trust me, my lord.'

'Speech so often employed by knaves and curs and assassins with a blade.'

The prisoner responded as expected, snivelling and shedding tears. Softening men was a skill and coercion a game that Cecil had refined over many encounters. Francis Tresham was too indolent and self-serving to prove a difficult catch. He was broken before he arrived.

Cecil stepped closer. 'You are not so pious as your venerable father, Sir Thomas.'

'He is a man of strong will and belief.'

'While you are a coward without morals?'

'I know my duty is to the King.'

'A sentiment not shared by your father.'

Tresham stared through his tears at the spy chief, resentment bubbling up. 'My father is an obdurate fool who squanders my inheritance and the fortune of the family, who through his unyielding ways brings fines and shame upon our heads.'

'Are you to be more reasonable?'

Tresham's eyes widened beseechingly. 'Place your faith in me and I will show you how.'

Cecil nodded. 'You have a chance to save your future or make the choice that ends it.'

'I choose to live, my lord,' Tresham babbled.

Cecil paused. 'Sir Robin Catesby is your cousin. He is engaged in a plot against the throne.'

'I know nothing of it, my lord,' Tresham pleaded.

'Yet you shall.' Cecil spoke slowly. 'You will hold yourself out as ally and friend, will be of solace and aid to your cousin and his gang.'

'What if he should suspect me, ignore my every blandishment and overture?'

'Arrange that he does not. Ensure he regards you with affection and trust.'

Tresham fretted. 'His companions may not be so pliant.'

The hunchback's gaze was unwavering. 'Oblige me and you will find me generous. Fail me in any fashion, give hint of what I ask, and you will earn my wrath and vengeance.'

And so a new recruit was engaged. Cecil was accustomed to succeed. With a single manoeuvre he would outflank the foe and unravel conspiracy, then lie in wait ahead. The King was proving the most tempting of bait and no armed papist would struggle free of the hook.

In a Highgate mansion, a Catholic Mass was underway. Here, just outside London, the celebrants were safe, could recite their Latin prayers and receive the Host and indulge in popish rituals that were banned throughout the nation. There would be no raid by pursuivants or arbitrary arrest, no pulling up of floorboards or excavation through walls in a merciless hunt for priests. For this was the Spanish embassy: as foreign soil, it afforded protection to the followers of Rome.

Don Juan de Tassis, the Spanish ambassador, understood why the pair of gentlemen had come. In this posting he had heard enough stories, wild plans and forlorn hopes to last a diplomatic lifetime. His previous existence, as court chamberlain in Madrid, had been easier; dealing with intrigue in Spain was much simpler than confronting the fractious politics and religious affairs of England. Spring might blossom outside, but there were precious few signs of Catholicism winning back this heretic land.

He sat in his study and appraised his two visitors. They were brave and committed men and doubtless believed in what they did. Too many of their kind had already ended on the scaffold. Yet the faithful were always welcome and the enemies of King James treated with courtesy and respect. Robin Catesby and his companion Thomas Percy would not have sought an audience without sound reason.

Catesby spoke. 'It is rare to find in England a place of such benign amity and warmth, Excellency.'

'You will ever have a friend here, Sir Robin.' The ambassador gave a patrician smile. 'Your brother in faith Tom Wintour has kissed the hands of my King. His fealty and love are not forgotten.'

'Neither, I trust, will you forget those who suffer for the cause in England and cry out for liberty of conscience.'

'We hear them.'

'Do you give answer?'

De Tassis hesitated. It was a thankless task placating English Catholics and managing their expectations. They wanted a miracle, and all he could deliver were platitudes and kind counsel. His hands were bound by a peace accord with King James and by the cold reality of present circumstance. 'What would you have me do, Sir Robin?'

'Only what we have already asked. To press your King to launch invasion, to send a force and sweep tyranny aside.'

'Would it succeed?'

'Catholics wait to rise, to overthrow James and restore the nation to its path of righteousness.'

'In two years of my embassy, I have seen no sign of it.' Another rebuff.

'Such signs are all about. The stars align and time is ripe and our brothers ready for their hour.'

'A hidden and formidable army or a ragged band of desperate souls?' It was a cruel question and one that needed to be asked. De Tassis rose, a grandee whose sympathy was tempered by pragmatism and whose long experience of dealing with England had tutored him to be cautious. The island race was a resilient foe. Perhaps the Catholic pair before him approached from a position of strength and possessed strategic vision. Or – more likely – they had no remaining option. Hope was rarely plucked from a hopeless situation.

He regarded the two men. 'As we speak, King James sends to Spain the aged Earl of Nottingham to countersign our treaty.'

'A treaty means little against our higher duty to the Lord.'

'Yet affairs of state cannot be ignored.'

'Nor matters of faith and the salvation of humankind.'

'Salvation?' The ambassador raised an eyebrow. 'Through rash action you will unleash in England the slaughter of all Catholics.'

'That is not our purpose, Excellency.'

'It may yet be the result. Keep with prayer and pilgrimage, Sir Robin.'

Catesby stayed Percy's restless irritation with a warning glance. There remained a chance to plead his case and channel his demands to King Philip. Spain had once been a worthy ally who with fire and sword fought Protestant evil. Zeal could ever be revived.

He met the ambassador's gaze. 'Where once the King of Spain sent a mighty armada, it seems his son is content to give commiseration.'

'Desist from insolent presumption, Sir Robin.'

'Forgive me, Excellency. It is my disappointment that speaks.'

'Would you have war again between our nations? Our treasure ships plundered by English privateers or King James's navy?'

'God calls us.'

'I answer to more temporal concerns.'

'Judgement is soon upon us, Excellency. There will be wailing and gnashing of teeth, a great cataclysm and a rending of the sky. A time when sinners are cast down and the good numbered with the saints.'

De Tassis was unmoved. 'As envoy of King Philip, I would rather be counted with the wise.'

'We are the spearhead, Excellency.' Resolve shone in Catesby's eyes. 'With or without your blessing, the will of Our Saviour shall be done.'

'Then you are alone.' The ambassador turned away, dismissing them.

As the two Englishmen crossed the gardens and ducked into the under-growth to avoid the prying gaze of watchers, Catesby comforted himself with his belief that to be tested was part of the journey. The Apostles had faced darkness and despair and the Spartans at Thermopylae encoun-tered overwhelming odds. De Tassis could stay undecided and remote; the great venture continued.

In a woodland clearing, Jack Wright waited with the horses.

'I wished for more in the embassy than sentiment and excuse.' Catesby said, as he swung himself into the saddle. 'But I received the Holy Sacra-ment and cannot complain.'

Percy was less sanguine, still smarting at the ambassador's curt dis-missal. 'We are betrayed, disowned, spurned as any contagion.'

'Yet as Christian soldiers we are content and freed of other cares.'

'Here sits one soldier who will not so easily forgive the cowardice of Spain.'

'Put it from your thoughts. It is England's course on which we dwell.'

They emerged from the woods onto the track and headed south for the city. In Flanders, Guido Fawkes would be busy acquiring horses and weapons to prepare for the coming conflict. Nothing Cecil and his forces could do would avert destiny or spare the King. Commitment outweighed everything.

'We have them.'

Hardy followed the progress of the small cavalcade. The swordsman Wright had unwittingly led him to this site, where he met two others eager to go unrecognised. Their bearing and gait had betrayed them even before a drover passed near to confirm and report with a hand signal. To the trio of plotters, nothing would seem out of the ordinary. *Find them, Hardy*, the King had commanded. On a corkboard, he had traced with coloured thread the bonds between these men and their link to a cache of gunpowder. Robin Catesby, Thomas Percy and Jack Wright, riders bound for London and incriminated by a clandestine visit to the Spanish ambassador Don Juan de Tassis.

'They did not come to pray.' Hardy addressed Carter and Swiftsure riding at his side. 'I vouch too they sought more than Spanish silver to pay their families' recusant fines.'

Ahead and out of sight, Catesby and his lieutenants ran a gauntlet of surveillance. Carters working to replace a wheel, a rat-catcher and his dog, a gentleman and his mistress venturing to take the air on higher ground, all belonged to Hardy and provided eyes that would study and track and record.

The intelligencer called to another of his tribe, a wayside whore standing painted and gowned and alert for random trade. 'How seem they, Kate?'

'One was watchful and the elder scowled and I spied in the hand of their leader no less than the beads of a rosary.'

'You watched them well.'

She grinned. 'He was as handsome a devil as you and as muscled as a stallion. Would that he were no shameful Catholic.'

'If you are as fine a harlot as you are my spy, there will be many a smiling fellow.'

'I will take gratitude or pennies from any quarter.'

A laugh and a wave and Hardy moved on. Stationed at waypoints and crossroads were others awaiting the handover of the targets. The conspirators' destination could be critical to uncovering their intent.

Somewhere in the distance, a gang of youths and apprentices playing football spilt onto the roadway just ahead of the three Catholics. It was a rowdy affair, more brawl than match, reached in a welter of shouts and collisions and broken teeth. The leather-clad ball was almost forgotten in the scrap. At the sudden eruption of noise, Catesby's horse reared and unsteadied the rest, and an enraged Percy whirled to restore order, lashing out with his whip. Peace returned and the plotters rode on.

'Enough sweat and blood are spent.' Hardy grinned at the assembled players as he approached. 'You have earned your pay and my respect.'

'Add to them bruised bones and a limp,' a young man shouted from the back.

'They are part of our trade and compact.'

At their age he had been immersed in operations abroad, fighting for Drake and spying for Walsingham. The novice watchers here might never know war or the dangers he once faced. Perhaps it was a blessing. He thought of Adam, briefly glad that his absent son exchanged peril for waywardness and indolence. At least he would live.

Hardy and his companions maintained their pace, in time reaching the boundary wall of the deer park adjoining St James's Palace, where they dismounted to confer. The scouts would soon report. It was to this royal dwelling that Queen Elizabeth was brought when in 1588 the Armada had sailed and English troops had erected breastworks here to effect a final stand against the threatened invasion. Who could tell if a monarch might once again need such shelter.

'We have found their lair.' A mounted messenger cantered to give his news. 'Percy makes his home at the heart of the Palace of Westminster.'

Naturally he did, reflected Hardy. A traitorous plotter had no finer cover than the role of royal bodyguard and no greater vantage from which to launch an attack than a hollow deep within the ancient edifice. Everything until this moment had been a diversion, the skirmishes and scattered bodies mere play. Hardy now saw where all the threads joined up, where gunpowder and the King and his capital city would meet in grand cataclysm. One glittering event alone symbolised the power of the monarch, and a single detonation could obliterate it. The State Opening of Parliament was the target.

Skittles fell and the delighted laughter of Princess Elizabeth and her ladies eddied from the corridor. On a rain swept day in early May, it provided happy occupation for the royal entourage at Coombe Abbey. Lady Harington herself had briefly graced the occasion, gamely rolling the ball to scatter the pins and earning the applause of her audience. Now it was the turn of the young Lady Anne.

At the far end of the hallway, Adam stood back and smiled in support. 'Maintain your eye on the prize, my lady.'

'My eye will rarely stray.'

'Much depends on it,' he said with mock sternness.

She disguised her blush by stepping forward to release the ball. It rolled across the floorboards and struck the pins, and the princess hugged her friend in excited congratulation. Adam, who had proposed the game, served as referee, engaged in marshalling the players and maintaining good order. Everyone enjoyed his company.

The princess stepped towards him. 'And now you must show your skill.'

Adam bowed, his position secure and patronage reaffirmed, and took his turn. After a few moments, he left them to their pastime, the sounds receding as he climbed a stair and strode along a gallery. In a mirror, he caught a glimpse of the porter Smythe staring after him. It was hard to read the expression in the man's eyes, to gauge if it were a scowl or smirk playing on his lips. His adversary still loitered at the margin and menaced with his silence.

Enmity would have to wait. Adam strode to the stables and saddled his horse. The sky was clearing and the air fresh, and the bored guards at the gate called to him as a familiar face. He appreciated the banter. It meant they trusted him, and that was bound to have its use. None inside this enclave could imagine the scale of the threat gathering beyond. He rode through the parkland and out towards the heath.

'Fancy we should chance upon each other.'

The delivery was dry, the words spoken by a man seated on a dappled grey courser and screened by a thicket of beech. The location could vary, but rendezvous was needed for the regular debriefing.

Adam touched his hat brim in salute. 'Life here is quieter than in London.'

'It will not always be so.' The horseman peered at him. 'You do not lose your edge amid such comforts?'

'I am keen and ready as I ever was.'

'How is our contented brood? The young princess, her hosts and household? Your sweet beloved the Lady Anne?'

'All are happy and none the wiser. I leave them bowling at pins.'

'We placed you there for such a reason.' The man almost smiled. 'Does anyone grow jealous or begin to chafe at your presence?'

'A few young bucks mutter and the porter Smythe throws me direct black glances, but I think that I am safe.'

The man frowned. 'You are not impervious to a blade across your throat or thrust into your back.'

'A risk I shall embrace.'

They listened to the birdsong and the gentle rhythm of the day, alert for any sound of danger. The horseman drank brandy from a flask and proffered it to Adam. 'Did you deliver the horses to John Grant?'

'I did.' The young man took a swig. 'Not a single pursuivant was at my tail.'

'Isaiah Payne is still smarting at the elusiveness of his quarry.'

'It seems we are again to run him ragged.'

'You play too many games. Remember you are out here on your own.'

Adam handed back the flask. He could hardly forget it. The messenger headed back to London as he headed back to the royal pen via a circuitous route. At one end of the track lay Coombe Abbey and a few miles behind him the country seat of Robin Catesby at Ashby St Ledgers. Two worlds and a religious divide, and he precariously bestrode the whole.

Some way into his journey, he became aware that another rider was shadowing his progress.

'Our prodigal is returned.'

The troop captain welcomed his old comrade back to the fold with a warm smile and an embrace. It was comfortingly familiar terrain for Guido Fawkes. About him was the small encampment, the tents and hovels that served as a field base for the English regiment in Flanders. Here on the outskirts of Brussels the exiled and disaffected of Albion could gather, Catholic volunteers committed to waging war for Spain and spreading their faith with violence. For bloody enterprise, there could be few more fertile areas from which to harvest support.

Fawkes surveyed the scene. 'It is a sight to quicken the blood and warm the heart.'

'Yet you desert us.'

'Desert?' The mercenary grimaced at the thought. 'I go where the need is greatest and the calling strong.'

'Your calling is as a soldier.'

'I do not forget, and nor do I abandon my religion or principle.'

'Forgive my doubting, Guido.' The captain laid a fraternal arm across his shoulder.

'There is another battle close, an event that will shake the world and see the downfall of a tyrant.'

'You speak of England.'

'Where else are liberty and truth so denied? Where else is our faith so trampled?'

'King James will rue gaining you as his enemy, Guido.'

They walked through the camp, old campaigners reunited. Fawkes greeted his brothers-in-arms, men he had led through skirmish and assault and inspired with his fervour. He was a quiet man, yet his courage was proven and his men crowded around with reminiscences and expressions of loyalty.

The captain nodded in approval. 'They would still follow you.'

'There is no bond like that between fighting men.'

'Yet you journey here for more than friendship.' The captain paused to regard him. 'Catesby asks that we provide whatever you desire.'

'He is a persistent and forceful man.'

'One who earns regard and is noted for his defiance of the little Scot.'

'And what defiance we plan,' Fawkes said with restrained satisfaction.

The captain laughed. 'Is it priests you demand?'

'I want war horses and muskets and campaign materiel. I want trained and armed men we may rely on.'

'It will take time to raise them, Guido.'

'That time is now.' Fawkes gripped the captain's arm and looked him in the eye. 'God and His saints will bring things to conclusion.'

'Without the support of Spain?'

His fingers tightened. 'We need no Spain to show our devotion, to unleash holy war and pierce the heart of the heathen Protestant.'

'You are right, Guido. All is possible.'

'And will be done.'

It was on these training grounds and through sieges and battles in the Low Countries that Catholic militancy had been forged and many of its soldiers returned hardened and ready to their homeland. The message now delivered by Fawkes would rouse any true believer from apathy or despair. While prospects for success might wither on the continent, there was hope anew in England.

The captain took a powder horn and musket and handed them to Fawkes. 'Show us that you do not shed the skills you learnt among us.'

Fawkes smiled. 'A challenge?'

'Think of it as a reward.' The captain tossed the mercenary a cartridge and stepped back to watch.

Fawkes had lost none of his speed or dexterity. The ball was efficiently rammed home and the powder added to the pan. Fawkes chose his target, the cooking pot at a hundred paces buckling to the impact. Cheers rippled in the camp.

Leaving the men to their tales and merriment, the captain proceeded to his tent. A rotund figure beloved of his men, he was a companionable drinker and rogue and yet the bravest of sorts. His soldiers depended on him. In turn he relied on them, counting on their talk and indiscretion and the letters they received from home. Another canvas shoe would soon be arriving on the desk of the spymaster Robert Cecil.

Throughout the spring of 1605, King James continued to rail against the Catholics and demand their obedience. On his order, fines again increased, and the pressure on recusant families would mount further during the summer months. The season ahead would prove hot and fetid and dangerous.

CHAPTER 13

'We've given you everything.'

Not quite, decided Realm. His victims were bound and naked and tied to chairs, a gemsmith and his wife and maid who did not yet fully comprehend the fate that was upon them. The gemsmith's crime was to be in possession of gold and jewels, to own a business in Cheapside which had come to Realm's attention. Down here in the cellar he could practise his arts without fear of interruption and explore what it truly meant to be a human. However loud their cries, it changed nothing.

Annoyingly, the man continued to plead. 'I beg you, free my wife and maid and we shall speak alone as men.'

'So they may raise the alarm? Run screaming from this place?'

'Your complaint is with me and none else.'

'There is no complaint.' Realm looked gently on the man. 'There is solely life and death and screaming at the gate.'

'What is it you want?'

'So many things. Hidden treasure and a final sigh, the colour of struggle and the warmth of a beating heart in my hand.'

The gemsmith thought he could engage; like any merchant, he believed a bargain might be struck. 'Anything you ask is yours.'

'Your fingers will be first.'

Realm was distracted by a whimper from the maid, a pretty-faced girl with round breasts, her flesh and vulnerability exposed. He went to stroke her and felt her flinch. He could not blame her for the response. Most would find the situation awkward.

'Why do you behave so?' The gemsmith was staring.

'Because it is my calling and my pleasure.'

'You are mad.'

'Yet still I convince others to place their trust in me.'

'Then they are fools.'

'Fools like you that in their torment shall learn of their mistake.' The renegade stepped to an open wooden chest and plucked from it a pendant encrusted with diamonds and rubies. His choice of jewellers had been wise. In this box alone were items of unimaginable value and beauty. A collection worth killing for.

He paused and regarded his audience. 'You think me a common thief? A cheap vagabond who stumbles on this moment?'

The man spoke with renewed hope. 'I think you a man who may have mercy in his heart.'

'Again you are deceived.' Realm returned the pendant to its place. 'These jewels are more than mere adornment and far exceed the value of your life.'

With fear and bile, words tumbled from the wife. 'You are a fiend, a demon, a monster.'

'And you a plain woman and scold that is soon to lose her tongue.'

'She means nothing by it.' The gemsmith attempted to placate their captor.

'Do you know what I intend? Do you know what is planned for this heretic nation and its King?'

'We are not privy to such things.'

'Search and you shall find.' Realm selected some items from the case and began to festoon the maid with precious stones. She had waited long for such largesse and now received a surfeit in the last minutes of her life. Two delicate gold and amethyst butterflies had alighted on her shoulders as her tears began to flow again.

'Let us go,' the gemsmith beseeched.

Realm ignored him. 'In her dying time, is she not rendered a princess? Raised from her common state and garlanded in dreams?'

'We do you no wrong.'

'That is of no interest to me.'

Walking among them, he touched their trembling flesh and bent to smell their animal fear. Such a sour and unmistakeable odour, like hogs sweating before the slaughter. Christian Hardy would never do these things and that was possibly his weakness. The renegade preferred to test himself and detach his thoughts from the consequences. A great comfort.

The maid was praying now, choking on the words. He joined in the recitation. '. . . And forgive us our trespasses as we forgive them who trespass against us . . .'

'Have you a notion of your sins?' Once more it was the wife who showed defiance.

'I have an inkling the Lord will not heed your Protestant mumblings or preserve you.'

'He will forever fight evil.'

Realm's retribution was swift as he tilted back her head and forced a handful of pearls into her gaping mouth. She gagged and swallowed, scattering the precious grains, her screams muffled.

'You offer pearls and now I give them back.' He released his hold and let her retch and weep. 'Perhaps you have no taste for finer things.'

There was little more to be said and much more to be done. They would die with a predictable lack of style and he would resent the blandness of it all. At least men like Hardy provided certain challenge. It was in this frame of mind that he took a knife and cut the maid's throat.

'Now we may talk.' He focused on the two survivors, shutting out the ambient noises. 'You have other jewels hidden in this place.'

'Why should I lie?' The gemsmith was gulping for air.

'Even in despair, a man may show perversity of spirit.'

'You have my word, I swear it.'

'I shall have all of you in a pail when I am done.'

Their misfortune was to have met him and to have wealth, to be both his prisoners and his confessors. They sat at the threshold and he would coax them across. He unfolded a cloth and laid out his tools, hearing the distant screeching and almost feeling pity. So rarely did people give willingly what he demanded. The obsidian blade caught the light and glinted with polished blackness. It would provide the perfect ending to the day.

An hour later, Realm packed his saddlebags and mounted up. It had been cooler in the cellar. His patient horse was glad to be moving from the close air and summer heat of the courtyard and leaving the City. The renegade dwelt briefly on the scene he had left, on the details that might turn the stomachs of lesser men. They had no need to test themselves as he did or become hardened to an existence devoted to subversion. Mopping up in the basement of the gemsmith would take a while.

A boy called out, 'A penny, sir? A ha'penny?'

After his recent good fortune, a lack of generosity would be churlish. He threw an emerald in the dirt and watched the child scrabble for it as though it were a crust of bread. Such a reward could either enrich or lead to murder. Life had many variables.

Close by Turnmill Street in Clerkenwell, he tethered his horse beside a rough-timbered dwelling and entered. Enough locals had been recruited to ensure that his stay was pleasant and surprises were few and that his presence aroused no interest. Prising up a board, he tipped his takings to join the piled artefacts below. Barbarity was simply a means, a habit needing to be fed, a store of screaming faces he glimpsed occasionally from afar. A man scarcely existed without his memories.

Lanterns moved through the undercroft beneath the House of Lords, marking the progress of the search. It had not been difficult to identify the modest dwelling in the nearby precinct rented by Thomas Percy or the storage space he had acquired, and Hardy would ensure that no part went unexplored. He held up his lamp and stared at the ceiling, recalling the tunnels he had once walked below the baiting pit at Paris Garden and the scent of urine and saltpetre that had led eventually here. Beyond his view was a chamber in which one day a King and his nobles would assemble to declare open a session of Parliament. The Globe Theatre had never been the target. It was Parliament House that Robin Catesby and his band of brother Catholics intended to blow to pieces.

'We have found it, Christian.'

He had been sure they would. The intelligencer followed the voice and discovered the burly form of Carter bending to examine a stacked mound of crates and firewood.

His lieutenant glanced up. 'Our gentleman pensioner has no wish to catch a chill this winter.'

'The blaze he seeks would banish any cold. How many casks?'

'Enough to put the fear of God into any living royal.'

'They do the same for me.' Hardy beckoned him away. 'Let it rest undisturbed. We have no plans to trigger the alert.'

'I will sweep back the dust we have disturbed.'

Hardy nodded. 'The longer matters lie dormant, the more heedless and unwary the foe.'

The big man frowned. 'Should we draw back?'

'They desire us lulled and we shall oblige.'

Sounds intruded in the evening stillness, a protesting voice growing louder as a figure in nightclothes was propelled stumbling by an unsmiling Black Jack. The porter resented being woken.

He glared at Hardy. 'What is going on here?'

'You are brought before me.'

'There is a better hour.'

'None that would suit my purpose.'

'Your purpose?' The face darkened further. 'I see no purpose save to vex and trouble me. On whose authority do you trespass?'

'That of Robert Cecil, Earl of Salisbury and Secretary of State.'

The porter had paled in the lamplight. 'I have done no wrong. Take me to his lordship and I will speak on oath.'

'His lordship sleeps and you will speak to me.' Hardy remained impassive. 'There may come a day when audience is granted.'

The threat was implicit and the porter's indignation had long since crumbled to confusion and despair. Surely he must be the victim of foul rumour or mistake. It was hard to mount a defence when the charges were not yet laid.

The intelligencer studied him. 'You bring rogues and villainy among us.'

'Not I, sir.' The porter shook his head. 'I guard this place, and my men patrol armed and ever vigilant.'

'What of your drinking and carousing? Your taking of money and bribes?'

'All is within the law.'

'Yet your spending is not within the level of your pay.'

'Is a fellow to be condemned for the fruits of his service?'

'It depends on how bitter the fruit and how diligent the service.'

'Few have voiced complaint, sir.'

'Praise is as hard to find.' Hardy observed the man's discomfort. 'Tell me of the gentleman who rents this undercroft.'

'Sir Thomas Percy? He is rarely to be seen. Yet he demands more room and his manservant busies himself on his behalf.'

'This manservant has a name?'

'It is John Johnson, sir. I have not seen him of late.'

'Describe him.'

'A listener and a dark and quiet man, restrained in his ways and seldom free with words.'

'You like him?'

'Often he has helped me and is given to acts of kindness.'

'Some say he is a soldier.'

'I thought so, but did not enquire.'

Hardy remembered a ghost from the previous year, a stranger who had watched a fumbled wine cask shatter before vanishing into the shadows. That ghost had acquired flesh and an identity. The mercenary Guido Fawkes had become the manservant John Johnson and the scope of his ambitions was laid bare.

Curiosity stabbed at the porter. 'Has Johnson committed some crime?'

'No less or more than you, should you breathe a word to any of our meeting.'

'Many rely on my discretion.'

'As you depend on your balls and throat.' Hardy fixed him with his lapis eyes. 'Fail in your promise to me and you will endanger the King.'

'King James is my sovereign lord and master.'

'He is vengeful towards those who disobey.'

The warning was unnecessary: obedience was guaranteed. The porter was unlikely to sleep soundly through the rest of the night. His was an existence of idleness and easy pleasure, of maintaining a light watch or turning a blind eye. He had been found wanting; worse, he had been rudely awakened and dragged from his bed and near accused of undermining the realm. All because of his generous spirit and on account of his befriending a loner. Escorted back to his quarters, the porter was grateful to be released from the interview. He would try to forget the unsettling events of this night.

Others too were troubled. As he raised his hands in benediction above the Sacred Host, Father Henry Garnet gave thanks for the gift of faith and yet knew that his prayers for peace might go unanswered. The times were against him. As Superior of the Jesuits he heard things, detected the nervous excitement among Catholics that change was coming and a decisive blow would fall. His was the old way, the path of suffering and the message that love would triumph if only men endured. No one now appeared to listen.

It was 16 June, the Feast of Corpus Christi. There would be no procession or public display, no proud affirmation of the old religion in the cathedrals and churches of England. Instead, in secrecy and fear a few of the committed gathered on this most holy day in a London house to celebrate the Eucharist and pledge their loyalty to Rome. Garnet felt their restlessness; he would try to urge restraint and warn against the folly of armed insurrection. For the sake of their survival, they must be strong.

He held aloft bread transformed into the body of Christ and dispensed it to his flock. They seemed grateful enough. Yet he saw in their faces what he had previously discerned in the countenance of John Grant at the manor of Norbrook: they had grown weary of hiding, impatient with passivity and a persecuted life. His mission was no longer theirs.

'Your eyes carry anger, my son,' he gently chided a young man after the service. 'Our Lord taught that we should embrace piety and forgiveness.'

Defiance flickered across the man's face. 'I embrace what best serves our cause, Father.'

'Your cause is to preserve the faith.'

'Is this preserving it, Father? Is this letting the Word of God shine forth?' There was a sardonic undertone to the voice as he looked around the cramped, hot room.

'Violence begets violence and rashness earns destruction.'

'Submission does the same.'

'Nowhere did Jesus preach the overthrow of Caesar.'

'Yet he attacked the temple and threw out those that did not belong.'

'Be wise, Everard. You have a devoted wife and family and everything to lose.'

'What I stand to lose through inaction is my dignity and soul.'

Another young gentleman chimed in. 'At the height of the Great Siege of Malta, did the Knights of St John not celebrate as we the Feast of Corpus Christi, Father?'

'Their faith never wavered.'

'Nor their devotion to arms in defeating the heathen Turk.'

The Jesuit had to concede that the man was right. Religion had sustained the knights in the heat of battle and delivered to them a victory. But their swords and pikes and wildfire had been as important as any prayer. It served to know history, to remember that the father of the feared intelligencer Christian Hardy had once fought on the shattered ramparts alongside those knights. Almost half a century on and the echoes still reverberated.

Garnet turned to a man standing silently to one side. 'What about you, Francis?'

Sir Francis Tresham smiled quickly. 'I am not one for fire and argument.'

Garnet pressed him. 'Your belief is strong enough to bring you here.'

'Nothing would keep me from a thing so precious.'

'Then I am glad you have in your blood some of the passion of your father.'

Tresham acknowledged this with the slightest of nods, perhaps embarrassed by the comparison. Contrast would be a better term, mused Garnet, for the son was not half the man his saintly parent was. The priest neither liked nor trusted this reprobate offspring, and disliked the look of calculation in his eye. Whoever depended on him would find him an unreliable ally.

He regarded Tresham with a searching gaze. 'What is your true conviction?'

The man dropped his eyes uneasily. 'To survive.'

'Or to profit?'

'Hard times demand a harder head.'

'Not courage and selflessness? Not a devotion to serving God?'

'We each have our path, Father.'

'As Catholics, ours is already chosen,' Garnet said sternly. 'It is to nurture and bear witness, to safeguard the peace and protect our fellow man.'

'Not all of us are Jesuit.'

'But we each owe allegiance to Rome and must submit to its authority.'

'Conscience too has its voice.'

'Be careful how you heed it.'

Unlike his cousin Catesby, Francis Tresham spoke without real emotion. It was as though he played a game, was toying with matters for which he had no real concern. Conscience was merely a word. Garnet was unsure which one he feared the most, the charismatic zealot or the amoral chancer. He reminded himself to write again to the new pope, Paul V, urging him to issue a proclamation condemning any Catholic who sought to overthrow the English throne. If King James were as concerned as he, the royal court would at present be in a state of pandemonium.

More barrels had been found. At the Lambeth residence of Robin Catesby, an agent had gained access to the back yard and returned over walls and gardens to make his report. The caretaker Robert Keyes was absent on business, and his journey home would be plagued by obstruction and incident, by a brawl and a toppled cart and by companions who encouraged drinking. There was time aplenty to investigate further.

Hardy queried the agent. 'I suppose no knot garden existed there.'

'Sixteen casks, Christian.' The man crouched beside him. 'Hogsheads and firkins and a flat stone with scorched black marks.'

'I wager powder and not red malmsey has caused them.'

The agent shook his head. 'London has never seen the like.'

'So let us tread with care.'

The quantity of gunpowder alone signalled the plotters' ambition. They were leaving little to chance. Combined with the cache in the Westminster basement, there would be thirty-six barrels, sufficient explosives to vaporise all life within several hundred yards of the blast. Divine right would not save the King. In a blinding instant the reign of James would be ended and the ruling structures of England with it. Through the smoke would ride the murderers cast as liberators, the likes of Catesby and Thomas Percy and their hireling Guido Fawkes. They did not intend to be merciful. Those who survived the initial explosion would be butchered where they lay; those who attempted to flee or hide would be captured for the slaughter. Catholics were plainly in a vengeful mood.

Hardy gestured to his men, and the team moved forward to retrace the path of the reconnaissance. They were disciplined and well rehearsed and carried on their backs scaling ladders and packs. Years spent fighting enemy agents at close quarters in the alleyways of Madrid, Lisbon and Paris had honed their proficiency.

They swiftly reached the yard and uncovered the barrels within the shelter. They moved cautiously. Keyes was no fool and might have left marks to detect intrusion or tampering. The veteran servants of the secret state would not be caught out by a Catholic quartermaster.

'We begin.' Hardy took a soft mallet and tapped free the peg of a hogshead. 'Do not forget: not a grain of powder may be missed.'

'What I do not forget is that my body may end up blown to pieces.' A lieutenant held wide the mouth of a sack. 'Nor do I forget the times you have endangered us one and all.'

'Would you have it any other way?'

The man grinned. 'I would cut off my balls were it different.'

Painstakingly the quantities of gunpowder were removed, replaced with the adulterated mix of charcoal and degraded saltpetre. Should a slow match be put to a sample, the test would indicate a failed batch. It would sow confusion among the conspirators, might serve to delay and disrupt their plans. Such sabotage created options for Hardy to pursue.

'The switch has been made.' Hardy stood and surveyed the result. 'And we leave no trace of our presence.'

Within minutes, the intelligence team had dispersed. The red-haired custodian Keyes would have no notion of what had taken place.

Hardy remained close to the scene, a traveller resting on a mounting block to eat his humble fare of bread and cheese. He chewed and watched without a nod or word, letting the boy approach until he sat beside him on the stone.

The child feigned distraction, swinging his legs and looking the other way. 'You are not here to eat, uncle.'

'Nor you, it seems.'

'I know that you are watching.'

'Then we are both of us guilty.' The intelligencer took another bite. 'For some time and from different places you have been observing me.'

'You spied me?' There was admiration in the voice.

'It was not difficult.' Hardy broke off a piece and offered it to the boy. 'I thought you would come near.'

Fingers snatched the morsel. 'Your eyes do not stray, uncle. They are set on the home of the tall fire-haired man.'

'What of it?'

'It will take more than bread to open my memory.'

Hardy flipped him a coin. 'Spill its contents or be gone.'

'He keeps his own company and is not ready with a smile. On occasion he threatens to beat me.'

'I would scarcely blame him.'

'Visitors call, making delivery or removing casks. Perhaps he is the servant of a vintner.'

'Maybe.' Hardy swung his gaze to the boy. 'A further penny is yours if you recall who brought the barrels.'

'A short man in a jerkin, dressed like a carter. Yet his horses were well fed and groomed and his voice and air were lordly.'

Sir Ambrose Rookwood, wealthy horse-breeder and Catholic gentleman, had strayed far from his Suffolk estate. It took a madman in a stable and a perceptive street boy in Lambeth to see through his disguise. Key plotters had been identified and the route of their black powder traced, their target laid bare as the Palace of Westminster and the King and his ruling elite. What had started as random incidents and names to sift and ponder had flowered to full conspiracy. The circle was complete.

The day was closing and the air heavy as Hardy took a wherry back across the river. There were deceptions to arrange and violent traitors to lull and a long summer and autumn to survive. Realm would hardly be holding fire. Yet Robert Cecil remained insistent. No harvest would occur until the rotten fruit had fallen.

'It's beautiful!' Beatrice gasped as he placed the diamond and ruby pendant about her throat, dazzled by his generosity and the lustre of the stones.

Realm was glad of her appreciation and growing fondness. That he had acquired the jewels through an act of boundless cruelty was incidental. Most precious objects had darkness woven into their history. He took a gem-studded brooch and leant to pin it to her gown.

'A butterfly?' She stared delighted in the mirror. 'What have I done to deserve such gifts?'

'For being as you are.'

'What I am is a widow, a commoner unused to such extravagance and display.'

'Is a man to be prevented from giving tokens of his regard?'

'You flatter and honour me, Will.' She glanced up at him. 'But it is too much.'

'Should I not be the judge?'

Her fingers caressed the pendant. 'A queen or princess would count her blessings to own objects of this value.'

'Rarity is deserving of rarity, Bea.'

'Yet how do you chance upon a trove so rich? How do you amass jewels beyond the means even of a potentate?'

'I could lie and talk of sea voyages and adventure.'

'Now you tease.'

He held and kissed her hand. 'With fondness and gentleness and respect for your concern.'

'Still you do not answer.'

'For the truth is too dull.' He kissed her hand again. 'Some jewels I trade and others belonged to my late wife.'

'It is scarce my place to wear them.'

'There is none more worthy, Bea.'

With a bow, he left her to her thoughts and the jewels. The latter would inevitably persuade. She was too trusting and kind, too lacking in judgement, too easily convinced. As a suitor who had become in recent weeks her lover, he had quickly grown to dominate her affections. Secrecy suited them both. Not in a thousand lifetimes would she perceive his purpose or glimpse his true identity behind his warm smile. A thousand lifetimes were unavailable. Realm stood in the garden and waited.

'You are a loving and generous man, Will Birch.' She came to him as he expected.

'I am guilty of love and little else.'

'Non one has ever bestowed on me such gifts.'

'Then put aside reluctance and embrace them.' He took her arms. 'One might suppose I had committed murder, you hesitate so.'

She laughed. 'My gentle Will do harm?'

'Deride me if you must. I know I am no match for other suitors.'

'It is because you are unspotted with blood that I welcome you to my side.'

Merchant and widow walked together, pausing to smell a flower or to watch the bees working on the mallow. Their pace was unhurried. Her doubts were assuaged by his charm and attentiveness and her usual common sense subverted by his obvious wealth. He wondered how her cries would sound.

'You have spoken of Christian Hardy. Tell me more about your fighting man,' he suggested as they stood beside the stream.

'A lone ghost that walks abroad.'

'You are fond of him?'

'Of the parts I know.' She leant her head on his shoulder. 'But his life and duties engage him in ways I never shall.'

'He is a fool to forfeit you.'

'Or he is just a soldier and servant of the Crown.'

'His loss is my advantage, Bea.'

They kissed with feeling, expressing with a touch what they could not say in words. Realm kept his gaze on the woods. Somewhere in the shadows, his men were maintaining watch in case the enemy showed. Hardy might be engaged in chasing down conspiracy, but he had often proved himself a master of surprise. A musket ball would cut short an unseemly interruption.

Gentlemen and their ladies rode out on Hampstead Heath, while in their London homes the tapestries were furled and silver packed in readiness for the summer exodus. Like King James himself, many would busy themselves with diversions in the countryside.

CHAPTER 14

Again he noticed the horseman trailing him. It had become routine, the presence sometimes betrayed by no more than the thud of a hoof or the skyward flurry of birds. Perhaps it was intended to unsettle or warn or to map the pattern of his journeys. Whatever the motive and however he responded, a rider always appeared. They were good at what they did.

Adam would continue his business and attempt to draw the threat close. If caught or questioned he had a ready answer; a player and musician had reason to wander with a mandolin strapped to his back. He enjoyed too the friendship and protection of the young Princess Elizabeth. Explaining the extra horses he often led might demand different skills.

The rider had stayed with him, within sight today, his face unknown to Adam. A persistent fellow. Adam had negotiated villages and moorland, dodging between flocks of sheep and convoys of wagons, and still the man followed. There was no attempt to hide. Danger sat like prickle heat at Adam's back as he encouraged the gelding to a canter, wheeling his horse round to face his pursuer.

'You press too close.' He held his sword at full extension, his arm steady and his gaze level. His adversary reined to a halt. Adam had decided to bring matters to a head. It would not do to let the issue drift, to be hounded to submission or mistake. Better to confront the devil than to run.

The devil was unperturbed. 'Will a minstrel slay me in cold blood?'

'If you have dispute with me, state it now.'

'I do not know why you should be aggrieved.'

'Yet you follow and observe and sit menacing on my tail.'

'A man is free to journey as he pleases.'

Adam's sword tip remained poised near the man's eye. 'It does not please me. You are at liberty to offer explanation.'

'Very well.' With unhurried ease, the stranger reached for a whistle on a lanyard at his throat and blew a single long note. Other men and horses emerged into the clearing. Adam stared. They had planned it well, could bring down his steed within twenty paces with a volley from their hunting bows and muskets. And he had thought himself the trapper.

'Lower and surrender your blade.' The scout held out his gauntleted hand.

Adam regarded the armed, encircling enemy. At least they had not killed him yet. A temporary surrender would give him time to ponder the uncertainties of his trade. Whoever arranged his capture had predicted well the course of his travel and character of his response.

They bound his wrists and led him on his own horse, retracing familiar paths, their progress conducted in silence. Possibly they sought a more isolated site in which to mete out their justice. It boded ill that they had not covered his eyes.

'Reacquaintance is sweet.'

In the forest clearing stood the giant porter of Coombe Abbey, apparently delighted with the events he had initiated. Leaning on a quarterstaff, a wide-brimmed hat shading his brow, he contemplated his prisoner with brute appreciation. 'You thought me ponderous and dull-witted, a beast too slow to catch you.'

Wincing, Adam was hauled from the saddle to stand before him. 'An error I confess to.'

'What more will you confess?' The staff whipped around to strike the young actor in the abdomen. 'Why, you do not kneel.'

'To a menial?'

It earned a second blow and Adam dropped gasping to the ground. He struggled upright and was felled again, a foot planted on his head to push his face into the earth.

He spat out a mouthful of dirt as they hoisted him to his knees. 'I have had worst fare in taverns hereabouts.'

'Now is the time to taste humility.' Smythe crouched down to study him. 'Your handsome ways will count for naught when your corpse is gnawed by rats.'

'I am at a loss to know my crime.'

'Nevertheless, it shall cost you dear.' The porter grinned at the thought. 'There are those you slight by your very presence, young gallants whose position and honour are challenged by an upstart in their midst.'

'It is my banishment they seek?'

'With regret, it is your death.'

Smythe stood, the tip of his staff grinding deep into the forest litter. It would take an age for anyone to find the remains of his victim in so secluded a place. Adam lay still. The men around him had no need to mask their faces, for he would not live to identify them. Their grim intent seemed to suck the light from the woods.

The porter went on, 'You have become the problem and I am appointed to deal with it.'

'A man should have a chance to defend himself.'

'You, a man?' Smythe laughed. 'You are a stripling, a beardless youth, a rutting dog brought low.'

'What then will be your epitaph?'

The porter's eyes narrowed in animosity. 'Perhaps little, save that I was more worldly and sure-footed than you.'

A motion of his hand and Adam was lifted and forced to walk deeper into the shadows. There had once been a dwelling here, but the foundations were now crumbled, and the ragged mouth of a disused well lay treacherous and overgrown.

Smythe took the confiscated mandolin and let it drop into the void, the instrument jarring in its plunge. 'Let us hope you make a sweeter sound.'

Adam strained against his bindings. 'There will be justice, Smythe.'

'Not for you. You are a wanderer, a performer who grows restless and takes to the road looking for excitement elsewhere.'

'I have friends.'

'The Lady Anne?' The porter shrugged. 'She will assume she is betrayed and her callow lover strays abroad seeking new conquests.'

'They will search for me.'

'None will even miss you.'

Adam was edged closer to the brink and a halter and length of rope tied beneath his arms. His captors intended his death to be agonised and lingering, his suffering compounded by the squalor and darkness. The immediate gratification of a hanging was being sacrificed.

Smythe whispered in Adam's ear as he cut free his hands, 'We would not wish you to succumb too quick.'

'Heaven forbid I should disappoint,' Adam said through lips numb with terror.

'At least you may play your mandolin.'

A boot kicked him over the rim.

The stench of decay and dead things surrounded him and crawled into his senses. Far above was the glimmer of the world he had departed and down here his tomb. He wallowed chest-deep in a chill and stagnant pool, balancing precariously on rotten timbers and sharing the space with the decomposing carcasses of bats and birds. In time he would weaken and slip, give up the fight and submit to the inevitable. Yet while he had breath and will he would persevere.

Escape was beyond his reach and contemplation. He had already felt the walls, pressing his fingers into the shallow cavities, scraping with blind concentration to create a handhold or ledge. Futile endeavour could either buoy the spirits or accelerate despair. His situation allowed him to reflect on his mistakes, on the stages of the journey that had led him to this, and on his underestimation of the porter Smythe. The man had not forgiven him their initial altercation. Now none would remember Adam Hardy. Should he be informed of Adam's disappearance, his father would doubtless scarcely shed a tear, would swallow his disappointment and regret. The boy had been wild and destined for misfortune.

He called out, listening to the words die before they made it to the surface. About him was the wet coiled weight of the severed rope. The taunts and curses of the men who had left him here were the last human sounds he would hear. One day strangers might chance upon his mouldering bones and wonder at their find. Hours passed.

'*Adam . . .*'

An angel watched over him, the shout distorting to a whisper and a rope ladder tumbling within his reach. He grabbed and clung, kicking free of his mire and hauling himself upward, labouring fast in his ascent. There was no telling if Smythe played a trick and tortured him with false hope of a reprieve. Whatever he faced, the prospect of daylight and fresh air outweighed any possible hazard.

'Robin?' He squinted disbelievingly at the face peering over the rim. 'You have come to my rescue?'

'I have not ridden here to throw you back. My scouts are everywhere.'

His saviour's hands pulled him from the opening, supported him as he retched with exhaustion and relief. Thomas Bates was there too, the manservant acting as sentry and tending the horses.

Adam shook his head. 'Am I the ghost or is it you?'

'Neither of us is yet buried.' Catesby held his shoulders to survey him. 'Though the rankness of your clothes suggests you perished long ago.'

'Some I meet of late have not been so discerning.'

'You are in gentler company now.'

'That I know.' The young man embraced his smiling saviour. 'My thanks can barely convey my gratitude.'

'No gratitude is needed, Adam. Catholics suffer and we help each other as we may.'

'Once you pulled me from a prison and today you have drawn me from a well.'

'It is a pattern we must seek to break.' With a smile, the older man patted his cheek before walking to the horses. 'You are too precious to lose to foul design or accident.'

'So you have often said.'

'You doubt me?' Catesby glanced back across his shoulder.

'I crawl from a London dungeon a common Swaggerer and from here a ragged and stinking beggar.'

'A Swaggerer who saves priests, a beggar who delivers horses and warns of danger and is a friend to every recusant.'

'What next is my duty?' Adam asked.

Catesby turned, both humour and hardness in his eye. 'I see no better course than to return to Coombe Abbey and the side of your Lady Anne.'

Adam looked at him surprised. 'Will this tomb not beckon me once more? Will Smythe and his men not make good their threat?'

'They will know they are observed; they will wonder at the force opposing them and conspiring to set you free.'

'They may be spurred to act more decisively.'

'Or will tread with caution.' Catesby could persuade the most obdurate of people. His confidence and strength of character inspired and would overcome objection. It was a power he used with calculation and effect.

Adam stared down at his soaked apparel. 'Your humble servant is reborn.' He paused. 'You have my gratitude, of course, Robin. But I face peril and death for you without condition or complaint; much is demanded of me but nothing explained.'

'For your safety I hold back the full truth.'

'Men still seek to murder me.'

The ringleader paused. Security was paramount, the competing elements of violent overthrow hard to balance when expectation and speculation gathered by the day. At this stage, a minor lapse could bring catastrophe.

Adam nodded as though he understood. 'You regard me as a boy, a groom, a mere servant and no equal.'

'One for whom I show concern and to whom I threw a ladder.'

'So that I may better run to your call.' The young man was not ready to mount up. 'Even at the edge of my grave I kept my silence, Robin.'

Everything was a risk. The young accomplice had won his spurs and the right to be informed why he had penetrated Coombe Abbey. Catesby was decided.

'We plan to snatch and crown as Queen of England the Princess Elizabeth.'

'There is toil for you, Negro.'

Robert Keyes stowed the oars and jumped ashore. Tethering the boat at the foot of the stairs, he called again to the man. Perhaps the creature did not hear or comprehend, or perhaps he merely possessed the sullen insolence of his kind. Sixteen barrels of gunpowder waited to be offloaded and the quartermaster had little patience and no time for pleasantries. It was the early morning of 20 July, and the final consignment of explosives had crossed the river to Westminster. Haste had overcome caution.

'Assist me and you earn a penny.' Keyes prodded the African with his boot and gestured to the craft. 'Refuse and you will receive a beating.'

There was the semblance of a reply as the large Negro stirred and clambered upright. His loss to the Spanish plantations was the gain of English Catholics, decided Keyes with wry amusement. The beast might have scant vocabulary or thought, but he had the brawn and sinew of three men.

Another voice intruded in the dawn. 'You win for yourself a slave.' From the half-light emerged Fawkes, the custodian come to take delivery.

Keyes regarded him. 'I feel ill at ease on this side of the Thames.'

'Then let us make it quick.' The quartermaster nodded to the longboat. 'I bring what you require.'

'Trust I shall use it well.'

They commanded the African to assist, directing him to land the kegs and transfer them to a handcart. Whoever was his master was the fortunate beneficiary of his docility and brute strength. Once the shipment was unloaded, the mute servant was dismissed with his penny.

In the undercroft beneath the House of Lords, Keyes marvelled at the tiered wall of casks. Curiosity had drawn him in and enthusiasm overcome his initial reluctance to stay. Together with Fawkes he had achieved this, had guarded and ferried and created a high altar to transformation. The magnitude of the project could awe a man to silence.

Fawkes too considered their creation. 'As God took seven days to forge the world, I in His name shall take a second to change it.' The mercenary began to reconstruct the screen of firewood and sacks of coal. 'It seems the home of Sir Thomas Percy will be supplied well this winter.'

'His loyal steward John Johnson is the most diligent of men.'

Fawkes inclined his head at the use of his cover name. There was truth in what his comrade said. He had excavated and maintained watch and kept his nerve through months of waiting, had journeyed far to gather others to the fight. No one else had put themselves so close to the source of danger.

The quartermaster bent to assist, the two men labouring together to erect the facade. Catesby and his companions relied on this pair's steadfastness and efficiency, and they would not disappoint. Soon it grew light outside and Keyes was obliged to draw his rare visit to a close. 'Game is set, Guido.'

'All that is required is that I should play and put the match.' Fawkes tugged a final prop into position. 'Be on your way, brother. At some later date we shall meet.'

'I will not hazard in which world.'

They parted company and Keyes returned to his emptied boat, another man about his business in the waking moments of the day. The Negro had gone. Casting off and manning the oars, the quartermaster headed back to Lambeth. He didn't spare the African another thought.

Black Jack was indeed engaged in other duties, moving through the passageways of Westminster until he reached a heavy and weathered door. Its key was already in his possession. He entered the building and climbed the stairs. Christian Hardy was waiting to hear his news.

So the enemy had finally stepped closer to their goal. It was to be applauded in a way, an act of madness or brilliance that took courage to pursue. Either Catesby and his coterie were fools or King James was the drooling idiot for creating them. This abandoned dwelling was as fine a place as any from which to observe the coming show.

Within the hour, Hardy also made a journey. Anonymous on a wherry, he was carried a short distance downriver to a landing stage at Whitehall and was granted entry through its water gate. The guards were briefed and would offer no challenge. These summer months were for idling, for watching the river traffic, counting the days and growing bored with the absence of the King. When monarchs toured their realm, their vacated palaces languished.

The cellar was like no other, a cavernous affair immense and pillared and fit to host a vast banquet. Yet neither courtiers nor public descended here and it sat far from the view of prying eyes. For that reason it well suited the spymaster Robert Cecil.

'My intelligencer sends word and I reply.'

'You desired to be informed.'

The little hunchback's manner was as cold as his surroundings. 'Is our city not full of poison and contagion in this summer heat?'

'His Majesty is wise to keep his distance.'

'A course I scarcely discourage. It provides us a chance to follow the stream and peruse its waters, to determine where to cast the line.'

'There will be a rich haul, my lord.'

'I count it only when it lies dead and gutted.' Cecil stared towards a rack of wine barrels. 'Tell me of the casks.'

'Keyes brought them across the river and he and Fawkes stowed them beneath Parliament House.'

'They must be pleased with their endeavour.'

'Catesby and Percy also.'

'How great will be their later surprise.' If he savoured the prospect, the minister did not share it with the likes of Hardy.

The intelligencer glimpsed the power behind the surface stare, the deeper secrets Cecil concealed. There would be events running parallel to those underway in Westminster and the spymaster was not telling.

'We have found their black powder and know it is merely the tip of their spear.' Hardy was probing. 'We also know they were seeking foot soldiers to fuel their battle in the streets.'

'Your own battle is that which I assign.'

'What if Catesby and his captains should choose another, my lord? What if there is a wider uprising to contest?'

Cecil's face was blank. 'Deal with what you see and not with what you suppose.'

'A plot to kill the King and therefore to replace him.'

The Secretary of State was forced to whip in his hound. 'Do not press me or push your fortune.'

'Ashby St Ledgers is the key.'

At once Hardy detected the truth and the brief pulse of anger that it sparked in Cecil. He had gained an insight and it irked the hunchback in his lace collar and dark finery. So that was it, a planned insurrection in the Midlands with Robin Catesby at its head. The Princess Elizabeth at Coombe Abbey was to be either a victim or a pawn.

Cecil came slowly towards him, his words and footsteps careful. 'Pry only where I ordain it and keep within your bounds.'

'Intelligence is my trade.'

'Be then wise and intelligent in your manner. There is enough work for you here.'

'With the powder laid? With Realm hidden in some burrow?'

A sliver of black obsidian appeared between the fingers of the spy chief. 'This fragment suggests a different tale.'

'Where was it found?'

'At a place of slaughter, the home of a Cheapside gemsmith and his wife.' Cecil let the piece drop and shatter on the flagstones. 'He acquires wealth and leaves a multitude of corpses in his wake. The renegade is not finished in his purpose and nor are you.'

Realm accumulated wealth and corpses, Hardy reflected. Much the same could be said of the Secretary of State. The intelligencer was certain that when events had played out and Cecil stood triumphant, more grandees would have vanished from their noble mansions on the Strand.

Some thirty horsemen charged across the field, their swords outstretched, giving voice to their aggression. The hessian sacks filled with earth and straw stood no chance against them. One day the enemy would be flesh and bone, the county militias or the defenders of Coombe Abbey. It was important to train for any eventuality.

'We cut them well.' Catesby wheeled his mount and shouted his encouragement. 'You will make a fine troop of cavalry yet.'

A recruit expertly disembowelled his target. 'Would that they were the bellies of true foes.'

'Such a day will come, you have my word.'

Another hacked at his imagined adversary. 'Why, my prey is as bloodless as any Protestant, Robin.'

'A Protestant may bring all manner of force against us.'

'Yet we endure,' the man said proudly.

'Never lower your guard and you will live the longer.'

Tom Wintour and Jack Wright cantered along the line, elated by the action. The assembled men had no inkling they were the kernel of a larger force forming to kidnap a princess, spread rebellion and change the course of history. A glorious summer day of exuberance and comradeship would go unsullied by the detail.

Wright sheathed his sword. 'We should not tarry, Robin.'

'Thus counsels my strong and watchful shadow.' Catesby looked about him. 'Are we not gentlemen riding out for sport?'

'We are also Catholics armed and mounted in a shire with many spies.'

His commander nodded. 'Very well, Jack. Our sport is done and we disperse. You and Tom each take your men and I shall lead the rest.'

Orders were relayed and the group divided and set out homeward along the skein of country tracks. There was little to draw the eye or alert the sheriff, for even recusants were permitted to take the air.

'In a drumroll of hooves, Adam steered his horse into view and galloped towards the riders. He had been patrolling the area as a roving scout, and now brought word. The enemy was about.

'Two miles hence, Robin.' The young man panted his report. 'Pursuivants lie in wait. Payne is at their head and they number fifteen strong.'

'A paltry few against those with faith and fire.'

'He will not be deterred.'

'As I shall not be threatened.' Catesby waved his hand. 'I bid you go, Adam. Your face is too well known.'

Catesby and his men continued on their way, as careless as if they were returning from a day of sports. Adam's warning had been timely. Ahead, figures on horseback emerged into their path in an ambush intended to seem nothing of the kind. Leading them was Isaiah Payne, his body hunched and crow-like in the saddle.

He raised his hand as Catesby approached. 'What brings you here?'

'We are hunting.' Catesby motioned to the hawks carried by a few of his companions. 'It is no crime to enjoy sport and pastime in the field.'

The chief pursuivant let his gaze flicker among the group of men. 'I know who you are, Sir Robin.'

'Your notoriety is the greater, Payne.' The line drew laughter from the Catholics.

'Loyalty would better serve you.'

'Is that so?' Catesby straightened, his strong, upright figure towering over the wizened Payne. 'We are gentlemen and you are scavengers and lice.'

'Yet we are not Catholic.'

The two groups faced each other, the sharp end of a confrontation involving faith and the future of the nation. Both sides had belief and could muster more adherents. Much was at stake and the outcome was yet to be decided.

Payne offered a twisted smile. 'It appears we are outflanked by men with cavalry swords. But any retreat is temporary.'

His reconnaissance complete and identification made, Payne pulled his men back and let the enemy pass. There was no harm in stamping his authority and reinforcing the threat. Catesby trotted on, staring ahead.

'I know what it is that you do.'

Despair gleamed in the eye of the chief Jesuit. On his arrival home, Catesby had seen the sign that marked the presence of a secret visitor. He had climbed the gatehouse stair to find Father Henry Garnet awaiting his return in the upper chamber. The Jesuit's demeanour told him that the interview would not be comfortable.

'Is this where it began?' Garnet swept his arm around the room. 'Is this where madness started and you met to chart disaster?'

'What I told Father Oswald is bound by the seal of the confession.'

'You spoke more outside it.'

'Then I should learn the importance of discretion.'

'Absorb instead the meaning of catastrophe and the horrors you will wreak.'

'I see no other course.'

'For you do not think.'

'Where have your gentle musings led us? Has your prayer and pilgrimage spared us from destruction?'

'God will condemn you.'

'We are already damned.' Catesby stared hard at his friend. 'Now it is the turn of the chosen.'

'Rather it is the act of the lunatic and bewitched. You will kill Catholic lords, bring reprisal, obliterate the very faith you claim to serve.'

'While you and the Apostles sleep, my labour is not done.'

'More is the pity of it.'

Distance had grown between them, a realisation that compromise was finished and the ways of the past defeated. Matters were too far advanced. Garnet preached of a light in the darkness while a landowning zealot planned instead for explosion. Thirty-six barrels of gunpowder represented an insurmountable divide.

The Superior of the Jesuits strode forward to grip Catesby's arms. 'You believe you will be praised and thanked? Raised up and held in great esteem?'

'It matters not how I am regarded.'

'Men will curse your name for the woe to come.'

Catesby shook himself free. 'His Holiness in Rome has yet to denounce or discourage us.'

'He does not bless you either.'

'Our paths are different, but our goal is the same.' The ringleader spoke with defiant finality.

'Perhaps we are destined to unite only on the scaffold.'

Prophecy or surrender, Father Garnet could say no more. He would go on his way and continue his mission until the moment of the blast and the grimness of its consequence. Prayer was all he had.

In late July, the date for the State Opening of Parliament was finally set by royal proclamation for Tuesday, 5 November.

CHAPTER 15

There was an unease in her, thought Hardy. Where once his Beatrice had been welcoming, had cradled him with her laughter and concern, there was a strange formality. He blamed it on his many weeks of absence and the distractions of his work and trusted that matters would resolve. August was proving a trying month.

They meandered on foot back across the heath, making for her house at Templewood. From the high ground they had gazed down on the distant London vista and Hardy had thought of the barrels lodged beneath the House of Lords. Order ever hid chaos and events always trespassed on normality. Even now he was watchful, attuned to the possibility of attack.

Beatrice concentrated on the dirt track. 'Still you are drawn more to danger than to me, Christian.'

'I cannot burden you with private peril.'

'Nor bless me with your presence or share a fraction of my life.'

'Is this not a precious fragment?' He drew her closer to his side.

'I do not jest.'

'Yet you never before gave voice to such a complaint.'

'Only now do I learn to speak it.'

At least she showed emotion; that was easier to work with. She wouldn't feel aggrieved if she did not care. He would use this time to explain, to coax her back into acceptance of his ways. Habit could be comforting.

He swung around to face her. 'All the fault is mine. Forgive me, my lady, for my blunders.'

'With what ease you seek to persuade.' She was pushed almost to a smile. 'Yet I demand change, not apology.'

'Am I to make a promise I cannot keep?'

She sighed and proceeded on, at once exasperated and defeated by his teasing sincerity. No other man had his eyes or touch or latent ferocity. There was much to admire and more that troubled her.

'Tell me then, Christian. Where do you spend these months past?'

Walking at her side, he looked away. 'On the business of the King.'

'Would he die without you?'

'My task is humble.'

'Yet it takes you from me and returns you a stranger and a riddle.'

'You alone have powers to decipher me.'

'I yearn for a simpler code.'

This beautiful widow with her gentle ways had changed in the past months, become assertive. She stumbled on a stone and he caught her, glad for the excuse. As she tripped, a large diamond and ruby pendant on a gold chain swung clear of her bodice. She snatched for it and hid it quickly back inside her clothing.

Hardy was employed to be observant. 'Such a keepsake is no gift of mine, Bea.'

She flushed. 'A lady may wear what she pleases.'

'And then bridle at enquiry?' He viewed her with a smile. 'My intent was not to offend.'

'Then you are forgiven, Christian.' Still she didn't meet his eye.

'I admire fine things.'

He saw the flash of guilt before she looked down, and rebuked himself. Inquisition was unfair. His own dealings were scarcely beyond reproach. Beatrice was not his possession.

A group of horsemen appeared suddenly on the track ahead, and Hardy moved instinctively to block their approach. Ambush could happen anywhere. Beatrice recalled him to his senses, pulling him back with a touch and a word.

He let the riders pass unchallenged. 'Better vigilance than neglect, Bea.'

'Vigilance against what? Every shadow or horse? Is each old maid an assassin or schoolboy a spy?'

'Danger persists.'

'In your fevered head alone.' She gestured at the landscape. 'Or does a Catholic lurk behind that bush or tree? A regiment of Jesuits march across the hill?'

The forces that divided them were tugging again. Few citizens understood affairs of state; they faced challenge enough in their daily lives from plague and other dangers. Whatever the nature of the threat against His Majesty, other priorities abounded. Hardy did not expect his love to understand.

As they approached the house again, Carter and Swiftsure came into view on their horses. They greeted their return with a muted salute. From the lady's frown, they guessed their arrival had not improved the position of their master. Hardy motioned that they should wait and disappeared inside.

He later joined them alone and climbed into his saddle. 'You do my cause no good.'

'It seems you dig your grave deep enough.' Carter swatted away a fly with his outsized hand. 'She has a rare beauty, your mistress. Is not hope your watchword?'

'With you at my side it is more commonly despair.'

The former sailor laughed and touched the double-barrelled pistol in its sling across his chest. 'Your gratitude is poor.'

'As my memory is long.' Hardy picked up the pace. 'Where are we bound?'

'For the roving court of the King. Cecil bids us join the royal progress and guard the drooling Scot.'

Hardy frowned. 'His lordship wants us out of town.'

'I shall not complain.'

'Then you have yet to encounter James and his effete band of grotesques.'

'It is said he stinks.'

'He is as malodorous as he is small. But do not misjudge, for he is canny and quick.'

'You would lay down your life for him, Christian?'

'I would choose to lay down yours.'

The three men laughed. They were soldiers and cynics, fighting men who had shown their mettle and proved a match for any. The state was wise to rely on them. Yet if their duty was to the Secretary of State and the King, their loyalty was to each other.

Swiftsure was less enamoured with the mission and hunched stick-like on his mount. 'If King James rules by divine right, should not the angels protect him?'

'We are those angels,' said Hardy.

'Nothing heaven-sent is so ugly as Carter.'

'Or as expert with a pistol.' Hardy reached for a water bottle and tipped it to his lips. 'Yet Cecil commands and we obey. Where lies the King?'

'He heads for Oxford and brings with him Queen Anne and their son Prince Henry,' replied Carter.

Hardy was silent for a while. There was always the possibility that the gunpowder beneath the House of Lords was merely a diversion and the real plot lay elsewhere. Away from London, a rebel troop of horsemen could attack or a lone marksman take aim. History and experience taught that the desperate were also the bold.

'Once more we embark on the road.' Hardy glanced at his companions.

Carter grunted. 'I pray there will be strong women and double ale and violence.'

'In whatever order, you will find them. Though I am loath to leave London when Realm is about.'

'Like you, he will keep, Christian.' Swiftsure tightened his jangling bandolier of throwing knives. 'He wants you fresh for the kill.'

Back at her gabled home, Beatrice sat in the window seat of an upper parlour and studied the garden below. How complex love could be, and how sharp the sting of guilt. Yet there remained the balm of a more constant presence, of the benign and admiring William Birch. He would not vanish on dangerous escapades or consign her to isolation. Unconsciously she felt for the pendant and with her fingertips traced each exquisite angle. Two remarkable men vied for her affections and she was no closer to making a decision. In the orchard, the damson trees shimmered in a cloud of marauding wasps.

As he worked, Realm hummed a Spanish tune. It had been an age since he returned to England intent on settling scores. His masters in Madrid should not have been surprised by his departure; they had been the beneficiaries of his devoted service and passion for shedding blood. The odd foray and freelance action were part of who he was. Given the commitment of Robin Catesby and his band of militants, it would have been a dereliction of duty and pleasure to stay away.

Around him lay the fruits of his latest toil, the small casks of gunpowder sheathed with nails and leather bladders, waiting to be filled with naphtha. Solidarity with the Catholic cause was not his entire focus. There were other things besides, the small matter of revenge and the chance to acquire a fortune. He thought in passing of the widow Beatrice and how in kinder times he might have let her live. He cut a fuse and stood back to observe. Wherever he roamed and whatever he touched, devastation seemed to result.

The adaptation of Coombe Abbey from religious institution to stately dwelling had created forgotten passageways and dark and hidden nooks. No one had bothered to keep a record or map the subterranean labyrinth, and the princess's courtiers had more urgent pastimes. Occasionally, parties descended with lanterns and laughter to carouse or seek out ghosts. Yet the place was generally left to inquisitive rats and silence and the seeping dampness of the moat.

It was here, far from the gaze of Smythe and his patrolling watchmen, that Adam came to meet the Lady Anne, a late-night rendezvous beneath the Norman vaulting.

Anne kissed him, grateful her lover had returned. 'It cannot be right we meet like this.'

'Would you have it any other way?'

He pulled her close, silencing her response and quelling her unease. The light of a single candle and the threat of discovery added to the tension and the lure. They had proved before that passion paid no heed to risk. Anne was not to know how important she had become.

'So you permit me to breach the walls of Coombe Abbey.' His lips lingered at her ear. 'It seems by day I am an actor and by night a thief.'

'You steal much already.'

'Though I have yet in earnest to begin.'

She laughed and let her hands roam. 'Mr Shakespeare plainly tutors you in the worst of ways.'

'What is your own excuse?'

Laughing, they maintained their embrace, letting warmth and comfort and the moment flow.

He held her face between his palms. 'Does our little Princess Elizabeth sleep sound?'

'She reads the scriptures and says her prayers and slumbers like a lamb.'

'Without you, she is lost.' He gazed into her eyes. 'I depend on you as much.'

'You are then both my charges.'

'I wager I am more troublesome.'

It was her turn to caress. 'What trouble is the boy I love?'

'Smythe wishes rid of me, Anne.'

'A porter has no say or power of decision.'

'He has hands that itch to tear off my head.'

'As you have the wit to avoid them.'

He had not told her of the incident at the well or of his work for Catesby, avoiding discussion of anything that might alarm her. Trust was a fragile thing. Nothing could jeopardise his efforts or the progress of his infiltration: those were his orders and he would try his utmost to obey.

At a distant sound, he snuffed out the light and pulled her into a recess. She went to speak, thinking it a game or proof of his eagerness, but he tightened his grip and hushed her in a whisper. Someone had entered their domain; now she heard it too. They stood in the darkness, their breathing shallow and their senses straining, and willed the presence to recede. Chance or a random impulse to search might have brought the visitor, but Adam mistrusted coincidence. He watched the gleam of a lantern strengthen and fade on the wall opposite. Finally he exhaled in relief.

'They are gone.'

She did not move. 'You are certain?'

'As sure as any fox that outwits a plodding farmer.'

'We must take care, Adam.'

Catesby would agree. He had warned against unnecessary risk and yet needed his young acolyte at the centre of proceedings at Coombe Abbey. Without reconnaissance there was no intelligence and the intended kidnap would be compromised. The enemy remained vigilant.

Anne shivered. 'I should return to the royal chambers.'

'Are these surroundings not magnificent enough?'

'For the while, they lose their charm.'

'Do I?'

'Never.' Her confidence was returning. 'I would meet you in the midst of battle were it demanded of me.'

'Be cautious in what you wish.'

'I desire for nothing save that we be together.'

'Such things may be arranged.'

He searched out the candle and with a flint and wood shavings managed to relight it. Anne flared back into his vision, beautiful and softly lit, her hair burnished in the glow. There was no doubt he was a fool to leave, but he would be a greater fool to stay.

'Next time, we shall parade as peacocks above the ground, Anne. I still have a friend in Elizabeth.'

'Should we cause scandal or offence, her patience will soon cease.'

'A sobering thought.'

It did not dampen his spirit. They parted reluctantly, with embraces and renewed pledges of love. Adam descended to a deeper basement and worked his way through its derelict spaces towards the night beyond. Once outside, he paused and murmured a prayer of thanks that his luck still held, for he was convinced that it was Smythe who had come looking.

'It seems King James enjoys the hunt as much as we.'

Catesby regarded his two companions with a smile. They had met in the provincial town of Bath because events proceeded apace, because the gunpowder was laid and the date for detonation at last agreed. James had unknowingly announced his own impending execution. The capital was too infested with spies and contagion, and was no place in the summer for gentlemen to be seen. Tom Wintour and Thomas Percy had joined their leader to assess the conspiracy's progress and further prepare for the uprising. While a Protestant monarch obsessively rode out to improve his health, a group of Catholics were gathered to undermine it.

'They say he and his Queen are bound for Oxford.' Percy stood at the inn window and stared through a crack in the shutters. 'I never thought the Scot would pause and come to rest.'

Catesby leant back in his chair. 'All creatures must on occasion sleep.'

'Not this Satan, Robin. He flits and fidgets, sups and leaves, stands to rail against our faith and moves onward in a day.'

'Yet on the fifth of November he journeys to Parliament and there confronts his destiny.'

'We too confront our own.' Wintour would not meet his gaze.

'Does your blood not fire at the prospect?' Catesby was never one for doubt. 'Do you not already scent the change that we shall bring?'

Wintour hesitated. 'What you say is true, Robin. Yet still we are too few in number.'

'Our numbers may remain small for now, but our members are staunch and steadfast. Guido is ready at Westminster. Our stables are filling, and the young Elizabeth is closely watched.' Catesby spoke with conviction.

'Black powder and horses are only part of the greater scheme,' said Wintour. 'We need brothers we may rely on, wealthy disciples who will spread the word and inspire revolt.'

'When the King is dead, the world will arise.'

'Not necessarily to our cause.' Percy turned back from the window. 'The encounter at the Globe shows how our plans may be thwarted.'

'You draw too much from a single skirmish.'

'A skirmish that left our troops dead and the forces of the state alive.'

The ringleader heard their concerns and was grateful for their counsel. In spite of his apparent confidence, he knew that dreams were easy and their realisation hard and that the plan had weaknesses. Perhaps he should have given Jack Wright his head and permitted a mounted charge against the royal convoy. It would have been an incident complete with spirit and dash. Yet he still believed the silent approach was best and a sudden, massive blow the more conclusive. And they had come too far on this path to let uncertainty prevail.

He drew his sword and placed it on the table. 'We are bent to this fight?'

'As committed as we are to God.' Percy stepped back to the table and laid his blade on top of Catesby's. Wintour's joined them.

'You trust me?' Catesby looked into both men's eyes.

'We have never had reason to doubt,' Percy said.

'Then with your blessing I will bring others to our circle and let them into our secret.'

'The moment cries out for it, Robin.' Wintour nodded his support. 'Everywhere there is rumour of great happening.'

'Shame on us should we disappoint.'

Percy took his seat at the table. 'You say that Elizabeth is watched and stalked. Where is she to be taken?'

'To whatever haven we choose or find.' Catesby gave an assured smile. 'She is our rallying point and totem, a unifying symbol to whom all shall bend their knee.'

'And then?'

'When matters are decided and a new government imposed, a Catholic army will march on London and bring her for marriage and enthronement.'

Wintour mused aloud. 'So close to the scene of her family's murder.'

'Whether or not a single brick of the Abbey stands, we shall hail the new queen and the rescue of England.'

Soon after, ever cautious of observation, the men prepared to leave the inn and go their separate ways. Before departing, they once more crossed their blades and renewed their pledge. With their hands clasped on steel and their eyes closed, the trio made their devotions as questing knights had always done.

To a fanfare of trumpets, the royal party entered and the banquet began. For three days the King would bless the city of Oxford with his presence, would be entertained with exhibition and display and dramas presented in Latin and Greek. It suited James's intellectual vanity. Professors bowed low, the student body were brought to order and the streets and buildings had been scrubbed clean. For a few days at least, His Majesty would rest from the hunt and indulge in cultural pursuits.

Beneath a silk canopy and the Gothic splendour of the hall at Christ Church, he sat with his wife, Queen Anne, and son Henry and surveyed the academic throng. His would be a glorious reign and the arts and natural sciences would thrive. This was the difference between the light and the darkness, between the new age he ushered in and the backward and superstition-bound world of the Catholics.

He whispered to a steward, 'What matters does my son discuss?'

'The prince converses in Latin and French, Majesty. He speaks with animation of England and its place and of the need for future empire.'

'Do those about him listen?'

'It seems they are in thrall, Majesty.'

It was sobering intelligence that required digesting. James leant forward and stabbed at a slice of meat, a cue that others might follow. Jealousy simmered deep. He knew how mortals thought, understood that while his subjects fawned and bowed to him it was the eleven-year-old Prince Henry who effortlessly won their admiration and respect. Even at such a tender age the boy was handsome and commanding; as heir apparent he was both an asset and a threat. It would not do to let the rival camp grow too strong. His offspring spoke of England and its place, but perhaps he had yet to comprehend his own.

Musicians played and the conversation swelled. The King's thoughts turned to his fair daughter Elizabeth. She was a pious, clever girl and an effective proxy symbol of his power. She at least would cause him no sleepless nights or trouble.

He turned to his wife. 'How find you this life of academe, my Annie?'

'Each street and corner brings fresh revelation.' She smiled devotedly in response to his enquiry. 'I thank the Lord you take some respite from riding and the risk of a fall.'

'You are right, my Annie. Greek verse cannot do me harm.'

'Though it is no language I understand.'

'I could stay a lifetime here.' James caught the eye of a pale and fine-boned scholar. 'There is much to commend learning and letters and life among these fellows.'

Anne looked at him sympathetically. 'Royal duties preclude it.'

'And the call of the hunting horn would cut it short.'

He prayed that tumblers or dwarves might emerge to lighten the evening or a fire-eater burst from a sugared tower of pastry. These events could fatigue. Yet if his son persevered, so could he; if his son enjoyed sycophantic aesthetes eating from his palm, James would have them kissing his Scots rear. They did not have to like him, but simply to obey.

James rose and the chamber fell silent. It was a neat trick, never failing to restore his confidence and his thankfulness to the Divine.

'By right I am here and yet as humble servant also. We sit not as a King with his subjects, but as brothers and wise men conferring and I as a monarch willing to hear. You are the guardians of this flame and protectors of the truth. Ensure the spirit of learning stays pure and neither papacy nor pollutants despoil it.'

The scholars applauded and cheered as they were obliged to, would not let themselves or their institution down. The King stared at his son. Henry was on his feet and leading the applause. Doubtless he would slip back to his princely lodgings at Magdalen and leave royal matters to him. James gazed in benevolence on them all. Tomorrow, he would parade and strut and let the people see him, while keeping the royal guard close. None could truly be trusted.

'A man of both words and war.'

Hardy turned at the voice, recognising Shakespeare before he saw his face. The playwright smiled in genial welcome, his eyes appraising as usual, his domed head shaded by a wide-brimmed hat. He appeared to bear no grudge over the melee that had occurred in his theatre. 'Why is a denizen of the dark found here in the light.'

'Perhaps there is sound reason,' Hardy replied.

'Though where you go, a trail of debris surely follows.' The playwright seemed amused. 'Shall you do to Oxford what you did to my playhouse?'

'I will endeavour to limit the destruction.'

'It seems you owe me the silver cross at your throat.'

'A promise I will honour in time.'

'Then with beer, I shall accept.'

They moved away from the throng and navigated the tents and stalls that fringed the makeshift arena. On a temporary stage bedecked in flags, actors delivered their lines in Latin and played out a Scottish tale that traced the ancestry of King James back to the legendary Banquo. In *Tres Sybillae*, it was the brooding Macbeth with no heirs who was left out in the cold. From a balcony, the present King watched the dramatic conceit and graciously accepted the flattery.

Hardy and Shakespeare walked on. The intelligencer was happy to be noticed, to be marked by any recusant noble who might be in league with Catesby. It would draw attention away from events in London and convince the plotters they went undetected. Besides, gunpowder was not the sole way to usurp a throne.

The two repaired to a tavern and sat in quiet conference. Here there was none of the din of the Mermaid in London, or the gathering of men of opinion and influence. Yet the banter of students would mask their discourse.

Hardy supped his ale. 'You come to Oxford on an errand?'

'To note and learn and to watch the world about me.'

'Our tasks are not so different.'

'Conflict on stage is by its nature make-believe. Your stories speak a blacker truth.'

'As you entertain the King, so I stand ready to preserve his life.'

'A skill I admire and to which I will drink.' Shakespeare put the pewter goblet to his lips. 'But it is those who are devoured by your art of preservation that haunt me in my sleep.'

'Never have the innocent or unarmed fallen to my blade.'

'But have they suffered?' Shakespeare peered at him with searching intensity. 'Your eyes hold the solitude of one who injures those about him.'

Hardy concentrated on his ale. 'I try not to.'

Even Shakespeare, the diviner of souls, would not comprehend the scars and sacrifice or the recurring image of the mutilated remains that had once been a loving wife. So many missions and victims on a journey flecked with blood.

Hardy called for more beer and leant towards the playwright. 'I suspect there are few in your trade you do not know.'

Shakespeare smiled. 'They are either friends to embrace or foes to avoid.'

'You hear and watch and are privy to things, gain insight to the hearts of men.'

'I will not spy.'

'Nor do I ask.' Hardy's stare was unsettling 'My hot-headed son, baptised Adam Hardy, is acquainted with your friend Ben Jonson.'

'What of it?'

'A father deserves on occasion to hear news.'

'While a son on occasion will run from his father.'

'His welfare alone is my concern.'

'Such knowledge may keep him running.'

'That is my burden and my risk.'

Shakespeare reached and gripped Hardy's hand, kindness and empathy in his eyes. For a human moment they were fathers with shared concerns. 'Fear not for Adam.'

'Does he forage in a wilderness or howl on a barren heath? Languish somewhere in a dungeon?'

'He breathes and is well, carouses and drinks as merrily as we.'

'Is he fallen in with rogues?'

'Far worse, Mr Hardy.' Shakespeare shook his head with wry humour. 'He keeps company with royals and entertains a court at Coombe Abbey.'

Hardy put down his cup. Conspiracy had tilted and the world with it, linking Adam to the gunpowder treason and the future of a child princess. Hardy sat in silence. His son was reckless and untamed, a wandering youth without a thought or care beyond the tavern or whorehouse. Now he was at the heart of the fire. Dangerous times had become more hazardous.

Hardy stood. 'Duty calls me.'

'It is more curse than duty if it drives a man from his pot of beer.' The playwright looked up. 'My company offends you?'

'On the contrary, it enlightens.'

'Were that all my audiences were so grateful.'

Hardy moved to leave, and then turned back. 'You do me a great favour and I now return it. Keep far from the likes of Robin Catesby and you will not encounter harm.'

On 30 August, the King left Oxford and returned to his true passion of hunting. He would make the most of the season before affairs of state encroached once more on his pleasures and pastime.

CHAPTER 16

As James embarked on the next stage of his progress, a journey of a different kind was underway elsewhere. Some thirty recusants had gathered beyond London and were heading for north Wales, intent on pilgrimage to the shrine of Saint Winifred at the ancient site of Holywell. There they would pray, wash away their sins and find the strength to survive all manner of persecution. If the chaste and blessed Winifred herself had once been murdered and then triumphed over death, so too could the old religion overcome misfortune. This was the path of peace to which a few still clung.

Father Henry Garnet murmured his encouragement and shepherded them on. At least their travels took them through recusant territory and along an invisible network of sympathy and support. He would not relax his guard until he reached the shrine. Were they to be intercepted, it might herald the end of Catholicism in England. As Superior of the Jesuits, he would be a singular prize. There were other priests too, brave men pledged to their mission and spreading the Word, disguised among the group of lay brothers and gentry. Each was a beacon that kept hope alive, and a flame of sedition to be extinguished by the state.

A small man with a limp turned and grinned at Garnet in a spirit of fellowship. Most who saw him would dismiss the man as a worthless cripple punished by God for his misdeeds. But this worthless cripple had saved countless lives. He was the master carpenter and stonemason whose dedication and genius had conjured the finest hiding places for priests throughout the land. It was his trapdoors and feeding tubes, his refuges constructed behind walls and fireplaces that allowed the message to endure. In London, the hunchback Cecil deployed his dark forces, and here an equally small and damaged man nicknamed Little John defied him. There was reason to be grateful.

'We march well, Father.' A female disciple walked beside Garnet. 'One day we shall be an army.'

'So long as it is a force for peace.'

'There is little hunger here for war, Father.'

'Men may be persuaded.'

'Is this why we journey? So you may see how the land lies?'

'I fear the change about us.' Garnet strode on with measured tread. 'I fear that our brothers are pushed to the extreme and will lash out at their tormentor.'

'That tormentor I have of late entertained in my family home.'

The Jesuit nodded without surprise. While traversing his realm, the King and his family were not averse to breaking bread with those whose bones they would gladly crush. Perhaps James also gleaned intelligence and tested the loyalty of the stubborn Catholics. Whoever tasted the royal repast for poison must be a nervous individual.

Garnet glanced at the woman. 'How seemed the King?'

Her lips thinned. 'Happy to insult our faith even as he dined with us.'

'He is not noted for his manners or tact.'

'When is a barbarous Scot applauded for such?'

'I pray he will come to the light and to see reason.'

'If not, Father?'

She must have heard the whispers, decided Garnet. The recusant community was alive with gossip and anticipation, with creeping awareness that some drama was near. Most wished for a quiet life. Yet pilgrimage alone would not provide hope or hold the line or dissuade men such as Catesby from their brutal act. Trudging to a holy shrine might be little more than an exercise in futility.

He bowed his head. 'What do you hear, my lady?'

'Beyond the breeze and the call of birds?' His devotee knew what he meant. 'I am told a miracle is close.'

'Will it be a miracle when families are torn asunder and good people cast into prison under sentence of death?'

'We shall dwell with simpler things.'

'Simpler things ignore the truth.'

'Should we not on occasion be spared it, Father?'

Taking his arm, she stepped out with a firmer stride.

Garnet knew he would be lost without her kind, people of courage and commitment who toiled to arrange safe passage for the Jesuits. Recusancy depended on them. He sighed. 'How fortunate it is to be attended by such dear and loving friends.'

'The honour is mine to be among them.'

'It may be the last time we gather.'

'That is in the gift of God.'

'Or it is decided by the folly of men.'

Two months remained before the hour appointed for explosion, before catastrophe fell upon them. Catesby had revealed the truth. Despite the sanctity of confession, Garnet had been tempted to warn the hated Cecil of what might arise. Anything to save the Catholic faith. Yet it would be a compact with the devil and would mean the betrayal of those who had protected him and their condemnation to a grisly fate. No man of God or conscience could countenance it. He stared along the line and watched the resolute tread of his companions and the laden progress of their donkeys. Close by the shrine and springs at Holywell was a place named Calvary. All were headed there.

Aided by a hireling and directed by the glow of a single lamp, Realm dug with a shovel into the soil of the heath. He had performed such excavations in most places he visited; it was a form of ritual preparatory to the close. Some endeavoured to build priest holes and others expended effort on shrines and mausoleums. For him, selecting a plot and cutting the first sod was quite sufficient. No additional monument was required.

His accomplice cut away another root. 'You ask strange duties of me, cousin.'

'I pay you well.'

'Silver earns my silence.' The man spat soil from his mouth. 'Yet never have I dug so deep or in such secrecy. Is it to be bodies or treasure you bury?'

'My decision is not yet made.'

The renegade climbed out of the pit and sat on its edge, wiping his brow and slaking his thirst with a flask of watered wine. Working in these conditions parched the throat. He studied the straining back of his companion and wondered at the man's stupidity. Few paused to consider their fragility and the lingering presence of death.

'You toil hard, friend,' he commented.

'The sooner I am done, the quicker I shall rest my head upon the pillow.'

'True.'

'I have met many of your kind, cousin.' The man continued in his labour. 'All of them were felons and none remain living.'

'Then I am content to represent them.' Realm stood up.

'You have money and yet are no gentleman or merchant.'

'Who is not a knave? Who is so pure he may malign another man?'

Work progressed, the hole deepening and the mound of soil rising high above the surface. Realm supervised from above. Someone had to keep watch and judge when the operation was complete.

Finally he passed down a supporting plank. 'Our business here is ended, friend.'

'Lend me your bottle and I will drink to it.'

Realm threw the flask to him. He should be permitted his indulgence. Everything was as Realm wished and the spacious cavity ready to receive. The man drank gratefully and smacked his lips in satisfaction.

The renegade stooped. 'Reach up and I will haul you free.'

As he sought to clamber up, it was not a hand that met the labourer but the steel tip of a pick that buried itself in his mouth and emerged at the nape of his neck. The dead weight hung, the arms fluttering uselessly and the air bleeding out in a hiss. Realm let the body drop. It had been an efficient dispatch. Calmly, he added a layer of earth and laid more boards to seal the tomb. He had no doubt it was a temporary measure, for he was only at the start.

Commotion invaded the stable yard, the sound of hooves and harness and the shouts of riders mingling in a cacophony. Here at the country manor of Norbrook the numbers of men and horses grew daily, the stalls filling and excitement rising towards the moment when the command would be given. No one could be certain what awaited. Yet it could not be worse than a cowed existence beneath the polished heel of King James. At the Warwickshire home of John Grant, the Catholics were gathering for war.

'Smell the sweat and hark to the clamour.' Catesby breathed deeply and surveyed the scene. 'There is little like it, John.'

As usual, Grant was sombre. 'We must hope their loyalty survives the first encounter.'

'Trust in our endeavour, for we have no other recourse.'

'Should Parliament be allowed to sit, its laws against us will break our backs,' said Grant. 'Should the King emerge unscathed from the blast, the words on our headstones are already engraved.'

'Thus do we have sound motive to succeed.'

Grant continued to observe. Among those gathered were volunteers and their mounts landed from Flanders, men prompted by Guido Fawkes to lend themselves to the campaign. Catholics were answering the call to arms.

The ringleader glanced at his host. 'Where is young Adam?'

'He gallops the coursers and marshals our strays.'

'Soon I will count on him to place horse relays for our future escape from London.'

'So the time approaches.'

'It seems pilgrimage, too, draws near.' Catesby might have grimaced at the thought. 'Father Garnet busies himself in leading his friends this way.'

'He does no harm.'

'Though he may draw pursuivants to us? May pry and poke in our affairs and rail against our efforts?'

'There is no need for him to know.'

'Henry Garnet is rarely deceived.' Catesby whistled to a follower. 'We pursue a course far from the Jesuits' liking.'

'Then we must keep it from their view.'

They strolled back to the house. There were other matters to discuss. Grant led his guest to a cellar, the chamber reached by way of a trapdoor and false wall. Inside, light scattered from rows of breastplates and weapons. Like the stables, the armouries too were filling.

Catesby stared about him. 'Of such things are victories forged.' The commander stepped to remove a sword from its mount. 'Those who bear such arms and don the cuirass are doing so for Christ.'

'I trust He smiles on our venture more than Father Garnet.'

'As we have not abandoned Him, so He will not abandon us.'

In spite of his habitual sternness, admiration flickered in Grant's eyes. 'What you began is now rendered in flesh and steel, Robin.'

'We train and build and hold our nerve for the awakening.'

One spark was all it took, mused Catesby. More houses would be commandeered and their hiding places used to stockpile the paraphernalia of war. The plot had gained momentum, found new urgency. A pilgrim called Little John would soon be passing through. He would cast an expert eye over their plans and employ his tools to create bolt-holes fit for a princess.

Catesby's gaze alighted on a rack of priestly vestments, their hues garish against the metallic uniformity around them. Violence and worship were complementary forms. He went to inspect a robe in rich scarlet satin.

Grant watched him. 'It is the shade of martyrdom, Robin.'

'I will not baulk from donning such a mantle.'

'Nor I. In these final weeks, each man is called to serve.'

'May our pace be true and our spirits glad.'

Catesby looked around him once more, almost in awe at what had been accomplished and what was to come. They and not the Jesuits were the keepers of the flame, the guardians of the faith. Hope alone would fail to secure the future and prayerfulness never guarantee survival. Of this he was sure.

A fire burnt weakly in the clearing, barely chasing off the chill and dew. The pilgrims sat huddled, some reading the scriptures and others in prayer, resting their aching limbs. Father Garnet walked among them, raising their spirits with gentle words. What they did was brave and good and what they sought was a better world.

'Bless you, my son.' He placed his hand on the head of a follower. 'Go in peace and do as God commands.'

'I shall, Father.'

'We are weary and our feet blistered, but it is our will alone that matters.'

'We praise the Lord with each step.'

'An example to the doubters.' The Jesuit smiled and moved on, aware of how much they sacrificed and that they would follow him to wherever he ordained. At last they had reached Warwickshire. There were allies about, sympathisers who might feed and house them and give warning of dangers ahead. Yet it was not sufficient to dispel anxiety. For every friend there were ten enemies, men, women or children eager to win reward and perform their duty through betrayal. Even the trees might send their whispers on the wind to the spymaster Cecil.

He straightened at the bird call, and responded with a wave as a young man led a packhorse through the woods. He was a stranger, but in his handsome features was an openness and ready warmth that fostered goodwill and confidence.

Garnet came forward. 'We give you welcome, my son.'

Adam bowed. 'My name is Adam and I bring you provisions.' He began to open the saddlebags. 'My apology they are so mean.'

'We expect little and so it is manna.'

'Many wish you well and pray for your safe passage.'

'Yet there are those who do not.'

Adam paused. 'Be of cheer, Father. Pursuivants are no match for us.'

Garnet accepted the gift of roasted chickens and a ham. 'The house at Norbrook is generous with its bounty.'

'John Grant does not forget his brothers.'

'He has proved himself a thousand times our sentinel and saviour.'

With gratitude, the pilgrims started on their breakfast. They would not stay here long. The following days would see them sleeping in barns or beneath the stars, seeking cover near hedgerows or skirting towns, always maintaining their onward march. To tarry was to invite suspicion and enquiry.

After making his farewell, Adam threaded through the trees, mounting up as he reached the track. Further duties called. Just as he reached the edge of the wood, he glimpsed something, a movement and the sharp glint of steel. An intruder. Already his horse was rolling to a charge, Adam shouting and leaning to give chase. The figure was running, crashing through the thicket and stumbling headlong in his flight, shedding his cap and rudimentary camouflage.

'You are taken.' Adam hurled himself from the saddle and pinned his prey to the ground. Landing heavily, the figure gave a grunt, and a knife spun away.

Adam bound his captive's hands with twine before rolling him over. 'Even bloodied, I know your face.'

The young man looked at him sullenly.

'A pursuivant.' Adam pressed down on his chest. 'A scent hound of Isaiah Payne's.'

'So you will untie me.'

The captive was no older than Adam, a beardless London boy who had strayed into dangerous territory. They were not so different and yet had pursued alternative paths.

Adam leant close. 'You are brave.'

'And you foolish.'

'What do you see?'

'Enough.' The youth smirked. 'Papists in the woods and, I am certain, priests among them.'

'Such confidence could kill you.'

'Your carelessness will do the same.' The prisoner stared up, unblinking. 'Are you not the Swaggerer we seized one night in London? Will you not hang for your crimes?'

Adam paused and might have replied if Jack Wright hadn't called out to him. The enforcer approached fast on his horse. His rapier was drawn and his countenance dark.

'What happens here?' he asked curtly.

'Nothing of great moment.'

'Yet you have a prisoner, no doubt a spy who carries information to the enemy.'

'He is disarmed and is no threat.'

'Though he has a mind to scheme and mouth to speak and legs to carry him off.'

Adam stood up. 'You would slay him in cold blood?'

'In war there is always risk.'

'As there is also room for Christian mercy.' Adam looked from the ago-nised face of the captive to the unyielding gaze of the swordsman. 'He has his loyalties, as do we.'

'Remember then your own.'

'There is little I must prove, Jack.'

'Save your energy for the future and more important things.'

'Righteousness should prevail.'

'Security is all.'

Adam looked once more at the youth's face. 'I shall put it to Robin to spare him.'

'Appeal is denied.'

It took only a single sword thrust to the heart. In place of a prisoner to guard and feed, a corpse lay shuddering with a crimson pool livid on its chest. Wright was simply performing his function. What counted was the mission, the treason plot, the chance to strike a blow. The swordsman turned his horse and rode away.

There was a problem. In the undercroft beneath the House of Lords, Fawkes had discovered that his black powder was decayed. It must have been bad luck, a faulty batch that had worked its way into the supply. Without replacing these barrels there could be no certainty of explosion and too great a risk that King James and his coterie might survive. The mercenary preferred to wage combat with better odds.

The quartermaster Robert Keyes carried the message out to Coldham Hall in Suffolk and sent word to Catesby. He found Sir Ambrose Rookwood training his horses. Drawn naturally to conspiracy, the young gentleman agreed immediately to the request.

After several days, the ringleader himself arrived at Coldham Hall.

'I wondered how long before you alighted at my door.' Rookwood embraced Catesby and led him to his study.

'Keyes visited?'

'With demand for an arsenal of powder.' Rookwood poured his friend a glass of claret. 'You are travel worn, Robin.'

'I ride hard from Ashby St Ledgers.' Catesby drank fast to quench his thirst. 'You can find the gunpowder I seek?'

'I have done so before.'

'We need another source, supplies that are not watched by the hunchback Cecil.'

'There is much to be found in the shadows at Harwich.'

'You have my blessing to acquire it, Ambrose.'

'Again for use in Flanders?'

The question hung in the silence, a pivot on which the visit and the security of the gunpowder treason rested. Overthrow required finance and horses and explosives, and Rookwood could access them all. Deception had run its course.

'I have not told you every truth, Ambrose.'

'You come now to confess?'

'To ask for your support.' Catesby accepted another drink. 'As a brother recusant, my trust in you is entire.'

'It is a trust I shall not break.'

'I have your word on oath?'

'I swear it, Robin,' Rookwood spoke solemnly.

'Then I tell you of great events and of the overthrow we intend. We will bring down the tyrant James and place on the throne as Catholic queen the young Princess Elizabeth.'

'How will you achieve this?'

'Your black powder is the spark and revolt across the land its consequence.'

Rookwood's eyes shone and his hand trembled. 'At last we fight.'

'Everything is readied, Ambrose. Are you with us?'

'Life is too dull as a gentleman trader in horses.'

'Its end may be burdened with a welter of pain.'

Rookwood shrugged. 'There is only misery where there is no risk or meaning.'

Catesby was gladdened by the words. His instinct had been true and a new conspirator was inducted. Rookwood was an energetic soul with wealth and horses to his name. It was everything the ringleader wished for and part of the strategy agreed upon in Bath. The season was changing, and transformation was in the air.

Catesby refused the offer of a bed for the night, and Rookwood set off that evening for Harwich. Some fifty miles from his estate, the port provided both an anchorage for naval ships and shelter for countless smugglers. Peace with Spain ensured that while the warships were laid up, barques and transports multiplied and illicit trade thrived. A chain had been established, feeding goods from the coast through the den of cutthroats at Hadleigh up into Lavenham and on to the interior. Rookwood prospered in his dealings. None would question the motive of a horse-breeder come to purchase stock.

Hacking at a root with his billhook, Hardy tilted his hat against the low rays of the September sun and watched Robin Catesby pass. He had been waiting for the crisis with the gunpowder and the resulting dash to Suffolk, and had followed reports as Fawkes carried his message to Keyes in Lambeth and the red-headed quartermaster then sought out once more his kinsman Rookwood. That Catesby himself travelled down from the Midlands proved either the confidence or the desperation of these men. From the great chamber of Parliament to the rooms of a young girl at Coombe Abbey, the distance between was populated with the sound of hooves and the silhouettes of traitors moving into position.

Beatrice awoke, dimly aware of the candlelight and the shadowy presence in her chamber. She struggled to make sense of what she saw. Perhaps she still slumbered and inhabited some dream. There were things familiar and others strange, a glut of images that perplexed. She raised herself on her pillow and tried to rub from her eyes the sleep and confusion.

'You do not imagine, Bea.'

'Will?' she whispered, uncomprehending. 'It is you?'

'That's a difficult question difficult to answer.'

'What do you mean?'

'I owe you a description of what I have done and what is my intent.'

'Your intent?'

'So many questions from so dull a mind.' There was a new blandness to his tone. 'I am at my cruellest when I tire.'

'You frighten me, Will. I do not understand.'

'So I shall speak plainly. You are a prisoner and not long for this life.'

'*What*?' she stuttered, suddenly all too awake.

'Because there are limits to your use and time is ever pressing. Because I require you solely as a lure for the intelligencer Hardy.'

'Christian will have no concern for my plight.'

'You know him less than I.'

It always followed a pattern, thought Realm, the numbness in his victims seemingly mirroring his own, the conflict in their emotions leading to inertia. She was pulling the bedclothes up to her chin, her pretty face mobile with growing terror. Hardy was so careless with his lovers.

'There is no sanctuary, Bea. No hope, no escape, no answer to your pleas.'

'Have I done you wrong?'

'On the contrary, my lady. You have danced each step to perfection.' Realm studied the trembling face. 'It is why I rewarded you with fine and precious things.'

'What a fool I was to place my trust in you.'

'The sad lament of so many I meet.' He watched her gaze flit about the room. 'Yet you accepted jewels without murmur or enquiry.'

'I believed you loved me.'

'An error measured in blood. I have taken your knife and every object with which you may seek to do me harm.'

'I have my manservant and my maids.'

'Not as you would recognise.'

She pressed her face into the covers and began to weep. There would be plenty of time for more tears. Raw viciousness could match the efficiency and power of any immaculate Destreza swordplay. Each depended on control and technique.

'Open your eyes, mistress.' He was scattering the contents of a pail on her bed. 'Throw yourself wide to the humours that compel me.'

When her screams had abated, she sat hunched and whimpering. 'Why this?'

'You betrayed your servants, Bea.' The renegade picked through the human remains with the tip of his drawn sword. 'They had no heart or stomach for the fight.'

'In the name of Christ, what shall I do?' she sobbed.

He smiled. 'Pray.'

'Hail Mary, full of grace, the Lord is with thee.'

Their feet bare and their heads uncovered, the pilgrims descended the steps into the waters of the holy well and repeated the prayers of the rosary. Now they had reached their destination, they would wash away their cares, and rededicate themselves to the cause of God with the help of the Blessed Virgin and Saint Winifred.

Father Garnet led them through to the deeper springs. Worship was more important than war and water more purifying than fire. There was no gunpowder here, no wild talk of overthrow by men in thrall to madness. Peace reigned in these caverns while the world changed outside.

A pilgrim emerged, her hair damp and her eyes ecstatic. 'God called us to this shrine, Father. We did not stumble or turn back.'

'May His light and your example shine, Eliza.'

'Our strength is beyond all measure.'

'I pray it shall endure.'

'On every step of our way we found warmth and succour.'

'What we found was sorrow and lament.' Garnet spoke with quiet feeling. 'But as the blessed Winifred was granted life anew after her beheading, so shall we stand again despite the iniquities heaped on us.'

'Will the injustice end, Father?'

'I cannot say I shall live to see it.'

When the barrels detonated beneath Parliament House, what was left of the government would destroy without mercy the perpetrators and the innocent alike. In devising his scheme, Robin Catesby might as well have disembowelled by his own hand every fugitive priest. The Superior of the Jesuits had little doubt that the worst was yet to come.

A double eclipse occurred in early autumn 1605, the moon becoming obscured on 19 September and the sun on 2 October. The astronomical events provoked much comment and created a sense of foreboding. Soothsayers and theologians agreed that the twinned events portended no good. Working on his manuscript about a deposed and outcast king, William Shakespeare took note and absorbed the strange phenomena into the body of his play.

CHAPTER 17

'To fellowship and fair fortune.'

Catesby led the toast, at ease among his friends and raised above them on a table. They responded with loud cheers, recusants eager to drink and feast and leave their troubles elsewhere. Tonight at the Irish Boy Tavern on the Strand, the wine flowed and the dishes were heaped high and the gathering pulsed with a strange energy of release. Few had knowledge of the true meaning of the evening. It was 9 October and the plotters were bidding farewell to their innocent friends.

With an extravagant leap, Ben Jonson joined Catesby on his platform. He swayed a little, cheerily acknowledging the jibes and catcalls, resting his arm across the shoulders of his friend. 'Though by repute I run through any that offend me,' he grinned and peered out at the crowding faces, 'this night I vow only to murder the language of my birth.'

A voice called out, 'We encounter such massacre in each of your plays.'

'Then pray you will give me a hearing.'

A bawdy and forceful presence misted by tobacco smoke, Jonson launched into his speech, his audience still raucous. In spite of persecution, Catholics could yet throw the best of parties. Beside him, the chief conspirator listened to the merriment, but his face remained serious. He met the coded glances of Thomas Percy and Tom Wintour. Each of them would hold their own valedictory events in venues across London. Festivity was as good a way as any to gauge the mood and prepare.

Climbing down from his stage, Catesby moved among his guests, basking in their affection. They trusted and revered him. Perhaps they too had heard the rumours, the discreet mutterings that salvation was close. What they learnt would be fragmented. He squeezed an arm and stroked a face and leant to whisper in an ear. It might surprise them that a mile hence, in Westminster, a former soldier measured out lengths of fuse and played nursemaid to a powder store, and that a mere twenty-seven dawns remained before the world changed forever. Catesby carried his responsibilities with a certain lightness.

A figure accosted him. 'I have not witnessed such happiness in an age, Robin.'

'There is little more potent than shared faith and comradeship.'

'I salute you for harnessing both.'

Catesby received the praise modestly. 'I rely on others in all I do.'

'We keep our hope alive, Robin.'

'In time it shall be answered.'

His words faded in the din and he continued to walk among his guests. Tonight was for the laying on of hands; at a later date he would present a young and biddable queen. Many a catastrophic slip might lie in between. He wondered how many informants were present, the turncoats and potential traitors who swarmed to Catholic gatherings. They would find nothing here to alert them.

Jonson pushed his way through. 'What grand and generous entertainment, Robin.'

'My friends demand and I provide.'

The fiery playwright studied Catesby's face, recognising his own traits in another – impulsiveness and love of risk. For a fleeting moment, under the man's piercing eyes, Catesby felt his soul and intentions laid bare.

Taking his arm, Jonson steered him to a recess. 'Tell me truly, Robin. Do we meet in celebration or parting?'

'I have no gift of foresight.'

'People talk. There is rumour of violence and ferment, of great moment and overthrow.'

Catesby shrugged. 'Eclipses incite superstition and fear.'

'I speak of the work of men, not of heavenly bodies.'

'God may act through His servants on earth.'

Jonson stared close. 'Are you among them, Robin?'

'I will never abandon His children nor forget the meaning of the resurrection.'

'May your endeavours bring us joy.' Jonson reached for a goblet on a passing tray and drank its contents in one.

Approaching the tavern, Shakespeare paused. He saw the beguiling glow and heard the melded roar, could picture the scene within of brotherhood and good cheer. It was an environment he enjoyed, and the invitation tempted. Yet he lingered at the threshold, aware of his own doubts and the memory of a warning. The intelligencer Hardy had advised him to stay away from the likes of Robin Catesby.

Coming to a decision, the playwright hitched his cloak about his shoulders and turned on his heel. Survival was often a matter of judgement. The boisterous levity of the evening would be left to the less discerning.

In the yard of a brewer near Holborn, there was an engagement of a different nature. Jack Wright too had kept away from the Irish Boy. As the guardian of the conspiracy, he preferred the shadows and periphery where conviviality was not required. Realm had extended an invitation of his own and the swordsman was bound to accept. He stood waiting, recalling a previous time when the renegade had emerged from the gloom to deposit gold and treasure at his feet. Encounters with the man were never dull.

'So the day is nearly upon us.' The voice spoke softly from the darkness.

Wright turned towards it. 'Realm?'

He stepped from the shadows. 'It is not long before the appointed hour, when either the King or you are slain.'

'I am ready for whatever fate decrees.'

'Better to be its master than its slave, to lessen the dangers and improve your chance.'

'Once before you offered your counsel and aid and they led us to defeat.'

'No war is measured by a single bout.'

'It is scant consolation.'

'Yet you answer to my call.'

Wright could not deny it. There were things the renegade could provide, quick eyes and a dagger hand and a roving brief as outrider to events. He had given much, had scouted and killed, had earned his place on the battlefield. The conspiracy needed him.

The enforcer stared at the indistinct shape. 'What do you bring?'

'Devices to cause havoc. Explosive mines that may delay an army and disrupt the most committed pursuit.'

'Your industry is noted.'

'My work has scarcely begun.' Realm had not come for gratitude. 'Cecil still watches, and Christian Hardy remains at your back.'

'You have a plan?'

'More than you may ever discern. Be assured, the intelligencer has fewer heartbeats left than even the King himself.'

'Such promises I have heard before.'

'All of which I shall keep.' In spite of Wright's wariness, Realm's confidence was soothing. 'Go to your labours. I shall stop the hounds from snapping at your heels.'

'Is this then our farewell?'

'Think of it as the moment when a new coinage was struck.'

Once more Wright was left with a gift, this time a cart filled with ordnance primed to ambush and kill. He ran his fingers over the arsenal, admiring the renegade's ingenuity and application. Whatever providence decided, Wright and his companions were set to illuminate the world.

The plotters were not the only ones immersed in revelry. At Coombe Abbey a party was in train, courtiers and local grandees gathering at the behest of the young princess to dance and parade in their finery. There was to be a bonfire and masque, singing by minstrels, a chasing away of the autumn gloom. Everyone intended to surrender to the moment.

'Are they not pretty, Adam?' Princess Elizabeth pointed to the coloured lanterns floating ethereal on the moat. 'Do they not draw the eye as surely as the stars?'

'My neck at least is not pained to see them.'

She laughed and clung tighter to his arm. 'I am glad you are returned to us.'

'I too, Your Grace.'

'How shall we entreat him to stay, Anne?' Elizabeth turned to her lady of the bedchamber. 'How may we keep him from being lured to other parts?'

Anne glanced at her lover. 'I believe it is in the nature of players to roam.'

'He has wandered much of late.'

'Coombe Abbey is ever in my thoughts.' Adam bent closer to Elizabeth. 'As is my little sister here.'

'When next do you depart?' the princess asked.

'With your blessing, a few days hence. My absence will be brief.'

'Be certain I shall note it.'

It seemed strange to converse freely with the intended victim of a kidnapping, to have won her trust so completely that she placed her happiness without question in his hands. Betrayal was never simple. The same week, he would be leading teams of horses from Ashby St Ledgers and stabling them along the route to London. When the time came and circumstance demanded, Robin Catesby and his lieutenants would rely on such measures for their escape. Drink and frivolity helped ease the tension of the countdown, but Adam could not completely put it from his mind.

Anne recalled her role as chaperone. 'Princess, your guests await.'

'They may wait some more.'

'You would let them fret? Allow them to believe they are unloved or out of favour?'

'There is food and wine enough to please them.'

'It is your presence they desire.'

'While it is freedom I crave.' The princess looked to Adam for support. 'Tell my cruel shepherdess I do no wrong in standing here awhile.'

'Your court alone will judge.'

She sighed. 'You are right. A sneeze or glance may cause offence.'

'And your smile will brighten and reward.'

'Swear you shall sing and I will gladly go inside.'

'You have my solemn pledge, Your Grace.'

They made their way back, the little girl assuming again her regal persona. Men bowed and ladies curtsied and royal servants glided close. Adam was watchful, scanning the faces for any hint they intended him harm. There were some here who wished him disposed of in a well, yet all smiled pleasantly and hid their thoughts deep. The porter Smythe would be brooding in the background.

Adam leant to whisper to Anne, 'We are safer in our cellar lair than among this nest of serpents.'

'On occasion we must join them in the light.'

Their talk faltered, a gap opening in the bejewelled crush of bodies to reveal the presence of Isaiah Payne in plain and puritanical garb. His was not a festive contribution. Out of place in a conventional setting, at Coombe Abbey the pursuivant chief might have been mistaken for a theatre act.

His eyes were unhurried in their appraisal. 'From a tavern in Stratford to supping at court.'

'Like you, I frequent many places,' Adam replied.

'My attendance is directed by business of the state.' Still the man's gaze had not shifted. 'What is it that entices you?'

'Entertainment and a need to eat.'

'Your accent is not of this location.'

'Nor yours, I warrant.'

Payne licked his dry lips. 'You know what I do?'

'Few are unaware.'

'I am a chaser of demons and excisor of ills, a bearer of the truth.'

'There are plenty who claim you bring only misery.'

'They are poorly advised.' The pursuivant showed no flicker of humour. 'Are you of a similar mind?'

'Performing verse and song affords me little time to think.'

'I suspect you jest.'

'For the moment, it is no crime.'

'Who may tell what the future will usher?' There was a threat in the words. 'I have lost loyal men to the hazards of this shire and will not rest until I have victory.'

A tug at his sleeve summoned Adam away. He was grateful for the interruption and the company of Anne, for the beckoning wave of Princess Elizabeth commanding that he perform. The princess would accompany him on the virginal. It would be a touching scene and reinforce his status, completing his journey from street ruffian to court favourite.

Payne had not been fooled. His curiosity was too intense and his sombre presence lingered discordant in the crowd. Adam tried to banish his doubts. His cover held for now and the fondness of his patron might protect him awhile. Nevertheless, he would need to be careful.

Riding through the October rain on the churned mud and gravel of a London street, Sir Francis Tresham cursed the weather and his situation. He could sit in the saddle all night and still be paralysed by dread. At last his cousin Catesby had made his approach and revealed to him the outline of a treason plot that would either obliterate the King or destroy all English Catholics. And he had agreed to join. God help him in his choice and forgive him for his coming treachery. Men and history might judge him unkindly, but few mortals had ever encountered the bloodless spymaster Cecil in a basement of the Tower.

A squad of horsemen fell in alongside and escorted him the final mile to a residence near St James's. Word had been sent ahead and the state was not about to lose its asset. Ushered in without ceremony, Tresham removed his sodden cloak and stamped water from his boots. At least this time his wrists were untied and there was no hood over his head. It did not lessen the fear.

'A godless hour for godless things.' The Secretary of State was sparing in his welcome. 'Catesby approaches you?'

Tresham's face twisted. 'I wish he had not, my lord.'

'Your aged father has recently died and you are the heir. And lo, your cousin Robin appears.'

'You are not surprised.'

'I forewarned you of such event, am relieved the moment is come at last. At whose home were you ensnared?'

'That of Lord Stourton in Clerkenwell.'

'It is the most predictable of places.' Cecil appeared almost disappointed. 'Cousin Robin was persuasive?'

'He cajoled and flattered, entreated and begged, played on my loyalties as a kinsman and Catholic.'

'Naturally you were moved by his subtleties and tricks.'

Tresham nodded, a trace of bitterness in his voice. 'Since youth, he has prided himself on bending me to his will.'

'Then he will have gone to sleep this night a contented man.' Cecil peered at his guest. 'Tell me of his plan.'

'It is a thing of wickedness, my lord. An evil to arise on the fifth of November as His Majesty opens Parliament.'

'What form does this diabolic act take?'

'Explosion, my lord.' Tresham's agitation was sincere. 'Gunpowder that will wreak destruction and clear a route for the accession of the Princess Elizabeth.'

'She is but a young girl.'

'One who may be snatched, who may be tutored, who may be moulded to the service of the Catholics.'

Cecil displayed no emotion. 'How will the ringleader Catesby employ you?'

'He requests two thousand pounds and asks that I cede use of my country home, Rushton Hall.'

'We each make our demands.' The spy chief regarded his double agent, his calculations masked. The man was weak and unreliable and yet would be a linchpin of success. He would never comprehend his contribution to events or his expendable nature.

The hunchback withdrew a sealed envelope from a drawer and turned back to Tresham. 'Let there be no mistake where your duties lie.'

'I came straight to you, my lord.'

'Your actions are well noted.' Cecil continued to observe him. 'May I depend on you?'

'On my life, my lord.'

'A thing weighed in the balance this eve. You know Lord Monteagle?'

'Of course, my lord.'

'He is married to your sister, and is a Catholic noble eager to preserve his wealth and title and his friendship with the state.'

'I am loath to see him consumed in the dread blast of November.'

'So save him with an act of mercy.' Cecil held out the letter. 'Steal by darkness to his house and see this delivered anonymously to his hand.'

Tresham looked fearfully at the envelope. 'If it is a warning, do I not betray myself?'

'Think less and obey more and you will thrive, Sir Francis.' Cecil surrendered possession. 'You have lived these thirty-seven years. Endeavour to continue.'

Tresham departed and the minister was left to his thoughts and bundled papers. Protecting the realm and promoting his interest did not allow much time for sleep. About him lay his codebooks and digests, the reports from Isaiah Payne on equine clusters in the Midlands and from a farrier tasked with shoeing for the winter an unexplained number of horses. The trap was almost sprung.

He summoned a messenger and gave his orders, then stood at the window as rider and horse dashed into the night. Their destination was north, to the city of Coventry and the grand house of Coombe Abbey, there to alert the royal guard. Orchestrating the unfolding of events required finesse and concentration. Cecil was confident that the conspirators would prove his greatest allies.

It was raining harder as Tresham, the latest in their ranks, returned soaked and troubled to his lodgings.

'Surrender to me the silver cross.'

Hardy complied, removing the chain from about his neck and placing it on the rapier tip pointed at his chest. They were in woods to the north of London; a place frequented by the marginal and ignored. Few travellers passed this way. He could have fought, might have snatched and reversed the blade and moved into the attack. Yet there was method in his obedience. Rash action would not prevail. The crucifix slid down the blade towards its new owner.

Realm studied the object in the half-light. 'Does it not recall our meeting on the deck of the *Revenge*?'

'Time passes and the world is changed.'

'Yet again you are defeated.' Realm was matter-of-fact. 'You discovered the message I left for you in the house at Templewood?'

'Your tricks long cease to disturb.'

'I am certain they intrigued. Not unlike the mortal remains of your late wife.'

Hardy shook his head. 'Whether a head hung from a tree or entrails draped upon a table, your practice is familiar.'

'We must be thankful it drew you here.'

'Does Beatrice live?'

'While I survive, she is quite safe.'

'Your word means little to me, Reino.'

'Yet you bring me gifts.' A brief command and a henchman hurried to drag away the loaded sacks. A cursory inspection showed they held a fortune in gold and gems. The expedition to England had been profitable for the renegade. He perused Hardy's face thoughtfully. 'You take great risks.'

'Much remains at stake.'

'Your Beatrice?' Realm smiled. 'She was a slattern who gave herself too easily.'

'I do not wish her dead.'

'Did your heart beat faster as you entered her home? Did you imagine I had gutted and mauled her as I once did Emma?'

Hardy paused. 'There will come a time of reckoning.'

'You care and trust too much. Weakness is a curse.' Realm glanced towards his booty. 'I have lain patient these many years to take from you what you stole in the Americas.'

'So is it avarice that drives you? Not vengeance or a desire to kill the King?'

'I find it more compelling.' Realm stepped back a pace. 'Chase your ghosts and demons, Hardy. They are the company you seek.'

'Where is Beatrice?'

'When I am safely away from here, then you shall be told.'

Hardy was unconvinced. 'You cannot be trusted, Reino.'

'I am truthful to myself.' The renegade tied the packs across a horse and rose into the saddle of another. The two men exchanged glances, Hardy's eyes full of loathing. Without further comment, Realm wheeled his mount and spurred away, leading the other horse.

Hardy looked around at the three men left behind. In their eyes he saw what Realm's instructions had been. The renegade liked a neat solution. He had doubtless promised them a portion of his wealth, assured them the opponent would be unarmed, and urged them to take pleasure in their work. They scarcely required encouragement.

Hardy eyed them. 'You have your orders?'

'Do not waste your breath,' said the closest man, leering.

'Duplicity is the nature of your master.' Hardy took a step back and let them come to him. 'I see no fairness in this fight.'

'It is less fight than butchery,' the man jeered.

'Think then of your wives and children.' Hardy observed his opponents, men betrayed by their stupidity and footwork.

So they died. The first received a tree branch direct to his eye and a stiletto blade next into his gut, his discarded sword requisitioned to cut down his companion. As the last adversary rushed in, Hardy was upon him. It took a single blow from the butt of the weapon to ensure he would not rise again.

His breathing scarcely quickened, Hardy stood in the abrupt silence, alone with the carnage and the animal stench of blood. All in the name of the King. Events were in play.

A manservant paced fretfully in the dark outside his master's home. Excitement rarely ventured so far as the quiet hamlet of Hoxton to the north-east of London. Yet murmur spread and Catholics were tense with fierce anticipation. So he patrolled diligently with his lantern, alert to emergency or threat. It was about seven o'clock in the evening of Saturday, 26 October. Nothing to report.

'Who approaches?' He raised his lamp and squinted at the shape in the dimness.

'None but a friend.'

'I have no purse,' he said nervously.

'It is your ear and patience I desire.' The stranger came no closer. 'I bear a letter for your master, Lord Monteagle, and beg you take it to him.'

'At this hour? By this means?'

'Forgive my furtive manner. There is no other way.'

The manservant regained his composure. 'Is this some petition, a plea for alms?'

'I am nothing but the messenger.'

The letter was delivered and its bearer quickly withdrew. The servant hastened back into the manor. Rain was beginning to fall. In his parlour or music room, the master would be at study or play and yet would not chafe at the intrusion. A hint of intrigue demanded instant attention in these uncertain days.

'Fetch me more light,' Lord Monteagle addressed his servant as he slit open the envelope and unfolded the single page within. 'You say you did not know the man?'

'I did not see his face clearly, my lord, but I did not know him.'

'Yet he was insistent this item was brought to me.'

Surprises were unwelcome. At thirty years of age, his lordship had devoted his energies to maintaining his liberty, ensuring that the government knew his loyalties lay with the Crown. Catholic he might be, but he was wise enough to pledge his fealty to King James. A minor role in the Essex rebellion against the ageing Queen Elizabeth had taught him caution and to pick the winning side. He was lucky to have escaped with his life and a crippling fine. Being married to Elizabeth, offspring of the noted recusant Sir Thomas Tresham, had not been helpful.

The lamp was brought and its flame turned up high. Monteagle began to read aloud. '"My lord, out of the love I bear to some of your friends, I have a care of your preservation . . ."'

It deserved a second reading and another, the words emerging deliberate and slow as though repetition would enlighten. There was no mistake.

Monteagle glanced up. 'Is this a nonsense, Thomas? A jest?'

'It would be a dangerous one, my lord.'

'Dangerous?' Monteagle's face was pale with horror. 'It warns of a mortal blow befalling Parliament, suggests I absent myself in order to survive.'

'Perhaps you should ignore it.'

'And be complicit in treason and murder? Cast as knave in the drama that unfolds?'

'Your loyalty to the King is unquestioned.'

'This questions it well.' Monteagle shook the paper. 'This taints me, links me with conspiracy, besmirches my name with foul association.'

'None may accuse you, my lord.'

'Perception is all. I must act immediately.' Monteagle strode through the house, calling for his groom and the saddling of his horse. Whatever the hour and however poor the weather, he would ride at once into London and present the letter to Robert Cecil, the Earl of Salisbury. Better to be prompt than await the halter tightening on his neck, to ingratiate himself and blow wide open a plot than to bring down the hunchback's wrath on his head.

Without delay, his lordship set out alone, driven by fear and instinct. He left behind a household in uproar and confusion. Not long after, a second rider departed, carrying a message for the plotters.

'All is set.'

Excitement infected Tom Wintour's voice as he greeted Adam. They could congratulate themselves on their efforts to seed the route between London and Ashby St Ledgers with teams of horses. A rapid exit was being planned. Now at Dunstable, some thirty miles north of the capital, the pair had met to complete the chain. In less than a fortnight, the conspirators would ride as victors or fugitives to spread the word and incite revolt. Behind them would lie the blackened ruins of Parliament and ahead Coombe Abbey and the dawn of a new reign.

'From where do you ride, Tom?' asked Adam.

'Whitewebbs.' It was the recusant house from which Father Garnet had embarked on his Holywell pilgrimage. 'Robin awaits me there and I return to him this eve.'

'A long journey in bleak conditions.'

'What is mud when we have faith? Or mist and rain when God smiles on our enterprise?'

'It is a night for ease and drinking.'

'Such time may wait.' Wintour stared out from their shelter. 'You understand your duties?'

'They are difficult to forget.'

'Yet possible to mishandle. Much depends on you, Adam.'

The younger man was confident. 'Coombe Abbey rests peaceful and its courtiers are at play.'

'The Princess Elizabeth?'

'She earns the love of all with her spirit and sweetness.'

'One day she will bewitch the nation.' Wintour regarded his accomplice. 'You have come far from the Swaggerer boy I pulled from a gaol in London.'

'My hatred for James stays constant.'

'Thus do we prepare his downfall. As we speak, His Majesty roams Cambridgeshire in pursuit of quarry, blind to the fact that he is the hunted.'

'Tell Robin I shall not fail him.'

'As you must in turn inform our friends the game is now upon us.'

In manor houses ringing Stratford-upon-Avon and within striking distance of Coombe Abbey, gentlemen were gathering with their armour and horses. At Norbrook, John Grant was ready. Sir Ambrose Rookwood had stationed his supporters in the rented forward base close by at Clopton House, while at Huddington Court to the west, Robert

Wintour stabled more horses and made his preparations. Even in Robin Catesby's absence, his own country seat at Ashby St Ledgers had also become a muster point for men, weapons and stores. Another house had been commandeered. Owned by the recusant Throckmortons who conveniently sat in exile abroad, Coughton Court lay some ten miles out of Stratford. It was to this location that a handsome and dashing young gallant named Sir Everard Digby brought his family and servants. He was a latecomer to the conspiracy, but his was a critical role. Admired and popular and the ablest of horsemen, Sir Everard would lead the mounted assault to snatch Princess Elizabeth and change the royal succession. Like a claw extended, the Catholics were ranged against their target.

On 31 October, five days before the opening of Parliament, King James abandoned his hunting around the Cambridgeshire village of Royston and returned to the Palace of Whitehall in London.

CHAPTER 18

'"They shall receive a terrible blow this Parliament· and yet they shall not see who hurts them . . ."'

The King almost whispered the words, his gaze fixed on the text. At first he had studied the Monteagle letter in silence and now returned to the lines he deemed significant. Parliament was to be struck by an invisible hand and the warning was writ clear.

It was Friday, 1 November. Cecil had a private audience with his master. He watched James pace the gallery and saw his frown of concentration. There was an art to leading the King to a decision, to making the little Scotsman believe he alone unearthed conspiracy and controlled events. His Majesty was always grateful for an opportunity to shine. From sleight of hand and creative penmanship would come immense rewards.

Pink-tinged eyes viewed Cecil close. 'What think you of it, my beagle?'

'I am uncertain of its meaning, Majesty.' Cecil betrayed not a glimmer of deceit. 'It is Your Majesty who has the gift of insight.'

'Are these words not plain? Does this letter not speak of a terrible fate to befall Parliament?'

'It would appear so, Majesty.'

'Yet you bring me something of dread import.' James pointed to the page. 'Here it counsels the reader to devise an excuse and run to safety in the country. And here it speaks of some event and of God and man contriving to punish the wickedness of this time.'

'Lord Monteagle was most anxious and vexed.'

'Well might he be, my beagle. For he stumbles on the truth and I lay it bare.'

'Your wisdom and perception surpass all, Majesty.'

'It is why I rule and you still serve.'

Cecil bowed soberly. Revelling in the triumph of his own deduction, James would not scurry for sanctuary. He needed to be kept calm, to remain in London, to play his part at the centre of events. As Guido Fawkes tended his casks in the bowels of Westminster, so the King would parade in his lavish rooms and meet his councillors and choose his robes for the forthcoming state occasion at the House of Lords. Illusion was vital in these closing days.

'I crave your indulgence, Majesty. Both I and your council wait upon your discernment and decision.'

'A savage blow is aimed at us, a murderous plot by agents unseen.' The words slurred from James's mouth, his Scots accent stronger under stress. 'It will be a thing of cataclysm, employ powder and fire and annihilation.'

'You suspect the Catholics, Majesty?'

'No one else would dare such treachery.'

'So let us repay it and move stealthily against them, with measured steps.'

James frowned. 'Is haste not our ally?'

'It might yet be our enemy.' Cecil was smoothly persuasive. 'We must not alert them, cannot permit a single conspirator to escape the net we cast.'

'We wait? Do nothing?'

'Patience will reward Your Majesty. It will burnish your reputation and illuminate your strength, will lead us to the heart of this foul matter.'

'In four days I journey to Parliament.'

'By then we shall have rent wide every aspect of the plot.' The Secretary of State exuded confidence. 'Bide awhile, Majesty. I will deliver to you the heads of your foes.'

'Will they include noblemen and courtiers who bow and smile and profess to me their loyalty and love?'

'All shall be discovered.'

And all would lead to further power and wealth being vested in the hands of Robert Cecil, first Earl of Salisbury. The spy chief was relieved that his plan advanced. He would sanction a cursory search by the Lord Chamberlain of the area surrounding the House of Lords, but would ensure that the conspirators were not spooked by the government's behaviour. Perhaps they had already learnt of the letter. It made no difference. Cecil was certain the papist Catesby and his zealous brood were too deeply committed to their action to withdraw.

The King trembled a little. 'Outside these walls are men who hate me.'

'Your Majesty is revered.'

'Does reverence conjure high treason? Is it by custom expressed with a fuse and immolation?'

'Greatness will always beget envy and resentment.' Cecil was the master of the positive. 'Yet the esteem in which you are held by your subjects far exceeds complaint and dissension.'

'So long as there are Catholics, there will be attempts on my life.'

'Whilst so long as I have breath, none shall come close to harming Your Majesty.'

'What of my Queen? My children?'

'All will be safe, Majesty. I have already strengthened the guard about them and as a precaution removed them from the path of danger.'

'Do as you must, my beagle.' James smiled at his chief minister, warming to his role. 'These traitors believe me a timid mouse, but will find me the most savage of cats.'

He scratched at his crotch with absent-minded pleasure, distracted by thoughts of victory and revenge. At a glance he had solved a riddle and thwarted a great evil. England was fortunate indeed. Today was the Feast of All Saints, that moment of superstition in the recusant calendar when High Mass was celebrated and papists gave thanks to their pantheon of saints. No amount of prayer or intercession could help the conspirators now.

James let his gaze drift to a portrait of himself, high on the stateroom wall. 'God wills it I should live. He thus ordains destruction for any who defy.'

Sir Francis Tresham had intended to get drunk. But the joylessness of his situation had outweighed his thirst and he returned almost sober to his lodgings. Those who might condemn him had never faced his predicament; those who accused him of cowardice could never have seen instruments of torture in the Tower. To betray the King or his faith and friends, there was the rub. No easy matter. That his life and lands would be snatched away by the state had certainly influenced his decision. Still his soul was burdened and he trod heavily on the stair.

'Judas.'

A knife pressed against his throat and the voice of Tom Wintour spoke in his ear. News of the letter to Lord Monteagle had plainly spread. Tresham allowed himself to be propelled into his rooms, and caught sight of Robin Catesby awaiting his arrival. The reception would not be gentle.

'Sit.' Wintour forced him into a chair.

'Where is kinship?' Tresham gasped. 'Friendship? Our bond of trust?'

'I would ask the same.' Catesby spoke coldly.

'You wrong me,' cried Tresham.

'I hear hypocrisy.'

'It is I, your cousin Francis. What crime do I commit?'

'That of betrayal.'

'On my life and honour, I do no such.'

'Your honour is tainted and your life forfeit.' Catesby's eyes were hard. 'Tell me why we should not hang you.'

'I am innocent of your accusation.' Sweat had begun to pump from Tresham's forehead.

'Innocent of bearing a letter to Monteagle? Of revealing our plan to kill the King?'

'I did none of this.'

'Who else is so close to Monteagle?'

'All know that he is loyal to James.' Tresham leant forward and gripped the arms of the chair. 'All know he would not hesitate to sound a warning.'

'I invite you to our cause, and soon after, the cause itself is exposed.'

'Never have I failed you, nor would I now.' Tresham was earnest in his defence. 'I gave my pledge and it yet stands.'

'Though the dwarf Cecil has our secret.' Catesby's voice was flat.

'Seek your traitor elsewhere, Robin. I am with you as surely as when you first approached me.'

'Then I came as friend and cousin. This night it is as judge.'

'So judge others instead. I am blameless, I swear it.'

'You are?' His cousin's look was searching.

'My conscience is unsullied and my devotion to you true.'

'Where lies truth in a world of deceit and make-believe?'

'Do you not need my money and horses? Will you not reap benefits from what I may provide?'

'The price of your involvement is too high.'

'Consider me without prejudice and misperception, Robin. Every last measure of my loyalty is to you.'

Catesby was silent. He would not execute a man on mere suspicion, could not dismiss the argument of a cousin and childhood friend. This was Francis, the boy who had always worshipped him and followed his example. It was inconceivable that he had set out to sabotage the plot.

'Doubt will divide and destroy us, Robin.' Tresham was insistent. 'I stand forever at your side.'

'I shall hold you to your promise.'

'Should I disappoint, you will have reason to string me in a tree.'

The sentence was postponed. As they left Tresham's lodgings and walked into the night, Catesby and his lieutenant paused at the edge of an orchard to confer. There were many factors in play and a multitude of risks to balance.

'Do we delay, Robin?' asked Wintour.

'We do not.' The ringleader was emphatic. 'There is but one chance and we seize it as we may.'

'Even though Cecil receives warning and will muster a force against us?'

'A letter that describes an invisible blow is vague. A letter with unknown provenance that comes by night is as like to go ignored.'

'You believe this, Robin?'

'I know we have God and moment on our side. I know too that Parliament will enact more heinous laws against our kind and our duty remains to obliterate it.'

'I hope you are right.'

'Remember your vow and never falter.' Catesby placed a hand again on his friend's shoulder. 'We will listen for rumour and hint of discovery and meanwhile keep our nerve.'

Wintour succumbed to his certainty. 'Whatever is your demand, Robin.'

'My demand is for stalwart hearts and victory.' Catesby would not compromise, not so close to the goal. 'We proceed.'

On the Thames sat a trading barque ready to spirit them to foreign sanctuary should the danger mount and the authorities close in. Guido Fawkes had chosen the vessel as an option for escape, but none were yet thinking of fleeing.

Realm operated to a different schedule. His cart was laden and his treasure stowed and he was heading for the river. However Catesby and his gang of Catholic gentlemen fared, it was of little consequence to him. A timely departure was preferable to becoming enmeshed in eventual capture. There would be chaos and uproar, barricades and militias, turmoil that might see a passing stranger challenged or attacked. His instinct, pistols and gold were sure to carry him safe; nonetheless, come the hour of pageantry and detonation, he would be far distant.

He let the horse walk on, and thought of the city slowly waking and of Beatrice's corpse starting to moulder in its grave. His instructions had been specific. The frayed ends of a mission always needed to be tied. A light flurry of sleet brushed his face and he wondered at the heat and rage about to be unleashed. He would leave England to her destiny. From a house near Paris he would reinvent himself and buy position, would offer his talents to wealthy statesmen and apply himself to new labours. Even King Philip of Spain might forgive his transgressions if sufficient gold and gemstones were presented.

A rope dropped about his neck and dragged him from his seat, the cart rolling on unimpeded beneath the trees. He clutched at his throat, his legs kicking, his body turning in its frenzied fight for air. Nothing could explain it. Eternity stretched and images flickered and he believed he was already in the company of ghosts.

'How quickly fortune may turn.' It was Hardy's voice that echoed in his dying brain. Another ghost. 'Your ship at Tilbury must seem remote.'

The renegade was in no state to reply. They had let him swing awhile, cutting him loose only when his movement had weakened and death was close. He lay in the mud, choking and speechless and clawing his way back to consciousness.

Hardy pressed the flat of the katzbalger blade to Realm's cheek. 'First you will return to me the silver cross.'

'And then?' The gasping breath burnt his lungs.

'I shall decide between conducting my own torture and remanding you to Cecil.'

'You believe I will speak?'

'For what you have done, I intend you to die.'

'It will not bring you Beatrice.' Realm took the crucifix from his neck and dropped it in the dirt. 'It will not resurrect your long-dead wife.'

'Beatrice lives.'

Mockery sounded raw in his throat. 'You ever were so filled with hope.'

'As you are tripped by your conceit.' Hardy let the words and the katz-balger dangle. 'You used her as bait for me; rather, she was bait for you.'

'You are deceived.'

'Never by you, Reino. Your arrogance convinced you to adopt the name of William Birch, a man you killed as he searched your ship. Your folly allowed you to present as gifts the jewels you snatched from a gemsmith in Cheapside.'

'Little is changed by such deductions.'

'Yet I own your treasure and your fate.'

It had been a tense and complex affair, one set against the backdrop of wider conspiracy that had lured Realm back to his native home. Cecil would be pleased, although he would not learn of the recovered trove. In the grim recesses of espionage, finders always kept.

Hardy picked up the crucifix and looped it around his neck. 'Three men you put against me and they died. Two more perished at the grave where you meant to bury Beatrice.'

'I am not done.'

'Circumstance decrees you are.' Hardy directed a kick into his side, winding him. 'This is not Lisbon or some ship off the Azores.'

Face down in the mud, Realm retched and gasped. 'You forget our game is eternal.'

The intelligencer crouched close. 'Consider it now ended.'

Elsewhere, the conspirators would have received their final briefing and moved into position. They would not know that the King was safe and had no plans to visit Parliament or that his children were dispersed and well guarded. It was the Catholic traitors rather than Stuarts who were imper-illed. Hardy stood back as his men pulled the renegade to his feet. He had waited a lifetime for this prize, had waded through blood and barbarity and the silver mines of the Americas to bring this journey to completion. There was a bitter sweetness to the act.

A monster panted before him, unconcerned by its defeat, a prisoner with a face and demeanour trained to fox the memory. Just a codename on a corkboard. Realm had played so many parts, he was more composite than real person.

Hardy turned away. 'We shall not meet again.'

'A vow you cannot keep.'

'My duties lie in other places. You will be taken before Cecil.'

'Such an honour I scarcely deserve.'

'Every due you earn yourself.'

'And you?' The renegade watched Hardy sheath his sword. 'A wife or son can be lost without warning.'

It was Reino's last card and he had struck at his enemy in the only way remaining to him: he spoke of Adam.

'Fetch light! Bring wine!'

The hunting party had arrived in a riot of noise and urgency; hooves clattered, dogs barked, and men dismounted to a jangle of spurs. They were simply the advance group. Soon others would come, their carts heavy with armour and weapons and their coursers shod for action, a cavalry unit impatient to proceed. Here at the Red Lion Inn in Dunchurch village to the north of Ashby St Ledgers, a plot once hatched in a gatehouse room was finally reaching reality. Some ten miles distant across Dunmore Heath lay Coombe Abbey, the horsemen's intended target. It was Sunday, 3 November. The men's spirits were high and motivation strong and faith would not desert them.

'Thus at last we gather.'

There was relief in Sir Everard Digby's voice, an optimism and energy in his youthful features that enlivened all about him. Field sport was his passion. Like the King he detested, he was fearless in the saddle, would ride to hounds in any weather and take the highest fence. Doubt and introspection were not his way.

John Grant nodded, his clothes and hair damp from the journey. 'We must trust in God the foul weather will ease.'

'Rain is a friend that keeps at bay hostiles and pursuivants.' Digby handed the gloomy landowner a brimming goblet. 'We will feast and make merry as we may.'

'Our hour is close.'

'More reason then to enjoy the time remaining. Your men are ready at Norbrook?'

'Thirty ride from there tomorrow.'

The younger man smiled. 'With those from Ashby St Ledgers and Clopton and the friends I bring from Coughton Court, we shall number nearly a hundred.'

'Sufficient to raise a stir.'

'Enough to mount a campaign and seize the princess and raise the banner of our cause.'

'May the Lord guide our every step and be merciful to our enterprise.' Grant drank to his own prayer. 'You have seen Father Garnet?'

'He is difficult to avoid, for I give him shelter at Coughton. His High Mass for All Souls was the most solemn and touching of rites.'

'Perchance he suspects we too will be joining the dead.'

Digby did not deny it. Throughout the previous day, the sombre occasion of All Souls, the Superior of the Jesuits had been persistent in his questioning. Whether informed or merely chasing rumours, Garnet was no fool and would have been alerted by the horses in the stable yard and the earnest glances exchanged by the men. The stated cover of a hunting expedition would hardly survive close scrutiny. 'I hate to deceive Father Henry.'

'All sin is expunged by the good we do,' Grant said firmly. 'We are answerable for our actions to the Divinity alone.'

'How far I stray from the pilgrimage on which I embarked with him to Holywell.'

'He is a Jesuit and you are not. Leave him to his concerns and let us to the task before us.'

Others entered, friends and fellow recusants who had answered the call and crossed the threshold to embrace revolt. All were eager. There was Robert Wintour of Huddington Court, Tom's older brother, and their stepbrother John Wintour; Humphrey Littleton and his nephew Stephen; Sir Robert Digby, Everard's uncle; and Henry Morgan, a friend of Grant's. By the following nightfall, their number would be almost complete and the inn transformed into an encampment. Reconnaissance was already underway.

They drank and laughed and ate well long into the early hours. In this waiting time, it suited them to put worries from their minds. Sir Everard had brought seven servants to wait on his companions and, later, provide the core of what might be a travelling royal household. Carried in trunks in his chamber was the finest of clothing, doublets and cloaks threaded with gold, encrusted with pearls and edged with fur and lace. Protocol demanded sumptuous apparel for an audience with a future queen.

It had been a chill dawn and a colder day, hours spent hunched in a wood-shed or tending his horse and sheltering from the storm. Adam blew onto his hands and paced to keep warm. A man could go mad on a heath. The light was fading on the afternoon of Monday, 4 November. He had earlier met Sir Everard Digby to receive his orders and gorge on the rich scraps from his table, had witnessed the massing of a hunting party that would tomorrow evolve into a strike force. His duty was as its spearhead.

Now he closed on Coombe Abbey and scaled a wall, following a pro-cedure he had repeatedly rehearsed. They would not catch him: he was quick and skilled in infiltration. Often, hidden within the cover of a copse, he had watched the Lady Anne and her young charge wander in the gardens. Now he was returning.

'You will not find her.'

There was triumph in Smythe's voice, and a note of finality. This time there would be no argument, no equivocation, no result other than an execution. The sword in his large hand proved it.

The porter regarded his prey and adjusted the beam of his lantern. 'You are confused? I am not the fair maid you expected?'

'I fear you are less welcoming.'

'You fail to learn your lesson.' The porter scraped the tip of his blade on the flagstones. 'This is no well from which you may escape.'

'Again your mouth exceeds your prowess.'

'While yours shall see you slain.'

'A fat man with a lamp scarce frightens me, Smythe.'

'He will yet gut you with hard steel.' The blade flicked from side to side. 'The young princess is gone away, is taken with her ladies by royal guard to Coventry and safe quarters in the Guildhall.'

'Coventry?' Adam played for time.

'Such tidings vex you.'

'Uncommon things are of late become quite usual.'

Smythe leered. 'You sing and play among the court and yet carry the stench of a lie.'

'How quick you are to judge.'

'I am faster with a sword.' The porter hung the lamp from a stone projection. 'Pursuivants vanish, Catholic agitation grows and you appear at our gates.'

'Love may draw a man to a foolish errand.'

'Or is it hatred for the Crown?'

Adam studied his opponent and thought of a young girl carried in a rushed cavalcade beyond the reach of kidnap. Elizabeth would be sleeping tonight in a chamber once occupied by her grandmother the captive Mary, Queen of Scots. Again fate had turned and a future reign was thwarted. Sir Everard Digby and his hunting party would discover little to give them cheer.

'Armed men stand guard above, commanded to kill should you emerge.' Smythe closed and Adam danced lightly back.

'Then you spur me in my effort.'

'I presumed you would respond thus.'

'Oxen never change, Smythe. You are as brutish and plodding as when we first met.'

'There will be no further occasion.'

'A pity.' Adam insinuated himself within an arch. 'Our enmity is full of incident.'

'Your belly will soon be swollen with this blade.' Smythe rushed forward with a howl and the sword hacked at its target, aiming for flesh and connecting with stone, its wild progress marked by a shower of dust, a less emphatic finale than the porter had wished. He pushed on, undeterred and enraged. This was for the princess and the nobles who attended her, for past insult and failure. It was his duty as porter to defend Coombe Abbey.

He fell heavily, and his face was pushed into water foaming to his struggle. A setting that had suited Smythe now worked to Adam's strengths. He was the streetfighter, the vagabond and survivor with an avowed enemy in his grasp. Somewhere lay the sword, harmless.

Adam raised the man's head and listened to his liquid gulps for air. 'You have no wits, no sense, no use.'

'Mercy.'

'We are beyond it and far removed from earlier play.'

'I was mistaken.'

Adam spoke coolly in his ear. 'You left me to certain death in a well.'

'Such was my instruction.'

'This, you will find, is mine.'

He acted quickly, determined to extricate himself from his hostile surroundings before the alarm was raised. There remained a mounted force of Catholics and the potential for an uprising and unspoken events in London that would doubtless reunite him with Catesby. The evening was not yet begun.

Similar urgency infected the conspirators gathered in the private room of a tavern near Tyburn. It was their last meeting in these counting hours, a final briefing before the morrow, when the King and his ministers would disappear in a blinding flash. There was much to celebrate and enough to concern. The anonymous letter to Lord Monteagle had heightened the sense of risk and emphasised the unknown. Men caught in the eye of great events were often bemused at what they had started.

They regarded each other, pride and brotherhood quelling any fear. The ringleader Robin Catesby, Thomas Percy, adjutant Tom Wintour, enforcer Jack Wright and quartermaster Robert Keyes: on them rested the burden of responsibility for the coming fate of thousands. An artificial calm prevailed.

Percy attempted to reassure. 'All is quiet and the alarm is not raised. I travelled before noon to Syon House and there met my kinsman and patron the Earl of Northumberland. You will see I am still at liberty.'

'It means nothing.' Wright offered his customary objection. 'Could it not be a ruse or trap? Are we not lulled by the silence about us?'

'You worry, brother.'

'It is my duty.'

'I perform my own and say there is no cause for concern. Northumberland is a privy councillor, aware of all things and yet preparing to attend Parliament. Neither at Syon nor at his Essex House on the Strand did I encounter trepidation or suspicion.'

'Cecil lurks, I tell you now.'

Catesby laughed and slapped his riding gauntlets on the table. 'Doubt and fear are for times past. Tonight we ride north and our campaign begins and we await the burning of powder.'

'When do you journey, Robin?' asked Wintour.

'Sometime before midnight, with my manservant Bates.' The leader gazed around at his companions. 'Be saddled and ready and spur on as you may. Our rendezvous is settled and our goal determined.'

Wright shook his head. 'There is yet the matter of Prince Henry and his weakling brother Charles and their absence from the opening of Parliament.'

'We have not the power or resource to either seize or kill them,' said Catesby. 'Should they escape in the confusion, we will already be marching with our army.'

They believed him, and were in any case too far involved to voice further concern. Besides, not one of their number had been arrested and Fawkes still loitered undetected with his barrels. As a gentleman bodyguard to the King, Percy had investigated the welfare and security of the Stuart offspring. The princes would keep. So too the traitor who had warned Lord Monteagle.

Catesby muttered a prayer and stood up. 'Speech is done. Go now to your places.'

A final act was necessary. Percy passed his pocket watch to Keyes for later transfer to Guido Fawkes. The explosives man would use it to prepare the fuse and perfect his timing. When the gunpowder blew, the King would be above the blast and he and the Palace of Westminster would be erased.

A few hours later, Fawkes checked the timepiece. It was approaching midnight. The day had contained its share of incidents, including an encounter with a roving patrol who asked questions and mounted a superficial inspection of the undercroft beneath the House of Lords. Heightened security was to be expected before tomorrow's events. The soldiers seemed bored, their searching half-hearted. They departed without discovering what lay close at hand.

Dressed in a hat and cloak and with spurs fitted to his boots, the mercenary again shuttered his lantern and hid deep within the shadows. He did not expect to be disturbed. In the hours before dawn he would set the fuse and slip away, crossing the river and finding his horse before heading for the coast. A longer route was preferable to dodging informants and risking all in a dash to board a barque upon the Thames. Even as the King proceeded to his death, his killer would be under sail.

This was it. He shivered a little at the cold and wondered what was happening beyond the confines of his cellar. None could fault his devotion or his steadiness in the face of danger. For years he had worked to effect a miracle, and tomorrow a King was to gather with his bishops and nobles and then all would simply vanish. Praise be to God.

Out of the silence came the sound of wood splintering. Voices raked the stillness, harsh light flooding the undercroft. Fawkes pressed himself into the corner, his own understanding bitterly illuminated. They must have known, had waited and watched and left him to his own devices. It was the cruellest of fates. But he was a soldier accepting of misfortune, a holy warrior who would never submit. He thought of Catesby and his companions riding hard for the Midlands. His task now was to ensure their survival and escape.

'Your name?'

Men with muskets and drawn swords converged, their features obscured in the glare of lamps. A figure loomed in a fine doublet, wielding a rapier with an unpractised hand. The ceremonial puppet might be the first to die, mused Fawkes.

'I am called John Johnson.'

'Whom do you serve?'

'My master is Sir Thomas Percy.'

'Mine is the King.' The man bristled with self-importance. 'I am Sir Thomas Knevett, member of His Majesty's Privy Chamber and Justice of the Peace.'

Fawkes gestured to his surroundings. 'Peace is what you find here.'

'Yet you are dressed and spurred as though readied for flight.'

'Flight?' The mercenary feigned confusion.

'Thomas Percy is a papist and recusant and known supporter of sedition.' Knevett revelled in his own performance. 'And here you stand, his servant.'

'I tend firewood, that is all.'

The Justice peered towards the piled monument of sacks and timber. 'There is sufficient to warm a palace for a hundred years.'

Fawkes nodded thoughtfully. 'My master feels the winter chill.'

'Soon he shall endure the heat.' The command came almost as an after-thought: 'Seize him and search him well.'

Several of the soldiers rushed him. His reflex was to fight, and yet it ended as it was meant to, his face bloodied, his clothing torn and his hands bound fast behind his back. With a shout of triumph, the proof was methodically laid bare.

'Matches, touchwood, slow fuses, and a gold pocket watch of worth.' Knevett took ownership of the items. 'Unusual objects for a servant to possess.'

Fawkes remained defiant. 'I have many duties.'

'High treason sits among them. Now we shall unmask the whole.'

Quickly the soldiers removed the faggots and kindling to reveal the casks. Fawkes stood betrayed by the evidence against him. He watched with a sense of finality as a large Negro tossed aside a final layer of camouflage, and remembered seeing him about the precincts. All their planning and hoping was in vain and everything had been leading to this trap.

Knevett turned back to view his prisoner. 'Do you now tell me Percy has a thirst and these hogsheads brim with wine?'

'I shall speak no more.'

In time, they would force confession, ensure he cried out and beseeched the Lord for death. That was for another day. The hours had passed into Tuesday, 5 November. A plot had been foiled and a King would continue to reign.

CHAPTER 19

Tracking them was not difficult. Hardy had anticipated their direction of travel and assumed they would leave London before the fifth. Now he was on their tail. Only three rode in their party, the enforcer Jack Wright and manservant Bates attending the ringleader Catesby. There would doubtless be more now scrambling to make their departure. Adam, too, was in the Midlands and pursuivants were about, and wherever Isaiah Payne roamed there existed desperate threat. It was possible the spymaster Cecil had contrived everything.

Instinct told him he was gaining. Their horses would be tiring and they would seek to change mounts on the approach to Dunstable. Direct confrontation would disrupt their plans. He felt the tightness of the armoured doublet on his chest, the katzbalger and quiver of ash quarrels at his side, the hunting bow strapped across his back. At last the mission was live, his quarry on the move and the danger of Realm made safe.

Moonlight caught the road and the glistening puddles marking its length. His horse veered away from something at the side of the road, and he spied the object, a piece of clothing dropped by someone in a hurry. Hardy steadied the gelding and leant to retrieve it, lifting the fur-trimmed cloak to his cheek and nose. It was expensive and had not lain an hour. The traitors were jettisoning unnecessary weight, attempting to speed their journey. Inhabitants of a local inn might have noted their progress.

'It is late and you do not sleep,' Hardy called to the stablehand as he swung down from the saddle. 'You encounter travellers?'

'Three took fresh horses not half an hour past.'

'How did they seem?'

'Determined and short with their words, sir.'

'You have another mount to spare?'

'None that my master may offer.'

'Then rub my horse and give it drink and I will soon be on my way.'

He entered the stables and inhaled the sweet stench of straw and dung and equine sweat. These beasts had conveyed a trio of conspirators on the first stretch of their wild quest and would not be needed again. By the end of the chase, so much would be left in the past. Hardy patted the horses' necks and felt the cooling heat. An animal never lied. For the moment, the conspirators had their heads and a short lead, but before long they would be run to ground.

Once more astride his courser, he rode fast. His adversaries were unlikely to guess how close he was on their tail or how relentlessly he pursued them. Catesby had been brave and blind in his ambition. Survival demanded more.

A cask bounced towards him, its fuse lit and sputtering and its trajectory directed by the ruts in the road. He knew what it was, had in earlier assignments employed such devices to ambush his enemies or ensure his escape. The technique had been adopted by others. Pulling hard on the reins, he toppled the horse to its side, its body shuddering to the shock of detonation. For an instant he believed he himself had died and that his head was detached from his body. His vision was blurred and his hearing banished, and in the shimmering silence he became aware of the slow approach of a horseman. It took some time to shake free of his stupor and form words.

'Come near and you will die.' Even he was unconvinced by his weak and airless voice.

'This is no Bridewell fencing school, Hardy.' Wright stared down at him across the debris. 'Your swordsmanship and artifice mean little on the road.'

'You wish to put your own skills to the test once again?'

'I have neither time nor desire.' He looked down at Hardy's dying horse.

'Like all you intend, failure and darkness await you,' said Hardy. 'You and your enterprise are damned.'

'It shall not be by your hand. We have your son. Dwell on it and decide your move.'

Wright spun his horse and was gone, a shadow splashing headlong down the silvered track to catch his two companions. Hardy stared after him and rested the bow and quarrel. He was slowed but not yet excluded from the fight, would proceed with greater caution. Further explosives and other surprises might be positioned in his path. Perhaps they were a parting gift from Realm. He struggled upright and looked about. The horse was already dead.

'Stay back, I say!'

London was afire with rumour and commotion, the fever spreading from Westminster to the Strand and bringing shouts and lights into the streets. One word could ignite a fresh outburst of speculation, a single whisper cascade into a frenzy of fear. The King was dead, an army marched, the Spanish were invading. Consternation was overtaken by a different tale and extinguished by the facts. A plot had been foiled and an assassin caught and His Majesty by the grace of God was spared. Elation took hold. Citizens jostled and fought and swarmed to hear news. There must yet be conspirators at large.

Tom Wintour pushed his way unnoticed through the throng. He should have left, been northward bound with his brother fugitives. Yet curiosity held him, a dread fascination to learn the truth compelling him to hide among the crowd. It was Kit Wright, Jack's younger brother, who had roused him in his lodgings at the Duck and Drake and told him that Guido was taken. Half asleep, he had listened to the panting account, was wide awake by the time his feet hit the floor and he reached for his clothes. He had to be certain. While Kit hurried to warn Percy in Gray's Inn Road before fleeing himself, for the sake of Catesby and the greater cause Wintour would for the present remain and bear witness. That inn where they had once met to pledge themselves to treason and murder was now just a place on the Strand with a saddled horse and soon likely to be raided.

A soldier blocked his path, a pike held angled in his grasp. 'You have no passage here.'

'What causes such uproar?'

'It is the business of the Privy Council.'

'The council?' Wintour kept his challenge light. 'All about is talk a plot has been discovered.'

'We are commanded to keep order and guard approach to every part.'

'You do it well.'

'Everywhere is sealed and none may travel far.'

'Is the treachery contained?'

The gentleman's obvious breeding neutered any hostility. Plainly he posed no threat and was entitled to enquire, was deserving of a civil reply. These strange events had unsettled everyone. The soldier leant towards Wintour. 'A Catholic is apprehended with a hoard of black powder and had intent to kill the King.'

'His Majesty is safe?'

'We and the royal guard shall ensure it.' His grip tightened on the haft of the pike. 'Were I to find a papist dog, he would suffer to his final breath.'

'Who is this devil they seize?'

'A dark stranger, they say, a tall and scarred man now bound in chains and destined to face the wrath of the law.'

'May justice be done.'

As the crowd swelled, the line of troops pressed back. Whistles blew and reinforcements marched in to the beat of a drum. Wintour slipped away. His companions would be riding hard for the Midlands, thundering up Watling Street and throwing aside caution in their scramble to escape. Fawkes did not enjoy such a choice. Before long, the authorities would have names and dates and the outline of the plot and the cavalry would set out. The loyal lieutenant glanced back and observed the iridescence play about the base of the Parliament he wished destroyed. This was where hope ended and the final spasm of defiance began.

Not all were rushing to depart. A delivery was underway, courtesy of Realm, the cart manoeuvring slowly towards St James's Palace. Even royals needed provision; even their protectors could be fooled by papers with forged seals. The consolation prize for Catholic militants would be a detonation that won back the day and eradicated the young Prince Henry. It would leave his father's regime a little exposed and insecure.

The driver failed to notice the blade cutting through the oiled canvas and the large Negro emerging from beneath. He had his orders and they were to keep to schedule. Black Jack followed a different path and could be most persuasive.

There was good reason to wake the King. It was his victory to claim, his keen eye and powers of deduction that had solved the riddle and saved his throne. Self-congratulation was in order. In the early morning of Tuesday, 5 November, a day on which he had intended to journey to Parliament, a private audience had been prepared in the basement of his Escorial Palace. Unaccustomed to these darker reaches of his domain, he was wary in his descent. Guards were posted and the prisoner bound and he was in no danger. Still, the discreetly armoured doublet remained in place.

He stared at Fawkes from a distance. 'You seem much at ease in a cellar.'

'I have few cares or expectations.'

'Why so?' James let his mouth gape in enquiry. 'You are a Catholic committed to my destruction.'

'Satan confounds my plans.'

'As God in His wisdom spares me.'

'To what end?' The mercenary lifted his face and gazed at the monarch. 'So you may persecute and oppress? Hunt our priests and hound our religion to its death?'

'It is what the Lord demands.'

'In which book is it written?'

The King contrived a smile at the effrontery. He would not be distracted by insolence or swayed by disrespect. Moreover, the prisoner held his attention and provided diversion and interest. In a world of lickspittle courtiers, a sworn enemy was a find.

He continued to study the captive. 'Our destinies collide this night in ways you did not imagine.'

'I considered every consequence.'

'Did you?' James scratched his beard and leant against a pillar. 'Your sojourn here is but a wayside rest on your journey to the Tower.'

'Would that I had blown you to a thousand upon a thousand pieces.'

'Instead you languish chained and I stand before you whole.'

'The angels will weep.'

'My subjects rejoice.'

Fawkes narrowed his dark eyes. 'You are more demon than monarch.'

'And you a common traitor.' James pointed out 'Each one of your kind will be dug out and ferried to the scaffold.'

'There will be others after us.'

'They too shall be revealed. They too will be excised and our nation cleansed.'

'A Scotsman purify England?' Fawkes laughed harshly. 'You mire its every corner.'

James twitched at the accusation and the contempt behind it. He had misjudged, had expected less spirit in the prisoner and the interview to proceed as he directed. Unquenchable hatred was scored deep in the man's features. Fanatics were all the same. A voyage downriver on the misted Thames should help modify his views.

The King had recovered his poise. 'A warrant is issued for the instant arrest of your master Thomas Percy.'

'I doubt any shall find him.'

'You forget the loyalty of the people and vengeful reach of the law.'

'Neither will triumph over the might of faith.'

'Is this so, John Johnson?'

It was the little Scot's turn to mock and to gloat over what the night had brought. Events could have been so different. He was in the company of a confirmed enemy, a violent papist who maintained his pretence of name and occupation. A servant indeed. The truth would be extracted and the full extent of the conspiracy laid bare. Without further comment, the King took his leave and returned to the more comforting and familiar surroundings of the living.

They waited in the darkness, men stooped with fatigue, their faces raw and bodies numbed, their clothing stiff with the mud and spray of long travel. Eighty miles they had ridden in a day. Now they stood in the fields beyond the manor house, their heads bowed and the failure of their mission expressed as quiet grief. Here at Ashby St Ledgers a group of malcontents had met and a vague notion had blossomed to a plan. It seemed fitting that the conspirators returned to the origins of their crime. It was the evening of Tuesday, 5 November.

'I shall brook no misery or despair, my brothers.' Catesby patted his horse and called softly to his comrades. 'We have yet work ahead.'

There were murmurs of accord, the sound of followers too weary to offer argument and grateful to be led. Catesby had not lost his authority.

With him were his fellow fugitives, those who had streamed from London individually or in pairs and brought news of unfolding calamity. Thomas Bates and Thomas Percy, the brothers Jack and Kit Wright and the Suffolk landowner Sir Ambrose Rookwood. Joining them was Robert Wintour, who had ridden in haste from Huddington Court to deliver tidings that his brother Tom was safe and recently arrived. They were a select and committed band.

Their leader approached. 'Guido is captured, yet we are not. It falls to us to do our duty. We must again snatch the advantage.'

'Though we may not seize the princess?' muttered Kit Wright.

'The Lord gave us hands to wield sword and mouths to spread the gospel of our cause.'

'Robin speaks true.' Percy was vehement. 'At Dunchurch wait scores of horsemen armed and ready to give battle for the faith.'

'Are we not already in retreat, Robin?'

'We accept whatever is the circumstance.'

The situation was bleak, whatever the interpretation. Cecil would have started his relentless search for the perpetrators of the treason. The conspirators had little to lose in pushing on and pulling dignity at least from encroaching defeat. Dead men riding could yet do damage.

A sharp whistle signalled a new arrival. Adam cantered to greet his friends. He had been on reconnaissance north to the Red Lion, scouting ahead and ensuring the track was free of vigilantes or pursuivants. So far all was calm.

He delivered his report. 'No alarm is raised or soul about. Our passage to Dunchurch will go unnoticed.'

'How many of our brethren await us at the inn?' asked Catesby.

'Near a hundred.'

'Their mood?'

'They are eager and curious and spoiling for the fray. Sir Everard keeps their spirits high.'

'He knows we are to join him?'

'I told him as you asked.'

Hidden in the gloom, for a moment the leader was silent. Lives and destiny rested on his decision. He had not journeyed to this point in order to surrender, had not staked all to hesitate or quit in the fierce heat of adversity. God had kept him breathing for a purpose. Improvisation was their only recourse.

He addressed Adam as though they were alone. 'You served me well through much danger and earn your right to be released.'

'I will not walk away from friendship, Robin.'

'Someone must survive,' Catesby said gently. 'Know that in London we sought and failed to kill the King and no mercy will be shown us.'

'They will scarce thank me for my antics at Coombe Abbey.'

'You may take your chance and flee, find refuge in another country.'

'I would prefer to stand with you and fight.'

'Then we are agreed.' Catesby walked back towards his horse. 'King James endures and the young princess lies beyond our grasp. Yet we have more tricks to play. Gentlemen, we ride.'

Eight miles they travelled, exchanging few words, their attention on the road. The weather had closed in, ice forming on their clothes and sleet gusting in their faces. Catesby urged them on.

Their arrival was expected, the yelp of hounds and pinprick light of lanterns reaching out to greet them. The yard swirled with mounted horsemen and the strange exhilaration of uncertainty and impending action.

'You are come.' Sir Everard Digby did not hide his relief. 'Our company grows restless and confused.'

'I will give them clarity.'

'What should we do, Robin?' Digby kept his voice low. 'What course is left when Princess Elizabeth is conjured to Coventry?'

'You may still engage in war and rise to meet the challenge.'

'Some challenge it will be.'

'Are we not Catholics? Are we not despised lepers and outcasts ready to be conquerors?'

'Speak to us of events in London,' a man called out.

Few but Catesby could inspire in the midst of such misfortune or so capture the imagination. He stood in his stirrups to address them, his tiredness forgotten, his voice hoarse in its emotion, calling the men to arms and martyrdom. 'I will not deceive you. This day at noon was meant to be the last in which the King drew breath. Yet he lives and we are hunted and must salvage from the storm the justice and result we crave.'

Some cheered, but others cried out amid the general consternation, 'We are no army! We are lost!'

'On the contrary, you are saved.'

'You lead us to destruction!'

'I win you glory and regard.' Catesby spoke above the noise. 'Will you stand with me?'

Many bellowed in reply, 'To the end, Robin! To the end!'

They moved out, a torrent of cavalry flowing west. The hounds and the courtly clothes reserved for a gentler occupation were abandoned in the departure, along with any pretence that they were a hunting party. Catesby led and men followed, for they were as yet undefeated. Coombe Abbey was no longer the target.

His guards were not the most communicative, Realm mused. They plainly had orders from Hardy and were entrusted to deliver their prisoner unharmed as the intelligencer sortied forth on a new mission. The renegade pictured his adversary in pursuit of the Catholic conspirators. Such things were now beyond his interference or control.

Sheltering beneath an oak as they waited for the handover, the three stayed in their saddles, the burly Carter to his left and gaunt Swiftsure to his right. It would be difficult to manoeuvre free of the situation. No doubt each man had several kills to his name. They would not otherwise have been assigned to transport him.

He turned to Carter. 'You have the bearing of a seafarer.'

'You of a traitor.'

'A man betrays nothing if he commits his life to a cause.' The renegade was content to talk. 'It is happenstance I serve the King of Spain and not that of England.'

'And circumstance decrees you will be quartered on the block.'

'I have no regret. Your master Hardy provided me fair sport.'

'Christian was ever destined to outwit you.'

'He was?'

'We fought the dogs you sent against us and tracked each move you made.'

'I applaud your great endeavour.' The renegade shifted his attention to Swiftsure. 'What next in your journeying and adventure?'

'We go as we are commanded.'

'Then we are bound by similar things, sharing a world inhabited by Christian Hardy.'

A hand clamped on the back of his neck and squeezed him into silence. Realm was unconcerned. Exploring the boundaries of patience and permission was itself a useful exercise. He was learning all the time. These men were worthy of his company.

Carter spoke low in his ear. 'Do not press too hard your luck and sly intrigue.'

'I do no harm.'

'But we shall.' The big man had not released his grip. 'You are a prisoner and we the custodians.'

'Have you no ear for a tale? No eagerness to know the past of a condemned man?'

Carter was dismissive. 'The King survives and the conspirators flee and the gunpowder treason is ended.'

This explained much. Realm would dwell further on the intelligence and turn it over in his mind. The plotters had been ambitious and their plan ill-fated, the catastrophe befalling them long orchestrated by the spy chief Cecil and delivered by Hardy. Realm felt neither surprise nor great regret.

In the cold stillness, he heard the rumble of wheels that heralded the arrival of his transport. Another phase was beginning. He remembered El Papa Negro, the 'black pope', the horse-drawn coach of the Inquisition into which he had once been dragged in Lisbon. Possibilities were infinite and outcomes often varied from the ones decreed.

It pulled to a halt, a carriage with no windows, part-illuminated by lamps hanging at its front. Cecil preferred function to ceremony. As the coachman waited, an armed guard stood on the roof and beckoned with his firearm. 'You have the captive?'

'We are glad to surrender him,' said Carter. 'Watch him well, for he is never to be trusted.'

'We have yet to lose a prisoner,' said the guard.

Realm was transferred into the carriage and the door locked fast. The driver raised his whip. Behind him, the guard continued to observe the shadowy forms of Swiftsure and Carter. There was ever a bond between the secret servants of the state.

'You earn your pay and rest.' The guard cradled the stub body of his gun. 'Our night will be much longer.'

'The prize you carry is its own reward,' said Carter.

'What do you know of him, friend?'

'That he is the devil and the enemy of England. That it has taken a lifetime to entice and trap him.'

'Then he is the man we seek.'

'A man?' Carter shook his head. 'Few men behave as he.'

'Be glad your errand is done and he belongs to us.'

'His lordship will be content.'

'Cecil is not our master.'

Words and vapour hung in the instant before action. Carter and Swiftsure stood no chance. In a single movement, the guard knelt and levelled his weapon and its flared muzzle discharged. The shot spread and found its mark, the blizzard plume encompassing human and horse and bringing them down in a glutinous tangle. At such close quarters, nothing could survive.

Steadying the horses and flicking his whip, the coachman steered the transport on as his companion settled beside him on the seat. Another loose end had been tied.

An eventful day had turned to night. In the early hours of Wednesday, 6 November, the town of Warwick slumbered. The castle had been undergoing restoration and repair, its long abandonment ended and its wealthy new owner determined to acquire the trappings of hard-won status. For Sir Fulke Greville, poet and parliamentarian, ramparts and turrets provided the perfect statement and could embellish a comfortable home.

They could also draw the eye of desperate men and those requiring horses, conspirators who had galloped west some fourteen miles from Dunchurch. As Sir Ambrose Rookwood and his mounted entourage skirted the environs, another group, led by Catesby, was poised to venture closer.

'They sleep and no guards patrol the barbican or walls,' whispered Adam. 'Their portcullis too is unused.'

Catesby stayed crouching. 'It tempts us to rash action.'

'Do we strike, Robin?'

'We have no choice, for we are short of what we need.'

Already their number had dwindled to fifty, a fraction of the strength expected. Men had deserted, former friends and allies using the dark and frantic pace to splinter from the group, doubts and defections growing with the miles. Reason and realisation could often puncture a dream.

Not for Catesby. 'We must move silently and fast. We raid their stables by the eastern wall and seize what we may find in the courtyard. Our aim is yet to raise an army.'

'I shall tell the others to prepare.'

'Tread with caution, Adam.' The leader reached to grip his arm. 'None should resort to sword or musket unless we are in fierce retreat.'

Soon figures scurried through the gates of the castle, pausing briefly to listen for any response. Venturing inside the confines of a fortress held obvious dangers. Yet Catesby had belief in his companions and the efficacy of surprise.

It proved insufficient. A shot sounded from the Guy Tower, its report ringing off the stones, and a hammering bell joined the cacophony. The alarm had been raised. There were shouts, the puff and flash of powder discharge and the ricochet of musket balls.

'Make your escape! We are discovered!' His sword drawn, Catesby urged his followers back. They needed little encouragement, already tumbling from the castle mouth and the entrance to the stables. Few of the raiders had reached the stores or horses they sought.

'We live and thus we ride,' Catesby called out to the men about him as they scrambled to mount up. 'Keep your heads and your wits and we shall succeed. Nothing is lost and there is everything to gain.'

His words were barely heard in the general rout, his horsemen reduced to a scavenging rabble fleeing undisciplined from the scene. All that was left was to join them. Spurring his horse on towards the fields, Catesby glanced back at the walls. Swift departure was becoming a habit.

'How many did you see?'

Hardy stood in the courtyard at the base of the water gate and studied the ground about him. With him in the jagged light and razor chill of morning were the castle guards, elated by their triumph in warding off attack only hours before.

Their sergeant acted as spokesman. 'Confusion reigned. One moment there was stillness and the next they were upon us.'

'You had sentries?'

'There are always men on watch.' The sergeant shifted uncomfortably beneath the intensity of Hardy's gaze. 'It is true they must be kicked on occasion from their drink and sloth.'

'I do not blame their stupor. This place is little more than rubble and ruination.'

'Sir Fulke intends to restore it to full glory.'

'He is well served by you all.'

'A pity we had no kills.'

'Nor prisoners I may question.' Hardy pointed to the makeshift shelters of the craftsmen and labourers. 'What stores did the intruders seize?'

'Nothing that might aid them.'

'They took horses from the stables?'

'A few are gone, but will scarce be missed.'

Another interrupted. 'There is talk the enemy were Catholic rebels fleeing from the law.'

'The law is close behind them,' Hardy replied coolly.

'Every street in Warwick is patrolled and every gate is guarded,' the man continued. 'Every citizen arms himself and watches for the foe.'

'I doubt these desperate men will dare to venture back.'

Catesby and his outlaws were clutching at false hope. It showed in their rash actions and the wayward course they chose, in the needless risk they took by assaulting a part-derelict edifice. Yet the path they followed contained a logic Hardy had deciphered. His quarry was heading south for Stratford-upon-Avon, would be plotting a route between recusant houses and gathering supplies at Norbrook and Clopton. Then they would veer west the twenty miles to Huddington Court, the Wintours' family seat. From there they must turn north or face becoming trapped by militias advancing either side from Warwick and Worcester. Even apparent randomness had a pattern. Wales was their intended destination.

The sergeant stared at him. 'You are but one man and not the force of cavalry we expected.'

'Let others to their hue and cry. My toil keeps to the shadow.'

'I trust it will succeed.'

'Some will pray it does not.' Hardy paused. 'Tell me, sergeant. Do pursuivants pass this way in the hours since the raid?'

In London, the bonfires lit in celebration of the miraculous deliverance of the King had slumped to piles of ash and ember. There would be many sore heads and happy hearts. Yet in certain quarters, revelry had acquired an ugly aspect and mobs gathered outside foreign embassies to extract money and vent their rage and lay blame against Catholic nations for perceived connivance in the plot. Few would have heard the dull and far distant explosion during the night that left a cart burnt out and a body fragmented in a forgotten corner of a heath.

CHAPTER 20

'We shall yet have our reinforcements.'

It was spoken more in reflex than belief. Catesby stared through the panes, his gaze and thoughts confronted by the sheeting rain. About him in the upper parlour slumped the mud-spattered, exhausted forms of his companions. After fleeing Warwick, they had ridden for hours, navigating the flooded lanes and wind-scarred ridgeways. On Wednesday afternoon, soaked and dispirited, they had reached the small half-timbered manor of Huddington Court. Two days had passed since Guido Fawkes was captured; two nights had passed since they last slept. The ringleader would not succumb to self-recrimination.

At least here they could rest awhile. Throughout the house and sprawled in its old hall and barns, the rest of his party sought to warm themselves and sleep. The hours had crept on and soon they would be moving out again. One way or another, a violent death was probable for all. Catesby glanced at his timepiece. It was approaching three o'clock on Thursday morning. In the chapel room above, the family's Jesuit priest had emerged from his hide and was preparing to say Mass. There was no better way to bid farewell or ready men for the final act.

Catesby met Tom Wintour's eyes. 'You blame me, Tom?'

'We all shall follow you to the end.'

'I cannot guess where that may be.' The leader returned the watch to its pouch. 'How many stay with us?'

'I count fewer than forty.'

'Wars and rebellion have been started with less. But I had hoped for more.'

Percy looked up from his game of cards with Rookwood near the fire. 'They will be a match for our pursuers, Robin.'

'That must be our wish.' Catesby had seen the future. 'Yet we cannot forever dodge fate or hide from the truth. Guido will be broken and our names divulged and militias converge from every quarter.'

'I shall not be dragged by hurdle to the scaffold.'

'Nor I,' said Rookwood.

'Then we have the makings of a great battle.'

Their shared ordeal had brought them closer, gave edge and poignancy to an oath of brotherhood taken in a calmer time. It had been easy then to swear allegiance and pledge unswerving loyalty on the gilded hilt of a drawn sword. Hindsight was a merciless accuser. In the low light of the parlour, the pinched and haggard faces seemed already to belong to the afterlife.

Dozing by the door with a heavy rapier beside him, Jack Wright slid open an eyelid. 'This storm grants us cover, Robin.'

'It also slows us. Each mile we wade through the quagmire, we lose more men.'

'This is sent to test us.' Wright eased himself stiffly upright. 'Father Henry will comfort himself he counselled against our action.'

There was subdued and bitter laughter in the room, for Catesby had dispatched his manservant Bates with a message to Coughton Court and received in return the chief Jesuit's furious reply. Father Henry Garnet had never approved of their enterprise. Now he railed against their wickedness and demanded for the sake of the Catholic faith in England that they surrender to the law. His orders would go ignored.

Catesby nodded to the group. 'Remember that Jesus is with us even if the Jesuits are not. Remember too that while we are flesh to be corrupted by death, the beacon we light shall blaze eternal.'

'What will men say of us, Robin?' The youthful features of Sir Everard Digby had become suddenly aged and careworn. 'That we were fools? That we sacrificed all to misguided venture and selfish conceit?'

'Courage is no conceit and love of God can never be misguided.'

'People will condemn us.'

'There is not one whose blessing I seek, whose thought or word counts for more than our cause.'

There was a shout outside, the throwing of bolts and a shiver of cold air. They heard the stamp of spurred boots ascending, and Adam appeared at the door.

Catesby cast a paternal gaze over him. 'You are not drowned?'

'Rain is but the least of our foes.' Water streamed from the young man's hat and cloak and puddled at his feet. 'Word of our enterprise has reached the high sheriff in Worcester.'

'What did you find?'

'Taverns filled with rumour and an armed posse beginning to gather.'

'They will not ride before daybreak, and by then we shall be gone.'

'I heard the townsfolk call us fiends and demons, Robin. They wish us hounded to the gates of hell.'

'It is best then we outpace them.'

Worcester was a mere six miles to the west. Soon its militia would arrive, eager to win bounty and striving for the honour of first kill. No rivals from Warwickshire were going to steal their prize. It made for a fierce contest.

By turn, the conspirators climbed the stair to make their last Confession and receive the Holy Sacrament. It was in the name of God they toiled and for His sake they would persevere to the end. Thoughts of family, of grieving wives and children, consideration of the shame and hardship bequeathed to those they loved – nothing mattered against the radiance of the faith. In these moments before departure, men made their peace and settled on their fate.

As he walked through the house, Tom Wintour paused to glance into rooms redolent with memories of his childhood and more carefree times. Sentiment would bring nothing back. At the foot of the stairs, he ran his fingers over the carved banister finial of a falcon alighting on a tower. It was the symbol of the Wintours and of his past and of everything he left behind.

They mounted up and rode away shortly before dawn. Their heading was north.

He had stood on the high tower roof of Coughton Court and seen the lone rider approach, had known in that instant that the tidings were bad and his life work was over. All because of Robin Catesby, because men chose violence over peace, because reason would not prevail. From his rain swept vantage, Father Henry Garnet had clasped his hands in humble supplication and bowed his head to the inevitable. The manservant brought word from Catesby. He might as well have been a horseman of the Apocalypse.

'Do not weep, my daughter.' The Jesuit spoke gently now, trying to console Lady Mary Digby, her hands clutching at his shoulder and her sobs ragged in his ear. She deserved his pity.

'At every turn he deceived. He assured me he led out a hunting party.' She wept in anguish. 'My Everard is lost, become a traitor, renders me widowed and his sons fatherless.'

'We remain in the sight of God.'

'Yet God did not prevent this madness, nor stay Everard's hand.'

'Everard made his choice.'

'What choice is it that consigns me to disgrace? That so cruelly wrenches away my hope and life and love?'

'Be strong in faith, my daughter.'

'My pain and misery are too great.' She sagged beneath the weight of her despair. 'I believed him, Father. I trusted him.'

'Man is weak and his passion directed by whim and folly.'

'Did we not journey with you on pilgrimage to Holywell? Did my husband not seem content and committed to the path of peace?'

Garnet gritted his teeth. 'Sir Robin Catesby is most persuasive.'

'Damn him for what he does and a plague on his dissembling. Curse him for bringing ruin on our heads.'

Rage had replaced sorrow. She started up and strode to hurl a pitcher of wine across the room. The rented house was nothing but a lie, a theatre set, a convenient front for the high treason of her husband. The place where she had prayed had since become a prison.

Garnet watched the fury ebb as Mary Digby sank wretched to the floor. The sadness of others was the hardest to bear. He went to kneel beside her, appealing to Christ. He understood now that he himself could be no help to her or to any Catholic in England.

It was still raining at midday. A further diminished band had reached the manor named Hewell Grange and were engaged in ransacking it of money, weapons and gunpowder. It was there for the taking. The young master, fourteen-year-old Lord Windsor, was away. In his absence, the desperate fugitives menaced servants, broke down doors and ferried out their spoils, filling a cart they had sequestered from the stables. Only some twenty horsemen remained. Beneath the low and leaden sky and occasional shudder of thunder, they would seek to push on. Their leader was not ready to submit.

Yet their presence had brought spectators. A gaggle of villagers armed with mattocks and scythes stood hostile and silent outside the manor. Rapiers drawn, Jack and Kit Wright kept them at bay.

It was Catesby who rode over to reason and explain. 'It is for you that we do this, my friends.'

'How so?' The challenge was gruff.

'We stand for God and country. Join us in holy war to throw off your shackles and gain your freedom.'

'Is that what you offer us?' A yeoman shouted his contempt. 'With theft and plunder? With swords pointed at our chests?'

Catesby peered around at the small mob. 'There is no law when it falsifies the truth and devours lives, when innocent men are harried to their graves.'

'Where is your army?' sneered the man.

'It will rise and fight and prevail, for the love of our Lord and the sake of this nation.'

Another voice called out, 'Perchance too it will fall.'

'I would not endure so much without belief.'

'You will hang whatever, papist.'

'Not in this life will it happen.' Catesby sat proudly in the saddle. 'Nor will you have another chance to earn reward in heaven and the acclaim of your countrymen.'

He turned his mount and trotted back. He had failed in his quest to win support. His party would leave. They were like phantoms, bone-tired and grey, shivering with cold and devoid of the euphoric confidence with which they had started. Courage alone would carry them now.

Percy stared at him through bloodshot eyes. 'The locals are deaf to your call?'

'Such stubbornness is to be expected.'

'What sight do we present to them, Robin? What must they think on spying our ragged band?'

'We have tried and in itself it is enough. We have shed our blood and made our bid and will take any consequence.'

'Even Catholics spurn us.'

'It is not so bad to be despised.' Catesby gave a wearied smile. 'It is not so terrible to be part of the greatest endeavour of our age.'

'I never once forget my vow.'

'Nor I what Guido now endures for us.'

'He will be numbered with the saints, Robin.'

'So let us muster our force and proceed. Our pilgrimage is not yet done.'

The leader raised his hat and shouted a command and the cavalcade followed him out. The jolting wagon might have been a tumbril and its mounted escort a cortège. Behind them, the villagers silently observed their passage until the mist closed in and rain once more enveloped the scene.

'Your name.'

Fawkes barely heard. Stripped and laid out within the oak frame of the rack, he was a man at the end of hope and the beginning of his torment. Levers moved and rollers shifted and his limbs edged a little further from their sockets. The mercenary tried to breathe, to fight, to find relief for a body stretching beyond pain.

His audience sat unmoved. They studied him as though in court, hard men with harder eyes, his interrogators and jury. It was only a matter of time before he gave them what they asked, before the cogs moved and his body broke and he screamed from the depths of his soul.

A face hovered close, the voice insistent. 'You are no John Johnson.'

'I am.'

'Lies are no answer. Lies will bring you the worst.'

'John Johnson is my name.'

'I will swear that it is not.'

'Then it is you who lies.'

Sir John Popham, Lord Chief Justice, gave a curt nod to an assistant and listened to his instruction translate to a sustained and piercing howl. Rackings were never pleasant. Yet there was satisfaction in the process, the inevitability of confession, a reassuring certainty that another plot was countered and an enemy of the state brought low. The ageing and brutish knight watched the hands and feet of the prisoner quiver in their bindings. He hated Catholics.

'Spare yourself such agonies,' he growled softly at the captive. 'Again I ask your name.'

'Guido Fawkes.' It came bubbling from the white lips.

'Once more.'

'Guido Fawkes . . . Guido Fawkes.'

'Indeed it is. You are no servant?'

'I am a soldier.'

'A papist?'

Fawkes panted high in his throat. 'I embrace the true faith and cherish the old religion.'

'Like Percy? Like Catesby? Like Wintour and the brothers Wright?'

Questions came that already had answers. It was a demonstration of power, an indication that even as his tormentors systematically took him to pieces they were only confirming what they knew. Another joint popped.

'We have brought in the servants of known recusants, menials of Catholic gentlemen vanished from their homes,' Popham continued. 'They speak without much prompting.'

'Then you will not need me.'

'You are a traitor, Fawkes.'

'I made a stand.'

Popham gave another nod, and a keening wail coiled up from the basement chamber of the White Tower to the levels above. The conspiracy was unravelling, its members in full flight, and urgency demanded the application of extremes. A man as scarred and committed as Fawkes could withstand the manacles and more subtle forms of maiming.

The enquiry resumed. 'You strive to save your fellow traitors? To win them time for their escape?'

'I gave a solemn vow I would not speak.'

'Consider such promises void.' The Chief Justice's tone was brisk and businesslike. 'Your compact is since made with us.'

'Bitterness lies in the bargain.'

'And much suffering should you fail us.' Popham stared at the captive. 'Not one of your accomplices will endure.'

'Then I pray their end will be swift.'

'Where were you recruited?'

'In Spain and the Low Countries I was approached.'

'By whom?'

'Tom Wintour.'

'He brought you to London?'

'Yes.'

'For what purpose?'

'To reside in Westminster and guard and light the powder.'

'Its aim?'

'Murder of the King and his nobles and remedy for the contagion and evil in every corner of this land.'

There was courage in a man alone and wrenched apart and yet able to emit a residual spark of defiance. With perseverance, it too would be extinguished. The officers and secretaries settled into the rhythm of the evening and the Lieutenant of the Tower allowed himself a steadying sip of brandy. It would be a late and arduous session for everyone.

At his house on the Strand, Robert Cecil dimmed the lamps in his study and awaited confirmation from the Tower and the Midlands of all he already knew.

They had journeyed for sixteen hours since leaving Huddington Court. It was ten o'clock on Thursday evening as the remnants of their party crossed the border into Staffordshire and reached the small manor of Holbeche House. Their ride had been hellish, a faltering trek of twenty-five miles through incessant cloudbursts and mud. Their cart had toppled in the River Stour and spewed most of its contents. They were in no condition to go further.

'We will fortify the place.' Catesby still commanded. 'Barricade the doors and block the windows and choose your favoured vantage.'

'With what do we fight?'

'Your bare hands if needed. We do not travel this far to cower or submit.'

'Our powder is wet, Robin.'

'Then we shall contrive to dry it.' Catesby closed a pair of tapestry drapes. 'Light a fire in the upper parlour and fetch in our supplies.'

They still obeyed, their bodies stiff and weary. Villages were but waypoints on their odyssey and yesterday a time forgotten. Hanbury, Stoke

Prior, Tardebigge, Bromsgrove, Burcot, Lickey End, Clent and at last the hamlet of Kingswinford. This would be the conclusion.

Stephen Littleton, the house's owner and a faithful member of the mounted hunt, looked about him at the preparations. 'Who may have supposed my house would one day become a redoubt?'

Catesby shouldered a sodden bag of gunpowder. 'I know of few more noble uses.'

'And I none so sad.'

'We will yet repel the foe.' Catesby motioned to Adam. 'What do we see behind us?'

'Wraiths and ghosts and glimpses of over a hundred musket and horse,' replied the young man.

'It will be Sir Richard Walsh, high sheriff of Worcestershire, come to give us battle,' said Littleton.

'You are not troubled, Robin?' Adam asked.

'I welcome it, and will offer similar greeting to the militiamen of Staffordshire too.'

Their pursuers would have been slowed in their march by the night and weather, and were unlikely to begin their siege until the morrow. A few hours remained in which to pray or summon reinforcements.

Catesby turned back to Littleton. 'I beg you, Stephen. Go with Tom Wintour to every farm and great house hereabout. Call them to arms and bring all true Catholics here to do their duty.'

'Have we not tried such device? Will any number replace those that now desert?'

'We may but strive.'

Wintour and Littleton departed, another pair of horsemen slipping into the night. It was a token gesture and they already knew the mission was futile. Their first destination would be the home of John Talbot, Catholic grandee and landowner and perhaps a tepid sympathiser of the cause. Only a handful of the faithful remained at Holbeche House, men exhausted beyond care and the limits of endurance.

Slowly the remaining few carried the damp sacks of powder upstairs and laid them before the hearth. This night was for stumbling men to do foolish things. An ember spat from the fire and caught the powder. The blast engulfed those closest. There were screams and shouts and writhing bodies aflame and the falling debris of explosion. Above the epicentre a beam was shattered and a section of roof blown away, and about it smouldering ruin. It was hardly the detonation the conspirators had intended or for which they had toiled so long.

His face scorched and his hands and clothing burnt, Catesby crawled through the wreckage to tend to his companions. Sir Ambrose Rookwood and the rider Henry Morgan lay dazed but conscious and would survive. It was John Grant who suffered most, his eyes gone, his features disfigured and his body horribly maimed. God had turned his back and there was nothing to be done. As his friends bore him downstairs, the stoic master of Norbrook made no whimper or complaint.

'You do not stay?'

In the small chamber off the hallway, Catesby looked up from his chair with understanding in his eye. He had asked much of his companions and could neither blame nor condemn. In the shadow land between life and death, every man had the right to follow his conscience and do as he wished. But he glimpsed their shame and felt their heartache.

Sir Everard Digby bowed his head. 'I am tired and can labour no more, Robin.'

'I shall be forever grateful for your company and friendship.' The leader glanced to Robert Wintour. 'Much have you toiled also.'

'It is too late for regret.'

'Where shall you go?'

'To any place that militia or pursuivants do not visit.'

Catesby nodded. 'I wish you then God speed and give you my thanks.'

'Others will accompany us.'

'I expected no less.' Catesby's blistered hands waved vaguely at the news. 'Even my manservant Bates has run for the cover of the night.'

Tears pricked Digby's eyes. 'And you, Robin? What is your intent?'

'I resolve to die here.'

Catesby rose and followed the men from the room, watching as others filed by and readied themselves to climb down a narrow shaft set into the floor. Beneath the dwelling lay a cellar tunnel leading out into the grounds, built to provide an escape for any cornered recusant. Enemy scouts might already patrol outside.

Catesby kissed a gold crucifix and raised it in salute. 'Everything we do has been for the honour of this Cross. Forget not why we rode and the history we created.'

For a brief moment, his gaze shifted to Adam with a wordless instruction. The young man had loitered on the stair and was not among the fugitives crowding to depart. A single look bade him well and freed him of his obligation. Someone had to act as guide.

When they were gone, Catesby went to kneel in communion beside his injured friend John Grant and wait for the coming day.

'And so you appear again.'

There was no mistaking the voice of Isaiah Payne or the wizened form that aimed a pistol at Adam's chest. The small company of fleeing conspirators shrank back into the derelict dovecote that housed the tunnel mouth. Arrayed before them were shadows ghostly lit by lanterns. It would be an unequal contest.

Again came the rasping and triumphant voice. 'You did not think we would leave such bounty to militiamen alone? Did not believe you would remain beyond our grasp?'

'I am not privy to the work of elves and goblins,' replied Adam.

'Such swagger and bravado.' Payne kept the pistol steady. 'It earned you a beating on the streets of London and will gain you worse punishment here.'

'Whatever is your sport.'

'My sport is to have you silenced, to see a louse transfixed and writhe its last.'

'Is it not custom to bring a man before a justice?'

'Some are lost or damaged first.' The chief pursuivant was no stranger to summary execution. 'You ran and fought and offered fierce resistance.'

'It is no tale I recognise.'

'Nor one you shall live to refute. Our practices range far beyond convention and the common law.' Those practices had carried Payne far and permitted him to hunt priests and traitors across the land. His endeavours had now brought him to Adam and a group of fleeing Catholics. He gazed on his catch, satisfied. 'I have scoured too many houses to be deceived by a recusant tunnel.'

'We are a poor prize for your efforts.'

'I shall find consolation.' The trigger finger tightened. 'You should not have set so challenging a scent.'

Yet the pursuivant had left a trail of his own. The blunt double head of the crossbow quarrel buried in his back, its impact shocking the man into a sharp and sudden cry. Adam stared, confused, and the other pursuivants fell into panicked disarray. Payne was down and would never rise again. The space where he had stood was filled by another figure. Christian Hardy stepped forward, cradling a hunting bow. He now assumed command, addressing Payne's men.

'Put up your weapons before more blood is shed. In time you will see sufficient Catholics die.'

Reluctance showed. 'We have our duty, Hardy.'

'You also have your lives. Value them and forget what you have witnessed.'

'There will be answer for what you do.'

'Far worse for you should you resist or speak of this event.' The intelligencer casually lifted the bow. 'I too have men devoted to the kill.'

Payne's former crew required no reminding of Hardy's repute. Cowed, sullen and denied their usual bounty, the pursuivants retrieved the corpse of their leader and vanished into the gloom.

Sir Everard Digby stared at the stranger. 'We must thank you.'

'I am no friend to you.'

'Yet you save us from certain capture.'

'To what avail, you must decide. Your days and freedom are numbered.'

'At least you give us a chance.'

'It is all that any possess.' Hardy shrugged and stood aside for the small band of broken, weary men to file past him. One stayed unmoving within the dovecote. He had been seemingly transfixed since Payne fell.

Alone together in the fragile silence and with the rain once more falling, Hardy and his son stood reunited. The hunt had been long and both were weary. Talk of gunpowder and treason was for some other night.

'What brings you, Father?'
'I come to claim you back.'

Tom Wintour was the first to be hit. Unsuccessful in his final drive to gather recruits, he had returned during the night determined to die with his confederates. Now, as he ventured out to reconnoitre, a musket discharged at close range and his right shoulder was instantly shattered. It was late morning on Friday, 8 November, and a company of two hundred Worcestershire militiamen had the house surrounded. Robin Catesby's loyal lieutenant would curse the hour he was not killed outright.

From around the low wall framing the front courtyard, volleys of shot opened up. Lead tore through leaded panes and splintered wood and threw out clouds of brick dust. A show of force was necessary to break the spirit of resistance. Sir Richard Walsh, high sheriff, was not tempted to raise his head above the parapet.

The response soon came. Jack Wright bounded down the shallow steps, his sword drawn for battle. He did not get far, a musket ball ripping through his chest and bringing him down. Not even the plot's enforcer could withstand the withering point-blank fire. His younger brother was next, Kit running low to draw the guns and test his mettle and falling mortally wounded. The smoke cleared and the guttural moans of dying men sounded weak and plaintive in the air.

Another man had decided to make a dash for the stables. Weakened by his burns and bracketed by shot, Sir Ambrose Rookwood limped out in a futile gesture of defiance. He was quickly halted by a round to his thigh. He slumped against a wall, unable to do anything but watch the final events play out.

Smoke drifted in the house as the curtains caught alight. Catesby, Percy and Wintour gathered in the hall.

'They seek to flush us out.' The leader drew his sword and regarded his two companions. 'I swear they will not take me.'

Percy shivered with the energy of the moment. 'I stand with you, Robin.'

'And you, Tom? Will you die with us?'

'My sword arm is no help.' Wintour pressed a bloodied rag against his wound.

'No matter, it is a staunch heart and steady eye that counts.'

'Then you have my company.'

Catesby looked from one to the other. 'I could not ask for more. I am glad I meet my end with the bravest and closest of my brothers.'

'We too are blessed, Robin.' His face pale, Wintour looked at his leader with devotion.

'Though God deserts us, we stay loyal to him and are bound by our duty to the cause.'

Percy saluted with his blade. 'To the true faith.' His friends echoed the words.

The trio murmured a last prayer as Catesby turned the lock and swung wide the door. What had begun as discontent and crystallised to direct action would peter to a close at the entrance to this modest house. There was a frozen moment, a pause before the onslaught, a deep intake of breath.

'Shall we, gentlemen?' The three stepped out to martyrdom.

A marksman obliged, dropping Catesby and Percy with a single shot as back to back they descended the step. The fight was over. Attackers rushed in to seize the building and start their pillage, the dead and dying brutally stripped by militia searching for plunder. Even silk stockings would fetch a price. Wintour took a beating and a knife to the belly and Rookwood a kick to the head. Inside the house, the blinded John Grant and burnt Henry Morgan were unceremoniously trussed as prisoners. Some would be needed alive to warm the dungeons of the Tower and provide the public with the later spectacle of their grim demise.

Face down in the hallway, a slick of blood behind him and his fingers clasped about a picture of the Virgin Mary, the ringleader was in his final throes. Willpower had dragged him back inside and fervour had not deserted him.

'Let the bones you have broken rejoice.' His whisper was lost amid the uproar. 'Take not thy Holy Spirit from me, for I am a sinner that returns to you.'

The voice stilled as the sinner expired, and a man stooped to pluck the papist bauble from his grasp. Such items would make a fine trophy for the spymaster Cecil.

Circumstance decreed a swift transaction; neither party would loiter. At the Folkestone jetty, a trading vessel under the colours of the Hanseatic League waited to set sail. There was little that was unusual in the scene and nothing to draw comment, save that the flag she flew was one of convenience and her master and crew were Spaniards. For the sake of a lasting peace and to avoid further incident, Cecil had ensured that ambassador Don Juan de Tassis was informed of the whereabouts of a captured English renegade. Exporting a problem was often the best way to contain it.

Hurried aboard, Realm glanced back to the quayside and his prison coach. He would not miss its coffinlike interior or the horrors to which it might have transported him. Spain too was intolerant of those who disobeyed and who pursued vendetta and private agenda at the expense of diplomatic calm. His confession would be sought and doubtless a grievous punishment applied.

Leaning back against a bulkhead, he heard the casting off and the snap of canvas and felt the swell beneath the keel. So many missions had begun or ended this way, with fearsome odds and unresolved danger and the shadow of Hardy still present in his mind. England and its intelligencer would keep. There was always the next time, the prospect of encounter, the chance to inflict more harm. Realm watched the men haul on the sheets and respond to the shrill blasts of the whistle. Each to their own. The eternal game continued.

ENDING

Ceremony and bloodletting were a common pairing. Through the streets of London the grim procession came, four horses dragging wicker hurdles on which lay the bound prisoners and winding with measured tread from the Tower to Old Palace Yard in Westminster. It was 31 January 1606, and an execution was in train.

Though the air was chill and the morning darkness lingered, a vast crowd pressed in along the route to see the traitors and jeer them on their way.

'You papist dogs! You jackals! You'll soon bleed upon the block!'

'Do you repent? Will you show remorse?'

'Shame on you, traitorous whores!'

'Burn in the flames of hell!'

Puritans and prostitutes jostled for a vantage, and soldiers clustered watchful in doorways. Spectacle had its dangers. There could be armed recusants hidden in the throng, Catholic zealots driven to facilitate escape or with the blade of a knife release the captives from their misery. Grief-stricken womenfolk too might win the sympathy of the masses and upset the smooth running of the occasion. Only the previous day, the distraught wife of Thomas Bates had thrown herself weeping on him as he was carried towards his death in the churchyard of St Paul's. The authorities would brook no further embarrassments.

They could be pleased with the result so far and the elimination of the first batch of prisoners. The previous day had seen Everard Digby, Robert Wintour, John Grant and the manservant Bates in turn ascend to the scaffold. Each had provided a degree of entertainment, some wishing the King long life and others unrepentant. All had perished devout and Catholic. Those who praised His Majesty the loudest received the longest time on the rope and were spared the horrors of full consciousness when cut down and removed to the block for disembowelment. Yesterday's workload had been a clearing out of the latecomers and bit players to conspiracy and rehearsal for the main event.

As he was paraded past his former lodgings in the Strand, Sir Ambrose Rookwood opened his eyes and glimpsed his wife leaning from an upper window. He called out, straining at his rope bindings, 'Pray for me, my sweet Elizabeth! Pray for me!'

'I will, and be of courage!' Her voice was strong above the din. 'Go with God and let Him bring you to His everlasting light!'

The mournful convoy lurched on. They were a select few, a consolation prize for the government and people since the ringleader Catesby, his deputy Percy and the feted swordsmen Jack and Kit Wright had opted to die elsewhere. Perhaps the ghosts of the already departed stalked the current proceedings. If so, they would have witnessed the horses and their loads turn into Whitehall for the final approach. Tom Wintour, Ambrose Rookwood, Robert Keyes and Guido Fawkes were bound for the Parliament buildings they had with single-minded commitment once sought to destroy.

Assembled and waiting were their audience, the nobles and hierarchs who would have been among the victims. They were curious to see these devils brought into the open and eager to be present as they were cast into the pit. Fine theatre was promised.

'Behold the heart of a traitor.'

His apron spattered, the executioner raised aloft the bleeding heart he had ripped from the chest cavity of Tom Wintour. It had been a grisly affair. Pale and prayerful and refusing to admit his wrong, the conspirator had earned neither the approval of his audience nor an extended hanging. His screams had been loud and constant during his castration, evisceration and butchery. Now his organs blackened in the brazier fire.

Crossing himself repeatedly, Rookwood mounted the scaffold. He did well, delivering a speech sufficiently contrite to bring him several minutes on the rope. By the time he reached the block, he was near death and less able to feel the crude plunge of the knife. Again the fire billowed smoke.

Following close behind was Keyes, the red-headed quartermaster unremorseful and climbing the ladder without hesitation or fear. He had always known the risks. At the top and with the halter about his neck, he jumped. His intention was to snap his neck, to cheat the hangman of his performing turn, to choose the moment of his passing. But instead it was the rope that broke. Furious and fully conscious, he was dragged struggling to the block and pinned down while they untidily gutted him.

Finally, the appearance of the archdemon himself and the climactic finale to the entertainment. Fawkes was changed. He was no longer the tall and upright soldier or the mythic plotter in his lair, but a hunched and broken cipher hobbling on the flagstones and aided by his guards. Few words would be forthcoming. Painfully he inched upwards on the steps and was steadied by the hangman. This was the conclusion to his treason and his trials. Then the leap, the gasp of the crowd, the tautness in the rope. Guido Fawkes had succeeded in depriving all of a magnificently prolonged drama.

There were the customary pleasantries to follow, the protocol that came with such occasions. Everyone wished to be seen and to be heard discoursing loudly on the great gunpowder treason. Still the fire burnt close to the block and the odour of blood and cindered flesh lingered.

Christian and Adam Hardy walked in silence from the scene and side by side through the precincts. The intelligencer had brought his son for a reason, to show without words the fragility of life and the stark consequences of ill-judged action. It was a lesson the young man was unlikely to forget.

At the entrance to the small dwelling where Fawkes had once resided, Robert Cecil appeared in his fur-trimmed robes. The Secretary of State had anticipated their arrival.

Hardy inclined his head. 'Justice is done, my lord.'

'It is rarely complete, and our task is ever arduous.' The hunchback's stare was neutral. 'Threat remains and Jesuits abound.'

'Father Henry Garnet is captured.'

'There will be others. The martyrs of today nourish the foul deeds of tomorrow.'

'Then we must be careful whom we kill.'

An eyebrow might have arched. 'A traitor is a traitor.'

'The eye may deceive and the mind ill inform.'

'Or is it the tongue that undermines a man?' Cecil regarded his intelligencer's face. 'Your skills are known to me, Mr Hardy. So too your boundless offence.'

'I sacrifice much, my lord. Two of my trusted lieutenants are dead.'

'Such are the dangers we confront.'

'Some are to our front and others to our back. Some conspired to free the renegade named Realm.'

'Greyness shrouds the paths we walk.' The Secretary of State was sanguine. 'It is the same greyness that has devoured my chief of pursuivants, Isaiah Payne.'

His point was made and the scores were equal. One pursuivant for Carter and Swiftsure. Both spy chief and intelligencer comprehended the rules and accepted the exchange. There was little delicacy in their game. Yet it maintained the balance and natural order and ensured that the King and his progeny survived. Against that, the victims were incidental and the deceiving of Beatrice of no consequence.

'What of you, fellow?' Cecil studied Adam silent beside his father. 'Do you rejoice in these executions and the morality of our tale?'

'I give thanks the reign of King James endures.'

'A wise and politic answer. It is with this spirit of reflection I now repair to the house behind to confer with my most reliable agent.'

Hardy made to step forward. Yet it was his son who strode to follow the spymaster, the younger man assured of his reception and eager to assume his rightful place. There was no backward glance. From the start, it had been Adam that penetrated the heart of conspiracy and the halls of Coombe Abbey, that kept vigilant watch over Princess Elizabeth, that betrayed Catesby and his band and led armed militias to the door of Holbeche House. Catholic plotters had never stood a chance.

Among the crowds returning to the Strand, William Shakespeare listened to the laughter and tried to shed from his thoughts the events of the day. He had broken bread or shared a drink with many of the dead.

As flies to wanton boys are we to the gods, he reflected. They kill us for their sport.

On his short perambulation of the Tower wall, Sir Walter Raleigh paused and took a nip of firewater from his flask. His prison had become quieter of late. Before him, the boats still offloaded and the wherries dodged about and somewhere enemies of the state either plotted or were being killed. There was routine in everything. He glanced upriver and wondered when the next crop of heads would seed the skyline above London Bridge.

ACKNOWLEDGEMENTS

My profound thanks are owed to the following for contributing in so many ways to the arrival of this book:

Sarah, Lizzy and Michael: for accompanying me in my research.

Professor Hugh Edmondson: for welcoming me to his beautiful home at Huddington Court.

Ivor Guest: for permitting me access to the crucible of the plot at Ashby St Ledgers.

Diane Williams: for making time and throwing wide the doors of Holbeche House.

Pamela Bromley: for her keen insight into the events and history of Warwick Castle.

Charles Price: for teaching English and inspiring me at a young age to embrace the art of writing.

The Rolling Stones and Led Zeppelin: for providing the backbeat that drives everything I write.

HISTORICAL NOTES

In spite of his prevailing fear of assassination, **King James** survived all plots. He was to die in March 1625.

Princess Elizabeth later married Frederick, Elector Palatine and briefly King of Bohemia. He was deposed in a year, earning Elizabeth the sobriquet the 'Winter Queen'. Exiled to The Hague and then widowed, she finally settled in England after the end of the Commonwealth in England and the crowning of her nephew as King Charles II. Her son, Prince Rupert of the Rhine, had served as royalist cavalry commander during the English Civil War. She died in London in February 1662 and was buried at Westminster Abbey.

Prince Henry, seen as the great hope of the Stuart dynasty, never succeeded his father James. He died in November 1612 aged eighteen from an illness historians suspect was typhoid fever. Some have suggested poisoning as a possibility. Henry's younger brother Charles inherited the crown, an event that led subsequently to the English Civil War.

Father Henry Garnet, Superior of the Jesuits, was executed in St Paul's Churchyard on 3 May 1606. Moved by his suffering and anxious to speed his death, onlookers rushed forwards as 'hangers on' to drag down on his feet.

Robert Cecil, 1st Earl of Salisbury, continued to work tirelessly as adviser, spymaster, chief minister and Lord Treasurer to the King. He used the Gunpowder Plot to consolidate his power base and consign potential adversaries such as the Earl of Northumberland to the Tower. This most Machiavellian of men died from cancer in May 1612.

Sir Walter Raleigh endured in the Tower and was briefly pardoned by King James in return for his leading an expedition to Venezuela in 1617 to discover El Dorado. The mission failed. Worse, members of the expedition attacked Spanish positions on the Orinoco and Raleigh paid the price for Spanish anger and James's desire to maintain the peace. He was beheaded in Old Palace Yard at Westminster in October 1618. His embalmed head was presented to his wife.

William Shakespeare successfully negotiated the political and religious challenges of the period. Whilst he stayed aloof from trouble, his friend and drinking companion Ben Jonson was jailed in the aftermath of the Plot. It was advisable to shed all links to the memory of men such as Robin Catesby.

'**Realm**' is a composite of the many Catholic renegades and 'hispaniolated' Englishmen still active from the Elizabethan era. One, a certain Francis Limbrecke, served as a pilot to the Armada and was later caught spying on the English settlement of Jamestown in Virginia. He was hanged from the yardarm of the *Treasurer*, the ship that also carried Pocahontas and her child.